Domain

James Herbert was not just Britain's number one bestselling writer of chiller fiction, a position he held ever since publication of his first novel, but was also one of our greatest popular novelists. Widely imitated and hugely influential, his twenty-three novels have sold more than fifty-four million copies worldwide, and have been translated into over thirty languages, including Russian and Chinese. In 2010, he was made the Grand Master of Horror by the World Horror Convention and was also awarded an OBE by the Queen for services to literature. His final novel was *Ash*. James Herbert died in March 2013.

Also by James Herbert

The Rats
The Fog
The Survivor
Fluke
The Spear
The Dark
Lair
The Jonah
Shrine
Moon
The Magic Cottage
Sepulchre
Haunted
Creed
Portent
The Ghosts of Sleath
'48
Others
Once
Nobody True
The Secret of Crickley Hall
Ash

Graphic Novels

The City
(Illustrated by Ian Miller)

Non-fiction

By Horror Haunted
(Edited by Stephen Jones)

James Herbert's Dark Places
(Photographs by Paul Barkshire)

JAMES HERBERT

Domain

PAN BOOKS

First published 1984 by New English Library

This edition published 2012 by Pan Books
an imprint of Pan Macmillan
20 New Wharf Road, London N1 9RR
Associated companies throughout the world
www.panmacmillan.com

ISBN 978-0-330-52208-3

7 9 8

A CIP catalogue record for this book is available from
the British Library.

Typeset by SetSystems Ltd, Saffron Walden, Essex
Printed and bound by CPI Group (UK) Ltd, Croydon, CR0 4YY

Visit **www.panmacmillan.com** to read more about all our books
and to buy them. You will also find features, author interviews and
news of any author events, and you can sign up for e-newsletters
so that you're always first to hear about our new releases.

TIME: 12:37

DAY: Tuesday

MONTH: June

YEAR: The not too distant future . . .

PLACE: LONDON

One: Advent

Over Advent

They scurried through the darkness, shadowy creatures living in permanent night.

They had learned to become still, to be the darkness, when the huge monsters roared above and filled the tunnels with thunder, assaulting the black refuge – their cold, damp sanctuary – with rushing lights and deadly crushing weight. They would cower as the ground beneath them shook, the walls around them trembled; and they would wait until the rushing thing had passed, not afraid but necessarily wary, for it was an inveterate invader but one which killed the careless.

They had learned to keep within the confines of their underworld, to venture out only when their own comforting darkness was sistered with the darkness above. For they had a distant race-memory of an enemy, a being whose purpose was to destroy them. A being who existed in the upper regions where there was vast dazzling light, a place that could be explored safely only when the brilliance diminished and succumbed to concealing and pleasurable blackness. But even then the darkness was not absolute; different kinds of individual lights pierced the night. Yet these were feeble, and created shadows that were veiling allies.

They had learned to be timid in exploration, never moving far from their sanctum. They fed on night creatures like themselves, and often came upon food that was not warm, that did *not struggle against the stinging caress of the creatures' jaws. The taste was not as exciting as the moist and tepid moving flesh, but it filled their stomachs. It sustained them.*

Yet in this, too, they were cautious, never taking too much, never returning to the same source, for they possessed an innate cunning, born of something more than fear of their natural enemy; it was an evolution accelerated by something that had happened to their species many years before. An event that had changed their pattern of progression. And made them alien even to those of their own nature.

They had learned to keep to the depths. To keep themselves from the eyes of their enemy. To take food, but never enough to arouse unwelcome attention. To kill other creatures, but never to leave remains. And when there was not enough food, they ate each other. For they were many.

They moved in the darkness; black, bristling beasts, with huge, humped hindquarters and long, jagged incisors, their eyes pointed and yellow. They sniffed at the dank air and a deep instinct within craved for a different scent, a scent which they did not yet know was the sweet odour of running blood. Human blood. They would know it soon.

They tensed as one when their keen, long ears picked up a distant wailing, a haunting whining they had never heard before. They were still, many risen on haunches, snouts twitching, fur stiffened. They listened and were afraid, and their fear lasted for as long as the sound lasted.

Silence came and it was more frightening than the sound.

Still they waited, not daring to move, barely breathing.

A time passed before the thunder came, and it was a million times louder than the giant rushing things they shared the tunnels with.

It started as a low rumbling, quickly becoming a great roar, shaking their underworld, rending the darkness with its vio-

lence, tearing at the walls, the roof, causing the ground to rise up and throw the creatures into scrambling heaps. They lashed out at each other, clawing, gouging, snapping frenziedly with razor teeth.

More thunder from another source.

Dust, fumes, sound, filled the air.

Rumbling, building, becoming a shrieking.

More. More thunder.

The world and its underworld shivering.

Screaming.

The creatures ran through the turbulence, black-furred bodies striving to reach their inner sanctum within the tunnel network. Fighting to exist, deafened by the noise, squealing their panic, desperate to return to the Mother Creature and her strange cohorts.

The man-made caverns shuddered but resisted the unleashed pressure from the world above. Sections collapsed, others were flooded, but the main body of tunnels withstood the impacts that pounded the city.

And after a while, the silence returned.

Save for the scurrying of many, many clawed feet.

The first bomb exploded just a few thousand feet above Hyde Park, its energy release, in the forms of radiation, light, heat, sound and blast, the equivalent of one million tons of TNT. The sirens that had warned of the missile and its companions' approach were but a thin squeal to the giant roar of its arrival.

Within two thousandths of a second after the initial blinding flash of light, the explosion had become a small searing ball of vapour with a temperature of eighteen million degrees fahrenheit, a newborn mini-sun of no material substance.

The luminous fireball immediately began to expand, the air around it heated by compression and quickly losing its power as a shield against the ultraviolet radiation. The rapidly growing fiery nucleus pushed at the torrid air, producing a spherical acoustic shock-front which began to travel faster than its creator, masking the fireball's full fury.

As the shock-front spread, its progenitor followed, quickly dispersing a third of its total energy. The fireball grew larger, almost half a mile in diameter, leaving behind a vacuum and beginning to lose its luminosity. It started to spin inwards, rising at an incredible speed, forming a ring of smoke which carried debris and fission-produced radioactive isotopes.

Dust was sucked from the earth as the swirling vortex reached upwards, dust that became contaminated by the deadly,

6

man-activated rays, rising high into the skies, later to settle on the destroyed city as lethal fallout.

The angry cloud with its stem of white heat was more than six miles high and still rising, banishing the noonday sun, when the next missile detonated its warhead.

Three more megaton bombs were soon to follow . . .

1

Miriam stood transfixed.

What was happening? Why the panic? And that dreadful wailing noise of just a few minutes before. The sirens of World War Two. Oh no, it couldn't be happening again!

She was too stunned, too frightened, to move. All around people were pushing, shoving, running in fear. Of what? Aeroplanes with bombs? Surely that didn't happen any more. She should have paid more attention to the news. Should have listened more closely to her neighbours. Miriam recalled hearing something on the radio about tension in the Middle East; but she'd been hearing that for years and years. It didn't mean anything any more. It was just news, words, items read out by smooth-voiced young men and women. It had nothing to do with shopping at Tesco's and washing dirty sheets and spoiling grandchildren and living in Chigwell. And nothing to do with her.

Sixty-seven years old, wide-eyed and bewildered, Miriam stood on the corner of Oxford Street and Marble Arch. It should have been such a lovely day: hot, sunny, June; a day out, a special treat. A whole day just wandering around the shops looking – though not intensely – for a suitable present for Becky's wedding. Beautiful grand-daughter, nice sensible chap she was marrying, a wonderful match. Arnold, God rest him, God *forgive* him, would have approved. The boy – not handsome, true, but life was never too bountiful – had good manners and business sense. Becky would supply the beauty in the match, and if she, Miriam, knew her daughter's daughter, the driving power behind the man. A match made in heaven maybe not, for certainly the connivance of prospective (and prospecting) in-laws had laid the foundations. Call it an old-fashioned arrangement, but there were a few good families still left who followed the old ways.

What to buy? Not to worry – money was the main present. No forced thin-lipped thank-yous with such a gift. Something in glass or something practical for the wrapped present. Both. A set of crystal glasses, that would be ideal. She had smiled at her own solution.

The smile had vanished when the wailing began.

A young couple collided with her, knocking her back against a window. The girl went down and her companion roughly jerked her to her feet, one hand pushing against Miriam's chest. He shouted something, but Miriam could not understand, for her heart was beating too loudly and her ears were filled with the cries of others. The young couple staggered away, trails of mascara on the girl's cheeks emphasizing the blood-drained whiteness of her face. Miriam watched them disappear into the crowd, her breathing now coming in short, sharp gasps. She silently cried for her late husband: Arnold, tell me, tell me what's happening. There were no more wars, not here, not in England. Why are they so frightened? What were they running from?

The sirens had stopped. The screaming had not.

Stepping away from the wall, Miriam looked towards the lush green park. She had planned such a lovely, leisurely stroll through those grounds, a journey to the lake where Arnold had taken her so many years before. Had it been their first time of walking out? Such a silly woman: who used such an expression nowadays? Walking out! But it was such a nice term. So . . . so innocent! Had life been so innocent? Not with Arnold, God rest his devious soul. In other ways, a good man though. A generous man . . .

A push in the back almost sent her to her knees. No manners these days, no compassion for the elderly. No consideration. Worse. Rape the elderly, slash the baby, were the latest perversions. Such things!

The people were swarming down into the Underground station. Is that where I should be going? Would it be safe there? They seemed to think so. If only I knew what I should be safe from. Let them go; no sense in an old woman like me joining them. I'd be crushed and they wouldn't care. Tears began to form in her eyes. They wouldn't care about an old woman like me, Arnold. Not these people today, not these, these . . .

Something made her look at the sky. Her eyes were not too good, but was there something falling? An object, moving so fast; was that what they were afraid of . . .?

She blinked because her tears had stung her pupils, and in the time it took for that movement, Miriam and the milling, petrified tourists and shoppers around her ceased to exist. Their clothes, their flesh, their blood, and even their bones no longer were. Miriam had not even become ash. She had been vaporized to nothing.

The garage had always sold the most expensive petrol in town, yet it had always been one of the busiest. The owner, now busily stuffing his pockets with notes from the till – mostly tenners and fivers; pounds were no good for buying petrol in these oil-starved times – knew that position was all, that a prime location was the best asset any shop, pub or garage could have. His Maida Vale address and corner position were expensive assets rates-wise, but in business terms they could not be beat.

Howard turned sharply when a car in the forecourt tooted its horn. He couldn't believe his ears or eyes. The warning sirens had ceased and, if it wasn't a false alarm, within a few minutes the city was going to be blown to smithereens. So this bloody fool wanted petrol! He waved an irate hand at the motorist who waved back and pointed at his fuel tank.

Howard banged the till shut, leaving loose change in there. Hell, it was only money. He stamped to the door as the horn sounded again.

'Excuse me, can you fill her up please?' The motorist had wound down his window.

'Are you fucking serious?' Howard asked incredulously.

People were running past the garage, cars were bumper to bumper trying to move out of the machine-clogged city. He could hear the rending of metal as vehicles collided.

'I'm nearly empty,' the motorist persisted. 'I haven't got enough to get home.'

'Take the bloody train, mate,' Howard shouted back at him as he ran to his own car. He pulled open the door, then thought better of it. No way out in these jam-packed streets. Better to get below ground somewhere. Find a basement. Not much time. Shit, I knew it was going to be a bad day.

He ran back past the motorist who looked at him pleadingly. 'Please,' the man said, the word rising to a whine.

'For Chrissake, help yourself.'

Where to go, where to run to. Oh shit, nobody thought it would ever happen. Nobody ever really took it seriously. Everyone knew we were on the brink, but nobody considered it would really happen. It had to be a false alarm. Had to be!

'Leave the money on the counter,' he called back to the

motorist who had left his car and was holding the pump nozzle, studying it as though not sure of its function.

Howard looked right and left. Any building would do, anything with a basement. Wasn't that what they told you? Get downstairs. Paint your windows white, barricade yourself in with sandbags, get into the cellar, build a shelter, stock yourself up with food and water and stay down there until the all-clear sounded. All in the matter of four or five minutes. Oh Christ, if he only had the paint!

He reached a pub doorway. That would do, they had a big cellar, had to to store the beer. He pushed at the door, but it did not budge. Bloody hell, they couldn't close, it wasn't calling-time yet! He tried the public bar and banged at the glass in frustration when he found this door, too, was locked tight.

'Bastards!' he screamed, then turned to look back at his garage. The motorist seemed to have found out how to work the pump.

Howard cursed himself for having wasted time emptying the till. Edie was always calling him tight-bloody-fisted; maybe she was right. He should have been tucked away in some nice little basement by now. Still, it could be a false alarm. Nothing had happened yet. Yeah, that was it, he reassured himself. They'd made a mistake, bloody idiots. If anything was going to happen, it would have before now. He checked his watch and shook it. Couldn't have stopped, could it? Seemed a long time since the sirens had started. He grinned. What a mug! He'd acted like everyone else, running, panicking, telling God he was sorry. He tried to chuckle, but it came out as a choking sound.

Well, I'll tell you what, matey, you're gonna pay for that petrol. Howard began to walk back towards his garage, his little empire, shaking his head in resigned bemusement at the people rushing by. His two attendants, who had fled without his authority as soon as they had heard the sirens, were in for a rollicking when they returned. Huh! He could just see their sheep's faces now.

The motorist was climbing back into his car.

'Hold up, Chief!' Howard called. 'You owe me . . .'

The blinding flash stopped his words. His legs felt suddenly weak and his bowels very watery. 'Oh no . . .' he began to moan as he realized it actually was the real thing, there had been no mistake; then he, his garage, and the motorist, were scorched by the heat. The petrol tanks, even though they were below street level, blew instantly and Howard's and the motorist's bodies – as well as the bodies of everyone around them – were seared to the bones.

And even those hurled through the air began to burn.

Jeanette (real name Brenda) stared out from the eighth-floor window of the London Hilton, her gaze upon the vast expanse of greenery below. She casually lit the cigarette dangling from a corner of her lipstick-smeared lips while the Arab and his two younger male companions scrabbled around the suite for their clothes – the older man for his pure white robes, the other two for their sharply-cut European suits. The buggers deserve to panic, she thought without too much rancour, a stream of cigarette smoke escaping her clenched lips. According to the newspapers, they were the cause of all this, holding the world to ransom with their bloody precious oil, sulking at the merest diplomatic slight, doling or not doling out the stuff as the mood took them. Acting like a spoilt kid in whose house the party was going on: you can have a cake, Amanda, but you can't, Clara, 'cos I don't like you this week. Well now they'd all paid the price. The party was over.

She studied the scurrying people in the street below, the riders spurring their horses along Rotten Row, the lovers running hand-in-hand through the park. There were some, resigned like her, who were just lying down in the grass, waiting for whatever was on its way. Jeanette flinched when a pedestrian trying to cross the traffic-filled Park Lane was tossed over a car bonnet. The person – no telling whether it was a man or woman from that height – lay by the roadside, not moving and with nobody bothering to help. At least he or she was out of it.

Behind her the Arabs were screaming at one another, pulling on trousers, shirts, the old, fat man the first to look decent because he only had his long frock to wriggle into. He was already heading for the door, the other two hopping half-undressed behind him. Fools. By the time the lift came up it would be all over. And they wouldn't get far down the stairs.

At least the sirens had stopped. They were more frightening than the thought of the oblivion to come.

Jeanette drew in on the cigarette and enjoyed the smoke filling her lungs. Forty a day and it wasn't going to kill her. Her laugh was short, sharp and almost silent. And her looks would never fade. She glanced around the empty hotel room and shook her head in disgust. They lived like pigs and they copulated like pigs. How would they die? No prizes.

Still, she'd met a few on her Park Lane beat who were real gentlemen, who treated her with respect and a certain amount of gentleness. They were a bonus. These days she had learned to be less choosy. Her best years, although they hadn't fulfilled the ambition, were what she termed the 'up-

and-down years'. It had worked for a celebrated but unrated actress acquaintance of hers, a woman only famous for being famous, for being recognized because of the big wheelers she slept with. The strategy had landed that particular lady with a millionaire husband, who had soon divorced her, making the venture highly profitable. Countless pop stars and name photographers had added to her notoriety and bank balance. The technique was simple, although it could prove expensive.

The hotel Jeanette had used (as had her 'actress' friend) was further along Park Lane, its flavour more English than the Hilton. She had booked into the cheapest room possible (which wasn't cheap) and spent most afternoons and evenings riding the elevators. Down the guest lift (from the top) through the huge reception area or lounge, a short walk round the block to the service lifts, up to the top again, then back down via the guest lift.

She nearly always scored when just one man, or maybe two, occupied the elevator with her. A small, shy smile from them, a word about the weather, an invitation to take tea, or a drink in the bar, perhaps dinner, and that was it. She was home and dry. Of course it didn't take long for the hotel staff to cotton on, but any such establishment, no matter *how* high-class, allowed a certain amount of licence in such things. So long as there was no trouble, the hookers weren't obvious, no money went missing, the management turned a blind (yet watchful) eye. Jeanette had never got the live one, though. Plenty of almosts, but never the McCoy. Now it was just a little bit too late; her looks were not as fresh, the bait not as succulent. Hence the Park Lane/Mayfair 'beat'. Assignments were often made by phone, but nowadays it paid to pound the pavement. She could do without these sessions with three or more participants, though; they were a little too exhausting.

She turned back to the window, pressing her forehead against the cool glass. The cries from those below drifted up and her eyes began to moisten. Is this all it amounted to? Is this where it all led? Eight floors up in a hotel bedroom, naked as the day I was born, sore from the abuse to every orifice in my body by the three clients. Some climax, some joke.

Jeanette pushed herself off the window pane, stubbing out the cigarette on the glass. Maybe there was something better waiting. Maybe there was nothing. Well, even that was better.

She tried to blink when the world became a white flash, but her retinas had already shrivelled to nothing. And her body and the glass had fused into one as the building fell backwards.

As the heat wave spread out from the rising fireball, everything flammable and any lightweight material burst into flame. The scorching heat tore through the streets, melting solids, incinerating people or charring them to black crisps, killing every exposed living thing within a radius of three miles. Within seconds, the blast wave, travelling at the speed of sound and accompanied by winds of up to two hundred miles an hour, followed.

Buildings crumbled, the debris released as deadly missiles. Glass flowed with the winds in millions of slicing shards. Vehicles – cars, buses, anything not secured to the ground – were tossed into the air like windblown leaves, falling to crush and maim. People were lifted from their feet and thrown into the sides of collapsing buildings. Intense blast pressure ruptured lungs, eardrums and internal organs. Lamp standards became javelins of concrete or metal. Broken electricity cables became dancing snakes of death. Water mains burst and became fountains of bubbling steam. Gas mains became part of the overall explosion. Everything became part of the unleashed fury.

Further out, houses and buildings filled with high-pressure air and, as the blast passed on to be followed by a low-pressure wave, the structures exploded outwards. Anyone caught in the open had their clothes burnt off and received third-degree burns from which they could never recover. Others were buried beneath buildings, some to die instantly, many to lie beneath the rubble, slowly suffocating or suffering long lingering deaths from their injuries.

One fire joined another to become a destructive conflagration.

Police Constable John Mapstone was to remember his fifth day on the Force for the rest of his life. He'd always had a bad memory (fortunately, required educational standards for the Force were dropping by the year) but, because his life was only to last for a few more minutes, this proved to be no handicap.

As soon as he heard the sirens begin their bladder-weakening wail, he knew where the crowds would be headed. He quickly forgot about the two Rastafarians loitering by the outside displays of the jeans shop and made his way towards Oxford Circus Underground station, keeping his stride firm and controlled, although swift. A glance back over his shoulder told him that the Rastafarians had taken the opportunity to snatch a pair of jeans for themselves, plus a canvas shoulder-bag. Good luck to you, he thought grimly. Wish you well and long to wear them.

He tried to maintain his poise as he was jostled by the crowd, wishing someone would turn off the bloody sirens that were inciting the pandemonium. The red and blue signs of the London Transport Underground were directly ahead and he was already engulfed in a heaving mass of arms and legs.

'Steady on!' he told the people around him. 'Just take it nice and easy.'

Perhaps his face was too fresh and pink, his manner too youthful; nobody took notice of his reassurances.

'There's plenty of time to get under cover.'

He tried to keep his voice low-pitched, remembering his training, but it kept rising towards the end of each sentence. The blue uniform is a mark of authority, the training sergeant had told the recruits in a loud voice that had resonated with that authority. People expect to be told what to do by someone in a blue uniform. This lot obviously hadn't heard one of the sergeant's lectures.

PC Mapstone tried again. 'Please don't rush. Everything will be all right if you don't rush.'

The staircase, one of the many smaller entrances to the Underground station, seemed to be swallowing up the mobs, and the policeman was gulped down with them. The clamour below was horrendous and he desperately looked around for colleagues, but there were too many people to distinguish any individual. A struggling convergence had been caused by the electronic ticket entrances, but people were sliding and climbing over them as fast as they could. Others were fleeing through the ticket-collecting exits, making for the moving stairs, wanting to be deep below street level before the impossible, the incredible, the 'nobody's-mad-enough-to-press-the-button', happened.

PC Mapstone tried to turn, holding up his arms, Canute commanding the advancing tide. His helmet was knocked askew, then disappeared among the heaving shoulders. He could only let himself go, moving backwards, his boots barely touching the ground.

If they would only act sensibly, he told himself. There was no need for all this. But the fear was contagious and soon it would chip away at the fragile barrier of his own calmness. He became part of the herd.

His back struck something solid and he was dimly aware that he had reached the metal turnstiles. By now, the restricting cushioned arms of the ticket machine had been twisted from their bearings by the immense pressure of the crowds and Mapstone was carried over one side by the bodies streaming through. He managed to turn and land on his feet, and began to push his way towards the escalators, using his arms like a swimmer moving through thick, viscous liquid. The up-staircase had come to a halt because of the crowds treading downwards; the down-staircase appeared to be working normally. He was on it now and the movement, slow though it was, almost unbalanced him. He tried to grab the thick band of moving rubber that was the handrail, but there were too many people on either side. A body slid past on the immovable centre between staircases, the man obviously realizing it was the quickest way down. Another followed him. Then another. Another. Then too many.

A jumble of bodies slid down, going fast, arms flailing, grabbing at anything, trying to hold on to the upright bodies on the stairways. A desperate hand grabbed an arm and held on; bodies piled up behind; the weight was too much; the person on the stairs was dragged forward; the people in front began to fall; those behind began to tumble. PC Mapstone began to scream.

The staircase, its mechanism no longer able to cope with the overload, suddenly jolted to a stop. And then there was no control at all in the spilling, tumbling mass.

Many of those on the centre section fell into the people on the adjacent escalator, creating another human avalanche.

Mapstone, young, strong, but no longer eager, tried to keep upright, using his hands against the bodies in front, grabbing for the handrails on either side. It was no use. He managed to get one hand around the thick rubber band, but his arm was immediately snapped at the wrist by the crush behind. He shouted in pain and the sound was no louder than the shouts around him. His light was blocked out, sudden bright chinks appearing but disappearing just as quickly, creating a twisting, nightmare kaleidoscope in his vision.

Before the blackness took over completely, before his chest bones and ribs were forced back into his lungs, before his throat was squeezed completely closed by a knee that had no right to be in that position, and before all sensibility left his besieged mind, he thought he heard and felt a deep rumbling that had nothing to do with the chaos around him. A sound that seemed to rise up from the very bowels of the earth.

Oh yes, he assured himself. That would be the bomb. About bloody time too.

Eric Stanmore felt his knees slowly give way and he slid, his back against a wall, to the floor.

'Those crazy bastards,' he said aloud, his words and expression disbelieving. No one heard him, for he was alone.

Above him, standing six hundred and fifty feet over Totten-ham Court Road, paraboloid dishes collecting super-high-frequency radio beams transmitted from other, much smaller towers, each one a link in the chain of microwave stations strategically positioned throughout the country. The signals were channelled down to radio receivers at the base of the giant Telecom Tower, to be passed on by landline, or ampli-fied and retransmitted through an identical set of aerials.

His hands pressed against closed eyes. Had they known? Was this the reason for the sudden stepping-up of inspection and maintenance on all government communications sys-tems? Other threatened hostilities had caused similar drives in the past – more times than the public were ever aware of – and although the situation in the Middle East was grave, Stanmore had considered the latest directive as standard crisis procedure. He knew that the microwave systems would play an important part in the British defence in time of war, for there was no telling what damage other sections of the telecommunication network – underground cables and over-head lines – would sustain under enemy attack. The micro-wave system, radio beams passed on from one station to the next in line-of-sight paths, would prove invaluable if the normal system broke down. Even if relay stays were knocked out, the beams could be re-directed to others further along the line. The official reason for the system was to provide an unbreakable and economic (so-called) link between the three major cities of London, Birmingham and Manchester, but Stanmore knew that in an expensive operation (in progress since 1953 and at the time code-named *Backbone*) the net-work had been extended to cover many government installa-tions. A good number of S–RCs, sub-regional control centres whose purpose was to liaise and implement orders from the National Seat of Government and the twelve regional seats, were located close to such repeater stations, and Stanmore was well aware that a prime function of the system was to provide a failsafe connection between control centres. One of the most important in peacetime, although not crucial in wartime, was the tower he helped to maintain: the Telecom Tower in London. And it was the most vulnerable of all.

He knew there was no sense in trying to reach its base where adequate shelter was provided against such a world mishap – he almost smiled at the understatement, but his mouth and jaw had become rigid with tension – for the descent, even if he could get a lift to collect him, would take too long. The sirens had stopped now and he knew there wasn't much longer to go. His whole future spanned a matter of moments.

Stanmore began to tremble uncontrollably and sobs jerked his chest muscles as he thought of Penny, his wife, and Tracey and Belinda, his two little girls. His house was in Wandsworth, his daughters' school close by. Penny would try to reach the school as soon as she heard the terrible wailing of the sirens; she would never make it, though. They would all die separately, the girls bewildered, not understanding the full importance of the warning sounds, but frightened because the grown-ups around them would be frightened, and Penny would be in the streets, racing towards the school, exposed and panic-stricken. They had always planned in such morbid-thought moments of their marriage (the times perhaps when neither could sleep, when physical urges had been satiated and there was nothing left but to talk the small hours away) to barricade themselves in their home, to build a cushioned fortress under the stairs in the hallway, to follow the edicts in the local authority's Protect and Survive leaflet as closely as possible, and to stay there cocooned until the worst was over.

Neither of them envisaged – or, more truthfully, cared to admit – that there was a possibility that they would all be apart. They should have known, should have made some arrangement, some pact, to cover such a possibility. Now it was too late. They could only pray for each other and for their children. Let the rest of the world pray for itself.

He pushed himself to his knees and crouched there, his body tucked forward, hands still covering his face.

Don't let it be true, dear God, he pleaded. Please don't let it happen.

But it did happen. The huge tower was split into three sections by the blast, the top part in which Stanmore prayed travelling for a distance of almost a quarter of a mile before crashing to the ground to become unrecognizable rubble. Eric Stanmore had been vaguely and briefly aware of the floating sensation before displaced machinery and concrete had flattened his body wafer-thin.

Alex Dealey was running, his breathing laboured, perspiration already staining his white shirt beneath his grey suit. He hung on to the briefcase almost unconsciously, as if it mattered any more that 'sensitive' government documents could be found lying in the street. Or among the rubble which would be all that was left. He should have taken a taxi, or a bus even; that way he would have arrived at his destination long ago. He would have been safe. But it had been a nice, warm, June day, the kind of day when walking was infinitely preferable to riding in enclosed transport. It wasn't a nice day any longer, even though the sun was still high and bright.

He resisted the temptation to duck into one of the many office buildings that flanked High Holborn, to scurry down into one of their cool, protective basements; there was still time to make it. He would be so much better off if he reached his proposed destination, so much safer. Also, it was his duty to be there at such a catastrophic and, of course, historic occasion. Oh God, was he that far down the bureaucratic road that he could mentally refer to *this* as historic? Even though he was only a minion to the ruling powers, his mind, his outlook, had been tainted with their cold, logical – inhuman? – perceptions. And he had certainly enjoyed the privileges his office had brought him; perhaps the most important privilege of all lay just ahead. If only he had time to reach it.

Someone in front, a woman, tripped and fell, and Dealey tumbled over her. The pavement jarred his hands and knees and for a moment he could only lie there, protecting his face from the moving feet and legs around him. The noise was terrible: the shouts and screams of office workers caught out in the open, the constant belling of car horns, their progress halted by other abandoned vehicles, the owners having fled leaving engines still running. The awful banshee sirens, their rising and falling a mind-freezing, heart-gripping ululation, full of precognitive mourning of what was soon . . .

They had stopped! The sirens had stopped!

For one brief and eerie moment there was almost complete silence as people halted and wondered if it had all been a false alarm, even a demented hoax. But there were those among the crowd who realized the true significance of the abrupt cessation of the alert; these people pushed their way through to the nearest doorways and disappeared inside. Panic broke out once more as others began to understand that the holocaust was but moments away.

A motorbike mounted the pavement and cut a scything path through the crowds, scattering men and women, catching those not swift enough and tossing them aside like struck skittles. The rider failed to see the prostrate woman whom Dealey had fallen over. The front wheel hit her body and the machine rose into the air, the rider, with his sinister black visor muting his cry, rising even higher.

Dealey cowered low to the ground as the motorbike flipped over, its owner now finding his own course of flight and breaking through the plate-glass window of a shopfront. Sparks and metal flew from the machine as it struck the solid base of the window frame. It came to rest half-in, half-out of the display window, smoke belching from the stuttering engine, its metal twisted and buckled. The rider moaned as blood seeped down his neck from inside the cracked helmet.

Dealey was already on his feet and running, not caring about the woman left writhing on the pavement, not even mindful of the lost briefcase with its precious documents, only grateful that he had escaped injury and even more anxious to quickly reach his particular refuge.

The Underground station, Chancery Lane, was not too far away, and the sight gave him new hope. His destination was not far beyond.

Too soon the world was a blinding white flash, and foolishly, for he of all people really should have known better, Dealey turned to look at its source.

He stood there paralysed, sightless and screaming inwardly, waiting for the inevitable.

The thundrous, ear-splitting roar came, but the inevitable did not. Instead he felt rough hands grab him and his body being propelled backwards. His shoulder crashed against something that gave way and he was being dragged along. He felt himself falling, something, perhaps someone, falling with him. The earth was shaking, the noise deafening, the walls collapsing.

And then there was no longer burning white pain in his eyes, just the cool darkness of unconsciousness.

The initial nuclear explosions – there were five on and around the London area – lasted only a few minutes. The black mushroom clouds rose high above the devastated city, joining to form a thick layer of turbulent smoke that made the day seem as night.

It wasn't long before the gathered dust and fine debris began its leisurely return to earth. But now it was no longer just dust and powder. Now it was a further, more sinister, harbinger of death.

2

He kicked out at the debris that had covered his legs and was relieved to find nothing solid had pinned them down. He coughed, spitting dust from his lungs, then wiped a hand across his eyes to clear them. There was still some light filtering through into the basement corridor; Culver groaned when he saw smoke filtering through with the light.

He turned towards the man he had dragged in from the street, hoping he hadn't killed him in the fall down the stairway. The man was moving, his hands feebly reaching for his face; there was debris and a fine layer of dust over his body, but nothing too heavy seemed to have landed on him. He began to splutter, choking on the fine powder he had swallowed.

Culver reached towards him, groaning at the sudden pain that touched his own body. He quickly checked himself, making sure nothing important was fractured or sprained; no, everything felt okay, although he knew he would be stiff with bruises the next day – if there was a next day.

He tugged at the other man's shoulder. 'You all right?' he asked, twice attempting the question because it had come out as a croak the first time.

A low moan was the only reply.

Culver looked towards the broken staircase and was

puzzled by the sound he heard. As more dust and smoke swirled into the openings he realized he could hear a wind. He recalled reading somewhere that winds of up to two hundred miles an hour would follow a nuclear blast, creating an aftermath of more death and destruction. He felt the building shifting around him and curled himself into a tight ball when masonry began to fall once again.

Pieces struck his brown leather jacket, one large enough to cause his body to jerk in pain. A huge concrete slab that half covered the staircase started to move, sliding further down the wall its bulk leaned against. Culver grabbed the other man's shoulders, ready to pull him away from the advancing segment. Fortunately, the concrete settled once more with a grinding screech.

There was not much to see through the gaping holes of the ceiling above and Culver guessed that the upper floors of the building – he couldn't recall how many storeys the office block had, but most of the buildings in that area were high – had collapsed. They had been lucky; he was sure they had fallen close to the central concrete service column, the strongest part of any modern structure, which had protected them from the worst of the demolition. How long it would hold was another matter. And the choking smoke meant another problem was on its way.

Culver tugged at the shoulder nearby. 'Hey.' He repeated his original question. 'You okay?'

The man twisted his body and pushed himself up on one elbow. He mumbled something. Then he moaned long and loud, his body rocking to and fro. 'Oh, no, the stupid idiots really did it. The stupid, stupid . . .'

'Yeah, they did it,' Culver replied in a low voice, 'but there are other things to worry about right now.'

'Where are we? What is this place?' The man began to

scrabble around, kicking at the rubble, trying to get to his feet.

'Take it easy.' Culver placed a hand around the man's upper arm and gripped tightly. 'Just listen.'

Both men lay there in the gloom.

'I . . . I can't hear anything,' the man said after a while.

'That's just it. The wind's stopped. It's passed by.' Culver gingerly rose to his knees, examining the wreckage above and around them. It had seemed silent at first, then the rending of twisted metal, the grinding and crashing of con-crete, came to their ears. It was followed by the whimpers and soon the screams of the injured or those who were in shock. Something metallic clattered down from above and Culver winced as it landed a few feet away.

'We've got to get out of here,' he told his companion. 'The whole lot's going to come down soon.' He moved closer so that his face was only inches away from the other man. It was difficult to distinguish his features in the gloom.

'If only we could see a way out,' the man said. 'We could be buried alive down here.'

Culver was puzzled. He stared into the other's eyes. 'Can't you see anything?'

'It's too dark . . . oh no, . . . not that!'

'When I grabbed you out on the street you were looking straight into the flash. I thought you were just shocked . . . I didn't realize . . .'

The man was rubbing at his eyes with his fingers. 'Oh, God, I'm blind!'

'It may be only temporary.'

The injured man seemed to take little comfort in the words. His body was shaking uncontrollably.

The smell of burning was strong now and Culver could see a flickering glow from above.

He slumped back against the wall. 'Either way we're beat,' he said, almost to himself. 'If we go outside we'll be hit by fallout, if we stay here we'll be fried or crushed to death. Great choice.' The side of his clenched fist thumped the floor.

He felt hands scrabbling at the lapels of his jacket. 'No, not yet. There's still a chance. If you could just get me there, there'd be a chance.'

'Get you where?' Culver grabbed the man's wrists and pulled them from him. 'The world's just a flat ruin up there. Don't you understand? There's nothing left! And the air will be thick with radioactive dust.'

'Not yet. It will take at least twenty to thirty minutes for the fallout to settle to the ground. How long have we been down here?'

'I'm not sure. It could be ten minutes, it could be an hour – I may have blacked out. No, wait – we heard the winds caused by the blast; they would have followed soon after the explosion.'

'Then there's a chance. If we hurry!'

'Where to? There's no place to go.'

'I know somewhere where we'll be safe.'

'You mean the Underground station? The tunnels?'

'Safer than that.'

'What the hell are you talking about? Where?'

'I can direct you.'

'Just tell me where.'

The man was silent. Then he repeated: 'I can direct you.'

Culver sighed wearily. 'Don't worry, I'm not going to leave you here. You sure about the fallout?'

'I'm certain. But we'll have to move fast.' The man's panic appeared to be over for the moment, although his movements were still agitated.

Something overhead began a rending shift. Both men tensed.

'I think the decision is about to be made for us.'

Culver grabbed the other man below his shoulder and began to pull him towards the dimly lit staircase. The huge slab of concrete lying at an angle across the broken stairs began to move again.

'We haven't got much time!' Culver shouted. 'The whole bloody building's about to cave in!'

As if to confirm his statement, a deep rumbling sound came from the floor above. The building itself began to shake.

'Move! It's coming down!'

The rumbling became a roaring and the roaring an explosion of crashing timber, bricks and concrete. The wide basement corridor was a confusion of swirling dust and deafening noise. Culver saw the right-angled gap between tilted slab and staircase narrowing.

'Come on, up the stairs!' He pushed, shoved, heaved the stumbling man before him, lifting him when he tripped over rubble, almost carrying him up the first few steps. 'Get down! Now crawl, crawl up those bloody stairs for your life! And keep your head low!'

Culver wondered if the man would have followed out his instructions had he seen what was happening.

The side of the stairway was collapsing, its metal handrail already twisted and torn from its mounting; the blast-caused sloping roof over the stairs was slowly descending, slipping inch by inch down the supporting wall. Culver could just see the murky grey daylight creeping in from the streets faintly tingeing the top steps. He quickly ducked and followed the blind man's scrambling body, unceremoniously pushing at his ample buttocks. The man suddenly flattened as part of the concrete stairs fell inwards.

'Keep going!' Culver shouted over the noise. 'You're okay, just keep going!'

The descending ceiling was brushing against the top of his head now and Culver considered pulling out, going back. But the situation was even worse behind: the downfall had become an avalanche and he knew that most of the floors in the building must be collapsing inwards. He pushed onwards with renewed vigour, not bothering to shout encouragement that could not be heard anyway, just heaving and shoving, forcing his way through the narrowing tunnel. He was soon flat on his stomach and beginning to give up hope; the edges of each step were scraping against his chest.

Then the obstruction in front was clear: the blind man had made it to the top and was rising to his knees and turning, realizing he was free, one hand waving in front of Culver's face to help him. Culver grabbed the hand and suddenly he was being yanked upwards, the blind man shrieking with the effort, his mouth wide open, eyes shut tight. Culver's toecaps dug into the stairs, pushing, the elbow of his free arm used as a lever to heave himself up. The screeching, heard clearly over the background roar, was caused by the concrete slab tearing deep score marks in the supporting wall.

His torso was out and he curled up his knees, bringing his feet clear as the coffin lid all but closed.

He scrambled to his feet, pulling his companion with him, hurrying on, making for the wide doorway that was the entrance to the office block. The big glass double doors they had thrown themselves through only minutes earlier had been completely shattered by the blast; walls on either side of the hallway were beginning to crack.

They staggered out into the shattered, devastated world. Culver did not take time to look around; he wanted to be as far away as possible from the collapsing building. The blind man was limping, clinging to him, as though afraid he would be left behind.

Vehicles – buses, cars, lorries, taxis – lay scattered, disarranged before them. Some were overturned, some just wildly angled; many rested on the roofs or bonnets of others. Culver quickly found a path through the tangled metal, climbing between locked bumpers, sliding over bonnets, dragging his companion with him. They finally collapsed behind a black taxi, half the driver's still body thrusting through the shattered windscreen.

They gulped in mouthfuls of dust and smoke-filled air, shoulders and chests heaving, bodies battered and bleeding, their clothes torn and grimed with dirt. They heard the crumpling falling sound of the building they had just left, and it mingled with the noise of other office blocks in similar death throes. The very ground seemed to vibrate as they tumbled, their structures no more than concrete playing-cards.

As the two men began to recover from their ordeal, they became aware of the other, human, sounds all around them, a clamour that was the discordant outcry of the wounded and the dying.

The other man was looking around him as though he could see. Forcing himself to ignore anything else, Culver quickly appraised him. Although it was impossible to be sure, because of the white powdered dust that covered his clothes, he looked to be somewhere in his late forties or early fifties; his suit, dishevelled and torn though it was, indicated he was perhaps a businessman or clerk of some kind – certainly an office worker.

'Thanks for the helping hand back there.' Culver had to raise his voice to be heard.

The man turned towards him. 'The thanks are mutual.'

Culver could not manage a smile. 'I guess we need each other.' He spat dust from his throat. 'Let's get to this safe place you mentioned. Time's running out.'

The blind man grabbed his arm as Culver began to rise. 'You must understand we cannot help anyone else. If we're going to survive, nothing can hinder us.'

Culver leaned heavily against the side of the taxi, flinching when he saw the jumbled corpses of its occupants. There was a child in there, a little boy no more than five or six years old, his head resting against a shoulder at an impossible angle; a woman's arm, presumably his mother's, was flung protectively across his tiny chest. A fun day out shopping? A trip across town to the cinema, a show? Perhaps even to see Daddy in his great big office. Their day had ended when the cab had been picked up and thrown through the air like some kid's toy, its weight nothing to the forces that had lifted it.

For the first time he took in the devastation and his eyes widened with the horror of it all.

The familiar London landscape, with its tall buildings both old and new, its skyscraper towers, the ancient church steeples, its old, instantly recognizable landmarks, no longer existed. Fires raged everywhere. Ironically, he realized, the whole city could have been one vast conflagration had not the blast itself extinguished many of the blazes caused by the heat wave and fireball. The skies overhead were black, a vast turbulent cloud hanging low over the city. A spiralling column, the hated symbol of the holocaust, climbed into the cloud, a white stem full of unnatural forces. He looked around and for the first time understood that more than one bomb had fallen: two rising towers to the west – one well beyond the column he had been watching – one to the north, another to the north-east, and the last to the south. Five in all. Dear God, *five!*

He lowered his gaze from the horizons and slammed the flat of his hand against the taxi's roof. He had witnessed the stark face of ultimate evil, the carnage of man's own sickness! The destructive force that was centuries old and inherent in every man, woman and child! God forgive us all.

People began to emerge from buildings, torn and bloody creatures, white from shock, the look of death already on their faces. They crawled, staggered, dragged themselves from their shattered refuges, some silent, some pleading, some in hysterics, but nearly all separate islands, numbed into withdrawal from others, their minds only able to cope with their own individual hurt, their own personal fate.

He closed his eyes and fought back the rage, the scream- ing despair. A hand tugged at his trouser leg and he looked down to see the grimy face of the sightless man.

'What . . . what can you see?'

Culver sank to a squatting position. 'You really don't want to know,' he said quietly.

'No, I mean the dust – is it settling?'

He silently studied the blind man for a few moments before replying. 'There's dust everywhere. And smoke.'

His companion rubbed at his eyelids as though they were causing him pain. 'Is it falling from above?' he asked almost impatiently.

Culver looked up and frowned. 'Yeah, it's coming. I can see darker patches where the air is thick with it. It's drifting slow, taking its time.'

The other man scrambled to his feet. 'No time to lose, then. We must get to the shelter.'

Culver stood with him. 'What is this shelter? And who the hell are you?'

'You'll see when – if – we get there. And my name is Alex Dealey, not that it's important at this particular point in time.'

'How do you know about this place?'

'Not now, for God's sake, man! Don't you realize the danger we're in?'

Culver shook his head, almost laughing. 'Okay, which direction?'

'East. Towards the *Daily Mirror* building.'

Culver looked to the east. 'The *Mirror* isn't there any more. At least, not much of it is.'

The announcement had no visible effect on Dealey. 'Just go in that direction, past the Underground station towards Holborn Circus. And we keep to the right-hand side. Are all the buildings down?'

'Not all. But most are badly damaged. All the roofs and top floors have been skimmed off. What are we looking for?'

'Let's just move; I'll tell you as we go.'

Culver took his arm and guided him through the jungle of smashed metal. A red double-decker bus lay on its side, crushing the cars beneath it. Figures were emerging from the shattered windows, faces and hands smeared with blood. Culver tried not to hear their whimpered groans.

An elderly man staggered in front of them, his mouth and eyes wide with shock. As he fell, Culver saw the whole of his back was a pincushion of glass shards.

Bodies, mostly still, lay strewn everywhere. Many were charred black. He turned his eyes away from limbs that protruded from heaped rubble and beneath overturned vehicles. His foot kicked something and he almost retched when he saw a woman's head and part of one shoulder lying there, the rest of her nowhere in sight.

Shattered glass crunched under their feet and even in the false dusk it glittered everywhere like spilled jewels. The two men skirted around a burning lorry, shielding their faces from the heat. Something fell no more than thirty yards away from them and from the squelching thump they knew it had to be a body; whether the person had jumped or accidentally fallen from a high window of one of the more intact office blocks, they did not know, nor did they care to know. They had a goal to reach, something to aim for, and neither man wanted to be distracted from their purpose. It was their only defence against the horror.

Another building on the opposite side of the road collapsed completely, sending up billows of dust and smoke, engulfing the two men in thick clouds. An explosion nearby rocked the ground and they fell to their knees. Coughing, choking, Culver hauled Dealey to his feet once more and they stumbled on, a cold determination keeping them moving, awareness of the sinking poison their driving force. Others were moving in their direction. Now many were helping the injured, leading them towards the only place they felt could be safe. Groups carried those unable to walk, while those who could crawl were left to make their own way.

'We're just passing Chancery Lane Underground station,' Culver said close to Dealey's ear. 'Everyone seems to be taking shelter down there. Everyone that's left, that is. I think we ought to do the same.'

'No!' Dealey's expression was grim. 'It will be too crowded to get through. We've more chance if you do as I say.'

'Then where is this place? We haven't got much more time!'

'Not far, not far.'

'Tell me what the hell we're looking for.'

'An alleyway. A wide, covered alleyway that leads to a

courtyard and offices. There's a big open iron gate at the entrance. It should be just a few hundred yards ahead.'

'I just hope to God you know what you're doing.'

'Trust me. We'll get there.'

Culver took a last wistful look at the opening leading to the Underground tunnels, then shook his head once. 'Okay, we'll do it your way.'

The nightmare continued, a dream far worse than any Culver had ever experienced. Destruction to a degree he had never imagined possible. A mad, stumbling journey that tore at his mind and made him weep inwardly. Havoc. Madness. Hell exposed.

A woman – no, girl: even in her dishevelled state he could see she was just a girl – rushed at them, tugging at Culver's jacket, pointing and pulling him towards an overturned car.

Dealey held Culver back. 'We've got to get under cover,' he said grimly. 'We can't stay out in the open much longer. Even now it might be too late.'

Culver jerked his arm away. 'We can't just leave her. She needs help.'

The blind man snatched at the air, trying to grab hold of him. 'You can't help any of them, you fool. Don't you see that? There are too many!'

But Culver had allowed the girl to drag him away. As they approached the overturned car, the girl crying hysterically and refusing to let go of his arm, he saw the body lying half beneath it. One arm lay across the man's chest, the other was flung outwards, his hand clawed, already stiffening. Culver knelt beside him and fought back the sickness. The body was that of a young man, perhaps the girl's boyfriend; his eyes stared sightlessly towards the blackened sky and his tongue protruded from his open mouth as if trying to escape. His stomach had split and his intestines lay exposed and steaming.

'Help him,' the girl pleaded through her sobs. 'Please help me get him out.'

He held her shoulders. 'It's no use,' he said gently. 'He's dead. Can't you see that?'

'No, no, it's not true! He'll be all right if we can get that thing off him. Please help me push it off!' She threw herself at the overturned car and strained against it. 'Please help me!' she cried.

Culver tried to pull her away. 'He's dead, don't you understand? There's nothing you can do for him.'

A hand lashed out at him. 'You bastard, why won't you help me?'

Dealey crawled towards them, their voices his only guide. 'Leave her. She'll never listen to you. We've got to save ourselves.'

Culver tried to hold on to the distraught girl. 'Come with us, we can find somewhere safe.'

'Leave me alone!' she cried.

'There's nothing you can do,' came Dealey's anxious voice once again.

The girl thrust Culver away and sank down beside the dead man. She threw herself across his chest and her small shoulders heaved with her sobs.

He knelt. 'If you won't come with us, get down into the Underground. The air will be contaminated with radioactivity soon, so you've got to get under cover.'

There was no indication that she understood.

Culver stood and wiped an arm across his eyes. He caught sight of Dealey on his hands and knees; he stepped towards him and helped him up. 'How much further?' he shouted, irrationally beginning to hate the man.

'Not far. We should be nearly there. Cross a small side-street, go on a bit more, and we're there.'

Culver yanked him around and led the way, Dealey's grip on his arm hard, as if he would never again let go.

After a short distance, Culver said, 'There's a break in the kerb here. This must be the side-street, only now it's just piled with rubble. The buildings on one side have collapsed into it!'

'Just ahead, then. Not far.' A look of hope was on the blind man's face.

They had to move out into the vehicle-littered roadway to skirt debris and Culver suddenly caught sight of the alley-way's entrance. 'I can see it. It looks as though it's still intact.'

Their pace quickened, both men desperate for refuge. They plunged into the darkness of the entrance and tripped on rubble lying there. Culver pushed himself onto hands and knees, then moaned aloud. 'Oh, Jesus Christ, no.'

Dealey looked towards the sound of his voice, eyes closed tight against their pain. 'What is it? For God's sake, what is it now?'

Culver slumped against one wall and closed his own eyes. He drew his legs up, resting his hands over his knees. 'It's no good,' he said wearily. 'The other end's blocked, piled high with debris. There's no way we're going to get through.'

3

They were running again. Frightened, exhausted, wanting to wake up, to see the sun streaming through parted curtains, wanting the nightmare to end. But they were running. And around them the fires raged, the dead lay still, the injured writhed their agony. The nightmare refused to end.

The steps leading down to the Underground station were heaped with rubble; the round metal handrails were wet with blood. It wasn't as crowded below as Culver imagined it would be; he guessed that most of those who had reached the station had gone further down, away from the ticket area, into the tunnels. As far away from the crazy world above as possible. Even so, there were still many people scattered around the gloomy circular hall with its ticket kiosk, machines and few shops.

'We may need light,' Dealey told him, the irony not lost on him. If only his eyes did not hurt so much. If the stinging sensation would just go away. He forced his mind to concentrate. 'We have to get into the eastbound tunnel.'

'We should have tried this other entrance in the first place,' Culver said, quickly looking around. Other figures were still staggering into the Underground station.

'No, only under extreme circumstances are secondary access points to be used.'

'Extreme circumstances? You've got to be kidding!'

Dealey shook his head. 'Only in an emergency. I knew the station – the tunnels – would be filled with people. It would have been too dangerous to use; now we have no choice.'

'Are you saying this ... "shelter" ... is only available to certain people?'

'It's a government shelter. There isn't room for the public.'

'That figures.'

'The government has to be practical. And so do we.' Dealey's voice became tight, as though he were fighting to keep control. 'I'm giving you a chance to live through this; it's up to you whether or not you take it.'

'You can't make it without me.'

'Possibly not. It's your choice.'

For a few long, sightless moments, Dealey thought that the other man had walked away from him. He breathed a silent sigh of relief when he heard him speak.

'I doubt there's going to be much left to survive for after this, but okay, we'll find the shelter. I'd still like to know how you know about this place, though. I take it you work for the government.'

'Yes, I do, but that's not important right now. We must get into the tunnels.'

'There are some doors on the other side of the hall. I can just about make it out in the darkness; one could be the stationmaster's office, so we're bound to find a torch or a lamp of some kind.'

'There's no light down here?'

'Nothing. Just daylight – what there is of it.'

'The emergency lighting may still be working in the tunnels, but a torch might come in useful.'

'Right.'

Dealey felt a hand on his arm and allowed himself to be

led across the hall. The cries of the injured had died down, but a low coalescent moaning had taken its place. Something clutched at his trouser leg and a voice begged for help. He felt his guide hesitate and Dealey quickly pulled the other man to him. 'You haven't told me your name yet,' he said to distract him, walking on, keeping the other man going.

'Culver,' came the reply.

'Let's concentrate on one thing at a time, Mr Culver: first, let's find a torch; second, let's get to the tunnels; third, let's get into the shelter. Nothing else must sidetrack us, not if we want to live.'

Culver knew the blind man was right, yet it was difficult to disregard his own misgivings; would it really be worthwhile to survive? Just what *was* left up there? Had most of the northern hemisphere been wiped out, or had the strikes concentrated only on major cities and strategic military bases? There was no way of knowing for the moment so he closed the questions from his mind, just as he kept further, more emotional, thoughts at bay. Only the mind-numbing shock would see him through, so long as it did not affect his actions; for now, nothing else but finding a torch mattered.

The ground trembled briefly and screaming broke out once more.

The two men stopped in their tracks. 'Another bomb?' Culver asked.

Dealey shook his head. 'I doubt it. An explosion not too far away, I think. It could be just a fractured gas main.'

They reached the first door and Culver twisted the handle. Locked. 'Shit!' He took a pace back and kicked out. Once more, and it gave. Another, and it was open.

Culver went in, Dealey following close behind, a hand on his guide's shoulder. A voice came from the darkness. 'What d'you want? This is London Transport property, you're not allowed in here.'

Culver was not surprised at the irrationality. 'Take it easy, we only want a torch,' he reassured the man whom he could just see crouching behind a chair in one corner of the tiny room.

'I can't let you . . .' his voice broke. 'What's happened out there? Is it all over?'

'It's done,' Culver said, 'but it's not over. Is there a torch in here?'

'There's a flashlight on the shelf, to your right, by the door.'

Culver saw it. Reached for it.

The crouching man raised an arm to protect his eyes when Culver flicked the switch and shone the beam in his direction.

'My advice to you is to get into the tunnels,' Dealey said. 'You'll be safer there.'

'I'm all right where I am. There's no need for me to leave here.'

'Very well, it's up to you. Are you the stationmaster?'

'Mr Franklin is dead. He tried to control the crowds. They were panicking. He tried to hold them back, tried to make them form queues. Instead, they trampled him. None of us could help. Just too many!'

'Calm yourself. The crowds have gone, most are below in the tunnels. And the nuclear attack is over.'

'The attack? Then it really happened, they really did it? They dropped the Bomb?'

'Several, I should think.'

Culver decided not to mention the five separate cloud stems he had seen; he would tell Dealey later, when they were alone.

'Then we're all finished.'

'No, not if everyone stays under cover for now. The worst damage from radiation should be over within two to four weeks, and by then the authorities should have everything under control.'

Culver almost laughed aloud, but the effort would have been too much. 'Let's get out of here,' he suggested instead.

'I can only repeat: you'll be safer in the tunnels,' Dealey told the crouching man, who gave no reply.

Culver turned the beam away, switching it off as he did so. The flashlight would be useful: its casing was made of heavy-duty rubber and the lamp reflector was wider than normal. 'We're wasting time,' he said quietly.

If Dealey was surprised at his guide's sudden resoluteness he did not show it. 'Of course, you're right. Let's hurry.'

They made their way through the ticket barrier towards the escalators. There were three and none was working. Culver noticed that the ticket hall had filled with more people, most of whom appeared to be totally disorientated, their movements uncertain, their eyes blankly staring. He told Dealey of what he saw.

'Is there nothing we can do for them?' he whispered harshly.

'I'm afraid not. I only hope we can help ourselves.'

Concentrate. The stairs. Have to ease our way over to them. Ignore the old woman sitting on the floor rocking her blood-covered head backwards and forwards. Forget about the kid clinging to his mother, yelling for her to take out the horrible pieces of glass from his hands. *Don't look* at the man leaning against the wall vomiting black blood. Help one and you had to help another. Help another and you had to help everybody. Help everybody and you were finished. Just help yourself. And this man Alex Dealey, who seemed to know so much.

They were soon at the top of the centre escalator. Bodies were sprawled all the way down, sitting, lying, some just slumped against the handrails. He could just make out dim emergency lights below.

'We'll have to be careful going down,' he said. 'The stairs are packed with people and we'll have to work our way through them.' He released the blind man's arm and clamped Dealey's hand around his own. 'Hold tight and stick close.' He pushed his way through to the stairs.

Men and women looked at them, but no one objected. Some even tried to move aside when they realized Dealey was blind. It was slow progress and Culver was careful not to trip, allowing his companion to lean on him, to use his strength for support; one slip and they would never stop rolling.

They were halfway down when people below came pouring from the platform entrances.

They clawed at those on the escalators, trying to get on to the stairways, calling out, screaming something that Culver and Dealey could make no sense of. The renewed panic was infectious: the confused mass on the stairs rose as one and began to beat their way back up, punching out at those who blocked their path, pushing their way over those who lay injured.

'What now?' Dealey asked in frustration as they were shoved aside by the group just below them. 'What's happening down there, Culver?'

'I don't know, but maybe it's not such a good idea after all.'

'We have to get into the tunnel, don't you understand? We can't go back up there.'

'You know it and I know it; try telling them!' A fist struck him in the chest as a man struggled to get by. He staggered back, but resisted the urge to retaliate. Instead, he shouted above the din, 'There's only one way down, and it's going to be dangerous for you!'

'It can't be more dangerous than what's behind us!'

Culver pushed him against the rubber handrail and lifted his legs onto the centre section, jumping up himself, holding on to the rail with one hand, his arm crooked under Dealey's, the flashlight still grasped tightly. 'Use your feet to control your slide and I'll try to keep hold of the rail!'

The descent began and both men soon found it impossible to maintain a regulated speed. The arm-lock Culver had on Dealey became too difficult to maintain; his other hand slipped from the handrail and they plunged downwards, feet striking the climbers on the stairs, so that their bodies twisted, their descent becoming completely uncontrolled. It was a frightening, helter-skelter ride towards another, unknown terror, a heart-churning rush into fresh danger.

Their fall was cushioned by the desperate figures massing around the bottom of the escalators. They landed in a flurry of arms and legs, wind knocked from them, but striking nothing hard which could cause serious damage. Culver was only slightly dazed and the flashlight was still gripped firmly in his hand.

'Dealey, where the Christ are you?' he shouted. He pulled at a hand rising from the bodies beneath him and released it when he realised it wasn't the blind man. 'Dealey!'

'Here. I'm here. Help me.'

Culver used the flashlight to pinpoint the voice's source; the emergency lighting was very limited. He found Dealey and tugged him free.

'You okay?' he asked.

'I'll find out later,' came the reply. 'So long as we can both walk, that's all that matters for the moment. We must find the eastbound tunnel.'

'It's over there.' Culver pointed the beam in that direction as though the other man could see. 'Westbound is on a lower level than this.' The flashlight was almost knocked from his hand as someone hurtled by. The congestion at the foot of the escalators was growing worse and both men fought to resist the human tide. Culver helped up one of the men who had cushioned his fall moments earlier.

He pulled the man's face close to his. 'Why is everyone running from the tunnels? It's the only safe place!'

The man tried to get away from him, but Culver held on. 'What is it? What's in there?'

'Something ... something in the tunnel. I couldn't see, but others did! They were cut, bleeding. They said they'd been attacked in there. Please, let me go!'

'Attacked by what?'

'I don't know!' the man screamed. 'Just let me go!' He tore himself free and was instantly swallowed up by the crowd.

Culver turned to Dealey. 'Did you hear that? Something else is in that tunnel.'

'It's mass hysteria, that's all, and it's understandable under the circumstances. Everyone's still in a state of shock.'

'He said they were bleeding.'

'I'd imagine there are not too many people who *haven't* been injured in some way. Perhaps a rat or some other creature got trodden on in there and bit back. Whoever was bitten obviously panicked the others.'

Culver wasn't convinced, but he had no intention of returning to the world above where the air would be laden with radiation-contaminated particles by now. 'We'll have to fight our way through.'

'I'll do what I can to help.'

'All right. Get behind me and hold tight. I'm going to push my way in – you can put your weight behind me. Keep pushing, no matter what.'

Culver shielded his face with his arms, the torch held before him as an extra guard, and together he and Dealey forced their way through the mob like swimmers against a strong current. It was hard going and both men were soaked with sweat before they reached the outer fringes of the crowd. There they found others who had not joined the throng, those who were wary of what lay behind them, but who realized the danger from above. And then there were those who could not move: the injured, the dead.

'The platform's through here,' Culver said as they reached one of the platform's entrances. He glanced back at the escalators, at the thick mass of shuffling bodies, the stairs crammed with a struggling, heaving crowd. One slip, he thought, and hundreds will be crushed. He was glad not to be among them. And then he noticed there were more pouring from the shorter staircase leading up from the westbound platform; they frantically joined the mass, their shouts mingling with those of the others. He was curious: why should the panic have spread to a totally different tunnel, the one *below* the eastbound?

'We can't stop here, Culver. We must keep going.' Dealey was leaning against the smooth, yellow-tiled wall, his portly frame sagging, clothes in disarray. Culver pushed the disturbing thought from his mind and led the other man out onto the platform. There was no train on the track.

'D'you think there's still power in the lines?' Culver asked worriedly.

'I doubt it. Didn't you say that only the emergency lights

were on? I think the main power has been cut. Is there a train in the station?'

'No.'

'Then the trains are probably stuck in the tunnels; I think we can assume the tracks are dead.'

'You assume it. I'll walk between the lines.'

'Take me to the tunnel entrance. To the, er, left, the east. We have to go back down the line.'

'Look, I'm not so sure. Those people seemed pretty scared of whatever was in there.'

'We've been through all that.'

'People were running from the other platform too, the one below this. How do you explain that?'

'I don't need to. We have no choice but to find the shelter.'

'We could stay here. It's deep enough underground to be safe.'

'Not necessarily. It isn't sealed; there are openings, vents, all along the tunnels where radiation can penetrate.'

'Are you always so pessimistic?'

'I'm sorry, but it's pointless pretending optimism under these circumstances. From now on, we must consider the worst possibilities if we're to live.'

'How far into the tunnel is this entrance?' Culver looked towards the round arch of the dark tunnel, his brow furrowed in anxious lines.

'Eight to nine hundred yards. It won't take us long.'

'Let's get on with it then.'

The platform entrance was not far from the tunnel itself and the two men approached the black gaping hole cautiously. Culver stepped close to the platform's edge and shone the flashlight into the darkness.

'It looks clear,' he called back over his shoulder to Dealey.

'If there was anything in there the crowds probably scared it off long ago.'

'Let's hope you're right.'

Dealey had felt his way along the side wall and had caught up with Culver. 'How do your eyes feel?' Culver asked him.

'Bloody sore, but not as bad as before. The stinging is slowly fading.'

Culver nodded and pointed the beam straight into his face.

'Can you see anything at all?'

Dealey blinked. 'No. It hurt even more for a moment, though. Did you shine the light at me?'

'Straight into the pupils. They shrank.'

'It could mean nothing.'

'Yeah, keep up the pessimism. Grab my shoulder, and keep your left side against the wall; we're going down.'

The air was cool, clammy, in the tunnel, and they could see the emergency lights stretching one after the other into the blackness, their dim glow barely making an impression. It felt to Culver as if they were descending into a void, an emptiness that was itself threatening. Perhaps it was just the unnatural stillness after the turmoil above; or that he felt an unseen presence, eyes watching him from the shadows. Perhaps his nerves were just stretched to breaking point. Perhaps.

The tunnel curved slightly, the single chain of lights ahead disappearing. The dim glow from the platform behind vanished as they rounded the curve, leaving them in total isolation. Their footsteps echoed hollowly around the arched walls.

Culver noticed there were gaps in the wall to his right; he shone the beam in that direction and light reflected back from another set of tracks.

'I can see another tunnel,' he told Dealey, his voice strangely loud in the confines of the shaft.

'It must be the westbound. Keep your torch to the right – I'd hate to miss the shelter.'

Dealey's weight dragged against him now and he knew the man was near to exhaustion. His eyes must have hurt like hell and the mental agony of not knowing if he was permanently blinded couldn't have helped much. Again, he wondered who the man was and how he knew about the shelter. Obviously he—

Something had moved in the darkness ahead. He'd heard it. A scurrying sound.

'Why have you stopped?' Dealey was clenching his arm tightly.

'I thought I heard something.'

'Can you see anything?'

He swung the torch around in a wide arc. 'Nothing.'

They went on, their pace quickened despite the tiredness that dragged at them, their senses acutely aware, a sudden, awful foreboding growing within. Culver frantically searched for the opening, the doorway that would lead them to safety. There were recesses in the wall, but none held the magic door. Surely they must be near. They'd walked more than eight hundred yards. It felt like eight miles. They had to find it soon. Jesus, let them find it soon.

He fell. Something was lying across the line. Something that had tripped him.

'Culver!' Dealey shouted, suddenly alone. He stumbled forwards, arms outstretched, sightless eyes wide, and he, too, fell over the something that lay across the line.

His hands touched metal and quickly recoiled. At least they were now certain of one thing; there was no power in the line. His hands scrabbled around in the darkness. Felt something. Soft. Sticky soft, a head, a face.

'Culver? Are you all right?'

His guide's voice came from further away. 'Don't move, Dealey. Don't touch any more.'

But it was too late. His groping fingers had found the eyes. But there were no eyes. Just deep, viscous sockets that sucked at his fingers as he withdrew them. He fell back and his hand touched something else. It was warm, and it was abhorrent. It was something slippery and it belonged inside a body, not outside.

'Keep still!' Culver's voice commanded again.

Dealey's throat was too constricted to allow speech.

Culver, lying sprawled across the outer track, shone the flashlight around them. Bodies littered the tunnel. Black shapes moved among them, feeding off them.

They crouched, eluding the beam. Or scuttled away, back into the shadows.

'Oh, no, I don't believe it.' Culver's voice was a moan.

'Tell me what's there, Culver. Please tell me.'

'Keep still. Just don't move for a moment.'

Slowly, very slowly, he pushed himself into a sitting position. The light flashed across a bristle-haired humped back; the creature tensed, fled.

He half rose, the flashlight held before him. Its beam fell upon a human foot, a leg, a torso, the wicked yellow eyes of the animal squatting on the man's open chest. The creature plunged its bloodied snout deep into the wound, pulling flesh free with huge incisor teeth.

It stopped eating. It watched the man with the torch.

'Dealey.' He kept his voice low, but could not control the tremor. 'Move towards me – *slowly* – just move slowly.'

The other man did exactly as he was told, the fear in Culver's voice all the warning he needed.

Culver carefully reached for him, remaining crouched, avoiding any sudden movement. He drew the crawling man to him, then moved back so that they were both against the tunnel wall.

'What is it?' Dealey whispered.

Culver took a deep breath. 'Rats,' he said quietly. 'But like I've never seen before. They're big.' He wondered at his own understatement.

'Are they black-furred?'

'Everything's black down here.'

'Oh God, not again, not at a time like this.'

Culver glanced at him curiously, but could not see his expression in the darkness. He did not want to take the beam away from the dead bodies or the shapes that moved among them. His eyes narrowed. 'Wait a minute. There were a couple of outbreaks of killer Black rats some years ago. Are you saying these are the same breed? We were told they'd been wiped out, for Christ's sake!'

'I can't see them, so I can't say. It's hardly the time to discuss the point, though.'

'Yeah, I'm with you there. But what do you suggest – we shoo them away?'

'Can you see the shelter door? We must be close.'

Reluctantly, and very slowly, Culver swept the beam across the carnage. He winced when he saw the tangle of torn human forms and fought back nausea as the creatures steadily chewed at their victims. He had never before realized that blood had such a strong odour.

He froze when he saw one rat stealthily creeping towards them, its long body kept low, its haunches hunched and tensed. The torch beam reflected in its eyes and the creature stopped. It moved its head away from the glare, then moved back a few paces. It slid back in the darkness, unhurried and unconcerned.

'Have you found the doorway yet?' Dealey hissed urgently.

'No. I got distracted.'

The light resumed its slow journey, revealing too much, each new horror chilling him to his core, causing the hand guiding the torch to tremble so that the very cavern seemed to quake. He deliberately aimed the beam along the wall he and Dealey rested against; Dealey had said the doorway was on the right-hand side of the eastbound tunnel. He hated the idea of allowing darkness to conceal the gorging creatures once more, for he felt somehow it was only the light holding them back, as if it were a force-field of sorts. Deep down, he knew he was wrong. They had not been attacked because the vermin were content with their kill for the moment; their hunger could be satiated without further effort.

But if they felt threatened the slaughter would start again, and this time, he and Dealey would be the victims.

Oh Christ, where was that bloody shelter?

The slow-swinging beam came to a halt. What was that?

He moved the light back a few feet.

It came to rest on a figure standing in one of the openings dividing the two tunnels.

She was perfectly still, eyes staring directly ahead into the brickwork of a column opposite the one she leaned against. Her clothes were torn, dirt-smeared; her hair matted, unkempt. She did not appear to be breathing, but she was alive. Alive and shocked rigid.

'Dealey,' Culver said, keeping his voice low. 'There's a girl on the other side of the track. Just standing there, too scared to move.'

He tensed as a black shape appeared in the opening, at the girl's feet. Its pointed nose twitched in the air before it leapt off the small ledge to be among its gluttonous companions.

'Find the door, man, that's more important.'

Culver grimaced, a smile without humour. 'You're all heart,' he said.

'If we find the shelter, then we may be able to help her.'

'She could collapse at any moment, and if she does she'll fall right into them. She'd have no chance.'

'There isn't much we can do.'

'Maybe not.' Culver began to rise, his back scraping against the brick wall, the movement slow, easy. 'But we're going to try.'

'Culver!' A hand grabbed his sleeve, but he shook it off. He began to move away from the slaughter, backing off in the direction they had come.

'Stay there, Dealey,' he whispered. 'You'll be okay. They're not ready for dessert just yet.' His black humour did not amuse even himself.

When he felt he was at a safe distance – although a few hundred miles would have felt safer – Culver crossed the track. Then began the cautious, deliberate walk back, keeping the beam low, not wanting to disturb the unholy feast. His footsteps light, Culver stepped through one of the openings onto the adjacent track, hoping none of the creatures was lurking there. Less intimidated by the bloodletting because now it was out of view, he made faster progress.

The girl scarcely blinked at the glare as he reached her from the other side of the opening. He stepped up onto the small ledge and faced her.

'Are you hurt?' he asked, raising his voice a little when there was no response. 'Can you hear me? Are you hurt?'

A tiny flicker of life registered in her eyes, but still she gave no acknowledgement of his presence.

'Culver,' came Dealey's hissed voice from the other side of the tunnel, twenty feet or so back from the opening Culver and the girl stood in. 'I can hear them getting closer. You've got to help me. Please find the shelter.' He sounded desperate, almost tearful, and Culver could understand why. The sucking guzzling of the vermin was nauseating as well as terrifying, and the cracking of small, brittle bones cruelly accentuated the horror.

Becoming impatient with his own caution, Culver quickly swung the wide beam along the opposite wall, starting at a point further down the tunnel. There was more than one recess set in the brickwork, but none held a doorway, until – *there it was*! Almost opposite. A goddam iron bloody door! Unmarked, but then it would be!

'Dealey! I've found it!' It was difficult to keep his voice low. 'It's just a little ahead of me, about thirty yards from you. Can you make it on your own?'

The other man was already on his feet. He began to inch along the wall, feeling with his hands, his face almost pressed against the rough brickwork. Culver turned his attention back to the girl.

Her face was smeared with blood and dirt, although he could see no open cuts, and her eyes remained wide and staring. She might have been pretty, he couldn't tell, and her shoulder-length hair might have looked good with the sun reflecting highlights, but again, it was hard to tell and not the uppermost consideration in his mind. When his hand touched her shoulder the air exploded with her scream.

He staggered back from her thrusting arms, his head striking the column behind. His eyes closed for just an instant, but when they opened she had gone. He swung the torch and found her again. She had fallen among the half-eaten bodies, startling the black vermin so that they scurried away. And now he saw just how many of the creatures there were.

Hundreds! My God, more. Many more!

'Dealey, get to the shelter! Move as fast as you can!'

The girl was trying to rise, trying to crawl away from the glare, and the rats had stopped, were turning, were watching her, were no longer afraid.

4

He jumped, slipped, lay sprawled, the flashlight gone from his grasp. His hands were in a sticky mess and he quickly withdrew them, afraid to see what they had touched. The girl was only a few feet away and he lunged for her ankle to prevent her moving any further, for the beasts were waiting for her just beyond the circle of light.

She screamed again when he gripped her leg and pulled her back. His other hand scrabbled around for the torch, ignoring the wet, mushy things he touched in the darkness. He grabbed the handle, but the girl was fighting against him, kicking, turning and beating at him with her fists. The taste of blood was in his mouth and he turned his head aside to avoid the blows. A weight thudded against him and he felt something tear at his thigh.

He cried aloud and brought the heavy flashlight down hard on the rat's spine. It squealed, high-pitched, piercing, but its teeth would not release their grip. The flashlight came down again, harder, harder, again, and the creature's claws scrabbled at the dust beneath it. It released its hold, squealing, the sound of a baby in pain. Culver struck again and it staggered sideways. But it did not run.

Culver jumped to his feet, the fear overcoming his exhaustion; he stamped on the creature's skull, his boot crunching bones, squashing the substance beneath. The rat writhed, twitching spasmodically between the human bodies it had been feeding off, its screeches becoming a mewling sound, fading as it died.

He saw the other rat just before it leapt and brought the torch round in a crushing swing, striking the black, bristling body in mid-air, his whole weight behind the blow, losing balance as he followed through. He was on the ground again, among the corpses. Why didn't the creatures attack in force? What were they waiting for? The answer flashed into his mind as he scrambled to his feet: they were testing his strength! The first two were just the advance party; the rest would follow now that they knew how weak their opponent was! There was no time to wonder at their cunning.

He pulled the girl up, holding her around the waist, and flashed the light around the tunnel.

They were waiting there, watching him. Dark, hunched monsters, with evil yellow eyes. Slanted eyes that somehow glinted an unusual intelligence. Their bodies quivered as one and he knew they were ready to strike.

The girl pulled against him and he clamped a hand over her mouth to prevent her from screaming again. He ignored the pain as she bit into him. In the periphery of his vision he saw Dealey edging his way along the wall.

'It's just a few feet ahead of you,' he said, fighting to keep down the hysteria. 'For Christ's sake, Dealey, get that bloody door open.'

Culver began to make for the recess himself, forcing the girl to go with him, moving inch by inch, careful not to stumble over a body, to slip in the blood. Fortunately, the girl seemed to realize what was happening. She was still tense, stiff, but she no longer fought. He eased his grip over her mouth.

The rats had started to creep forward.

He risked a look at Dealey. The blind man had reached the door. But he was sagging against it. His face was turning in Culver's direction. His eyes were closed tight and his mouth was open in a silent moan of agony.

'Dealey?' Culver said, still moving towards him.

'The keys. The keys were in my briefcase!' His last words were screeched and his fists began to flail at the door's metal surface.

'Don't!' Culver warned, but it was too late. The screams and the banging had spurred the black creatures into attack.

Culver cried out as the leaping bodies slammed into him, his arms instinctively protecting his face. Both he and the girl went down under the weight and a million razor-sharp teeth seemed to sink into his skin. He kicked, thrashed out with his arms, shouted his pain and terror.

The tunnel shook. Dust and bricks fell from the ceiling. The explosion ricocheted around and around the curved walls, spiralling towards them, heaving the earth. Three hundred yards away, the tunnel collapsed, flames roaring through in a great ball that billowed outwards.

The vermin screeched, their attack on the two humans forgotten. They cowered to the ground, a mass of dark quivering bodies, completely still, they themselves now rigid with fear.

Culver rose to his elbows and swiped at a rat nestled on his lap. It fell to one side with a snarling hiss, but did not retaliate.

Another explosion, louder than the first, and the fireball expanded, raced towards them along the tunnel, filling every inch, a swelling yellow that scorched the walls.

The creatures ran, scrabbling over the bodies, slithering past or leaping over Culver and the girl, squealing in alarm, they themselves the hunted now, the fast-approaching billowing flames the merciless hunter.

Culver was on his feet, lifting the girl, the vermin forming a dark-flowing river around his legs. He ran with her, just a few feet, praying that the recess in which Dealey knelt would offer some protection, the wall of fire hurrying to meet them, eager to incinerate them in its fiery embrace.

It was too near, they could never make it! He jumped the last few feet, the dead weight of the girl unnoticed in his panic.

They crashed into the metal doorway as the flames reached them and Culver felt the searing heat against his skin, licking at his clothes.

It was hopeless. The narrow refuge could offer little protection as the fire swept by. They would all be burnt to a crisp.

And then he was tumbling forward with the others, falling into a different light, the metal door giving way, the scorching flames at his back, dropping, tumbling, over and over and over, never wishing to stop, the world just light and pain and sound . . .

And then blackness.

5

'Oh, Jes—'

A gentle hand forced him back down onto the narrow bunkbed.

'It's all right,' a voice equally gentle said. 'You've got a nasty wound in your leg; we're dealing with it.'

Culver looked up into the white face that seemed to hover above him. The woman was frightened – he could just detect the glimmer of alarm hiding behind her outwardly calm gaze – but she worked steadily, professionally, swabbing away the blood from the gash in his thigh.

'You were lucky,' she told him. 'Whatever did this just missed the artery.'

'You sure?'

She didn't smile. 'If the artery had been severed we'd have both been painted bright scarlet by now. And you'd be considerably weaker than you appear to be. No, the blood's deep red and it's flowing rather than spurting, so it's not too serious. What did this, anyway?'

He closed his eyes, but the memory became even sharper. 'I don't think you'd believe me.'

The woman stopped working momentarily. 'After today, after this madness, I'm prepared to believe anything and anybody.'

A silence fell between them, one which Culver eventually broke.

'There were rats in the tunnels,' he said. 'But like no goddam rats I've ever seen before.'

She looked at him curiously.

'They were big, some as big as dogs. They ... they were feeding off people who'd fled into the tunnel.'

'They attacked you?'

He nodded. 'They attacked. It's hard to think ... I don't know how . . .'

'Some of the engineers heard you pounding on the emergency door. You literally fell in among us.'

He tried to look around him. 'Just who ... what is this place?'

'Officially it's the Kingsway telephone exchange. Equally officially, but not for public knowledge, it's a government nuclear shelter. You happen to be in the sick bay at the moment.'

Over her shoulder, Culver could see other two-tiered bunkbeds. It was a small room with grey walls and ceiling; strip-lighting glared overhead. There were other figures around a bed further down.

The woman followed his gaze. 'The girl you brought in with you is being treated for shock. I took a look at her first – she doesn't appear to have sustained any serious injuries, just minor cuts and bruises. Her hair is a little singed, but you must have protected her from the fire out there.'

'Fire?'

'Don't you remember? The engineers said the tunnel was ablaze for a few seconds, a fireball of some kind. You'd have all roasted if the door hadn't been opened at the crucial moment. As it was, you were lucky you were wearing a thick leather jacket or your back would have peeled . . .'

'Where's Dealey?'

'. . . the skin on your hands and the back of your neck is scorched . . .'

'He didn't make it.' Culver sat up.

A hand splayed against his chest and eased him back down again.

'He made it. He's talking with the CDO . . .'

'The what?'

'Civil Defence officer. Dealey wanted me to take care of you and the girl first.'

'You know he's been blinded?'

'Of course. With luck, it may only be short-term; it depends on how long he looked into the flash. I assume that's how it happened?'

'Yeah. And it was only for a split-second.'

'He may be fortunate, then. It'll be a long wait for him, though.'

She busied herself tending his wound and for the first time he was aware of his naked legs.

'If it was a rat bite we'll need to disinfect. You'll need an anti-tetanus jab, too,' she muttered. 'Feeling strong?'

'Not particularly. Who are you?'

'Doctor Clare Reynolds.' Still no smile. 'I'm only here for a meeting with Alex Dealey and several others which was scheduled for this afternoon.'

'You work for the government?'

This time a brief, tight smile flashed. 'I was drafted in when the situation reached crisis point. Normal precautions; nobody thought it would escalate to this. Nobody.'

She turned to a small trolley by her side and poured fluid onto a small pad. Wisps of premature grey mingled with the dark auburn of her hair, which was cut short in a practical rather than glamorous style. Her features were pinched taut – not surprising in the circumstances – and her pale skin seemed almost anaemic, although that could have been due to the harsh lights above (or again, the circumstances). He noticed she was wearing a wedding ring.

She turned back to him. 'This is going to sting,' she warned, brushing the soaked pad into the gash.

'Shhhhh—' Culver gripped the sides of the bunk '—iiiiit!'

'No masochist you. Okay, it's done. No need for stitches, just a pad will do. We don't want to bury any infection. You've a mass of smaller wounds and abrasions but no serious burns from the fire. I'll treat them and then I want to put you out for a short time; you've been through a lot.'

'I'd rather you didn't.'

'Sure you would. Just think yourself lucky to be out of this for a while. What's your name, by the way?'

'Steve Culver.'

'Pleased to know you, Mr Culver. I think we'll be seeing a lot of each other.'

'What happened, Doctor? Why did they *let* it happen?'

'It all comes down to greed in the end.' Some of the forced stiffness went out of her. 'And envy. Let's not forget our old friend envy.'

She finished dressing the wound, and administered the anti-tetanus injection; then she reached back into the trolley for a Diazepam-filled syringe.

He awoke to find a different pair of eyes staring down at him. Her blonde hair fell around her face, a face that was still marked and grimy from the ordeal in the tunnel. Her eyes were wide, and unlike the doctor's cried out her fear. A hand clutched at his shoulder.

'Where am I?' she asked, almost in a whisper. 'Please tell me.'

He struggled to sit up and his head rode a coaster. Her hand tightened on his shoulder, digging into the flesh.

'Take it easy,' he begged. 'Just give me a minute.'

Culver slowly eased his back against the wall behind and waited for the spinning to stop. His head began to clear, making way for jumbled thoughts to rush in. His senses sharpened rapidly as he remembered. The dread drifted down into the lower regions of his stomach like a ship sinking to the sea bed. He looked at the girl, then pushed a hand between her hair and cheek.

'You're safe now,' he told her softly. He wanted to hold her, to hug her to his chest, to tell her it was all a bad dream that had ended. But he knew it was just beginning.

'We're in a government shelter,' he said. 'The entrance was in the tunnel near where we found you.'

He watched her shudder.

'I remember.' Her voice, her gaze, was distant. 'We heard the sirens. No one could believe it was really happening, but we ran, we hid. We thought the tunnels would protect us. Those things . . .' She broke and he pulled her to him.

Her sobs were muffled against his chest and he felt his own emotional barrier, a shield that was tissue-thin, beginning to tear. There was a closeness between them – he was sure it was shared – an intimacy imposed by what they had both been through, a desperate touching of spirits. Culver held on to the girl and fought against his own despair.

After what seemed a long while, her shuddering stopped, although she continued to tremble slightly. She pulled away from him.

'Were . . . were you the one who helped me? Out there, when those . . . *Oh, God, what were they?'*

'Vermin,' he answered, keeping his voice calm. 'Rats that must have been breeding underground for years.'

'But their size! How could they get to that size?'

'Mutants,' he told her. 'Monsters that should have been wiped out years ago when they first appeared. We were told that they had been, but it looks like we were misinformed. Or deceived.'

'How could they survive, how could they breed, how could they go unnoticed?' Her voice was rising and Culver could see she was beginning to lose control again.

'Maybe we'll find the answers later,' he answered soothingly. 'The main thing is that we're safe now. Whatever's above, whatever's in the tunnels, can't touch us here.'

He would never forget the haunting shadow that touched her face at that moment. 'Is ... is there anything left ... above?'

He could not answer. To have done so, to have had to *think* of it, would have broken him. Push it away, Culver, save it for later. It was too much to take right now, too much to envisage. Keep away thoughts of black-charred children, torn bodies, crushed, bewildered children, a devastated, ravaged city, country – world? – contaminated, shrieking, *children, children, children*!

He had cried out then, not loudly, not frenziedly; a piteous sound that was faint, but nevertheless, an outpouring of anguish. And now it was the girl who comforted him.

The doctor came for them a little later. She stopped for a moment in the doorway of the small sick bay, briefly wishing that she, too, had a pair of arms to fall into, someone who would hold her, tell her things would be all right ... if only she knew if Simon ... mustn't think about it, mustn't even consider her husband's death.

'How are you both feeling?' she asked, professionalism stifling rising emotion.

They looked at her as if she were some weird alien, perhaps the creator of the havoc above; but the man, Culver, recovered quickly.

'How long were we out for?' he asked as they separated.

'About six hours,' Clare Reynolds glanced at her wristwatch. 'It's now just after seven. Evening.'

She approached them. 'Now tell me how you're feeling. Any aches, pains, you think I should know about? You?' She looked at the girl.

'I'm just numb.'

The doctor now looked even paler to Culver, if that were possible, but she managed a sad smile. 'We all are mentally. How do you feel physically? Do you hurt anywhere?'

The girl shook her head.

'Good. Do you want to tell us your name?'

The girl sat upright on the edge of the bed and wiped a hand across her eyes. 'Kate,' she said.

'Surname?'

'Garner.'

'Welcome to the survivors' club, Kate Garner.' The icy tone hardly sounded welcoming. 'How does your leg feel, Mr Culver?'

'Like it was bitten by a rat.' Culver raised his knees beneath the single blanket and rested his wrists over them. 'What's been going on while we were asleep?'

'That's why I'm here. A meeting is about to start in the shelter's dining room. You'll find out all you want to know there. Are you fit enough to get dressed?'

Culver nodded and realized that, for the moment at least, he had put something behind him. The pain, the tormenting images, could be kept in cold storage for a while. They would never leave him, of that he was sure, but for the time being they could be suppressed. A cold fury was taking hold inside and he knew it would help sustain him throughout whatever was yet to come. For a while.

The doctor reached up to the bunkbed above, then tossed his clothes into his lap. 'Jacket's a little burnt and your jeans and shirt are somewhat torn, but no need to worry – the meeting won't be formal. Kate, could you come over to another bed? I just want to have another look at you.'

Culver quickly dressed, wincing at the pain sudden movement caused. He must have been more bruised than he realized, and the whole of his thigh had stiffened. He found his tan boots beneath the bed and grunted as he bent to lace them up; it felt as though someone had slammed a medicine-ball into his stomach. He stood, using the upper bunk as support until he felt steady, then joined the doctor and the girl.

'Everything okay?' he asked, looking from one to the other.

'No serious damage.' The doctor stood. 'Let's join the others.'

'How many "others" are there?' Culver said. 'And who are they?'

'Engineers mostly, technicians permanently based here to operate the telephone equipment. The rest are ROCs – members of the Royal Observer Corps – and one or two Civil Defence people. More should have joined us at the first warning of attack, but . . .' she shrugged '. . . such clinically devised plans don't always work out in practice. Especially when a whole city is in a state of panic. There are nearly forty of us in all.'

She led them from the sick bay and both Culver and the girl gasped at the size of the area they had entered.

'Impressive, isn't it?' Dr Reynolds said, noticing their astonished looks. 'It would take well over an hour to walk around the whole complex. I won't bore you with a list of technical equipment housed down here – mainly because I don't understand most of it myself – but we have our own power plant *and* two standby plants. We also have our own artesian well and purification plant, so water won't be a problem. That's the switching unit area to the left and the power plant is just ahead of us. Further on is the kitchen, dining room and welfare department; that's where we're headed.'

The harsh glare from the overhead neon lights added to the atmosphere of machine-sterility; no warmth reflected from the grey-green walls. A quiet hum of power indicated electronic life in the non-human world, but Culver noticed that no individual machinery appeared to be functioning. He briefly wondered if there was anyone else left to communicate with.

Eventually, after what seemed like a long journey through confusing corridors, a different kind of humming reached his ears, but this was distinctly human: it was the sound of many voices in low-pitched conversation. The three of them entered the dining room and heads swung round in their direction, all conversation coming to a halt.

6

Dealey sat at one end of the room, white pads held by a bandage covering his eyes; at the same table, positioned at a right angle to the three rows of dining tables, were two blue-uniformed figures, one female, and two other men in civilian clothes. One of the latter whispered something to Dealey, who stood.

'Please come forward, Mr Culver,' Dealey said. 'And the young lady, too. Dr Reynolds, if you would join us at this table.'

Many of the people in the room were wearing white overalls and all looked pale and tired. They watched Culver and Kate curiously, almost as though they were interlopers gatecrashing an exclusive club. Two seats were offered them and they took their places close to the top table. The doctor sat next to Dealey.

Two mugs and a coffee pot were pushed towards Culver and he nodded his thanks, pouring for himself and the girl. No sugar or milk was offered. The buzz of conversation had started again and, as he raised the mug to his lips, he was aware of the barely suppressed stridency that prevailed. He glanced at Kate; she was gazing into the dark brown liquid as if it would somehow reveal some insane reasoning for all that had happened, some crazy logic as to why man should choose to shatter the very earth he lived upon. He wondered what she had lost personally – husband, family, lover? No wedding or engagement ring, so perhaps lover or even lovers. Parents, brothers and sisters. The memory of them all had to be bombarding her emotions, a relentless tormentor that only oblivion itself could vanquish. Everyone in the room was going through the same ordeal, the loss of relatives, loved ones, the sense of waste, futility, the fear of what lay ahead for themselves. Culver felt the coldness spreading through him like a creeping night shadow.

He sipped his coffee, realizing he was probably more fortunate than those around him, his losses back there in the past, the worst of his suffering carefully stored away, the lid shut tight. And though he had fought to survive that day, he wasn't sure it really mattered so much to him.

Dealey was conferring with the doctor and the civilians on either side, all three keeping their voices low, conspiratorial. The blind man looked weary, the unhealthy pallor of his skin heightened by the harsh overhead lighting. Culver had to admire his stamina, wondering if he had taken any time at all to rest after their arduous and gut-wrenching ordeal. He must be in pain from the injury to his eyes, and the mental anguish of not knowing whether or not the damage was permanent must in itself have been draining. He seemed different from the frightened, disorientated man that Culver had dragged through the wreckage, almost as if his badge of office (whatever office that might be) had reaffirmed the outward shell, officialdom his retrieved armour. Dealey looked up at the assemblage, his head moving from right to left, as if picking up threads of conversation.

The man next to him stood. 'Can I please have your attention?' he said, his words calm, measured, a rebuttal of the pernicious hysteria that skitted around the room from person to person like some quick-darting gadfly.

Conversation stopped.

'To the few who don't already know me, my name is Howard Farraday, and I'm the first line manager or senior engineer of the Kingsway telephone exchange. At the moment, because there is no one of senior position here, that makes me the boss.' He attempted a smile that was barely successful. He cleared his throat. 'Since further excavation work, begun in the 1950s, Kingsway has had a dual role: that of automatic exchange, carrying some five hundred lines, and as a government deep shelter. Most of you will be aware that the first ever NATO transatlantic cable terminates here.' He paused again, a tall man whose normal stature would have been described as robust had not the events of that day dragged at his shoulders and hued shadows of weariness around his eyes. His voice was quieter when he continued, as if his earlier confidence was fast draining from him. 'I think you'll also have been aware of the increased activity regarding Kingsway over the past few weeks; standard procedure, I might add, in times of international crisis. Although ... although the situation was regarded as serious, no one imagined this ... this ... that events would escalate to such disastrous proportions ...'

Culver shook his head at the jargonized description of the genocide. The coffee was bitter in his mouth and the wound in his thigh throbbed dully. His rancour, his deep-felt hate for those who had instigated the devastation, was frozen within for the moment with the rest of his emotions.

'... because of the increasing hostilities in the Middle East, and Russia's invasion of Iran, all such government establishments have been receiving similar attention ...'

The man droned on and what he said meant little to Culver. Words, just words. Nothing could adequately convey the horror, the dreadful loss, the ravages of what was yet to come. Once more his eyes were drawn to the girl; her gaze was still cast downwards, both hands clasped tight around the coffee mug, oblivious to its heat. His fingers curled around her wrist and at first there was no response; then she looked his way and the mixture of anguish and anger in her eyes bored into his own steadied emotions. He exerted soft pressure and now her expression was one of confusion: she seemed to be silently asking him why had it happened, why had they been spared? Questions he asked of himself and questions to which there were no answers. Man's madness to one, God's will to the other. No real answers.

Farraday was gesturing towards the seated man on his left '. . . senior Civil Defence officer, Alistair Bryce. Next to me here, on my right, is Mr Alex Dealey who is from the Ministry of Defence, and next to him, Dr Clare Reynolds, who has been associated with this particular establishment for some time now, so many of you will already know her. Then we have two Royal Observer Corps officers, Bob Mc-Ewen and Sheila Kennedy, whom you may also have seen from time to time on inspection duty. There should have been several other, er, officials, with us today – a meeting had been planned for this afternoon. Regrettably, they did not reach the shelter.' He swept back a lock of hair that dangled over his forehead, his upper body tilting backwards as if to assist the manoeuvre. 'Perhaps, Alex, you would like to continue.' The tall man slumped rather than sat, his hands clenched tight on the table before him, his shoulders hunched. Culver had the impression that Farraday's address had ended not a moment too soon; the man was ready to crack.

Dealey did not rise. And there was something chilling about listening to a man whose expression was hidden behind a white mask.

'Let me start,' he said, his voice surprisingly filling the greyish-green-walled dining room without raising itself beyond conversational level, 'by saying I know how each and every one of you must be feeling. You're afraid for your families, your loved ones, wondering if they have survived the nuclear explosion. Afraid, too, for yourselves: is this shelter safe from fallout, is there enough food, water, what will be left of the world we know?

'Two things I can reassure you of immediately: we are all well protected here, and there are provisions to last for six weeks, probably longer. As for water, those of you who are employed here will know that the complex has its own artesian well, so there will be no risk of contamination. I think it's important to stress these factors to relieve your minds of just some of the terrible burden they are bearing.'

There was still an uncomfortable, unnatural silence around the room.

'Mr Farraday has already mentioned that I'm from the Ministry of Defence. Actually I belong to the Inspector of Establishments division and I suppose you could call me a government shelter liaison officer – one of the chaps who sees that our underground defence units are in running order and in a permanent state of preparation.'

He leaned forward on the desk as if taking the whole room into his confidence. 'It's because of that specific role that I have full knowledge of every underground shelter and deep shelter, both public and governmental, in London and the surrounding counties, and that I can assure you that we are neither *alone* nor isolated.'

At last there were murmurs among the gathering, at last a reaction. Dealey raised a hand to bring the room to order.

'Before I give you general details of these shelters and operations centres, I think it best we appraise our present position and, of course, I'm sure the questions uppermost in your minds must be what exactly has happened, and what is the extent of the damage to our country?'

He placed both hands flat on the table. 'Unfortunately, we have no way of knowing the answers.'

This time the murmuring was stronger, and angry voices could be heard over the general buzz. Farraday quickly cut in.

'Communications with other stations have temporarily been lost. For the moment we cannot even make contact with the underground telecommunications centre near St Paul's, which is less than a mile away.'

'But the tunnel network should have protected the system,' a black engineer sitting close to Culver said sharply.

'Yes, you're quite right: the cable tunnels and deep tube tunnels should have afforded ample protection for the communications system. It would appear that the amount of damage nuclear bombs could cause has been badly underestimated and that vital sections in the network have been penetrated.'

Dealey spoke up. 'From information gathered before communications failed, we believe at least five nuclear warheads were directed at London and the surrounding suburbs.' He licked his lips, betraying the first signs of nervousness since the meeting had begun, and his next words came quickly, as though he were anxious to impart the information. 'We're not absolutely sure, but we think those targets were Hyde Park, Brentford, Heathrow, Croydon and the last somewhere northeast of the city. The nuclear weapons themselves would have been a mixture of one and two megatons, ground bursts and air bursts.'

Culver was confused. 'Wait a minute,' he said, raising a

hand like a child in a classroom. 'You're talking about a cable system being knocked out, right?'

Although their recent conversations had been fraught, mainly shouted, Dealey recognized the voice. 'That's correct,' he replied.

'Then why can't we communicate by radio?'

Farraday gave the answer. 'One of the effects of a nuclear blast is something we call EMP – electro magnetic pulse. It's an intense burst of radio waves that can destroy electrical networks and communication systems over an area of hundreds of miles. Any circuits with sensitive components such as radios, televisions, radar, computers, and any systems attached to long lengths of cable – telephones, the electricity power grid – are subjected to incredible surges of current which overload and destroy. A lot of the military equipment has been EMP-hardened by putting sensitive circuits inside conducting boxes and laying cables deep underground, but it looks as though even that hasn't been so effective.'

'Jesus, what a fuck-up,' Culver said quietly and those near him who heard nodded their agreement.

Dealey attempted to still the disquiet that was rumbling around the room like muted thunder. 'I must emphasize that these conditions are only temporary. I'm sure contact with other shelters will be made very soon. Mr Farraday himself has assured me of that.'

Farraday looked at him in surprise, but quickly recovered. 'I think we can safely assume that other such shelters have been left intact and are already trying to link up.'

Culver wondered if his statement was as dissatisfying to others as it was to him. He was startled when Kate, her voice dulled but clear to everyone in the room, suddenly said: 'Why was there no warning?'

'But there was a warning, Miss, er . . .' Dr Reynolds leaned towards him and whispered the name '. . . Garner. Surely you heard the si—'

'Why didn't anybody know it was going to happen?' This time there was an icy shrillness to the question.

There was a short, embarrassed silence at the top table before Dealey answered. 'Nobody, not one person in his right mind, could imagine another country would be foolish enough – no, insane enough! – to begin a Third World War with nuclear arms. It defies all sensibilities, all logic. Our government cannot be blamed for the lunatic suicidal tendencies of another nation. When the USSR land forces invaded Iran with a view to overrunning *all* the oil states, they were warned that retaliatory steps would be taken by the Combined World Forces . . .'

'They should have been stopped when they took total control of Afghanistan, and then Pakistan!' someone shouted from the back.

'I'm sorry, but political debate is useless at this time. Remember though, at the time of the Afghanistan conflict, there was no Combined Forces, just NATO and the Alliance Pact. Simply, the Western powers did not have the muscle to turn back the Russians; or at least we weren't confident enough to exercise whatever strength we had. It was only when the Gulf States finally decided that the West was the lesser of two evils, that we were able to deploy our forces in strategic positions.'

'But if we hadn't starved Russia of grain and then oil in the first place, they would never have been desperate enough to invade!' the same voice came back.

'Mr Dealey has already said this is not the time for such a discussion,' Farraday interrupted, fearing the meeting could so easily get out of hand. Hysteria was thick in the air; the smallest upset now could turn it into outrage and perhaps even violence.

'It may not even have been the Russians who fired the first missile, so until we know more let's not argue among ourselves.' He instantly regretted his words, realizing he had just implanted a fresh seed of thought.

Dealey quickly tried to cover the mistake. 'The point is that nobody imagined the situation had reached such a critical state. Our own government was making provisions for war, just in case, against all odds, it did break out.'

'Then why weren't we, the public, told that it was so imminent?' Culver's cold anger was directed solely at Dealey, as though he, the representative figure of government authority, was personally responsible.

'And create nationwide panic? What good would that have done? And besides, nothing was certain; the world has had more than its share of false crises in the past.'

And the world had cried 'wolf' too many times before, Culver thought sourly. The girl was shaking her head, a slight, mournful movement that bespoke bewilderment as well as despair.

'I repeat,' Dealey went on, 'the prime motive for us all is survival. We've managed to live through the worst, now we must cope with the aftermath.' His eyes seemed to bore through the white gauze covering them, defying every man and woman in the room to deny the rhetoric. 'Retrospection in our present circumstances can be of no constructive value whatsoever,' he added unnecessarily.

The uneasy silence indicated reluctant agreement.

'Now perhaps our CDO can advise us on what will happen over the next few weeks.' Dealey sat back in his chair, his masked face inscrutable, only the quick darting of his tongue across already moist lips again betraying an inner nervousness.

The senior Civil Defence officer decided he would carry more authority if he stood. Alistair Bryce was a small, balding man, whose jowls hung in flaps on either side of his round face; heavy pouches under his eyes completed the impression of a face made up of thick, spilled-over liquid. His eyes were sharp, however, and never still, bouncing quickly from left to right like blue pinballs.

'A few words, first, about what's likely to have occurred above us. What I'm going to say will frighten you, will distress you, but the time for lies is long-gone. If we are to survive, we have to work together as a unit, and we've got to trust each other.' His eyes took a more leisurely sweep around the room. 'I promise you this: our chances for survival are good; only our own fear can defeat us.'

He drew in a long breath as though about to plunge into deep water, feeling, in a metaphorical sense, this was the case.

'Anywhere between sixteen and thirty per cent of people in the Greater London area will have been killed outright. I know official figures lean towards the lower estimate, but as I said it's time for honesty. My opinion is that the number of dead will be at least twenty-eight per cent, and that's on the conservative side.'

He allowed a little time for the unsettling information to sink in. 'Another thirty to thirty-six per cent will have been injured by the blast alone. Many will have been crushed or trapped in buildings, or cut by flying glass. The list of various types of injury would be endless, so it's pointless to itemize. It's enough to say that burns, shock and mutilation will be widespread, and many will have received permanent or temporary eye damage caused by retinal burns from the initial flash.

'Blast pressure from each of the bombs will have damaged approximately seventy-five per cent of the Greater London area: most tall buildings and many bridges will have collapsed, and the majority of roads will have been blocked by rubble, fallen telegraph poles and lamp posts, and overturned vehicles. About thirty per cent of the houses in the city and suburbs will have been reduced to rubble, and over forty per cent too badly damaged to be repaired in the immediate future. I hardly need to say there probably won't be an unbroken window left in the capital.'

Bryce's face looked drained of blood, his overhanging jowls resembling empty money pouches. Perversely, he seemed to be taking refuge behind his own cold facts, as though the words had no real meaning, but were the considered statistics of an imagined war. It was a stance that enabled him to cope with his own emotion. 'Fire damage will be extensive and I'm afraid our fire services will be little more than useless. It may be that most of London above us is in flames.'

The cries, the sighing moans of despair, could no longer be contained. Several men and women were weeping openly, while others merely sat grim-faced, staring straight ahead as if seeing something beyond the room, beyond the shelter. Perhaps the suffering that was out there.

Kate had slumped forward on the table and he drew her close, using soft pressure against her initial resistance. She, along with Dealey and himself, had probably gone through more horrors that day than anyone else in the room, for they had been out there in the destruction, running for safety with the crowds, taking refuge in the tunnels. Almost eaten alive by rats. He wondered how much more her mind could take without losing grip totally.

Bryce raised both hands to quieten them and said reluctantly, 'There is still a consequence of the attack that must be dealt with. I know it's difficult for every man and woman in this room, but the reality of what has happened and what is going to happen must be faced now. If we are all aware of the worst effects of nuclear war, then nothing will be unexpected, nothing more will further demoralize us. Hopefully,' he added ominously.

'The next problem for every survivor of the blast is fallout. Most of the city's population would have had less than half an hour to get under cover before radioactive dust fell. Those still unprotected within six hours of the attack will have received a lethal dose of radiation and will die within a matter of days or weeks, depending on the individual dosage. And of course, anyone injured by the blast or its effects will be even more susceptible to radiation. Unofficial figures indicate that around four million people within the Greater London boundaries will be dead or dying within two weeks of the attack, from a lethal dose of more than 6,000 rads.'

Farraday's voice was shaky when he spoke and Culver had the impression that he asked the next question for the benefit of his staff rather than his own curiosity.

'Can you tell us how many will be left alive after all this?'

Eyes riveted on the Civil Defence officer. He was thoughtful for a moment or two, as though silently counting bodies.

'I would say, and this is purely a rough judgement on my part, that barely a million Londoners will survive.'

He paused again, his eyes cast downwards, as though expecting uproar; but the hushed silence that filled the room was even more daunting.

'We can't be sure of any of these figures,' Dealey said, his voice hasty but sombre. 'No one can really predict the results of a nuclear attack because there are no precedents – at least, not on this scale.'

'That's perfectly true,' Bryce accepted, 'but my observations are more than mere conjecture. There have been many well-researched reports, official and unofficial, on just this subject over the past few years, using the devastation inflicted upon Hiroshima and Nagasaki as a basis for speculation. The sophistication and advanced striking power of modern weapons were obviously taken into consideration, along with the living conditions of today's society. I'm basing my assumptions on a compromise between government and independent calculations.'

'Nevertheless, we cannot be sure.' Dealey's rebuke was unmistakable. Culver guessed that there had been an earlier, more private meeting between those at the top table, a clandestine conference to decide just what the 'masses' (there was now a tragic irony in that word) should be told. It seemed they hadn't all been in agreement.

'We've got families out there!' It was a wild shout and Culver turned to see a small man at a centre table who had risen to his feet, his fists clenched, a moistness to the anger in his eyes. 'We've got to get to them! We can't leave them out there on their own—'

'No!' There was a brutal coldness to Dealey. 'We can't leave this shelter to help anyone. It would be fatal.'

'Do you think we care about that?' This time a woman was on her feet, her tears unrestrained. 'Do you think there's anything left for us here? Any life for us to live?'

Other voices joined hers.

'Please!' Dealey's arms were raised once more. 'We must not lose control! It's only if we survive – and other units like ours – that we can help the people outside. If we panic, then the survivors of the blast will have no chance at all. You must understand that!'

Farraday leapt to his feet. 'He's right. If we leave this shelter too soon we'll be subjected to lethal doses of radiation poisoning. How will killing ourselves save those on the outside?'

They understood the logic of his argument, but such high emotion was not subservient to hard fact. There were more shouts, some of them abusive and particularly directed towards Dealey, as a Ministry of Defence employee.

It was Dr Reynolds who calmly brought the room to order.

'If any of you go out from this shelter now, you'll be dead within a matter of weeks, possibly days.' Her voice was raised just enough to be heard over the clamour. She too was standing, her hands tucked into the pockets of her open white tunic, and it was probably the uniform of her profession that gave her some credibility. She represented the physical antithesis of Dealey, a man who was the puppet of a government that had brought their country to war. Their vehemence towards Dealey may have been unjustified (and most of those present realized this despite their anger) but he was *there*, one of the faceless bureaucrats, within their reach, within striking distance.

Dr Reynolds was well aware of whom the rising hysteria was aimed at, and in some respects could understand it, for these shattered people needed something tangible to blame, *someone* to be held responsible. Dealey, as far as they're concerned, you're *it*!

'I can tell you this,' she said, the noise beginning to subside. 'It won't be a pleasant death. First you'll feel nauseous, and your skin will turn red, your mouth and throat inflamed. You won't have much strength. Vomiting will follow and you'll suffer pretty excruciating diarrhoea for a few days. You may start to feel a little better after this, but I promise you it won't last.

'All those symptoms are going to return with a vengeance, and you'll sweat, your skin will blister and your hair will fall out.

'You women will find your menstruation cycle will ignore the usual rules – you'll bleed a lot, and badly. You men will have pain in your genitals. If you do survive – which I doubt – you'll be sterile, or worse: the chances are that any offspring will be abnormal.

'Leukaemia will be a disease you'll know all about – from a personal point of view.

'Towards the end your intestines will be blocked. You might find that the worst discomfort of all.

'Finally, and perhaps mercifully, the convulsions will hit you, and after that you won't care very much. You'll sink into a brief coma, then you'll be dead.'

The eyes behind the large glasses were expressionless.

Jesus, thought Culver, she didn't pull her punches.

'There are other milder results of irradiation if you'd like to hear them.' She was coldly relentless, deliberately frightening them into staying. 'Food won't do you any good – you won't be able to extract essential nourishment. All the tissue in your body will age dramatically. There'll be a contraction of the bladder, bone fractures that won't mend, inflammation of the kidneys, liver, spinal cord and heart, bronchopneumonia, thrombosis, cancer and aplastic anaemia which will lead to subcutaneous haemorrhaging – in other words you'll bleed to death *under* the skin.

'And if that isn't enough, you'll have the pleasure of watching others around you dying in the same way, watching the agonies of those in the more advanced stages, *witnessing* what you, yourself, will soon be going through.

'So if you want to leave, if you want to expose yourself to all that, knowing you'll be too ill to help others, I don't see why we should stop you. In fact, I'll plead on your behalf to allow you out, because you'll only cause dissension in this shelter. Any takers?'

She sat when she was sure there wouldn't be.

'Thank you, Dr Reynolds,' said Dealey, 'for explaining the reality of the situation.'

She did not look at Dealey, but Culver could see there was no appreciation of his thanks.

'Perhaps now that you've heard everything at its pessimistic worst, we can continue on a more constructive note.' Dealey briefly touched the bandages over his eyes, as though they were causing discomfort. 'I said earlier that we were not isolated here in this shelter. I know our lines of communication have been temporarily cut, but at least we're secure in the knowledge that there are many others who will have survived the blast in shelters such as this. And all these within the central area are connected by either the Post Office tube railway or the London Transport Underground system.'

'It stands to reason that if our radio and telephone connections have been knocked out then these tunnels will have been destroyed too,' someone called out.

'True enough. I'm sure a few of the tunnels have been damaged, perhaps even destroyed completely, but there are too many for the whole system to have been wrecked. And also, certain buildings have been constructed to withstand nuclear explosions, buildings such as the Montague House "Fortress" and the Admiralty blockhouse in The Mall. I won't give details of all the bunkers and what are called "citadels" that have been built since the last World War, but I can tell you that there are at least six shelters on the Northern Line tunnel system alone, below stations such as Clapham South and Stockwell . . .'

Culver had the feeling that however candid Dealey was appearing to be as he listed other sites in and around London, he was still holding back, still not telling all. He mentally shrugged; it would be hard to trust any 'government' man from now on.

'. . . and a National Seat of Government will be set up outside London, and the country divided up into twelve regional seats, with twenty-three sub-regional headquarters . . .'

Was anyone in the room really listening to Dealey now?

'. . . county and district controls . . .'

Did any of it make sense?

'. . . sub-district controls, which will liaise with community posts . . .'

'Dealey!'

Heads turned to look at Culver. Dealey stopped speaking, and the tell-tale tongue flicked across his lips.

'Have you told anybody about the creatures out there?' Culver's voice was level, but there was a tightness to it. Kate beside him stiffened.

'I hardly think it need wor—'

'It's got to worry us, Dealey, because sooner or later we've got to go out there into those tunnels. The main entrance is blocked, remember? The tunnels are our only way out.'

'I doubt they'll stay underground. They'll scavenge for . . . food . . . on the surface. And in that case, they'll die from radiation poisoning.'

Culver smiled grimly. 'I don't think you've been doing your homework.'

Farraday broke in. 'What's he talking about? What are these creatures?'

This time it was Dr Reynolds who spoke. She removed her glasses and polished them with a small handkerchief. 'Dealey, Culver and Miss Garner were attacked by rats outside this shelter. It appears they were particularly large and, to say the least, unusually ferocious. They had attacked and were devouring survivors who had taken shelter in the tunnels.'

Farraday frowned and looked back at Culver. 'Just how large were they?'

Culver opened his arms like a boastful fisherman. 'Like dogs,' he replied.

More silence, more stunned dismay.

'They will be no threat to us,' Dealey insisted. 'By the time we leave this shelter, most of these vermin will be dead.'

Culver shook his head and Dr Reynolds answered. 'You really should have known this, Mr Dealey. Or perhaps you wanted to forget. You see, certain forms of life are highly resistant to radiation. Insects are, for instance. And so, too, are rats.'

She replaced the spectacles.

'And,' she continued in almost a sigh, 'if these creatures are descendants of the Black rats that terrorized London just a few years ago – and from their size, I'd say they were – then not only will they be resistant to radiation, but they'll thrive on it.'

7

A noise.

He listened intently.

A scratching sound.

He waited.

Nothing. Gone now.

Klimpton tried to stretch his body, but there wasn't room even to straighten his legs. He flexed the muscles in his back and twisted his neck from side to side, refraining from groaning, not wanting to wake the others.

What time was it?

The digital figures of his watch glowed green on his wrist. 23.40. Night.

There was no other way of telling night from day, not there, not in their small dusty prison.

How long? Dear God, how long had they been down there? Two days? Three? A week? No, it couldn't be that long. Could it? Time didn't count for much when shadows failed to move.

But what had woken him? Had Kevin cried out in his sleep once more? What did the boy think of the grown-up world now?

Klimpton reached for the small pen-light he carried in his shirt pocket and flicked it on, sheltering the small beam with his hand. The urge to switch on the larger lamp hanging from a peg just above his head was strong, but he had to conserve the batteries; no telling how long they would have to stay down there. The candles, too, had to be saved.

He shone the light towards his son, the pin-point of light barely touching the boy's eyes. His sleeping hours had been erratic and restless enough without spoiling what now appeared to be a deep slumber. Kevin's face was peaceful, his lips slightly parted, only a dust smear on one cheek giving evidence that all was not quite normal. A slight movement of the wrist and another face was revealed close to the boy's, but this was old, the skin grey, like dry, wrinkled paper. Gran's mouth was open too, but it held none of the sensuous innocence of his son's. The opening – hardly any lips any more – was too round, the cavern too black and deep. It seemed every breath exhaled let slip a little more of her life. And, face turned towards her, his son drew in that escaping life in short, shallow intakes, as though quietly stealing his grandmother's existence.

'Ian?' Klimpton's wife's voice was distant, full of sleep. He turned the light towards her and she closed her barely-opened eyes against it.

'It's all right,' he whispered. 'Thought I heard something outside.'

She turned from him, snuggling further down into the sleeping bag. 'It was probably Cassie,' she mumbled. 'Poor dog.' Sian had already returned to her dream before he switched the torch off, and he was hardly surprised; like him, she had only slept fitfully and not for very long since they had been ensconced in the improvised shelter.

Ian Klimpton sat there in the dark beneath the basement stairs, his ears sensitive, eyes watching the blackness. There had been many noises through the dark hours, the wreckage above them settling, distant thunder, far-away explosions that still managed to make the remains of his house shiver. Sometimes it felt as though the trains were still running below the foundations, but he was sure this couldn't be so. Everything above – and even below – must have been destroyed by the bombs. At the very least, there could be no more power to run trains.

Thanks to him, his family had been saved. Sian had scoffed when he had studiously read the Home Office's survival booklet and he himself had felt embarrassed by his own attention to it. Nevertheless, he had taken it seriously. Not at first, of course. His initial inclination when the booklet had fallen through the letter-box onto the doormat was to glance through it, then toss it into the waste bin; but something had made him keep it, to hide it between books in his study. A rational fear that someday the instructions might come in useful. And later, tension around the Gulf States had caused him to retrieve it and study the directions more thoughtfully.

The booklet had advised householders to find a protected refuge in their own houses, a cellar or cupboard beneath the stairs. Klimpton's house had both: the steps leading down to the basement area had a cupboard beneath them. To go to such lengths as whitewashing all the windows of his house would have made him the laughing stock of the neighbourhood, even when the world crisis was reaching breaking point, but internal measures could be easily taken without public knowledge. Things like collecting one or two plastic buckets (for sanitation purposes as well as storing water) and stocking tinned food, not upstairs in the larder where it would disappear through daily use, but down in the basement itself, on a shelf where it would be forgotten, unless (or until) it was needed. Keeping sleeping bags and bedding somewhere handy, somewhere they could be conveniently grabbed from should the emergency arise. Having more than one torch – and a lamp – plus a supply of batteries. Candles. Containers. Portable stove. First-aid kit. Other items like magazines, books, comics for Kevin. Toilet paper. Essentials, really.

Of course the clutter under the stairs had to be cleared. And a tattered mattress brought down from the loft to lean against the outside of the cupboard door. He was thankful, too, for the old chest-of-drawers that stood battered and unloved in one corner of the basement; that would afford added protection with the mattress against the door. He hadn't blocked up the small basement window whose top half was at street level, and there had been no time to do so when the sirens had alarmed the district. But he had done the best for his family, and they had survived the worst.

Perhaps there was more he could have done. He could have built a brick shelter in the cellar. He could have piled up sandbags against the stairway. He could have reinforced the ceiling over their heads, kept the bath and sinks filled, built a stronger lean-to against the stairs. He could have moved the family up to the Scottish Highlands.

No. He had carried out his duty. Not many men would have done more. And most of all, he had been with his family when the bombs were dropped.

Klimpton was of the new breed of businessmen. His office was his own study, his master and tool the computer he kept there. He could contact every major office of the company which employed him in any part of the world with just a few deft finger punches of the keyboard. No office politics, no commuter travelling, no grovelling to the boss. Even so, it was a busy life and one he enjoyed. It meant he saw a lot more of Kevin.

The scratching sound again.

Somewhere outside, in the basement itself.

Was it the dog? Had Cassie found a way into the cellar?

Impossible. Klimpton had had to lock their pet out, much to the distress of Kevin, for there was no way they could have an animal living with them. It would have been too unhygienic – and Christ, it was bad enough already without having a dog messing all over the place. And Cassie would need precious food as well. They had had to listen to her howling after the bombs had fallen. Then the whimpering, the whining, for days – could it have been a week? – with Kevin more upset by the noise than by the holocaust. They hadn't heard Cassie for a long time now, though, and Klimpton wondered if the dog had wandered off to another part of the house, if there was another part standing. Or was she slumped against the cellar door, nose pushed towards the draughty crack beneath, weakened, frightened? Dead?

Maybe she'd got outside and was trying to get through the basement window.

He shifted his legs, groaning as bones wearily protested. The only way he could sleep was in an upright position; there just wasn't room for them all to lie down.

They were supposed to stay inside the refuge for at least forty-eight hours, and inside the house, preferably the basement, for much longer; two weeks at least, maybe more. The sirens would sound again when it was safe to come out.

He could risk leaving the cupboard now, he was sure. They must have been inside for at least a week. And the stink from the plastic bucket, dosed with disinfectant and covered with a polythene bag though it was, would make them all ill before much longer.

The others needn't be disturbed. He could push the door open just enough to squeeze through with the bucket. The mattress, wedged against the chest-of-drawers, would provide an escape tunnel. He could check on the dog while he was out there.

Klimpton shrugged himself loose from the covering blanket and groped for the larger torch he kept by his side. His hand closed around Gran's bony ankle, but she did not stir. Her flesh was cold even though the atmosphere inside the cupboard was warm and clammy. She refused to get into the sleeping bag proclaiming it was too much like sleeping in a straitjacket and that she couldn't breathe bound up like that. So she used it as a mattress, having a blanket wrapped around her instead.

He found the torch, then groped for the plastic bucket with its full contents (it was embarrassing for all of them to squat over such a thing in front of others, even though they were family and despite having the lamp turned off – darkness couldn't cover sounds nor smother smells – but Klimpton would not give in to their protests and allow any of them outside the refuge). The bucket was easy to find in the dark – practically everything was within reach – and he lifted it by its wire handle. His nose wrinkled in disgust.

Half-turning, Klimpton pushed against the small door to his right, only the pressure from the mattress outside giving some resistance. He leaned his shoulder more firmly into the wood and the gap widened.

Sian moved restlessly behind him. 'Ian?' she said, both weariness and urgency in her voice.

'It's okay, go back to sleep. Don't wake the others.'

'What are you doing?'

'Getting rid of this damn bucket,' he whispered back.

'Is it safe? Isn't it too soon to go out there?'

'We're all right in the cellar. As long as I don't stay out too long.'

'Please be careful.'

'I will. Sleep.'

He had to squeeze through the opening sideways, the chest-of-drawers allowing little more than a twelve-inch clearance. The bucket was pushed before him.

Once he had wriggled himself outside he switched on the torch, waiting for the dazzle in his eyes to fade before venturing further. The mattress, forming a soft, narrow lean-to over him, smelled musty and dank and he dismissed thoughts of what must be crawling around inside it; all those years in the loft must have turned it into a wonderful home for little creeping things. The concoction of smells from bucket and mattress made his stomach want to heave, but then the stench of his own vomit would have made matters even more uncomfortable for them all. Klimpton swallowed hard. The sooner he was out in the comparative openness of the cellar the better.

He wondered if there would be any cellar left. Perhaps the whole house had fallen in, leaving the basement open to the skies. To the fallout. Stupid. They would surely have known if that were the case. It had been quiet down there. The distant rumbles were just that: distant. And the air was heavy, stale. The old Islington houses were solid, built in a time when mixtures for bricks and mortar were not skimped. Foundations were solid. Walls were steadfast. Probably not too much of London was left up there, but Klimpton knew there was a certain protection in rows of houses, depending on which direction the blast or blasts came from. His own big terraced house was roughly in the middle of a block, so he might have been lucky, unless the front or the back was exposed.

With a sigh of relief, he was free. He pushed the bucket as far away as possible and rested for a moment, his shoulders clear of the protective corridor. Fearfully, he raised the torch, dreading what he might find, expecting the basement to be in ruins, ceiling caved in, debris everywhere. Perhaps the night sky peering in. He silently cursed himself for doubting his earlier rationalization. The light beam confirmed his reasoning.

The ceiling, though large chunks of plaster were missing, had withstood the impact. Klimpton quickly swept the beam around the basement and stopped when it fell upon the small window. Rubble had poured through, smashing both glass and frame, creating a slope of debris. At least the opening was completely filled, leaving no room for fallout dust to sneak in.

Using elbows and knees, he pushed himself clear of the tunnel and stood, his chest heaving with the exertion, surprised that such a small effort had left him so breathless. All the hours of cramped inactivity combined with the stale air they had been forced to breathe had taken their toll.

The scratching sound again.

His chest stopped its swelling, his breath only half-drawn in. He swung the torch into a far corner. Nothing there. Then along the base of one wall. An old bicycle of Kevin's, a three-wheeler. Broken laser-beam space rifle leaning against it. Sian's ancient washing machine – bin men had refused to take it away. Record player, the old type you could stack up eight discs on, valves dead and dust-furred inside. Another corner. Light bouncing back off an old frameless mirror. Nothing more. The next wall, leading back towards the stairs. Nothing. No junk, no discarded furniture, just ... just ... something that shouldn't be there.

A shadow. But nothing to cause it.

He steadied the torch, peered closer, and—

Scrabbling sounds from above!

Frantic. Claws against wood.

The stairs. It came from the top of the stairs.

And then a whimper. A mewling, begging whimper.

Klimpton let the half-breath go, then drew in a full slow breath. Cassie had heard him down there. The poor old bitch was trying to get to him. He shone the torch up the stairs and the scratching became more frenzied. She could probably see the light beneath the door. He'd better calm her down before she woke the others.

Quietly as possible, Klimpton climbed the wooden steps, at once relieved and disappointed that Cassie was still alive. Alive she posed a problem.

A small, excited yelp as he approached. The clawing increased. As his head drew level with the foot of the door, he leaned forward, one hand resting against the top step, his mouth moving close to the gap under the wood.

Below him, something moved from the unusual shadow in the wall.

'Cassie,' he said quietly.

A small, tired bark came back.

'Good girl, Cassie,' he soothed. 'Keep it quiet, there's a good dog.'

The whimpering, the pleading, continued.

'I know, Cassie, I know, girl. You're scared, you want to be with us. But I can't let you in, not just yet. Understand, I want to, but I can't.'

The rejection was painful, and the urge to open the door was almost irresistible. He had to be hard, though, had to be firm. Human beings were more important than pets. The dog would create too many problems down there, the hygiene risk would be too great. Cassie was becoming over-excited.

Another shape was born from the shadow. It lingered for a moment, a dark form concealed by the surrounding blackness. It moved, stealthily, joining its companion.

Klimpton wondered if he should open the door a little, just enough to reassure Cassie, perhaps calm her. The dog was losing control, becoming too frenzied.

'Hush, girl. Come on, Cassie, be quiet now.' His tone was harsher. The sound of the dog's paws against wood was a continuous rapid friction. 'Hey, cut it out!'

Cassie wailed while other things slid from the deep shadow that wasn't a shadow but a rent in the wall and floor, a fissure caused by the shifting of earth, the movement of concrete. The rupture reached down to the sewers beneath the streets.

The man on the stairs was unaware of the skulking, bristle-furred beasts, these creeping things, as they filed swiftly from the opening like smooth black fluid.

'Cassie, just shut up, will you?' Klimpton thumped at the door with the flat of his hand, but the dog yelped even more, all the weakness gone from her cries. Soon she began to growl and her master wondered if the ordeal had not driven her mad.

Sian's muffled voice came from below: 'Ian, what's going on up there? You've woken all of us.'

'Dad, is that Cassie?' came Kevin's voice. 'Please let her in, please bring her down.'

'You know we can't. Just go back to sleep.'

Klimpton knew the boy would now be crying in the arms of his mother or his gran. Bloody dog! As if they didn't have enough to worry about.

He pulled back as something solid thumped against the door, rattling the wood in its frame. Good Lord, the dog was throwing itself against the door in its desperation. He should have done something about the animal before they came down there. Should have cut its throat (oh no, he couldn't see himself doing that) or locked it in a cupboard. But there had been no time, no time to think, no time to act sensibly.

Thump.

'Stop it!' Klimpton shouted, banging his fist against the wood. 'You stupid bloody pest.'

One of the night creatures stood poised at the foot of the stairs, its yellow eyes glinting, a reflection from the torch beam. Two long-clawed feet rested against the bottom step and its back was hunched, giving it an arched appearance. It studied the man for long moments, until its snout twitched, sniffing the air. It moved away from the step and sniffed its way around the plastic bucket, attracted by the aroma of excrement and urine. The sounds of movement close by diverted its attention.

Its night-seeing eyes distinguished the black tunnel from the lesser denseness of the cellar. Different odours drifted from there. The animal approached in a small scurrying movement, poking its long snout into the opening. Further sounds excited the creature, for they were living noises. And instinctively it was aware that the animals who made the sounds were weak. Its jaws opened to reveal long, sharp teeth that dripped with wetness.

The rat entered the tunnel, its body, with its wide powerful haunches and hunched back, fitting comfortably. One of its companions followed. Then another.

The pink, scaly tail of the last rat slithered snake-like through the dust of the cellar floor before disappearing into the inner blackness.

Above, Cassie was barking frantically, running away from the door, then returning with a crashing thump, throwing herself so hard at the wood that Klimpton felt sure she would burst through. He was frightened by her actions, fearing that if she did break into the cellar, she would run amok. Her screeching bark was near-demented, and Klimpton shuddered to think of the effects of a bite from a mad dog.

He staggered back at the force of the next throw, grabbing the handrail to keep his balance. How the hell could he pacify her, how could he soothe her? How could he make her damn-well stop? Wasn't their nightmare enough?

A scream. From below.

Sian!

Kevin!

He turned on the stairs and the torch beam swung downwards.

Klimpton almost collapsed. And if he had, he would have fallen among them.

For the cellar was alive with thick, furry bodies, a black carpet of moving shapes, squirming, leaping over each other's backs, never still, long pointed noses raised here and there to sniff the air, eyes caught in the glare of the torch, glinting yellow like those of cats, a terrible mass of writhing vermin, so big, so huge, like nothing he'd ever seen before, monsters, hideous . . .

'Nooooo!' he cried when his family's screams broke through his shock. Looking over the handrail he saw the creatures disappearing into the mattress tunnel to the shelter. His family was screaming beneath his feet.

Klimpton ran down the steps, leaping the last few, landing among the rats, stumbling, falling to his knees. He lashed out with the torch and the creatures scurried away. He was up, kicking out, screaming at them, tearing at the chest-of drawers, pulling it aside, ignoring the teeth that sank into his calf muscles. He pulled at the mattress and the cupboard door swung away with it.

Nothing made sense in the torchlight. All he could see

was a jumble of struggling shapes, something white here and there, something white but smeared with dark red, and the red was his family's blood.

A weight thudded against his back, but he did not feel the razor teeth slash his skin, tearing flesh away with his shirt material in a large, loose flap. He did not feel the mouth that tightened around his thigh, the long incisors seeking the warm liquid within. He did not feel the claws that raked the back of his legs, nor the snapping jaws that gained purchase between them.

He only felt the pain of his wife, his son, his mother.

Clawed feet scurried up his back, reaching his shoulders, teeth finding a hold on his neck, knocking him forward so that he fell into the opening to join his family in their blood-drenched refuge.

At the top of the stairs, the door rocked against its frame as Cassie threw herself against it, the blows becoming more rapid, more forceful, the wood rattling against its frame, the air filled with yelps and screams and squealing.

As the screams eventually faded, so the blows became weaker. And when the sounds in the cellar were only feeding noises, the dog's barks became a wailing moan. And when the blows stopped and the door was still, all that could be heard was a muffled, whimpering sound.

And from below, a rapacious gnawing.

8

'How is he?'

Dr Reynolds, whose eyes had been cast downwards in thought as she closed the sick-bay door behind her, looked up in surprise. She smiled at the girl and Kate saw the tiredness behind the smile. And the anxiety.

Clare Reynolds leaned back against the door, hands tucked into her tunic pockets, a familiar gesture. 'He'll pull through,' she answered, and Kate realized the anxiety was for more than just Culver; it was for all of them.

'The radiation penetration was minor – less than a hundred rads, I'd say.' The doctor took out a cigarette pack and offered it towards Kate. 'Do you smoke? I haven't noticed.'

Kate shook her head.

'Sensible.' Dr Reynolds lit her cigarette with a slim lighter. She drew in a deep breath and closed her eyes, face towards the concrete ceiling. The gesture of removing the cigarette and exhaling a thin stream of blue smoke was almost elegant. Her eyes opened once more.

'Thanks for helping out over the past few days.'

'It kept me busy, and that helped me.'

'That seems to be a problem in this place: very little to do for most of the staff. For some it induces apathy, for others, discontent. They need something other than death and destruction to keep their minds occupied.'

'Farraday's tried to keep them busy.'

'Any luck with communications?'

'Not as far as I know. It could be that we're all that's left.'

Dr Reynolds studied the girl thoughtfully. She looked better than when she had first arrived, but the fear was still there, that barely-disguised brittleness, a reed that could snap at any moment rather than bend. Her hair was clean, a lively yellow, her eyes softer now, but still uneasy. The torn blouse had been replaced by a man's shirt, hanging loose over her skirt. On one side, high on her chest, a film badge was pinned, a dosimeter that everyone in the shelter had been instructed to wear; at the end of each week, these were to be analysed by the small radiological department housed in the underground complex. Dr Reynolds could not quite understand the need, for there were enough ionization instruments strategically placed around the shelter to give full warning of any radiation leakage, but she assumed they were used for psychological effect, a reassurance to the wearer. What reassurance should they begin to become cloudy?

'Would you like a coffee?' she asked. 'I'm desperate for one. It'd give us a chance to talk.'

Kate nodded and Dr Reynolds pushed herself away from the door. They headed towards the dining area.

'Will Steve be all right?' Kate asked again, not satisfied with the doctor's previous answer.

An engineer stood aside to allow them room to pass along the narrow corridor and Dr Reynolds nodded her thanks, smiling briefly. 'Oh, yes, I think he'll be fine. Although the radiation dose was comparatively minor – the worst physical effect apart from the nausea and dizziness was to render him sterile for a day or two, and I'm sure that didn't bother him in his condition – I'm afraid it considerably lowered his resistance to infection from the rat bite. Fortunately, the powers that be thoughtfully provided an antidote to the disease this particular beast—'

Kate had stopped. 'Disease?'

The doctor took her arm and kept her walking.

'Some years ago, this breed of rodent – a mutation, as I understand it – infected anyone it bit with an extreme form of Leptospirosis. A cure was found soon enough, and it was thought that the beggars had eventually lost this extra weapon in their nasty little arsenal. It seems the medical authorities were never quite sure, though, so they decided to play it safe should the worst ever happen. I found our life-saver among the medical supplies.'

'Then why wasn't I infected? And Alex Dealey?'

Dr Reynolds shrugged. 'You weren't bitten – at least not deeply. You suffered scratches, mostly. But I injected you and Culver after I put you out the other day. I wasn't taking any chances. And Dealey wasn't touched by them.'

'But he was ill.'

'Yes, but only from radiation sickness. Both he and Culver received roughly the same amount. Not enough to be lethal, but enough to knock them off their feet for a day or two. As you know, Dealey has recovered fully for the moment.'

'You mean it won't last?'

'Oh, he'll be okay – they both will. But the sickness is likely to recur within the next couple of weeks. It won't last long, though, not with the small dosage they've received.'

The *thrum* of the power generator reached their ears and was somehow comforting, an indication that technological civilization had not broken down totally. They passed the ventilation plant and Dr Reynolds gave a small wave to a group of engineers. Only one, a stocky blond man, returned the wave.

'Hope they're not planning a revolution,' the doctor commented, drawing on the cigarette.

The two women entered the kitchen area and Dr Reynolds poured two coffees from the unattended machine on the small counter. One or two groups were scattered around the dining area talking in lowered voices. Kate poured cream into her coffee, Dr Reynolds took hers black. They found a table by a grey-green wall and the doctor gratefully sank into a chair, flicking ash into the scrupulously clean ashtray as she did so. Kate sat opposite and looked intently into the big spectacles windowing her companion's eyes.

'How long will Steve be like this?'

Dr Reynolds blew a stream of smoke across the table, turning her head slightly to avoid Kate. 'You really care for him, don't you? I thought you were strangers before Doomsday.' 'Doomsday' was the title given to the previous Tuesday, used with superficial lightness, but the dark word appropriate to how everyone in the shelter felt.

'He saved my life.' It was a flat statement.

Dr Reynolds watched a fly land in the sugar bowl and wondered as it walked frustratedly over the wrapped sugar lumps if the insect had any idea of the catastrophe that had engulfed the world outside. She waved her hand and the insect flew away.

She looked back at the girl. 'Who did you lose?'

Kate's eyes lowered. 'Parents. Two brothers. I assume they're gone.'

The doctor leaned forward and touched her wrist. 'That may not be so, Kate. There's still a chance they survived.'

The girl shook her head, and there was a sad, tearful smile on her lips. 'No, it's better this way. I don't want to live in hope for them. And I wouldn't want them to have suffered. Better to believe they went instantly and with as little pain as possible.'

Dr Reynolds stubbed out her cigarette in the ashtray.

'Maybe that's the best way. At least you can't be disappointed. Did you have a lover, a boyfriend?'

'I did.' She didn't categorize. 'But that ended months ago.' The familiar pain was there, familiar to Dr Reynolds because she had observed it in the faces of so many in the shelter. She had seen it in her own reflected image each time she looked into a mirror.

'It's funny,' Kate went on. 'I can't remember his features. Each time I try to concentrate on how he looked, his face becomes hazy, like a badly focused picture. But in dreams it's so clear . . .'

'You know, Culver had nobody.'

Kate's attention returned, not swiftly, because memories sought to overwhelm.

'He told you that?'

'Not directly.' Clare reached for another cigarette. 'I wish I could give these up, but there doesn't seem to be much point, does there? I mean, what else could happen?' She lit up and shook the match into the ashtray. 'Couple of nights ago, when his fever was at his worst, Culver was crying in his sleep calling out something, perhaps a name – I couldn't catch it.'

'It could have been someone who died in the attack.'

'No, I got the feeling it was long before. He said over and over again: "I can't save her, the water's got her. She's gone, gone . . ." My guess is that this woman, girlfriend or wife, was drowned and in some way he feels responsible.'

'Why do you say that?'

'Just a feeling. I suppose his dreams reveal classic guilt symptoms. Perhaps they had a tiff and he wasn't around to drag her out of the water. Who knows? Whatever, he's still bothered by it. Maybe that's why he went for you out there in the tunnel.'

'Because of guilt?' Kate's eyes widened in surprise.

'No, no, not exactly. But it must have been very tempting to leave you there and sneak into the shelter. Let's face it, the odds were against all three of you surviving an attack from those monsters. Did you know he also pulled Dealey into safety when the first bomb hit? Maybe he's trying to make amends for something he didn't do in the past, or maybe he just doesn't care about himself. Maybe both reasons.'

'It could be he's just a very brave man.'

'Uh-huh. Could be. I haven't met many of those, though.' She flicked ash. 'Anyway, to answer the question you asked before we got re-routed: Culver should be up and around in a day or two. He's sleeping now, but why don't you pop down and see him later. I think you'd be welcome. In fact, I think you'd be good for one another.'

'It's too soon for that. Too much has happened.'

'I didn't mean it that way. I meant you could give each other some comfort, some moral support, if you like – God knows, each of us needs it. But as you implied, if it comes to sleeping together, it's precisely because so much has happened that from here on in, *nothing* will be too soon. Kate, have you any idea what we've got to face when we get out of this shelter? I'll re-phrase that: *if* we get out of this shelter.'

'I don't want to think about it.'

'You're going to have to. We all are. Because we may be all that's left.'

'Dr Reynolds—'

'Forget the formality. Call me Clare.'

'Clare, I'm not a fool. I've got some idea of what's happened outside and I know it's going to be grim – no, not grim, awful, God-bloody-awful – and I know that nothing will ever be the same again. I didn't care at first, but now I want to live through this, I want to survive, no matter what the world has become. For now, though, just for a little while, I need to adjust. Give me that time and I'll help you in anything you want. I can't promise I'll make a good nurse – I hate the sight of blood – but I'll do my best to help in any way I can.'

Clare smiled, patted Kate's hand. 'You'll do,' she said.

They drank their coffee in silence for a while and the doctor wondered how any of them would really cope once they were outside. The prospects were daunting, not least for members of her own profession, for she knew that at least half, if not more, of the city's hospitals would have been demolished by the blasts, and many, many doctors, nurses and medical staff would have been killed or injured. The demands on the services of those who survived were too enormous to contemplate.

The 'triage' system of selective treatment would undoubtedly have been put into immediate operation. The injured would be placed into three categories: those unlikely to survive after treatment; those likely to survive after treatment; those likely to survive without treatment. That meant that anyone with severe radiation sickness, or suffering from fatal burns or injuries, would not receive any treatment at all (or – and she knew this had not been agreed upon in discussions before the nuclear attack – merciful overdoses of morphia might be administered. She secretly hoped this would be the case). Even in normal times there were only enough burn units in the whole of the UK to deal with no more than a hundred severe cases at once, so what hope now?

Mass blood-transfusions for haemorrhages caused by radiation or injuries would be impossible; only five thousand or so pints of blood were stored in London for emergency use, and how many of those reserves would be left after the devastation? And how long would the Ministry of Health's drugs stockpiles of morphine, aspirin and penicillin last?

She tried to close her mind to all the possibilities crowding in, but they were ruthless harpies who refused to give her peace.

In the days, weeks, that would follow, other environmental hazards would arise. There would be millions of decomposing corpses, both human and animal, lying in the streets or under rubble, food for insects ... and vermin. God, there were supposed to be a hundred million rats, double the human population, living in England alone, only strict measures controlling their constant growth in numbers. Those measures would not exist any more ...

'Are you all right?' Kate was leaning forward anxiously. 'You suddenly went deathly pale.'

'Uh? Oh, just thinking. Just considering the mess we've got ourselves into.' She stubbed out the half-smoked cigarette, then lit another. 'Shit, I should stop doing that. Cigarettes might not be so easy to come by from now on.'

'Do you want to share your thoughts?'

'Not particularly, but since you ask ...' She rubbed her neck and twisted it in a circular movement, easing the stiffness. I was just mulling over the diseases that are likely to be rife when we eventually get out. Without proper sanitation, and with everything rotting up there, enteric infections—'

Kate looked puzzled.

'Sorry – intestinal infections could soon reach epidemic proportions. Some of the illnesses will be respiratory – pneumonia, bronchitis, that kind of thing – while others will be disorders such as hepatitis, dysentery, tuberculosis. I think typhoid and cholera will spread. Rabies, too, since we failed to keep it out of the country. Any sickness, you see,

111

any debilitation, will be exaggerated, and will lead to worse illnesses. Simple measles could become an epidemic. Any childhood infectious disease could wipe out thousands, maybe millions. Meningitis, encephalitis – that's a sleeping sickness caused by inflammation of the brain – even venereal diseases. The list is endless, Kate, just damn-well endless, and I don't think any of us – the government, the medical profession – can do anything about it! They've killed us all, maybe not tomorrow, nor the next day, but eventually. We don't have a hope in hell.'

It was all said in a flat monotone. An underlying hysteria in the doctor's voice would have been less frightening to Kate. Others in the room were looking in their direction and she wondered if they had heard, soft-spoken though Dr Reynolds' words had been.

'Clare, there must be some chance for us. If we can get to another part of the country . . .'

The other woman sighed deeply. 'I wonder just how much of the country is left. We've no way of knowing how many missiles were used against us. And whatever parts haven't been destroyed will be subjected to fallout drifting on air currents. Oh, Kate, I'd like to have hope, and I know as a doctor I shouldn't be talking like this, but all I feel is a despairing numbness inside, a huge dull-grey blankness. It won't allow room for anything else.'

Kate searched in the older woman's eyes for some sign of inner conflict, a softness, an indication of hidden tears perhaps, or even anger. But the eyes were expressionless. Not cold, not dead. Just void of all emotion.

Kate shuddered inwardly, and a chill touched her with the knowledge that the nightmare was not over. It had only just begun.

9

Culver looked around the sick bay, hoping he might find one of the other 'patients' awake, eager to talk. He was bored, annoyed at his confinement. The others were all asleep, as he guessed they would be, for they had been heavily sedated. Three engineers and one ROC officer had given way under the pressure so far. One of the engineers, a young man somewhere in his late twenties, had sliced his wrists with a razor blade. Only blood spilling beneath the toilet door had saved him. The woman, whom Culver had seen wearing the Royal Observer Corps uniform on the first day inside the shelter, had tried pills stolen from the medical store. The sound of her retching as they forced a rubber tube into her throat had roused him from a deep sleep the night before.

He sank back onto the pillow, an arm going behind his head to prop himself up. Five days he'd been out, according to the doctor, the radiation sickness hitting him first, then reaction from the rat-bite jumping in like some eager bully who wouldn't be left out of the fun. Well, he'd been lucky. The dose was minor although weakening, and Dr Reynolds had found something to counteract the infection. She had explained about the disease the vermin carried and as a precaution had inoculated everyone in the shelter against it. They were safe inside, she had said, but eventually they would have to surface and it was just as well to be prepared for *any* dangers that might be out there. Rats would be the least of their problems, Culver had thought.

He lifted the sheet to examine the bite. The wound was no longer dressed and looked an angry red. It felt sore, but not too painful. He'd live.

Letting the sheet drop back over his naked body, he stared up at the bunkbed above. As with the aftermath of any debilitating illness, everything seemed fresh, even the turgid colours of the sick-bay walls. The neon lights shone cleaner, brighter, the wires beneath the bed overhead sharp, their pattern precise. Even the filtered air smelled fresher. He could hardly recall the agonies he had gone through – save for the acute stomach cramps – but Dr Reynolds had told him he had become yellow as a Chinaman at one stage. Sudden spasms of muscular pains, constant vomiting, and delirium had been the results of the fever, all, she assumed, intensified by the radiation his body had absorbed. Fortunately, the antidote had worked quickly and much of the toxicity had been sweated out or flushed from him within the first couple of days. After that, total exhaustion held him in its smothering embrace and complete rest was the only cure for that.

Culver felt fit enough. Maybe just a little weak, but he was sure his strength would soon return when he was up on his feet. If only he knew where they'd put his clothes.

He pulled the sheets back and swung his legs onto the floor, then rapidly swung them back and covered his lower body, as the door opened. The girl entered and smiled when she saw him half-sitting in the bunkbed.

'You look good,' she said, walking towards him.

He nodded. 'I feel, uh, okay.'

She sat at the end of the bed, leaning forward a little to avoid the top bunk. 'We were worried for a while. I never realized the human body could lose so much waste in such a short period of time.'

'Yeah, well I'd rather forget about that. Did you look after me?' He seemed surprised.

'Dr Reynolds and I took it in turns. Don't you remember? She was with you *all* the time when your fever was at its peak, though.'

He rubbed the stubble of his chin. 'Sudden images flash into my mind.' He was silent for a few moments, then said: 'I remember you watching me. I remember your face looking down. You were weeping.'

She avoided his eyes. 'I didn't know how serious it was, whether you'd survive. You looked so awful.'

'You were worried?' Again he looked surprised.

Kate moved closer and ran her fingers through his tousled sandy hair, using them as a rough comb. 'There's a brightness to your eyes.'

'I guess it's all the vitamins our lady doctor is pumping into me.'

'She says that in a strange way you've been luckier than the rest of us.'

He gave a short laugh. 'This I gotta hear. Just how does she figure that?'

'You've been away from it. Your mind's been concerned with just one thing over the past few days: self-preservation. Even through your delirium it's been fighting, refusing to let go. And Clare – Dr Reynolds – says your mind's been doing something else too.'

Culver gently caught her wrist to stop her fingers moving through his hair. 'What would that be?'

'The brain is a remarkable machine, it can do several things at once. While it was helping you pull through, it was also adjusting.'

'Adjusting?'

'To everything that's happened. Oh, you've had your nightmares, some beauties by the sounds of them, but all the time your mind was accepting, going through everything that's happened, and, well ... digesting it, if you like. We've had to go through the same stages, but consciously. We've had to live through it over and over again and, as you can see, some of us didn't make it. There are others who still won't.'

He let go of her wrist and her hand dropped into her lap. 'Will you?' he asked.

'I'm not sure. At first I thought it would be impossible. Now I don't know. It's incredible what you can learn to accept. I don't mean that this nuclear war will ever be acceptable to any of us, but eventually I think our circumstances will. We'll live with what we have.'

Culver was startled by the change in her. But then she had still been in a state of profound shock in their first few hours inside the refuge. There had never been the chance for him to see what lay beyond that state. He brushed her cheek with the back of his hand. 'It seems we've had this moment before. Or something like it.'

Kate managed to smile again. 'Yes, when we first arrived. It helped me.'

'Me too. Want to try again?'

She blinked, and he guessed it was to clear the moistness in her vision. 'We're both wanted elsewhere,' she told him.

He raised his eyebrows.

'Alex Dealey wants to see you in the Operations Room.'

'So he's already set up a company command.'

'This place is more surprising than you think. Even the engineers who worked here on a day-to-day basis had no idea what the shelter comprised, exactly. Apparently much of the complex was out of bounds even to them.'

'Yeah, that makes sense. The authorities wouldn't want the word to get around that such underground bunkers existed. People might have read something into it and become frightened.' He grinned. 'You mean I can get out of this goddam bed without the doc slapping my bottom?'

'She won't condone any more malingering.'

He shook his head once, still grinning. 'She's changed her tune. One problem: do I go naked or do I make a toga out of this sheet?'

'I'll get your things.'

Kate quickly walked to a small door at the other end of the sick bay, glancing at the prone figures lying in the other bunkbeds as she did so. She disappeared through the door and Culver heard the sound of what must have been a locker opening then closing. She returned with some familiar items of clothing.

'Cleaned, but not pressed,' she announced, dumping them in his lap. 'Oh, and I did my best with the hole in your jeans. It doesn't look too good, but at least it's stitched.'

'You've been busy.'

'There hasn't been much else to do.'

He separated the clothing. 'Er, do you want to wait outside?'

She surprised him again by laughing, for there was genuine humour in the sound. 'Culver, I've washed you and wiped you and seen anything you've got to offer. It's too late to be coy.'

His feet touched the floor, but the sheet remained over his nakedness. He flushed red. 'This is different.'

Kate turned away, still smiling. 'Okay, I promise not to

peek; but I won't step outside. You may not be quite as strong as you think.'

When he stood, Culver understood what she meant. Dizziness hit him and he grabbed the top bunk. She was at his side instantly.

'Easy, Steve,' she said. 'It'll take a little while.'

He waited for his vision to clear, one hand on her shoulder, locks of her hair brushing against his fingers. He was conscious of her body's natural scent, its freshness, and the arm she had around him, the warmth of the hand on his hip.

'Thanks,' he mumbled. 'I should have listened. I'm coming together, though. If you could just hang on to me for a minute.'

She did, and was glad to.

'You could easily get lost in this place,' Culver remarked as Kate led him through the grey corridors. His legs still felt weak, his head still light, but there was a swift-returning vitality to his senses that made Culver wonder just *what* Dr Reynolds had been dosing him with.

'It's quite a complex,' said Kate. 'I don't pretend to understand any of their machinery, but apparently this place is a repeater station, according to the technician – sorry, engineer – who gave me a guided tour. I'm afraid intermediate distribution frames and motor driven uni-selectors don't do much for me.' Kate glanced at him. 'It's eerie seeing all this electronic equipment which isn't actually *doing* anything. I mean, you can feel it's alive, the current is still running through, but it's like some slumbering dinosaur, just waiting for something to rouse it.'

'Maybe it's already become extinct. This kind of technology may not play much part in our immediate future.'

'I don't think I could survive winter without my electric blanket.'

'Try a hot-water bottle. Or another warm body.'

She avoided his eyes and he suddenly felt foolish. Stupid remark, he scolded himself. He quickly went on: 'I take it they haven't managed to contact anybody yet?'

'No. They've even used a continuous punched tape on a telex machine, but nothing's come back. We've no way of knowing what's going on out there.'

'That could be for the best right now.'

The corridor opened out and they almost bumped into a small but broad-shouldered figure emerging from behind a ceiling-high row of apparatus. Unlike many of the men inside the complex, he was clean shaven and his light yellow hair neatly combed.

'Hiya,' the man said almost cheerfully. 'How you doing? Feeling better?'

'Yeah, okay.'

'Good. Catch you later.'

He passed them and strolled down the corridor, hands tucked into overall pockets and whistling tunelessly.

'He seems cheerful enough,' Culver said, watching the man's back.

'His name is Fairbank. He's one of the happier souls down here. Nothing appears to bother him. He's either supremely well-adjusted or crazy.'

'How about the others? From what I saw last time they didn't look too good.'

'Moods change all the time. It's contagious. One day the atmosphere's charged with an unnatural optimism, the next day you can feel the deep depression hanging in the air like a black fug. You've seen how disturbed some are in the sick bay. One or two others have been treated in there that you wouldn't know about – you were having your own problems.'

They were in a corridor again and he noticed a heavy-looking door with a small glass slit at face level. Built into the wall over the door was a red warning light, the light itself switched off. Kate saw him look through the glass.

'Would you believe they have their own broadcasting studio?' she said.

He rejoined her. 'Nothing surprises me any more.'

'Through here.' She caught his arm and wheeled him into a corridor on their right. 'That's the repeater standby plant ahead. Not much use when no phone calls are going through.'

They passed a room where rows of batteries sat in long tanks, with rectangular copper shapes above them which he assumed carried the current. Then they found themselves in a large open area which Kate told him was the main frame room. Identical racks of complicated switches and machinery stood in rows, forming narrow corridors; here and there monitors that he recognized as oscilloscopes stood by on trolleys, fault detectors made redundant because nothing was coming into the complex. Culver glanced up and saw masses of cables held aloft by a grid network, filling the ceiling area, an occasional metal ladder leading up to them.

'How much further?'

'Nearly there.'

They finally reached a closed metal door.

'HQ,' she said, pushing through.

The people gathered in the room were facing away from Culver, studying a wall-mounted map. He noticed other maps around the room, mostly of the UK, coloured pins decorating each one. One was marked with a gridwork of thick black lines.

Dealey was pointing at something on the chart before them, stubbing a chubby finger against the plastic-coated paper as if emphasizing a point. Culver couldn't quite register what was different about the man until Dealey turned to face him.

'No bandages,' Culver said. 'You can see?'

'As well as ever.' He pointed to a chair. 'I'm glad you're on your feet, but I shouldn't overdo it. Rest.'

Clare Reynolds came around from the desk they had all gathered behind. 'You look so much better, Steve. You had us worried for a while.'

'Thanks for taking care of me.' He was glad to sink into a seat.

'Kate became a dedicated nurse.'

He did not reply, but stared at Dealey instead. The Ministry man had shed his jacket but still wore a tie knotted up to the neck. Others in the room – Bryce, the ROC officer, and several others that Culver didn't know by name – were less formal in shirt sleeves and open collars. Only Farraday matched Dealey for neatness.

'It would appear we were fortunate enough to find cover just in time,' Dealey said, sitting in a chair behind the desk. The others were finding seats around the room, while Farraday leaned back against a wall, arms folded across his chest. 'A little longer and the radiation would have been too much. I want to thank you for getting me here.'

Culver brushed it aside. 'Like I said at the time: we needed each other. I'm glad your vision's okay.'

'Cleared up after the first couple of days. No permanent damage, thank God.'

Culver thought the man still looked drawn, weary, and

who could wonder at it? It was obvious that Dealey had taken leadership on his own shoulders, a responsibility that Culver didn't envy. He looked around the room and saw the same fatigue on the faces of the others. Perhaps the doctor had been right: he, Culver, had been well out of it for the past few days.

'We don't know much about you, Culver, except that you can take care of yourself pretty well.' Dealey was frowning, as if the compliment wasn't easy. 'May we ask what your occupation was before the attack?'

'Is it relevant?'

'I can't say until we know. We are a small group and any individual skill could be useful for our survival. There will undoubtedly be other groups – whole communities, in fact – and I would hope eventually all our resources will be pooled. For now, though, we have only ourselves to rely on.'

Culver smiled. 'I don't think my, er, particular occupation will help in those circumstances.' He added, almost apologetically but still smiling, 'I fly helicopters.'

Dealey leaned back in his seat and said, 'Ah,' the sound an interested sigh.

'Had my own outfit, nothing big. Just me with a partner to run the business side of things. Another pilot and a small ground crew. Nothing fancy.'

'What did you carry?' Farraday asked.

'Freight mostly, passengers now and then. We operated out of Redhill, convenient for London and the South, but I wouldn't say we were a threat to Bristow, the big helicopter company based in the same area.' He was smiling wryly.

Farraday was interested. 'What type of machines do you have?'

'Only three. Like I said, we're a small company. Our biggest is a twin-engined Westland Wessex 60, which we use

– sorry, I keep forgetting – *used* for carrying freight and aerial crane work. It could take up to sixteen passengers, so it came in handy for transporting businessmen, trade delegates, or work crews across the country. We've even carried a few rock bands and their entourages to gigs, not just for speed and convenience, but because I think they liked the impression it made. There was a smaller machine, a Bell 206B, that we used for smaller jobs, mostly surveys and freight. It carries four passengers, so we used it as our "executive" transporter.'

For a moment, Culver looked wistful. 'The baby was my Bell 47, just big enough to carry two. I've taught a lot of people to fly in that old machine, maybe not up to CAA-approved standards, but good enough so they'd never be a danger to themselves or anyone else. I rigged it up so I could spray crops too, and got a lot of work from local farmers.'

He found Dealey gazing at him in a peculiar way and realized the man was literally seeing him for the first time (unless he had visited him in the sick bay, which Culver somehow doubted). Whatever physical attributes Dealey had associated with Culver's voice were now being confirmed or denied.

'Just as a matter of interest,' Farraday said, 'what brought you up to London last Tuesday?'

'I've been trying to raise money for a new chopper, an old Bell 212 that Bristow was selling off. They weren't interested in leasing so I had to scrape up the cash. My bank was finally convinced the company was good for it.'

'You were asking for a loan from your bank wearing a leather jacket and jeans?' Dealey asked incredulously.

Culver grinned. 'Harry – my business partner – was the man who wore the suits. Besides, most of the begging had been done; the idea of the meeting was to clinch the deal.'

The grin disappeared. 'I was running late, something Harry couldn't stand too well. He must have been there, at the bank, waiting for me. Probably apologizing to the manager.'

'He may have been safe inside the building,' Dealey said, realizing what was going through Culver's mind.

Culver shook his head. 'The bank was close to the *Daily Mirror* offices. When we were out there I saw there wasn't much left of the *Mirror*, nor the buildings around it.'

A silence hung in the air, a silence that Culver himself broke. 'So what happens now? I assume the reason for this meeting is to discuss our future.'

Farraday moved away from the wall and sat on a corner of Dealey's desk, his arms still folded. 'That's correct, Mr Culver. We need to formulate a plan of action to cover not just the weeks we'll have to stay inside this shelter, but also when we leave.'

Culver looked around the room. 'Shouldn't everybody be involved in this? It concerns us all.'

Bryce, the CDO, shifted uncomfortably in his seat. 'I'm afraid a situation is developing between us, the "officials" if you like, and the Exchange staff. It's quite uncanny, but it's almost a minuscule encapsulation of how governments, since the last World War, have foreseen civil insurrection in the aftermath of a nuclear war.'

'You may have noticed,' Dealey put in, 'how many latter-day government buildings resemble fortresses.'

'I can't say that I have.'

Dealey smiled. 'The fact that you, and the public in general, haven't is an achievement in itself for the various governments who commissioned such buildings. They were built, of course, as strongholds against civil uprising or attempted *coups d'état*, and not just in the event of revolution following a nuclear war. Several even have moats around them – Mondial House in the City is a good example – or they may have recessed lower floors to make entry difficult. The most obvious is the Guards barracks in Kensington with its gun slits built into its outer walls.'

'Hold it.' Culver had lifted a hand. 'You're telling me there's a revolution going on down here?'

'Not yet,' Clare Reynolds broke in. 'But there is a growing resentment among the engineers and staff of the telephone exchange. They've lost so much, you see, and we, the "authorities", are to blame. It doesn't matter that we've lost everything too, and that we, personally, are not responsible for this war; in their eyes, we represent the instigators.'

'Surely not you, a doctor?'

'They're suspicious of *anybody* in authority.'

'Meetings like this, where they're shut out, can't be helping matters.'

'We've no choice,' Dealey said brusquely. 'We can't possibly include everybody in policy decisions. It wouldn't be practical.'

'They might feel that's how the world got into this sorry mess in the first place.'

Dealey and Bryce glanced at each other and the former said: 'Perhaps we were wrong about you. We thought as an outsider – a "neutral" if you like – you would be useful in bridging this unproductive division that's presented itself. If you feel you can't cooperate . . .'

'Don't get me wrong. I'm not against you. I'm not against anyone. What's happened has happened, nothing's going to make it different. I'd just hate everything to continue the way it has in the past, in a way that's led us to just this point. Can't you see that?'

'Yes, Mr Culver,' Farraday replied, 'we understand your intent. Unfortunately, it isn't as simple as that.'

'It never is.'

Dealey interjected: 'On your first day inside this shelter you witnessed for yourself the dissension among them. You saw how many wanted to leave, only Dr Reynolds' good sense dissuading them. We cannot shirk our responsibilities towards everybody, including ourselves, by allowing mob rule.'

'I wasn't talking about mob rule. What I'm referring to is group decision.'

'There'll be time enough for that when the crisis has passed.'

'This is a crisis that isn't going to pass.' Culver could feel his anger growing and he remembered Dealey urging him to leave Kate to the mercy of the rats in the tunnel. Throughout their ordeal, his priority had been one of self-preservation. 'We've all got a stake in this, Dealey, me, you – and those poor bastards outside that door. It's not for us to decide their future.'

'You misunderstand us,' Bryce said placatingly. 'We intend merely to plan, not decide. Our ideas will then be presented to everyone in this complex for discussion. Only after that will any decisions be made.'

Culver forced himself to relax. 'Okay, maybe I'm reading too much into this. It could be that yours is the only way, that we shall need some kind of order. But let me just say this: the time for power games is over.' With those words, he stared at Dealey, whose face was expressionless.

'We can take it, then,' Dealey said, 'that you will support us.'

'I'll do what I can to help everyone in the shelter.'

Dealey decided it would be pointless not to accept the rather ambiguous statement. He had hoped to find an ally in Culver, for any addition to their small nucleus of authority would help in the imbalance of numbers. If events had worked out as intended, many other 'outsiders' would have reached the shelter, and this particular problem would never have arisen. He was disappointed, imagining that perhaps earlier circumstances might have created a bond between himself and Culver, but he could see that the pilot distrusted him. Culver was no fool.

'Very well,' he said, as if to dismiss the dispute. 'Before you arrived we were pinpointing the city's shelters and their linking tunnels. The other maps around the walls locate the country's thirteen sites for regional seats of government and various bunkers, most of which will have been immune from nuclear attack, provided there were no direct hits. The grids indicate the communications lines between RSGs and sub-RSGs.' Dealey pointed to a particular chart showing the southwest of England. 'Over there you can see the position of HQ UK Land Forces, operating from a vast bunker at Wilton, near Salisbury.'

'Is that where the government will operate from?' Culver was already beginning to be intrigued.

'Er, no. There are several locations for the National Seat of Government, Bath and Cheltenham to name just two.' He appeared hesitant, and Culver saw Bryce give a slight nod of his head. Dealey acknowledged and went on. 'Although the facts have been carefully kept from public attention, several more-than-educated guesses have been made concerning the whereabouts of the government's secret emergency bunker. Most have been correct, but none has understood the magnitude, or the complexity of such a shelter.'

Culver's voice was low. 'Where is it?'

Dr Reynolds struck a match and lit a cigarette that had danced lifelessly in her mouth for some time. Farraday moved away from the desk and leaned against a wall, his arms unfolding, hands tucking into his trouser pockets. Bryce looked pleased, as though he personally had played some considerable part in the survival of his paymasters.

'Under the Victoria Embankment,' Dealey said mildly. 'Close to Parliament, and within easy reach by tunnel from the Palace, Downing Street, and *all* the government buildings packed into that rather small area of the city. The shelter itself stretches almost from the Parliament buildings to Charing Cross where another tunnel, one that runs parallel to the Charing Cross/Waterloo tube tunnel, crosses the Thames.'

'There are *two* tunnels?'

'Yes. The second, secret tunnel, is a bunker in itself, and provides a quick and safe means of crossing the river should the nearby bridges be destroyed or blocked.'

'How could such a place be kept quiet? How could it be built without people knowing?'

'Have you ever wondered why most of our cable tunnels and new Underground railway lines inevitably run over budget, and invariably take longer to build than planned? The Victoria and Jubilee lines are prime examples of excavations that have far exceeded their financial allocation and completion dates.'

'You mean they were used to cover up work on secret sites?'

'Let's just say that room for more than just Underground railway lines was made. And all the construction workers – at least those employed on the more sensitive sites – were sworn to secrecy under the Official Secrets Act before they were assigned.'

'Even so, there must have been leaks.'

'Quite so, but the D Notice prevented any media exploitation.'

Culver released a short, sharp sigh.

'So the élite got themselves saved.'

'Not the élite, Culver,' Dealey said icily. 'Key personnel and certain ministers who are necessary to pick the country up off its knees after such a catastrophe. And members of the Royal Family, naturally.'

'Would they have had time to reach the shelter?'

'Such provisions are always made possible for Cabinet Ministers and the Royal Family in times of foreign aggression, no matter what particular location they happen to be in. From the headquarters itself an escape route stretches for miles underground. It emerges beneath Heathrow Airport. From there, one can escape to any part of the world.'

'Unless the airport has been destroyed,' said Clare Reynolds, cigarette smoke streaming from tight lips.

'In which case, transport can be provided to another part of the country,' Dealey replied. He tapped unconsciously on the desktop with his fingers. 'As yet, we have not been able to communicate with the Embankment headquarters, and it's vital we make contact soon. We intend to send out a small reconnaissance party to explore the conditions above us when the fallout level permits. We also need to evaluate the state of the tunnels, which may provide a safer route to the main government shelter.'

He stared directly at Culver. 'We hope you'll agree to be part of that reconnaissance group.'

'Are you hungry, Steve?'

'Since you mention it, yes, I am.' He grinned at Clare Reynolds, who had asked the question. 'In fact, I'm starving.'

'Good, that's how it should be. You'll be good as new in a day or two.' She nodded her head in the general direction of the canteen. 'Let's get you something to eat, then I want you to rest for a while. No sense in overdoing things.'

She led the way, Kate and Culver following close behind. 'I could use a stiff drink after that long meeting,' she said, looking back at them over her shoulder. 'It's a pity the hard stuff is being rationed so frugally.'

'I could use a drink myself,' Culver agreed. 'I guess they didn't store much away down here, right?'

'Wrong,' said Kate. 'There's plenty, but Dealey thinks it wise to keep it under lock and key. Too much firewater no good for natives.'

'He may have a point,' the doctor said. 'The natives are restless enough.'

'It's really that bad?'

'Not that bad, Steve, but it's not good. Dealey may be suffering under a slight persecution complex because most of the resentment is directed towards him as the token government man. But large though this complex is, there's a certain amount of claustrophobia prevailing, and that coupled with a general feeling of melancholia, even repressed hysteria, could lead to an explosive situation. Too much alcohol wouldn't help.'

Culver silently had to agree. The atmosphere in the shelter did somehow feel charged and he could understand Dealey's nervousness. He felt tired once more, the meeting they had just left draining much of the buoyancy he had felt earlier. Culver had been surprised at the elaborate contingency plans that were regularly scrutinized, amended, modified and put into action throughout the decades of the cold war and détente eras, a festering, unspoken conflict, insidious in its durability. Now it had ended, mass destruction the terminator.

Dealey had once again defined the chain of command, but giving more details than he had at the first briefing Culver had attended.

The country would now have been split up into twelve regions, and each one could operate as a separate unit, a self-reliant cell. Under the National Seat of Government would be the twelve regional seats, under these, twenty-three sub-regional headquarters, which would issue orders to county controls, down to district controls and sub-district controls. At the bottom of the list, the last in the pecking order, were the community posts and rest centres.

Each region had its own armed forces headquarters, the regional military commanders and their staff housed in deep bunkers: these forces, working with police and mobilized Civil Defence units, would ensure the new emergency laws were obeyed. Warehouses, pharmaceutical and otherwise, even supermarkets, would now be under strict local government control. Certain buildings, motorways and key roads would be commandeered by the military. Mass evacuation had *not* been planned. In fact, it would be openly discouraged, for it would cause too much disruption in an already disrupted world, too much disorder to carefully laid-out plans.

Culver shuddered to contemplate the New Order that must have already taken over. Unless of course, the damage had been far greater than anyone had ever anticipated, the world itself dying and unable to respond to any kind of organization.

His thoughts were interrupted. The doctor had come to a halt as an engineer approached her and said something in a low, agitated voice. He turned without waiting for a reply and quickly strode back the way he had come.

'What's wrong?' Culver asked.

'I'm not sure,' Dr Reynolds replied, 'but there seems to be something interesting going on. Ellison wants me to hear something.'

She followed the retreating figure and came to the ventilation plant room.

A group of men, some wearing white overalls, others in ordinary clothes, were gathered around a large air duct, the shaft of which, Culver assumed, rose to the surface. He guessed filters removed any radioactive dust from the air intake. Fairbank was among the group.

'Something we should know about?' Dr Reynolds asked of no one in particular, and it was Fairbank who replied. There was a brightness to his eyes, but also an uncertainty.

'Listen,' he said, and turned back to the air duct.

Above the hum of the generator they could hear another, more insistent sound. A drumming, a constant pattering.

'What is it?' Kate asked, looking at Culver.

He knew, and so did the doctor, but it was Fairbank who answered.

'Rain,' he said. 'It's raining up there like never before.'

Two: Aftermath

Their time had come.

They sensed it, they knew.

Something had happened in the world above them, a holocaust the creatures could not comprehend; yet they were instinctively aware that those they feared were no longer the same, that they had been damaged, weakened. The creatures had learned from those who had hidden in the tunnels, killing and feeding upon the humans, satisfying a lust that had lain dormant for many years, repressed because survival depended on that repression. The bloodlust had been revived and set loose.

And the tunnels, the sewers, the conduits, the dark holes they had skulked in never knowing nor craving a different existence, had broken, allowing the world of light to intrude upon their own dismal kingdom.

They crept upwards, stealthily, sniffing the air, puzzled at the relentless drumming sound, emerging into the rain that drenched their bristle-furred bodies. The brightness dazzled their sharp eyes at first, even though it was muted an unnatural grey, and they were timid, fearful, in their movement, still hiding from human eyes, still apprehensive of their age-old adversary.

They moved out from the dark places and stole among the ruins of the city, rain-streaked black beasts, many in number, eager for sustenance. Hunting soft flesh. Seeking warm blood.

10

Sharon Cole thought her bladder might easily burst if she didn't do something about it soon. Unfortunately, the dark frightened her and she knew that beyond The Pit the darkness was absolute. All the others appeared to be sleeping, their breathing, their snores, and their murmured whimpers filling the small steep-sloped auditorium with sounds. If you couldn't sleep, the horror was ever-present; yet sleep and the nightmares allowed no peace.

They knew it was night only because their watches told them it was so, and dutifully, by agreement made between them all in the first days, they endeavoured to maintain a natural order, as if adherence to ritual would bring a semblance of normality to abnormal circumstances.

Only three precious candles kept complete darkness at bay, the men deciding the torch batteries were more precious and not to be wasted in hours of inactivity. One or two had suggested a *total* blackout at night, but the majority, as many men as women, had insisted on keeping some light through the sleeping hours, perhaps believing, like their Neanderthal forefathers, that light held back any oppressive spirits. Most rationalized that there should always be some light source in case of emergencies, and it made sense, but each of them knew they drew comfort from those small flickering flames strategically placed around the underground cinema.

Sharon shifted uncomfortably in the three seats she was sprawled across, the movement only causing the uneasy weight inside to press more insistently. She groaned. Oh God, she'd have to go.

'Margaret?' Sharon whispered.

The woman who lay in the same row as her and whose head almost touched Sharon's did not stir.

'Margaret?' she said, a little louder this time, but there was still no response.

Sharon bit into her lower lip. She and the older woman had formed an unspoken alliance over the past few weeks, a bond of mutual protection against the embarrassments as well as the hazards of their predicament. They were among a group of survivors, fewer than fifty in number now that several had recently died. Sharon was just nineteen, a trainee make-up artist from the theatre on the upper level, pretty, slim, and a pseudo-devotee to the arts; Margaret, fiftyish, round, once jolly, and a member of the brown-smocked corps of cleaners to the huge concrete cultural and business complex. Both had offered reciprocal comfort when the stresses of their existence had become too much, their frequent (but becoming less so) breakdowns managed as if by rota, relying on each other to be strong while one was temporarily weak. Both assumed their families – Margaret a husband and three grown-up children, Sharon parents, a younger sister as well as several boyfriends – were lost to the bombs, and both now needed a support, someone to cling to, to rely on. They had become almost like mother and daughter.

But Margaret was sleeping deeply, perhaps for the first time in so many weeks, and Sharon did not have the heart to waken her.

She sat and looked down at the dim rows, each one filled with restless bodies. One candle glowed in the centre of the small stage, its poor light barely reflected from the grey screen behind. To one side lay the hastily gathered and meagre provisions from the destroyed cafeteria two levels above the tiny, plush cinema known as The Pit. The food had cost dearly.

A security guard had led six others, all men, on a forage after one week's confinement, driven out by hunger. They had brought back as much unspoilt food as they could carry, as well as torches, candles, buckets (to use as water containers), a first-aid kit (which they had yet to use), disinfectant, and curtains for blankets. They had also brought back with them the cancer that was the nuclear bombs' deadly aftermath.

It was two days before they would talk about the destruction they had witnessed above – no living person had been found, but there had been an abundance of mutilated bodies in the rubble – and three days before the first of them went down with the sickness. Shortly, four were dead, and within days the last two were gone. Their corpses were now lying in one corner of the foyer outside, the curtains they had brought back their shrouds.

And the toilets were also in the black tomb of the foyer.

For Heaven's sake, Margaret, how could you be sleeping when I need you?

The reception area outside the theatre was regarded almost as an airlock between the survivors and the dust-diseased world above, only to be entered when necessary, the cinema doors kept permanently closed, to be opened briefly for access and then just enough for a body to squeeze through. The danger from radiation out there seemed minimal, for the main staircase, a narrow enough spiral, was blocked by debris (the search party had used the staff staircase which was behind a heavy door). Contained in the foyer were the telephone booths, long, curved seats around small fixed coffee tables, a bar (the stocks of liquor had been transferred to The Pit itself), the lift shafts and the invaluable public conveniences. The latter were invaluable because they provided a source of water (any day now the survivors expected the flow to trickle to a stop) and they meant sanitary hygiene could be maintained. In an effort to preserve the supply, flushing was allowed only at the end of every two days, and the possibility that the drinking water could itself be radiation-contaminated was disregarded on the grounds that if they didn't drink they would die anyway.

So, Sharon knew she would have to go out there into the high-ceilinged tomb where the dead men lay and walk by candlelight to the toilet. Alone.

Unless another female among the slumbering audience was awake and also needed to pee.

Sharon stood and hopefully scanned the rows of seats, peering through the gloom in search of another upright body. She coughed lightly to gain attention, but nobody acknowledged. It was strange how many hours most of them slept, albeit fitfully, despite the long days' inactivity. She supposed it had some psychological basis, an escape from the real, shattered world into another of dreams. Pity the dreams were usually so bloody awful.

Her bladder insisted time was running short.

'Hell,' she whispered to herself and carefully edged her way towards the aisle, avoiding contact with the occupants of the mauve and green seats. The row she had chosen with Margaret as their resting place – strange how each survivor had marked out their own territory – was close to the exit/ entry doors, so there were not too many stairs to climb to reach the back of the auditorium. The material of her tight jeans stretched against her knees and thighs as she cautiously mounted the steps, one hand using the wall on her left for guidance and support. She reached the candle burning by the door and dutifully lit another beside it from the flame, ignoring the flashlight placed alongside for emergencies.

Sharon opened the door a fraction, just enough for her slim body to slide through, the tips of her breasts brushing against the edge. The door closed behind her and she raised the candle high to look around the cold mausoleum.

Back inside the theatre, a figure quietly rose from the darkness.

Fortunately for Sharon, the feeble light did not reach the draped corpses in the far corner, but the smell of their corruption was strong. She quickly crossed the thick-carpeted floor, her steps leaving unseen footprints in the dust that had settled into the pile, heading for the closest toilet, the men's, desperate to relieve herself and equally desperate to be back among the breathing. The bodies could have been left inside the lift shafts or the staff stairwell, but everyone was reluctant to open any doors leading to the outside since the contaminated search party had been taken ill. Pushing briskly through the toilet door, relieved to be separated from the corpses, Sharon passed by the urinals and washbasins, making for the two cubicles at the far end. The mirrors above the basins reflected the candlelight and ghosted her presence.

Both cubicle doors were ajar and she was glad that tonight had been flushing night: the stench wasn't too bad. She entered one and, decorum unaffected by circumstances, pushed the bolt to behind her. Retracting her stomach muscles, Sharon released the top button of her jeans, unzipped, and gratefully settled onto the toilet. She sighed deeply at the relief. She gazed at the candle glow by the gap beneath the cubicle door for several long moments after the flow had stopped. The flame held faces, images, the pattern of her own life, all swimming incandescently before her in that small fire. People and memories, now consumed by a greater fire. Her eyes misted, the glow becoming softer, its edges even less defined, and she forced herself to stop thinking, to stem the spilling tears. There had been too much of that. When the sirens had sounded outside the concrete walls of the Barbican Centre, her only thoughts had been of her own survival. Nothing else – *no one else* – had mattered. The rush through the panicked crowds, running down the stairs, falling, picking herself up, ignoring the pain, intent on reaching the safest place in the entire complex, the underground cinema. The dash from the huge hall across the covered roadway to the staircase leading down, not using the lifts, knowing they would be crowded, fearing they would become jammed between floors. Others had the same idea, but not many. *Fortunately* not many. Crowding into the steep-tiered cinema, the blast rocking the foundations of the whole centre, shaking the walls, throwing the ground upwards, the incredible roar, the stifling heat, the . . .

The candle flame leaned towards her, flickering wildly. Disturbed by a draught. She thought she heard the swish of the main door as it closed automatically.

Sharon stood, pulling the jeans over naked hips. She zipped up and listened.

A footstep?

'Hello?' Sharon listened again. 'Hello? Is someone out there?'

Imagination?

Her own nervousness?

Maybe.

She stooped to pick up the candle, then unbolted the cubicle door. Her arm was outstretched, pushing the light into the darkness as she stepped through the door.

Sharon paused, listening once more. The blackness around her was more oppressive; the feeling of confinement, the sensing of millions of tons of broken concrete bearing down on the underground theatre, was almost unbearable. She suddenly felt that the air itself had become thick, somehow sluggish in her lungs, but sensibly told herself it was all nerves, that distress was the instigator and her own imagination was gullible to its suggestions.

But someone was in there with her.

She could hear breathing.

A harsh, short breath and the candle was out. Acrid smoke from the expired flame. A scuffing sound against floor tiles. A quavery sucking in of air. The stale smell of another body.

A hand touching her face.

Her scream was cut short as strong fingers covered her mouth. Another arm reached around her, enclosing her ribs. The expired candle fell to the floor as a head pressed against her own.

'Don't struggle,' came the urgent whisper. 'I'll hurt you if you do.'

It was then she knew the intent.

She panicked, her legs kicking empty air as her body was lifted. Sharon tried to scream again, but the grip over her lips was too tight. She bit down hard and tasted blood.

The man who had followed her from the cinema, the man who had covertly watched her through the traumatic weeks of their forced internment, who knew that civilization was at an end, that there was only death awaiting them all, who knew there was no law to punish him, nothing left to prevent him taking what he wanted, cried out in pain, but did not relax his hold.

One of Sharon's feet touched the edge of the washbasin and she pushed backwards with all her strength, sending them both crashing back into the cubicle she had just left. The man grunted as they went down, his head cracking against wall tiles. Yet still he clung to her.

The girl struck him with her elbows, squirming her body in an effort to wriggle free. His hand had left her mouth and his forearm was locked around her throat, squeezing her windpipe, frightening her even more.

'Please don't . . .' she managed to beg, the sound wheezing, the words barely audible. 'Please . . . don't . . . kill . . . me.'

His other hand was fumbling beneath her sweater, reaching for her uncupped breasts. Fingers closed around one risen nipple and the pain was excruciating as he squeezed. That same pain galvanized an instinctive reaction.

Their two bodies were half-slumped against the toilet wall, the back of Sharon's head against her assailant's chest. Her heels pressed hard against the floor, sending her body upwards and back in a violent motion, the top of her head cracking against the man's jaw, sending his head snapping backwards to hit the wall yet again. He howled and his grip loosened.

Sharon slid away, slithering along on her back, brushing off his clutching hands. She turned, was on her knees, her hand reaching out to feel a wall for guidance, the total darkness confusing, adding to the terror. Her fingers curled around the edge of a urinal and she pulled herself forward, making for where she knew the main door had to be.

She screamed loudly as his weight bore down on her.

He had landed on her legs and was slowly crawling up the length of her body, using his weight to pin her against the floor. She felt his hands on her back, on her shoulders, fingers now curling in her hair, pulling her head back. Then down, her nose bursting against the hard floor tiles. And again, her senses reeling with the blow. Resistance momentarily left her, although her arms still flailed limply. His hot breath was against her neck, his staleness smothering her. He pulled her round to face him and her nails tore at his eyes. He slapped away her hands and pulled at her sweater, exposing her body though it was unseen in the impenetrable blackness. She screamed again and a fist squelched against her already bloodied nose. Sharon groaned as invisible hands groped at her clothing.

Neither of them heard the scratching at the door.

The man lowered his head and his teeth found the soft flesh of her stomach. He bit her and she shrieked. His mouth left a sticky trail of saliva across her skin as his lips sought her nipples. A hand pulled at the button of her jeans and they opened, the zip descending halfway. Trembling fingers pushed it further. The same hand probed and she tried to squeeze her thighs together, but his leg, thrust between her knees, thwarted her. A new pain as the rough fingers entered.

In the darkness behind them, the door leading into the foyer slowly opened under the gathered pressure of the black-haired creatures. A sleek, hump-backed body crouched low against the floor, eased its way through the gap. Others, excited by the fragrance of sweet, running blood, pushed from behind. The corpses on the far side of the foyer, their curtain shrouds torn away, their white bodies covered with smaller, moving shapes that chewed and gnawed their rotting flesh, were now forsaken for something more alluring, a sustenance the vermin were becoming familiar with: the moist freshness of living organs.

The man had raised himself to his knees and was tearing at his own clothing, ripping off buttons, shoving underpants and trousers down over his hips in one movement, the total darkness stimulating him to an even greater frenzy, his mind creating the image that lay beneath him, his touch realizing its substance.

Sharon's eyes were closed, though it made no difference in the absence of light, and blood flowed into her mouth. She heard his movements above her, his grunts, the murmured animal sounds. And part of her was aware of the draught that tickled at her scalp.

The man began to lower himself and she felt his warm, dribbling penis settle against her stomach. She moaned and turned her head away from his foul breath, her cheek scraping against his rough beard.

'Please ... don't ...' It was almost a whisper, a last desperate pleading. Briefly, and in a distant area of her mind, a place where situations can be considered with detachment, aloofness its own protection, she wondered why she cared after all that had happened. With so many hundreds of millions dead, why should her single feeble body be sacrosanct? The answer was obvious, and she knew it before the question was really begged. *Because it was hers! They could kill off the whole fucking world, but her body belonged to her!*

As the tip of his penis pushed against the tender opening between her thighs, one hand grabbed at his hair and yanked, twisting his head round; the stiffened fingers of her other hand jabbed wildly for his eyes. She felt sickened when the untrimmed nail of her index finger sank into something soft and movable.

He lurched away, his turn to scream, his pulped eye popping from its socket as the girl's finger withdrew. The eye lay on his cheek, hanging there by the threads of its retaining muscles. He fell into the space beneath the wash basins, hands reaching for the dangling eyeball.

But the rat reached it first.

The muscles were severed by a clamping of jaws and a rapid shaking of the vermin's head, and the eye was swallowed virtually unscathed. The creature, whose natural habitat was darkness and shadows, lunged with barely a pause for the opening from which bloody juices streamed. It buried its pointed snout deep into the empty socket.

Sharon thought the man's screams and thrashings were because of the injury she had caused him. She kicked out at his body, not realizing she was striking other, scuttling forms. Sobbing, she pulled at her jeans, tugging them back over her hips, her back against the smooth floor. Something sharp snapped at a leg and she thought he had bitten her again. Her other foot struck out and connected with something solid. Her leg was released.

She staggered to her feet, a urinal giving her support. Blindly, she hurled herself towards the door, praying she was moving in the right direction. The man's screams filled the small toilet, bouncing off the walls and ceiling, amplified in the tiled chamber, and she felt no remorse for the injury she had dealt him. Through her own sobs and his screams she failed to hear the squealing.

She tripped against something low to the ground, imagining it was one of his flailing limbs, and her head struck the edge of the half-open door. Only momentarily did she wonder why the door was still open, for her main thoughts were on reaching the safety of the cinema where the other survivors would protect her, where Margaret would comfort her, would rock her soothingly to and fro just as her own mother had done when she was little and helpless.

But her mind could no longer ignore the squirming, wriggling creatures beneath her feet, the high-pitched squealing, the sharp, tearing pain as daggers ripped at her legs.

She saw light, for the cinema doors had been opened by those inside who had heard the terrible screams, who were now screaming themselves as a thick, black-running river poured into the small theatre.

Sharon staggered over the flowing bodies, running with the rats, all control completely gone, not knowing what else to do, just flowing with the stream.

And when she toppled over the top stair of the steeply-tiered theatre, the jaws of one creature clamped around an arm, another clinging to her back, teeth and claws entwined in her hair, it was like cresting and plunging with a small but forceful waterfall.

A black, consuming waterfall.

11

The weight of the .38 Smith and Wesson Model 64 strapped inside its holster was uncomfortable against the side of his chest, but then Culver was unused to carrying such a weapon. Dealey had informed him it carried six bullets rather than the five its predecessor, the Model 36, had carried. Culver saw no reason for his having to fire off even one bullet: the war had already been fought and there could be no enemy and surely no victor. Dealey had agreed but had added that the dangers would be from within. Culver felt disinclined to pursue the point.

He shone the flashlight ahead, its beam reflecting goldly off the water-dripping tunnel walls. The others – Bryce, Fairbank, and the ROC officer, McEwen – waded behind him through the knee-deep water, wary eyes constantly seeking out cracks or niches in the curved brickwork where dark creatures could lurk.

Mercifully, the murky water covering the Underground railway tracks also hid the rotted remains of those who had been slaughtered near the shelter's secret doorway. It had been unfortunate that Fairbank had accidentally kicked something loose beneath the surface, for white bones had risen like ghosts from a liquid grave. The four men's steps had been more careful after that, each one pushing from his mind the thought of skeletal hands reaching for them from the dirty, flowing water.

Despite their trepidation, however, it was a relief to be beyond the confines of the shelter. In the four weeks they had been trapped inside, morale had sunk even lower and attitudes had varied between deep despair and sluggish apathy. Until the past few days, when a bitter tension had replaced both moods.

Many of the engineers and exchange staff resented Dealey's refusal to allow them to leave, particularly when Bryce had admitted that the extraordinarily heavy rainfall that had not ceased for a moment since it had begun weeks before, should have all but washed away the worst of the fallout.

Yet Alex Dealey had insisted that everyone should remain where they were and wait for the all-clear sirens. If the unremitting downpour could be heard by means of the air shafts, then so would the sirens. But Culver sensed there was more to the Ministry man's objections, almost as though giving way to the mob meant relinquishing not just his own self-given authority, but the power of government rule itself. And only chaos would take its place.

As yet, retention of command had not quite become an obsession with Dealey, but it had certainly developed into a capricious objective. Perhaps, too, this pursuance of a familiar and orderly regime was a way of saving himself from complete despair, for it seemed that each survivor, prisoner to the holocaust, strove to find some semblance of their old existence in this new world. It showed in various ways: Dr Reynolds practised her profession with dedicated care, even though her attitude at times seemed cynical; Farraday worked at his machines, keeping them running, urging his staff to help him make the breakthrough in communications, even issuing a work rota so that no engineer had a completely idle day; Bryce constantly checked the stores, the weaponry, consulted emergency documents, even maps as though they would provide a sensory link with other survival stations; Kate helped Clare Reynolds, helped Farraday, helped Bryce, helped Dealey, kept herself constantly busy, a personal assistant to all of them.

Culver did not think too much of the past. But even he did not change into the other clothes provided from the shelter's stores; he kept his torn jeans and worn leather jacket.

The idea of the reconnaissance was to boost morale a little, possibly to dissipate some of the tension, rather than just an attempt to make contact with the outside world. Culver realized it was too soon for the latter, that if there were survivors above, they would still be in a state of shock. And many would be dying. Yet he was glad to go. Before, when the idea had first been mooted, he was reluctant and might even have refused if a decision had had to be made there and then; but now the Exchange, huge though it was, was like a prison to him. It was the same for many others, for there had been no shortage of volunteers for the mission. Dealey had been selective, using Bryce as representative of authority, McEwen almost in a military role, Fairbank as worker delegate, and Culver as a neutral, perhaps even an intermediary. It was a nonsense to Culver, but he was prepared to go along with Dealey's little games if it meant breaking free of the shelter for a short while. In fact, the group's time limit was two hours, and if the ionization instrument carried by McEwen registered an unhealthy amount of radiation still around, then their return to the Exchange was to be immediate.

Yet their departure had not raised the spirits of the other survivors as much as Dealey and his closer associates had hoped. Culver had felt uneasy as he prepared to leave and had studied the faces of the engineers and workforce as they gathered round to wish the departing team good luck. They showed interest but little excitement. Perhaps there was some dread in their gaze.

In Kate's eyes there had been fear, and the fear had been for him alone.

'I think I can see the station!'

It was Fairbank who had called out, jerking Culver from his thoughts. All four men shone their flashlights straight ahead.

'You're right,' Culver said, his voice low, not reflecting Fairbank's excitement. 'I can make out the platform. Let's get out of this water.'

Their pace quickened and the tunnel echoed with splashing sounds. In his eagerness to be free of the overwhelming darkness and the sluggish, black water that was a tangible part of it, Bryce tripped over a concealed track, going down heavily, but just managing to keep his torch above the surface. Culver and Fairbank waited as McEwen, nearest to him, helped the Civil Defence officer to his feet.

'Take it steady,' Culver warned them. 'No point in busting something before we even see daylight.'

They proceeded more cautiously, walking single file in the middle of the flowing stream, keeping between the unseen rails. The stench in the tunnel was foul and the other three had no wish to take a similar ducking. Culver only moved to the side when the platform was close. He paused, climbed up and shone his light along the platform while the others waited. The station appeared to be empty.

He turned to the others and found he had nothing to say. It was Bryce who suggested they move on.

Culver helped each one onto the platform and they did not stop again until they had reached the opening leading to the escalators. The only sound was that of flowing water, a disturbed hollow gushing that echoed eerily around the tiled walls. They turned their lights on posters announcing new films, the finest whisky, the prettiest stocking-tights, and felt acutely saddened for things past. An Away-day was now a journey beyond existence, not a trip to another town, another county.

Culver remembered the screams, the panic cries, of just a few weeks before and his chest ached as though there was pressure from within. He had half expected the platform to be filled with bodies, perhaps even one or two survivors among them; the emptiness was somehow more frightening. The sudden thought that possibly there had been survivors who had returned to the surface, who had already begun to adapt, had even begun to rebuild some kind of life, cut into his fear; not decisively, but enough to raise his hopes just a little. That barely formed optimism lasted but a few fleeting moments.

'*Oh my good God!*'

They turned to see McEwen standing by the corner of the small exit archway. He was aiming his torch towards the escalators beyond. The three men approached McEwen slowly as his hand began to rise, the torch beam travelling up the stairway. Fairbank moaned aloud, Bryce sagged against a wall, Culver closed his eyes.

Bodies were sprawled on the stairways as far as the light would reach. There were more, many more, piled up at the bottom of the three stairways, dishevelled bundles, decomposing, stains of dark blood, dry and crusted, spilling like frozen lava from the heaped forms. And even from where the four survivors stood they could see the corpses were not intact and that their mutilation had little to do with rotting flesh.

Limbs did not decompose before the rest of the body. Surface organs – noses, ears and eyes – did not just fade away. Stomachs did not split as though intestines had broken free from dying hosts.

Bryce had begun to vomit.

'What happened to them?' Fairbank asked incredulously. 'There's no bomb damage down here, nothing to cause those inj...' He broke off abruptly, realizing what the others already knew. 'No, it couldn't be! Rats wouldn't attack this many people.' He stared wildly at Culver. 'Not unless they were already dead. That has to be it! The radiation killed the people first and the rats fed off them.'

Culver shook his head. 'There's dried blood everywhere. Corpses don't bleed.'

'Sweet Mother of...' Fairbank's knees began to sag and he, too, leaned against a wall. 'We'd better get back to the shelter,' he said quickly. 'They may be still around.'

McEwen was already backing away towards the platform. 'He's right, we've got to get back.'

'Hold it.' Culver grabbed his arm. 'I'm no expert, but by the look of them, these people were attacked some time ago. If the rats were still around I think there'd be a lot less left of the corpses. They'd be...' he fought down his own nausea '...a regular food supply for the vermin. My guess is that they've moved on, maybe searching for fresher food.'

'You mean they can afford to be choosy?' Fairbank's voice was too weak to sound scornful.

'I think we should go on. If the bastards are anywhere, they'll be behind us in the tunnels.'

'Oh, great. That'll give us something to look forward to.'

The engineer shone his torch back in the direction they had come from.

Bryce, wiping his mouth with a handkerchief and still using the wall for support, said, 'Culver is right: we should go on. These vermin have existed in the darkness for so long the world above will be alien to them. They'll hide where they feel safe and attack only the weak and defenceless. These poor unfortunates may have already been dying before they were set upon.'

He managed to straighten and his face looked haunted in the torchlight. 'Besides, two of you have guns; we can defend ourselves.'

Culver could have smiled at the thought of two handguns fighting off hordes of monster vermin, but the effort would have been too much. 'We've come so far, almost to the point of no return, if you like. If we go back now, we'll have achieved nothing. If we get to the top of those stairs, then at least we'll have some idea of what the world has left to offer. Who knows, it may be teeming with human life again. Perhaps they're even creating some order out of the mess.'

'Yeah, I'd love to believe it but I'd have to be fucking mad.' Fairbank slapped the palm of his hand against the smooth wall. 'You're right in one thing, though: we've come this far so let's go on. I want to see daylight.'

'But we'd have to climb through those dead bodies.' McEwen looked at the other three as though they were insane.

'Keep your eyes off them,' Fairbank suggested.

'How d'you stop smelling them?' There was more than a hint of hysteria in the ROC officer's plaintive cry.

Culver was already walking away. 'You've got a choice: come with us or walk back on your own.'

Bryce and Fairbank pushed themselves away from the

wall and followed. After a brief moment of hesitation, a moment when his face pinched tight and his bowels considerably loosened, McEwen went after them.

Culver could not keep his gaze from the first few bodies; they held a peculiarly morbid fascination for him, a compulsion to see how much damage could be inflicted upon the human frame. It was the things that crawled between the openings, the gashes, the empty eye sockets, that made revulsion the catharsis of his curiosity rather than the mutilated flesh. He tried not to breathe in too deeply.

They climbed the stairs, forcing themselves to step between the corpses, deliberately keeping their eyes unfocused, their torch beams never lingering too long on one particular spot. Culver wondered how long the generators operating the emergency lighting had continued to run: had these people died in total darkness, feeling only the slashing jaws and talons, or had they witnessed the full terror of their assailants? Which would have been worse: unseen demons gnawing away at your squirming body, or black carnivorous beasts, seen and thereby understood, tearing you apart? Culver slipped and his knee thudded against the chest of a man whose face was just a gaping hole.

Culver recoiled, almost backing into Bryce who was just below him on the stairs. Bryce grabbed the handrail for support, preventing them both from toppling back down the escalator. Recovering, Culver continued to climb, but an abhorrent question could not be pushed from his mind: why would the creatures burrow so deeply into a man's head when softer flesh and organs were more accessible?

He stopped and surveyed the pile-up of bodies before him. They would have to be lifted clear and the idea of touching them did not appeal.

'Help me,' he said to Fairbank, who was next in line

behind the Civil Defence officer. Bryce moved aside to let the engineer pass.

'Christ, do we have to?' Fairbank complained. 'Can't we climb over?'

'And risk all of us tumbling down to the bottom in an avalanche of corpses?'

'Since you put it that way . . .'

The first body they lifted was that of a woman and, with nothing much left inside her open abdomen, she was as light as a feather. They carefully avoided looking at the featureless face.

'Put her onto the section between escalators – she'll slide down.'

Fairbank did as instructed and watched the body swiftly descend into the darkness below. 'There's a ride she couldn't enjoy,' he said, and froze as Culver looked at him sharply. He cast his eyes downwards, avoiding Culver's icy gaze. 'Sorry,' he mumbled. 'It's . . . it's bravado, y'know? I'm shit-scared.'

The other man turned away, reaching for the next corpse. It was another woman, but this one had some substance to her and was not as easy to lift, even though her breasts were gone, her stomach hollowed. Both men grunted with the effort and when an arm fell around Culver's shoulder in a lover's casual embrace, he had to bite into his lower lip to prevent himself from screaming. All her fingers were missing.

When her body had careered off into the blackness, twisting sideways as it sped down, they reached for the next. For a few seconds they could only look at the tiny child, her curled body untouched. The heavy woman had protected the little girl from scything teeth, but her weight and the weight of others had been suffocating.

Culver knelt and brushed a lock of pale yellow, almost white, hair from her cheek. The others watched, not knowing quite what to do. Fairbank looked at Bryce, who gave a slight shake of his head.

Finally, Culver laid the child on her side and arranged her unmarked limbs so that her body was at rest. Perhaps the others expected to see tears in his eyes when he rose, perhaps remorse, his face crushed with grief; they were not prepared for the tight-lipped grimness, the anger that exuded a frightening coldness. For the first time Bryce saw something more in this somewhat laconic stranger who had arrived in their midst so dramatically just a few weeks before, something he realized Dealey had appreciated from the beginning. Dealey had tried to use Culver during their time of self-enforced internment, had tried to gain his confidence, make him part of the 'officials' team, but Culver would have none of it. Neither would he side with the others, those whom Dealey secretly referred to as 'the civilians'. He remained his own man and, as such, was trusted by both parties, if not accepted. Bryce thought that Culver could not have cared less, mistaking his attitude for apathy; now, for the first time, he saw that Culver's impassivity paradoxically covered an intensity of feeling which only a moment such as this could unveil. Once seen, you were aware that it had always been there and was the quality that made you feel slightly uneasy in his presence. It was a subtle thing and Bryce guessed only extremes made it recognizable. He could not understand why this sudden revelation had assumed a special importance to him, but Bryce was somehow relieved to know the man was far more complex than he had been given credit for. Strangely, he felt safer in his company.

Culver was pulling at another body, this time a man whose eye socket was enlarged as though something had bored straight through. Fairbank moved forward and helped the pilot lift the body onto the makeshift slide. As he did so, he glanced upwards towards the top of the escalators, a movement catching his eye.

'What's that?'

The others followed the direction of his gaze. A black shape was moving towards them, sliding down in the same manner as the corpses they were disposing of. It gathered momentum as it drew nearer.

Fairbank backed away from the handrail, fearing the worst. McEwen drew his revolver.

Culver raised a hand as if to stop the ROC officer firing. 'It's okay, it's a body.'

Fairbank gave a quick sigh of relief and stepped towards the handrail again, hands outstretched to catch the sliding figure.

'Let it go,' Culver said quietly but urgently.

The engineer raised his eyebrows in surprise and withdrew his hands. As the sliding figure went by he understood Culver's command. The corpse was headless.

This time he staggered back from the handrail. They all followed the descending body with their torch beams.

'What could have done that?' Fairbank asked breathlessly.

'The same that did all this,' Culver said, waving his torch at the carnage above and below them. 'Come on, there's room to get through now.' He stepped over two corpses, using a handrail for balance.

'Wait a minute,' said Bryce. 'They could still be up there. Something caused that body to move.'

Culver went on, his pace quickening. 'Maybe we disturbed it,' he called back over his shoulder. 'It could have been resting on the handrail and movement down here made it shift. Or maybe it just rotted itself free.'

The three men left behind glanced anxiously at each other, then moved as one after Culver. McEwen kept the .38 clear of its holster.

There were two more human blockages before they reached the top and these were cleared quickly and with little thought. Bryce wondered how soon the mind adapted itself to circumstances, how quickly it impersonalized itself from such enormous tragedy. The aching sickness was still there, but they were gradually becoming anaesthetized to the horror. Not completely, but enough not to be distracted by it.

At last they were at the barriers leading to the escalators. They shone the lights around the circular ticket hall and their spirits sank still further as the nightmare was reinforced.

The round chamber, sunk just below the city streets, was nothing more than a huge open grave. Culver rejected the idea: it was more like a slaughterhouse.

There were two entrances where a steady torrent of rain poured through, diffusing the greyish light of day. The tangled shapes before them could have been hewn from rock, so still, so colourless, were they.

Many of the blast survivors had obviously staggered or dragged themselves down into the station, seeking refuge from the killer dust they knew would soon fall. He remembered those whom he and Dealey had met fleeing from the tunnels; had they thought it safe to linger here in the ticket hall, that their very numbers would keep the vermin away? It would have been packed with the injured, the dying. The smell of fresh-flowing blood would have been overpowering, attracting the creatures below.

There were doors leading off from the hall – he and

Dealey had entered one when they had first fled from the holocaust – and several were jammed open with the bodies of those who had tried to escape. He wondered how the station worker who had told him where to find the flashlight had fared, and turned the torch on that particular door. It was off its hinges.

Fairbank had walked over to the ticket office, a long isolated booth near the centre of the round hall, careful to step over husk-like corpses and brushing away flies that buzzed greedily over them. He detested these swarming parasites as much as the creatures who had wrought such slaughter. And almost as much as the men who had sent the missiles.

The office door was open, a man's body sprawled half-out as though he had tried to flee from something inside. Fairbank pushed at the door until it nudged against something solid on the other side. The gap allowed him to see all he wanted to.

Terrified survivors must have cowered inside when the vermin had attacked, assuming they would be safe, that the creatures would not be able to break through the booth's toughened glass. But he saw that two panes were completely shattered while others had cracks from top to bottom. The explosions above had probably caused the cracks, weakened the glass, to break through must have been relatively easy for the rats.

He wrinkled his nose at the smell spilling from the confined space and saw something that momentarily stopped his breathing, if not his heart.

'Jes – hey, over here!'

The others, preoccupied with their own disturbing observations, turned towards the booth. He waved them over.

They crowded into the doorway, their combined lights showing every detail of the carnage inside the ticket office. They soon spotted what had taken Fairbank's breath away.

The black rat was huge, almost two feet in length. Its scaly curved tail offered at least another eighteen inches. Its fur was stiffened, dull and dry with death, its massive haunches still hunched as though the rodent was ready to leap. But there was no life in the evil yellow eyes, no dampness to the mouth and incisors. Yet still it emanated a deadliness, a lethal malevolence that made three of the men shudder and back away, even though its neck was twisted at an awkward angle, its skull indented unnaturally.

Only Culver moved forward.

He stooped and examined the dead beast closely. Someone had fought back, had battered the rat to death. That person was probably also dead, killed by the creature's companions, but at least he or she had not given in easily. Possibly there were other dead vermin out there, lying among the bodies of the humans they had attacked, corpses of both species decaying together.

There seemed to be little weakness in the creature, even in its present state. Yet the skull was caved in. How hard had it been struck? He touched the outer rim of the dent, and the bone beneath his fingers moved inwards. It was brittle and thin. And there was no sign of blood. The blow had not even broken the skin, yet it had presumably caused the rodent's death. Culver turned the body over and found no other wounds. So possibly the vermin had paper-thin skulls – at least, this one had. Where did it leave him? Nowhere. It might be feasible to win a battle with one or two of these creatures by crushing their heads, but they moved around in packs – large packs.

He straightened and coldly kicked the bristle-furred corpse before leaving the booth.

His companions were watching the booth warily as Culver carefully picked his way towards them. He slapped away flies and other insects, averting his eyes as they landed in the open wounds of the dead and laid their eggs. How fast would these insidious insects multiply now they had no opponents? And what epidemics would they carry and spread among those left to survive? Once the rain had stopped, this other, tiny-sized menace would take to the air to breed, develop and devour. Only winter would stem their tide, and then only temporarily.

Culver faced Bryce. 'How many of these vermin have been living in the sewers and tunnels? And for how long?'

The Civil Defence officer had to look away; once again the glint in Culver's eyes was intimidating. The voice was low, controlled, but the anger was barely suppressed.

'I don't know,' he answered, frightened by everything around him and frightened by Culver's tone. 'There were no reports of them that I know of.'

'You're lying. They're too big and too many to have stayed concealed for this long.' His face was only inches away from Bryce's. The other two men looked on, themselves interested in the answers.

'I swear I know nothing of them. There were some rumours, of course . . .'

'Rumours? I want to know, Bryce.'

'Nothing more than that! Just hearsay. Stories of large animals, perhaps dogs, roaming the sewers. Nobody gave the stories any credence. In fact, the reports were that rats were becoming scarcer down there in recent years.'

'Yeah, ordinary rats. Didn't anybody stop to wonder why?'

'You . . . you mean these creatures drove the others out?'

'It's possible. Come on, Bryce, you're a government man – you must know more. Were there any disappearances, sewer workers and the like going missing?'

'That's always happened, Culver, you must understand that. There are hundreds of miles of tunnels beneath the city, and the sewers have always been dangerous through flooding, cave-ins. And animal life has always existed down there. God alone knows what has prowled the tunnels through the decades . . .'

'Bryce . . .'

'I'm telling you the truth! I work for Civil Defence, nothing more! If anyone knows something, it'll be Dealey.'

Culver stared at the older man for a few more moments before the tenseness left his body. 'Dealey,' he said, almost as a sigh. He suddenly remembered again the flight into the tunnels just after the nuclear bombs had detonated, when he had told Dealey, then blind, that there were huge rats around them. Dealey asked if they were black-furred, and had said something like, 'No, not now,' as if he knew of them. He might just have been referring to the previous times when the mutants had rampaged; or he might have known they were still in existence.

'Maybe he'll do some explaining when we get back,' Culver said and turned away from Bryce. 'Let's see what's left upstairs.'

Together they clambered over the dead, each man keeping a wary eye for any black moving shapes among them. They saw one or two rat carcasses lying among their victims, but Culver noticed something more. He looked around at Bryce and their eyes locked. Something passed between them, a sensory acknowledgement, and neither one mentioned their observation to the other two who were more interested in the opening ahead.

The rain bounced hard off the metal-edged steps and fallen masonry, sending up a low splattering spray. The sound was intense, almost violent.

'They've destroyed the skies, too.'

It was a strange and poignant thing for Fairbank to say, and it sent a shiver through each of them. They stood by the opening, becoming damp with reflected rain, even though not exposed to its full force.

Bryce spoke to the ROC man. 'Check the geiger. In here first, then outside.'

McEwen switched on the machine hanging over one shoulder by a strap, realizing he should have checked the atmosphere for radiation at each stage of their exploratory journey. Too many shocks had overwhelmed such a precaution.

Brief, separate clicks came from the ionization instrument's amplifier and McEwen quickly reassured Culver and Fairbank. 'It's normal. It's just picking up very high-energy particles natural to the atmosphere. See – it's irregular, weak, nothing to worry about.'

'Care to take a shower?' Fairbank pointed with his thumb at the pouring rain.

McEwen looked less sure of himself. He took the geiger counter from his shoulder and pushed it out into the downpour.

'It's warm, the rain's warm!' He quickly withdrew his arms and brushed off droplets as though they were acid.

'It's all right,' Bryce quickly said. 'Nothing's registering on the counter.'

'Then why is it warm?' Culver asked, regarding Bryce suspiciously.

The older man shrugged. 'Who knows what's happened in the upper layers of the earth's atmosphere. Perhaps the rain is cold around the equator now.' He became a little angry. 'You keep treating me as though I'm in some way to blame for all this. I'm just a tiny, insignificant cog in a huge government wheel, Culver. My job has always been to protect lives, not destroy them, and as such I've had more battles with Whitehall ministers than I'd care to relate to you. The Civil Defence Corps was due to be scrapped totally just a few years ago, until we roused public opinion enough to prevent it.'

Culver was about to respond when Fairbank interrupted, nodding towards the rain-soaked stairway and saying in a no-nonsense voice: 'I'd like to take a look up top.'

Culver's smile was slow in coming, and his eyes neither changed expression nor left Bryce's. 'Yeah,' he said. 'I think we'd all like to see what's left.'

He stepped out into the rain.

It felt good, so good. A cleanser, a purifier. He turned his face upwards, closing his eyes, and the heavy raindrops pelted his face. McEwen was right; it was warm, unnaturally so. But it was alive and it was wonderful. He climbed the steps, the others close behind.

Culver reached the top and stopped while the others caught up with him. They looked around, their faces white with shock, the warm rain battering their bodies, its sound the only sound.

It was Bryce who fell to his knees and cried, '*No, no, no . . .*'

12

Many years before, when Culver was no more than a boy, someone had shown him a sepia print of Beaumont Hamel, a small town in a sector of the Somme front. The old photograph had been dated November 1916 – the time of World War I – and the image had stayed frozen in his mind ever since.

The battle long over, just thin trees remained, bare and stunted, without branches, their tops jagged charcoal. No grass, not one solitary blade poking from the solid mud. No buildings, just rubble. No birds. No growth. No life. Only desolation, total, unremitting. And unforgiving.

If he could have stepped into that picture, if he could have actually stood in that granite mud, breathed the charred and gas-tainted air, he had known that nothing would have stirred, the scene would have remained a frozen still, the reality imitating the reproduced image.

He had just stepped through that frame and found the concrete equivalent to the sepia waste.

The ruined city lay humiliated and crumbled around them, nothing moving except the relentless rain. Not every building had been completely demolished, although none had escaped anything less than excessive damage; those remaining stood like broken monoliths amid the mountains of rubble, misshapen parodies of man's construction powers. Some rose up with innards exposed, gigantic doll's-houses with one wall removed so that furniture and decor could be viewed; all that was missing were the tiny dolls themselves. Of others, only skeletal frames were left, the steel girders twisted, buckled, yet still proclaiming their resistance to whatever forces their makers could thrust upon them. There appeared to be no definite order by which one building had collapsed completely while another had remained partially erect, although the damage seemed worse in the distance, as if the power of the shockwaves had reduced as they swept outwards, each preceding office block or dwelling absorbing a fraction of the force, dissipating the fury, affording a small protection to its neighbour.

Among the rubble, like tossed-away toys, lay cars, buses, other vehicles, some merely black-stained husks, completely burned out, others smashed into irregular shapes. The roads – what could still be discerned as roads – were metal graveyards, full of silent, defunct machines. Most lamp posts were bent, many doubled up like matchstick men with stomach pains; some, torn from concrete roots, lay stiffly across other wreckage, defeated but unbowed. Office equipment, furniture, television sets, tumbled from the debris, shattered and somehow incongruous in their exposure.

Also shattered, but far less incongruous because the search party had almost become used to them, were the misshapen bundles that had once been living, moving humans. They lay everywhere: in cars, in overturned buses, among the debris, in the roads. Many were huddled in doorways – whatever doorways were left – as if they had crawled there to await the poisoned air's descent.

The four survivors were relieved that the insects were held at bay by the rain torrent.

Shock upon shock hit them, sweeping through in waves,

their numbed minds mercifully dulling the rapid, horrifying visions. Yet the full impact of one sight could not be defused, for it was literally a panoramic statement of what had come to pass, a cruel affirmation of the devastation's magnitude.

Standing at street level in the heart of the nation's destroyed capital, they could now see the land's natural horizon, a view that before had always been obscured by a raggedy, concrete skyline, a growth-chart of varying greys against a blue background. Gentle hills that encircled much of London were no longer hidden, and to the east and west there was open space, broken only by a few upright buildings and the higher mounds of rubble.

It was awesome, and it was intimidating. And each man experienced a terrible loneliness, a longing for the world they had lost, for the people who had died.

Above them the sky was black and low, the new horizon silver. The warm rain drenched them and could not wash away their fears, nor their deep-felt misery.

Bryce was on his knees, his bowed head against the litter-strewn pavement.

McEwen's tears mingled with the rain on his cheeks.

Fairbank's eyes were closed, his head tilted slightly upwards, his body stiff.

Culver looked around, his feelings locked inside.

To the east he could see the round structure of St Paul's, its dome gone, the walls cracked and broken, huge sections missing. He was puzzled, for although there had been little time for observation when he and Dealey had fled after the first explosion the damage had not seemed this bad. Then he remembered that other bombs had been dropped – five had been estimated – and was then surprised the city had not been totally flattened. There seemed to be less damage to the east and sections of the south-west, but the rain made everything too hazy to be sure. The lower portions of several buildings within the immediate vicinity were fairly intact, although mounds of rubble that had once been their upper floors created slopes from them.

In the distance he could just distinguish red glows where some parts still burned, or where fresh fires had broken out. As if to confirm his thoughts, light flared from the north as though an explosion had occurred. The heavy rain was fortunate, not just because it helped clear the radiation dust, but because it had also kept the fires under reasonable control. What was left of the city could easily have become one raging inferno.

He walked over to McEwen and prodded his arm. 'Try the geiger, see if anything's registering.'

The ROC officer seemed glad to have something more to think about. A surge of clicking erupted from the machine and the needle flickered wildly for a second or two. 'It's okay,' McEwen quickly reassured him. 'Look, it's settled down. There's a certain amount of radiation around, but it's below danger level.'

He wiped his face to clear its wetness, the tears and rain.

'Fairbank?' Culver glanced at the engineer standing nearby.

There was a strange smile on Fairbank's face when he opened his eyes and turned towards the others. It was sad, yet a peculiarly satisfied expression, almost as though the tragedy was no surprise to him.

'What now?' Fairbank asked.

'Let's get Bryce to his feet, then have a quick look round. I don't want to stay out here any longer than necessary.'

Together they lifted the Civil Defence officer, who leaned against them for several moments for support. His strength returned slowly, but his spirit would take much longer.

'Any suggestions,' Culver said, 'as to where we should look?'

Bryce shook his head. 'There's nothing left to see. There's no hope for any of us.'

'This is just one city,' Culver replied sharply, 'not the whole bloody country. There's still a chance.'

Bryce merely continued to shake his head.

'There's a store over there,' Fairbank said, his voice loud so that it could be heard over the downpour. 'It's a Woolworth's – I used to pass it every day. There'll be food, clothing, other things that might be useful.'

'We don't need anything for the shelter yet, but it might be worthwhile taking a look,' Culver agreed.

'Leave me here,' said Bryce. 'I've no stomach for rummaging among the dead.'

'No chance. We're sticking together.'

'I won't be able to make it. I'm ... I'm sorry, but I must rest. My legs seem to have gone. The stress ...'

Culver looked at Fairbank, who shrugged and said, 'He'll only slow us down. Leave him.'

'Stay here, then. But don't wander off. We're going straight back into the tunnel when we return. Remember, the idea was to get back within two hours – we won't have time to start looking for you.'

'Yes, I understand. I won't move from this spot, I can promise you that.'

'You might be better off out of the rain. Try one of the cars over there, but keep a lookout for our return.'

Bryce nodded, relieved to be left alone. He watched the others making their way through the ruins of what once had been one of London's busiest thoroughfares. Clambering over rubble, weaving between inanimate traffic, their figures soon blurred by the rainfall. Then they were gone and the acute loneliness they had all felt only moments earlier pressed harder on him, almost crushing in its ferocity.

The feeling of being the last person alive on the chastised planet was overwhelming, even though he knew his companions were not far away. His whole being cried out, in pity, in anguish; but mostly in despair. How much was there left of the human race, and what could its future be? Slow oblivion? Or would eventual procreation breed generation upon generation of debilitated and atrophied offspring, possibly even mutants, degenerates? Who would survive in the plague-stricken lands where even food that could be scavenged might contain the very seeds of lingering death? There was no way of knowing how massively destructive the conflict had been, whether any nations had been left unblemished, any countries untouched. They had failed even to learn the extent of their own homeland's ravagement.

The rain was like thousands of question-marks saturating his mind. There were no answers. Not yet. And perhaps, for this small band of survivors, there never would be.

Bryce pulled up his coat collar, clutching the lapels to his chest, a symbolic gesture; the downpour was tepid, but it chilled his inner core.

There were many vehicles to shelter in; he walked over to a car nearby, its door hanging open as if the owner cared little for security as he fled the havoc – Bryce almost smiled at the thought of someone meticulously locking his vehicle while the city crumbled around him. The windscreen was shattered and he brushed glass fragments from the front passenger seat, relieved to find no bloodstains among them. He climbed in and the rain rattled its steady drumbeat on the metal over his head, splatters still reaching him through the opening, but adding no discomfort to his already soaked person.

A folded newspaper lay at his feet, sodden pages merged into one soft, mildewy lump. He glanced down, then bent to retrieve it, perhaps wistful for a remnant of natural order, a memento of yesterday's comfortable existence. All crispness long-vanished from its malty-grey leaves, the midday *Standard* threatened to disintegrate when he picked it up.

At first he frowned at the 72-point headline that said: PM URGES: STAY CALM.

Then he began to laugh.

And he laughed so much that tears flooded his eyes, and they were tears of mirth and bitterness, neither emotion giving way to the other.

And his shoulders jerked with the effort.

One leg stamping at the footwell.

Making the car judder.

Causing something in the back seat to stir.

13

Fairbank was the first to slip through the opening leading down onto the store's shopfloor. Mounds of debris, a hazardous mixture of masonry, powdered concrete and glass, had all but covered the wide display windows and swingdoors, but the three men had clambered up towards the dark opening heedless of the danger. Fairbank's enthusiasm to taste once again the confectionery delights denied to them among the shelter's plentiful but unexciting rations, to don a clean shirt, put on fresh underwear, was too keen for him to be discouraged by his two more cautious companions. And Culver himself had to admit the prospect appealed after their weeks of austere confinement.

He warned, however, that everything could be spoiled by now, and that clothing and other items might well have been ruined by fire.

'Just one way to find out, Culver,' the engineer had replied, grinning, the earlier emotional shock apparently overcome for the moment. Culver surmised that the man was either completely insensitive or a natural survivor, his durability perhaps a strong quality in such times. He had followed Fairbank's scampering figure up the incline.

At the top, Culver turned to McEwen. 'We'll need the geiger counter in here; the place could be full of radiation.'

Somewhat reluctantly, the ROC officer climbed the slope.

They watched Fairbank slither down the other, much steeper side, using their torches to guide him.

He settled at the bottom, waving his own torch around. 'Christ,' he exclaimed, 'the stink in here!'

'We can smell it from here,' Culver told him before sliding into the gap. McEwen quickly followed and all three squatted in the disturbed dust, peering into the gloom, their lights penetrating the darkest corners.

'Ceiling's caved in at the far end,' McEwen observed.

'Everything looks safe otherwise,' said Fairbank. His voice took on a lighter tone. 'Hey, d'you see what I see?' His beam had caught multi-colour wrappers in its glare. He was up and at the sweets counter before the other two had a chance to rise.

'Don't scoff them all, Bunter, you'll make yourself sick,' Culver advised, unable to stop himself from smiling.

'Crunchie bars, Fruit and Nut, Walnut Whips – Christ, I'm dead and this is Heaven.' They heard him chuckle and began to laugh themselves.

'Bournville Plain, Dairy Milk, Pacers, Glacier Min—' his voice broke off.

By then, Culver and McEwen had joined him and they, too, were examining the array of bright wrappers that a fine layer of dust only faintly subdued. They soon discovered what had brought his exaltation to a sudden halt.

'Someone else has been at 'em,' McEwen commented.

'Someone or something.' Culver picked up a loose wrapper, a vision of black-furred creatures snuffling their way through the chocolate bars and sweets sending a prickly coolness along his spine.

'Rats?' Fairbank regarded him with wide eyes.

'Maybe.' Culver popped open the small restraining strap of the shoulder holster.

'They'd have done more damage, made a bigger mess,' said McEwen.

'He's right,' Fairbank agreed, but there was still a nervousness to him. 'Let's grab as much as we can carry and get out.'

'Thought you wanted a new shirt?'

'I can live without it.' He began to stuff chocolate bars into his overall pockets.

'Wait a minute.' Culver stayed Fairbank's hand midway between counter and trouser pocket. 'If it's not vermin it may be something more important.'

'People?'

Culver shone his torch along the litter-filled aisles. The store's interior stretched a long way back, opening out halfway down in an 'L' shape. No light came through the collapsed ceiling in the far corner, off to his left. The smell that assailed them had become all too familiar over the past hour or so, and Culver had no real desire to investigate further. Unfortunately, conscience told him he had to. Maybe a morbid curiosity added its weight, too.

His footsteps sounded unnaturally loud in the store that had now become a vast cavern.

Fairbank shrugged and went after him, still snatching goodies from the counter as he passed and squeezing them into his already full pockets. He spied a set of shelves containing handbags, holdalls and – even better – suitcases, and made a mental note to grab one on their way back.

McEwen found the idea of being left alone in the shadowy consumer grotto unacceptable and swiftly caught up with the other two.

Culver in the lead, they drew near the corner where the store widened. An electrical department came into view, plastic-coated wires hanging loosely from their spools like oversized cotton thread, light sockets, switches and lamps lying scattered as if swept from their displays by angry hands. Beyond that, the record and hi-fi department looked as if the choices had not been appreciated: album sleeves littered the floor, stereo equipment lay scattered. Bodies, some still moving, lolled in the mess.

Damp fingers, disembodied by the darkness, curled around Culver's wrist.

He recoiled by instinct, the others intentionally, for they had seen the hideous figure just before it had touched him.

Culver wrenched his arm free and staggered back against a nearby counter, but the figure went with him, unbalanced, claw-like hands clutching at Culver's clothes. The man fell to his knees, preventing himself from sinking further by hanging weakly on to the pilot's leather jacket.

The man's voice was a thin, rasping sound. 'Help ... us ...'

Culver stared down at the emaciated face with its wide, staring death-camp eyes, the torn lips, cracks filled with dry blood, gums exposed and teeth decayed brown. A few sparse tufts of hair clung to the man's scalp. His skin was puckered with fresh sores and there was a thin line of dried blood trickling from both ears. Fright gave little room for pity in Culver.

The man groaned, although it was more of a throat-singed croak. He seemed to shrivel before them.

Overcoming his revulsion, Culver caught the collapsing figure, and gently lowered him to the floor. The man's clothes were torn and bedraggled; they smelled of excrement.

'Please ...' The voice was weaker this time, as though the effort of seizing Culver's wrist had taken most of his remaining strength. '... help ... us.'

'How many are left alive here?' Culver said, his mouth close to the dying man's ear.

'I . . . don't . . .' His head lolled to one side. 'Don't . . .'

Culver looked up at his two companions. 'Radiation sickness,' he said unnecessarily. 'He won't last much longer. Try the geiger, see how bad it is in here.'

McEwen switched on the machine and they jumped when its amplifier discharged urgent, burring clicks. The needle jumped wildly before settling just beneath the quarter-way mark.

'Too many rems,' McEwen told them hastily. 'It's dangerous, we've got to leave immediately.'

'I'm on my way,' Fairbank said, beginning to turn.

'Wait!' Culver snapped. 'Take a look at the others. See if we can save any of them.'

'You gotta be kidding – oh shit, look . . .'

They followed Fairbank's gaze and saw the shuffling shapes emerging from the shadows, most of them crawling, some stooped and bent, stumbling as if with age, a whining coming from them that was more frightening than piteous. In that moment of abject fear, it was hard to think of these unsteady, shambling figures as fellow humans, wretches who had had no time to shelter properly from the disaster and its disease-carrying aftermath, for they came at the three survivors like lepers escaping their colony, like hunched demons rising from unhallowed earth, like the undead reaching out to embrace and initiate the living . . .

It was too much for Fairbank and McEwen, one trauma too many in that day of traumas. They backed away.

The ravaged faces, fully revealed in the torches' combined glare, pleaded for pity, for compassion, for relief from their suffering.

'Culver, there's too many of them. We can't help them all!' Fairbank's voice was shaky with its own special pleading.

'We can't stay here,' McEwen added from further away. 'The radiation count is too high! If we don't leave now we'll end up like these people!'

One figure, a woman, finding some last vestige of strength, lurched forward and clung to Fairbank.

'... *nnleasennnnnn* ..' she implored.

He reflexively pushed her away and she fell to the floor, a weak cry escaping her. Fairbank took a step towards her as if instantly regretting his action, a hand reaching out. The moans of others changed his mind.

'It's no good, Culver,' he said wearily. 'We can't help them. There's too many.' He turned and broke into a stumbling run towards the front of the store, chocolate bars and sweets tumbling from his overloaded pockets.

A hand scraped against Culver's cheek. He flinched, but did not pull away from the feverish man he knelt beside.

'Don't ... leave us ...' the man whispered.

Culver took the hot trembling fingers from his face and held them. 'There's nothing we can do for you right now,' he told him, and added lamely: 'We've got a doctor among us. If she's agreeable, we'll bring her back; she may be able to do something for you.'

The man's grip suddenly strengthened. 'No ... no ... you can't ...' His other hand, wavering but determined, clutched at Culver's collar.

Another weight fell across the pilot's shoulders.

Culver toppled onto his side, the other person bearing down on him, the man beneath pulling, refusing to let go. Culver groaned, a sharp, harsh sound, almost one of pain, and he struggled against them, quickly shrugging the weight from his shoulders, grabbing the other man's wrists and slowly prising the hand away from his jacket. The man's other hand, still gripping his, was less easy to dislodge and for one insane moment Culver considered using the gun. It would have meant instant release for him and instant relief for the radiation victim. But whatever it took for such an act, it was not in him. Not yet.

He squeezed the man's wrist unmercifully, and the claw-like fingers gradually opened. Culver broke free, rising to his feet, almost stumbling over a figure that had crawled up from behind. He avoided the grasping hand.

'I'm sorry!' he shouted, and then he was running, staggering after the others, his only thought to be away from this dark limbo between life and death and away from these poor wretches whose best hope was to die sooner rather than later.

He heard their wailing cries, and he thought he heard footsteps coming after him, but he did not stop to look around until he was at the foot of the slope. His two companions were already through the narrow opening at the top, Fairbank reaching back to help him, his face a confused mask of fear and shame.

This is crazy, Culver told himself. They're just people, our own kind, injured and disease-ravaged; not lepers, not unclean, and not dangerous. Why then were he, Fairbank and McEwen so afraid? He looked back and the answer was there. The shuffling, imploring figures were the incarnation of extreme human distress, the material results of the long-awaited, feared and fearful holocaust. The nightmare come true.

And who could face their own nightmare?

Culver leapt at the slope, Fairbank grabbing his hand and yanking him upwards. He was through the opening, warm rain and grey light enveloping him as he rolled down the other side, not stopping until he had reached the bottom, and even then rolling to a crouched position, facing the store as if expecting the dream to follow. Only Fairbank came sliding down to join him. McEwen stood a few yards away, poised to run.

'I guess there were just too many, right?' Fairbank said, clapping him on the shoulder.

Culver shuddered. 'Yeah, too many.' He straightened. 'We'll get back to them. Dr Reynolds can give them drugs, medicines, anything to ease it for them.'

'Sure,' Fairbank replied.

'Maybe one or two will pull through.'

Fairbank wiped rain from his forehead and nose. He spat into the muddied dirt at his feet. 'We'd better get to the shelter.'

He walked away leaving Culver staring up at the few visible letters of the store name and the narrow gap beneath. The mausoleum's name was WORT.

Culver caught up with the others as they squeezed between a bus, all its windows smashed, red paint in the front blistered and flaky, and a sky-blue van, the bottom of its side panels already showing rust. He tried to avert his eyes from the rotted corpse of the bus driver, thrown back in his cab, hands still on the driving wheel as though he had insisted upon carrying his passengers right up to the very doors of eternity. Culver tried not to look, but eyes can be skittishly curious. Glass shards impaled the figure, gleaming from the body like diamonds in an underground rock face, the largest segment neatly dividing the man's face in half. Something low in Culver's stomach did a mushy backflip and he forced himself to concentrate on the two men in front. McEwen was walking unsteadily, using the bonnets and tops of cars for support, geiger counter slapping against one hip, rain-soaked shoulders hunched forward. Fairbank, who had turned to see if Culver was following, was white-faced, deep creases stretching from cheekbones to jawline making his normally broad countenance seem suddenly thin, almost gaunt. He opened his mouth to speak, but a distant muffled *krumpf* had them all staring towards the west.

Less than half a mile away, the remains of a partly-demolished building were collapsing completely, the exposed floors tumbling in on one another like a card-player's thumb-shuffle. Clouds of dust billowed into the air, the rain only slowly beating them back to earth, the building becoming a pile of concrete and rubble amid a landscape of similar piles. Anything could have caused its surrender – an explosion of gas, the last rending of twisted and overloaded metal, the exhaustion of its own concrete structure. The building's final acceptance of the inevitable was like a death-knell.

The urge to return as quickly as possible to their sanctuary was strong within them, for more than ever it represented a form of survival. They hoped.

Skirting a five-car collision that resembled an artist's metal sculpture, they climbed another hill of debris and were relieved to see the Chancery Lane UNDERGROUND sign once more, a section of its blue and red symbol missing.

'It ain't much, but it's home,' Fairbank said weakly, in an effort to shake off his own despondency.

'Can you see Bryce?' Culver peered at the cars below, rain bouncing off their roofs forming misty haloes.

Fairbank shook his head. 'He can't be far – he looked pretty done-in when we left him.'

Culver noticed that McEwen was visibly trembling. 'You going to make it?' he asked.

'I just want to get away from here, that's all. It's like ... like one massive graveyard.'

'Pity some of the dead won't lie down,' added Fairbank in unappreciated black humour.

Culver ignored the remark. They all had different ways of coping; Fairbank needed to make jokes, no matter how lame, nor how tasteless.

'There he is.' Fairbank pointed, then frowned. 'At least I think it's Bryce.'

They descended warily, not risking a fall on the unstable slope.

'Over here,' the engineer said, leading the way through the tangle of machinery. Culver spotted the Civil Defence officer on the entrance platform of an empty double-decker bus. His feet were in the road, his body hunched forward over his lap, oblivious to the pounding rain. He appeared to have stomach cramps, but as they drew nearer, they realized he was clutching something.

McEwen caught sight of a familiar form sheltering in a doorway not far from the Underground entrance. For the first time that day he managed to smile. There wasn't much left of the building above the doorway, for the blast had sheered off the roof and upper floor but, although wrecked, the shops below remained, and it was here, in an open doorway, that the dog shivered over a scrap of food lying at its feet.

The mongrel – McEwen was no expert, but it resembled a German Shepherd mostly – looked forlorn and weak, its fur bedraggled, almost colourless with grime, ribs showing like struts through stretched canvas. Saliva streamed from its mouth, soaking the meagre rations it had managed to salvage from somewhere, and McEwen's heart went out to the dishevelled animal. After witnessing so much human suffering, the dog's plight stirred deep emotions in him for, unlike its masters, this creature was blameless, having no say in its own destiny, innocent of all guilt for the destructively sick world it inhabited. McEwen squeezed between two cars and made towards the animal.

The dog's head was bent low, too concerned for the raw meat at its feet to notice the man's approach.

Poor little bastard, the ROC officer thought. Half starved and probably still bewildered by everything that had happened.

He watched it wolf down one of the sausage-like scraps between its front paws. The food was red, bloodied, and McEwen wondered where it had found such fresh meat.

'Good boy,' he said, moving forward cautiously, not wishing to frighten the animal. 'Good old boy,' he repeated soothingly.

The dog looked up.

14

Bryce was in pain. He moaned and his body rocked quickly backwards and forwards in swift rhythm that sought to ease the hurt.

Culver and Fairbank saw there were scratch marks on his neck, blood flowing from the wounds with the rain. They rushed to him, Culver kneeling and grasping the CDO's shoulder.

'What's happened to you?' he said, using pressure to get the man to straighten. 'Did you fall?'

Fairbank looked around uneasily, then bent closer, hands resting on his knees.

Bryce looked at them as if they were strangers, a terrified, glazed expression in his eyes. Recognition slowly filtered through.

'Thank God, thank God,' he moaned.

They were shocked when they saw his face. The neck wounds stretched round to his cheek, where they became large gashes from which blood flowed freely. The thin line of blood, dotted with small bubbles of drying blood, stretched across the bridge of his nose as if he had been slashed with wire. One eyelid was torn, blood clouding the eyeball beneath red. 'Get me back to the shelter. Get me back as quickly as possible!'

'What in hell did this?' Culver asked, reaching for

a handkerchief to stem the seeping tide from the man's neck.

'Back, just get me back! I need help.'

'Culver, there's something wrong with his hand.' Fairbank had moved closer and was reaching for Bryce's arm. He tried to ease the injured man's hands from his lap, but met with surprising resistance.

'Bryce, were you attacked by rats?' Culver asked. 'Jesus, we thought you'd be safe out here.'

'No, no!' It was a shout born out of acute pain. 'Please take me back to the shelter.'

'Show me your hands. Let me see them.'

Culver and Fairbank pulled at the arms together.

Bryce had been clutching one hand with the other and, when they were withdrawn from between his blood-drenched lap, they came apart. The other two men flinched when they saw the fingerless right hand.

Fairbank turned away from the bloodied stumps, pushing his forehead against the coolness of the bus. Culver held the wrist of Bryce's injured hand. He folded the handkerchief, now rain-sodden, over the finger stumps, pressing them against the protruding bones.

'Hold the handkerchief against them,' he told Bryce. 'It'll stop the bleeding a little.' He guided the hand towards the other man's chest and placed the uninjured hand over it. 'Keep it there. Keep your elbow bent and your hand pointed upwards. Try not to move it.' He quickly ran his eyes over Bryce, checking for further wounds. He found them, but none was as bad. 'Where were they, where did they attack you from?'

'No, not rats.' It was an effort for Bryce to speak. 'It was a dog. A . . . mad . . . dog in the car. Rabid. It was rabid. That's why you've got to get me back.'

Culver understood and it was almost a relief. Bryce had come across a wandering dog and it had attacked him. Not rats. Not bloody mutant rats, but a lost, probably starving, dog! But if it had rabies, then Bryce was in even more serious trouble. No wonder he wanted to get back to the shelter – Dr Reynolds would have an antiserum, something that might save his life. If she didn't – Culver tried to push the thought away – then Bryce would be dead within four to ten days.

'Can you stand?' he asked.

'I . . . I think so. Just help me up.'

Fairbank forgot his nausea and helped Culver lift the injured man to his feet.

'Okay,' Culver assured Bryce, 'We'll get you back. There's bound to be an anti-rabies vaccine in the medical supplies, so don't worry. The sooner we get you there the better.'

'It's essential . . . that I'm treated before the symptoms begin to show. Do you understand that?'

'Sure, I understand. Try to keep calm.'

Through his pain, Bryce remembered the bitter irony of the newspaper headline he had read in the car just before the rabid dog had snapped its jaws into his neck. Keep calm, that was only annihilation knocking on the door. Keep calm, that was only Death tapping you on the shoulder. He began to weep and it was not just because of the throbbing pain.

They half carried him towards the Underground entrance, keeping a wary eye out for the animal that had caused the injury, avoiding open car doors where possible, kicking them shut first if there was no option but to pass by. The rain pounded ceaselessly, and even though it was warm, Culver felt a chill creeping into his bones. The outside world was as bad as they feared it would be; the city was not just crippled, it was crushed.

Culver and Fairbank both saw McEwen at the same time.

He was leaning forward, one hand extended, reaching for something crouched in a doorway. Something that was partly obscured by his own body.

McEwen smiled at the dog as he tried to coax it from the doorway. 'Come on, boy, no one's gonna hurt you. You just finish your food and then we'll see what to do about you. We could do with a rat-catcher.'

A low, warning growl came from the dog. Its head was still bent close to the food, and its eyes looked up at him with distrust. McEwen noticed there was a moroseness in those large brown eyes.

'Yeah, I know you're starving. I'm not going to take your food away from you. You just gobble it down, there's a good boy.'

Before the final scraps disappeared into the dog's jaws – snapped up and swallowed whole, as if it feared they would be taken away – the ROC officer noticed something odd. One of the two slivers of meat had what appeared to be a fingernail attached to it.

He hesitated, his hand poised in mid-air, suddenly not so sure that the animal should be patted. It looked a little wild-eyed now. And it was trembling, and its snarl was not encouraging.

There were red blood specks in the foamy white substance drooling from its mouth.

'McEwen!'

His head whirled round and he saw Culver running towards him through the rain, reaching for the gun in his shoulder holster. Everything became slow motion, the running figure, the turning-back to the dog, the animal quivering, moving forward, its back legs stiff as though semi-paralysed, the hunching of its shoulders, the bristling of its damp fur, the wide gaping jaws and blood- and saliva-filled mouth . . .

Culver stopped and aimed the gun, praying he wouldn't miss from that range. The dog was tensing itself to leap, but something was wrong with its haunches. Its own madness carried it through. It was in the air, yellow teeth exposed, ready to clamp down on the man's outstretched hand only inches away.

Culver fired and the shock wave jerked his arm back.

The mad dog spun in the air and landed writhing at McEwen's feet, jaws snapping, yelping, screeching.

McEwen stepped back, his feet moving rapidly over the wet pavement. He tripped over rubble, sprawling backwards.

The animal, mortally wounded, tried to reach him, crawling forward, its howls diminishing to a low snarling.

Culver moved in for the kill.

He aimed at the dog's head. Fired.

Then again, into the jerking body.

Again, and the body went rigid.

Again, and the body went limp.

He let his breath go and holstered the weapon.

McEwen was slowly rising to his feet and wearing a stunned, disbelieving expression when Culver reached him.

'Did it bite you?' Culver asked.

McEwen stared at him before answering. 'No, no, it didn't touch me. I didn't realize . . .'

'It attacked Bryce.'

'Oh, shit.'

'Help us get him back.' Culver had already turned away and was walking over to Fairbank and Bryce.

McEwen studied the inert canine body and bit into his lower lip. He had been so close, so fucking close. The realization dawned on him that nothing could be taken for granted any more, that the ordinary could never again be trusted. That was a legacy that had been left them. Just one of the many.

As with Culver, the chill was now inside McEwen. He hurried after the three figures as they disappeared down the steps leading into the station's ticket hall.

The sweet, putrid smell hit them before they had even reached the bottom step. Eagerness to get back into the shelter's cocoon safety, the same feeling a rabbit had for its burrow when a fox was on the prowl, battled with their reluctance to enter the gloomy interior with its infestation of glutted insects and rotting human cadavers. Bryce's moaning urged them on.

The awkward descent down the corpse-crowded escalator was almost surreal now that their initial horror had been muted by an excess of shocks. They had the feeling of creeping into the pit of Hades and that the dead littering their path were those who had tried to flee, but had not managed to reach the sunlight. Paradoxically, the four men realized that the hell was above them.

At one point, Fairbank and Bryce stumbled, nearly tumbling in what would have been a snowballing fall – the snowball comprised of gathering corpses – if Culver hadn't grabbed a handrail and used his strength to hold back the others. They rested for a short while before continuing, each man drained by what had proved to be a harrowing and arduous reconnaissance. They were mentally tired, too, for the trauma had its own special debilitating effect.

Nevertheless, none of them was keen to spend too long on the escalator: the slumped half-eaten shapes above and below were a gruesome reminder that they were not yet safe. They journeyed on, Bryce supported by Culver and Fairbank, McEwen leading the way, torchlight sweeping the stairway before them.

They heard the peculiar rushing noise long before they reached the bottom, and looked at each other quizzically before resuming the descent. The sound was emanating from the archway leading to the eastbound platform and as they drew nearer the four men began to understand its source. McEwen anxiously hurried ahead, the others hampered by the injured man.

The sound became a roar as they rounded the corner into the archway. McEwen's lone figure was standing at the edge of the platform, his torch held low. They reached him and they, too, shone their lights down into the raging torrent, its sound amplified by the circular walls and ceiling of the station platform.

'*The sewers must have flooded!*' McEwen shouted above the roar. '*All this rainfall must have been too much.*'

'*Too many cave-ins, caused by the explosions,*' Fairbank agreed. '*The water's had nowhere to run.*'

'*We must get back!*' There was panic in Bryce's voice.

'*Don't worry, we'll make it.*' Culver shone his torch into the eastbound tunnel, from which direction the water was pouring. '*It's not too deep, not waist-high yet. We can use the struts and cables inside the tunnel to pull ourselves along.*'

'*What about Bryce?*' said Fairbank. '*He won't be able to use his hand. I doubt if he's strong enough to fight the current anyway.*'

'*We'll keep him between us, help him along. One in front, two behind. He'll be okay.*'

Fairbank shrugged. '*If you say so.*'

'*McEwen, you get behind Fairbank, help him support Bryce*

as much as you can.' Adrenalin flowing through him once more, reviving his beleaguered body, Culver prepared himself for the ordeal ahead. *'We'll use just my torch – that'll leave your hands free. You set?'*

Fairbank and McEwen nodded, tucking their torches into their clothing. Bryce's had long since disappeared.

They walked to the end of the platform and Culver dropped down into the tunnel.

The water was icy cold and took his breath away for a moment. The current tugged at his lower body and it was an effort to move against it, much more so than he had expected. He grabbed one of the metal struts that ribbed the arched tunnel and pulled himself along, struggling to maintain his balance, hindered by the torch in his right hand. He stopped when the other three had dropped into the water. Bracing his back against the wall, he turned to them. It was difficult to talk, not just because the confined space reverberated with the rushing sound, but also because it was difficult to regain his breath. His legs were already numbed by the chill.

'Put your left arm through my right,' he told Bryce, crooking his elbow, still holding the torch in that arm. Bryce did so and Culver gripped tight so that their arms were linked. That way he could keep the light shining ahead while still supporting the injured man, and use his other hand to grab any holds along the tunnel wall that he could find. Providing both he and Bryce kept their backs against the wall, they would be all right.

They moved off once more, a bedraggled procession, the force against their legs becoming greater as they waded deeper into the tunnel. It was soon evident that Culver would not be able to use the torch and support Bryce at the same time; the weight on his arm was too great.

He brought them to a halt. *'You'll have to use your torch, McEwen,'* he shouted. *'Try to shine it ahead of us, against the wall on this side.'*

McEwen's light flicked on and Culver tucked his own torch into the waistband of his jeans. He linked Bryce's arm again, this time keeping his fist tucked tight against his own chest.

Perspiration was soon pouring from him with the effort of pulling both himself and the injured man along, despite the numbing coldness in his lower body. The first journey into the tunnel ran through his mind, the deep, hollow silence, the discovery of the bodies, the gorging mutant rats, the petrified girl. Kate! God, he wanted to see her again.

Bryce began to slip from his grasp.

'Hold him!' he shouted back to Fairbank as the injured man started to sink.

Fairbank grabbed Bryce beneath his shoulders and heaved him upwards. He held him against the wall, Bryce's mouth wide open against the dirt-grimed brickwork, gasping for breath. He tried to speak, but they could not hear his words.

'He's not going to make it!' Fairbank shouted to Culver.

Culver, too, rested against the brickwork and tried to recover his breath. He leaned close to Bryce and spoke into his ear. 'Not far now, only a little way to go. We can do it, but you've got to help.'

Bryce shook his head. His eyes were closed and he looked as if he were moaning.

Culver slid one arm from his jacket and slipped off the shoulder holster. Pulling the jacket sleeve back on, he tossed the flashlight into the swirling water, knowing there would not be room enough for both torch and revolver. He took the gun from its holster and tucked it securely into his jeans.

Somehow it was more important to him than the torch. He reached for Bryce's uninjured arm once more and tied the leather straps of the holster around his own arm and the Civil Defence officer's.

'*You've got to help me, Bryce!*' he yelled. '*I can't do it on my own. Lean into me and don't let the current pull you away! Fairbank, keep close! Keep bloody close!*'

'*I'm up your arse,*' Fairbank assured him, even managing a grin.

It was like travelling uphill with a typhoon around their legs and a dead weight pulling against them, but inch by inch, foot by foot, groan by groan, they made progress. After a while they saw that the floodwaters ahead were bubbling foam and the wrenching grip was now around their hips. The water was rising.

'*We've got to cross the tracks, get over to the other wall,*' Culver shouted back to the others, inwardly cursing himself for not having thought of it when the going had been a little easier. The rushing, liquid roar was almost deafening and he wasn't sure that the others had heard him. He pointed to the opposite wall and Fairbank nodded.

Culver let go of the thick cables that ran along the wall at shoulder level and, taking a deep breath in case he should fall, stepped out into the flow. He almost lost his footing immediately, so strong was the current. He staggered back, but hands reached out to steady him.

'*Let me go first,*' Fairbank shouted into his ear. '*We'll form a chain. Me, then Bryce with you hanging on to the cables at this side. We should be able to stretch right across. McEwen can go with Bryce, keeping behind him to hold him steady.*'

Culver gripped the top of the fixed cables and braced himself. '*Go ahead.*'

Holding on to the wrist of Bryce's injured hand, Fairbank

waded into the water, body leaning into the flow, McEwen stretching out from behind to help. Careful not to trip on the tracks hidden below, the engineer reached the centre of the tunnel, Bryce supported by the ROC officer, left arm still strapped to Culver's, going with him. Fairbank paused, struggling against the tide to maintain his balance. He felt as if icy arms had wrapped themselves around his legs and were trying to drag them backwards, maliciously eager to unbalance him. He knew if he were to make it to the other side he would need all his strength and manoeuvrability; he'd have to release the injured man's wrist.

'*Hold him!*' he shouted to the others, then plunged towards the opposite wall, jumping forward slightly, knowing the current would carry him back. The idea worked, but he had trouble finding a handhold, for he was down in the water, the current sweeping around his chest. He was carried several yards back before finding something to grip. There was a small recess in the curved wall and he grabbed its edge gratefully. Dragging himself up, he rested there for a short while, catching his breath, chest heaving. He could make out the shapes of the others, silhouetted by McEwen's unsteady torch. Bryce would not last long out there in midstream, for McEwen was having problems himself. Fairbank used the cables on that side to haul himself back.

When he was level with the other three men he took a firm grip on the top cable and stretched his body out towards Bryce, bending into the current as he did so. There was a gap of several feet still between them.

'*McEwen, you next. Grab my hand.*'

The ROC officer moved from behind the injured man, working his way steadily towards Fairbank. Once the gap had been bridged, they could all move across providing the engineer had the strength to hold them all.

His fingertips touched Fairbank's, palm slid across palm, fingers curled around wrists.

'*The torch, pass me the torch,*' Fairbank ordered. He uncurled his grip from around the other man's wrist and splayed his fingers.

Still holding on to Fairbank's arm with his right hand, McEwen placed the torch in the engineer's open palm, the movement slow and deliberate, the current threatening to dislodge them at any moment. The positioning was awkward and the light was never still, but it afforded them some visibility.

The strain on Culver at the opposite side of the tunnel increased, for only his strength now held Bryce. He could feel the Civil Defence officer weakening by the second.

'*Hurry!*' he shouted across to the others. '*He can't last much longer!*'

McEwen grasped the injured man's wrist, keeping his eyes off the bare stumps of the fingers, the makeshift bandage long since gone, concentrating only on pulling Bryce towards him.

Culver moved away from the brickwork, a foot brushing against a rail beneath the swirling dark waters. He stepped over it, nudging Bryce ahead of him, his body angled against the current. He let go of the cables, stretching his arm forward for balance. The pressure was tremendous and he noticed that the water was up to his waist.

Fairbank pulled and Culver pushed and they might well have made it had not something rammed into McEwen's midriff. The object spun around so that its length jammed against all three men midstream.

When McEwen looked down and saw the wide rictal grin of the dead man, the lifeless eyes somehow conveying the agony of drowning, something snapped inside. He screamed and both hands lost their grip.

The merciless water snatched him away before he could regain his balance.

The sudden total burden of Bryce's weight was too much for Culver's own precarious balance. Both he and Bryce plunged backwards.

Fairbank, shoved against the wall, could only watch in dismay as the three men hurtled back along the tunnel, only heads and occasionally shoulders bobbing above the surface. McEwen's screams could be heard over the roar.

He pressed himself back against the shiny brickwork and closed his eyes. 'Oh Jesus,' he said. 'Oh Jesus.'

Culver went under, his body spinning beneath the churning surface. Something was pulling him down, a weight that hardly struggled against the force that tore at them. Whether Bryce was unconscious or merely shocked into immobility there was no way of knowing, but regret that he was tied to the injured man stabbed at Culver's disordered thoughts like a taunting barb. He choked on the water that filled his throat, his lungs, forcing his way back above the foaming surface, spluttering, coughing, wheezing for breath.

He pulled at the limp body, dragging it up, Bryce's head rising next to his, unseen in the darkness but jerking violently as if he too were gasping for air.

Culver felt the straps around their arms loosening, Bryce's body beginning to slip away. It would have been a relief to have let the burden go, to use all his unencumbered strength to reach safety, but old, unrelenting memories stirred inside, rising through the panic like dark shadowy ghosts.

He reached beneath Bryce's shoulder and struck out for the side of the tunnel, digging his heels into the firm ground below. Carried along by the momentum of the water and his own efforts, he crashed into the wall. He desperately clung to the other man as their bodies were spun round, once, twice; on the third spin his grasping hand found purchase. They had been swept back as far as the metal-ribbed section of the tunnel, the station platform probably just a short distance away in the darkness. Culver clung there, holding Bryce to his chest with his other arm, gasping in air and praying that the surge would not grow any stronger.

When he had regained his breath, he called out for McEwen, but there was no answer. Maybe he couldn't hear above the noise. He might have found a hold somewhere and be hanging on for dear life just out of earshot. Culver doubted his own hopes, for inside the station itself the walls were smooth with nothing to cling to. Unless McEwen had managed to scramble onto the platform, he had no chance of preventing himself from being swept through into the next tunnel. Light suddenly skimmed along the surface of the broiling water from the other direction, the glare dazzling him.

Fairbank! Fairbank was still back there! This time he called out to the engineer, but again doubted his voice could be heard.

Bryce began to stir and Culver drew him upwards, so that their faces were level.

'*Can you move, Bryce? We've got to get back along the tunnel before the water rises any further.*' A thought struck him, one that he pushed away, refusing to worry over it at that stage. One thing at a time, Culver, just one thing at a time.

Bryce tried to reply, but the words were inaudible.

Holding the Civil Defence officer's arm tightly, Culver began to edge his way forward once more. A shape rushed by, reflected highlights from the torchlight giving it some form. Another shape, and this time its face was pointed upwards, protruding from the water like a death mask. Oh God, thought Culver, somewhere else in the lower regions of the city others had been taking shelter, perhaps in another station further along the line, perhaps in the tunnels themselves – possibly even the sewers – and they had been flushed out by the flood. Another body sped by, arms outstretched and hands clawed as if the corpse was still angry at its fate. Perhaps by now the whole of the Underground system had become one vast catacomb.

The light was closer and Culver realized that Fairbank was coming back for them. He renewed his efforts, fighting against exhaustion as well as the tide. Fortunately, Bryce had revived enough to help himself a little.

The journey was easier for Fairbank, who was travelling with the flow, and soon he was next to them, shining the light directly into their faces.

'Thank God you're all right,' he yelled. *'I thought that was the last I'd see of you.'* He shone the torch past them. *'Where's McEwen?'*

Culver could only shake his head.

Fairbank stared into the distance, hoping to see the lost man. He soon gave up the search. *'You ready to try again?'* he asked Culver.

'Is there a choice?'

'None at all.'

'Then I'm ready.'

As the engineer turned away, Culver held his arm and pulled him close. 'I thought of something a moment ago.'

'Oh yeah?'

'What . . .' Culver struggled to voice the concern. 'What if we can't get back inside? What if the shelter itself is flooded?'

'Didn't you notice the door we left by? It's sealed. It'll hold out any water.'

'Not if they have to open it for us.'

Fairbank thought about it, then yelled back, *'Like I said, we got no choice.'*

Culver eased Bryce around him so that the injured man was in front. They kept him sandwiched between them as they made their way forward again.

It was a long, long, painstaking haul, but mercifully the force against them did not increase. They were aware of more bodies floating by, but by now corpses had become nothing new and nothing to spend thought on.

It couldn't have been hours – it only felt like it – when they reached the recessed door. They collapsed into the opening, careful to keep their feet and relieved that some of the pressure decreased slightly. Fairbank began pounding on the metal surface with the end of his torch.

Culver felt Bryce beginning to sink once again and he held on to him tightly, knowing he would not be able to keep his grip for too long; now that they had reached comparative safety his strength was fading fast. Last time it had been fire he was trying to escape from, this time it was its opposite – water.

'Open up, you bastards!' Fairbank was yelling. *'Open this fucking door, you shitheads!'* He pounded harder, rage giving him the energy.

Bryce was slipping away and Culver resolutely held on to him. He suddenly felt incredibly weak, as though his last remaining ounce of strength had decided enough is enough, there was no more.

He forced himself to stay erect by sheer willpower and it was only when that instinct had also decided to desert him that he felt the metal behind him giving way.

The door opened and he, Bryce and Fairbank were washed through with the torrent.

Hands reached for them as they tumbled over the floor. Culver came to rest between a large locker and a concrete wall and he lay there, resting his back in the corner, watching the figures struggling to close the metal door against the floodwater. It was a hardfought battle, the water cascading in and threatening to flood the whole complex.

More figures rushed forward to help and he saw Dealey standing nearby, watching anxiously, water already lapping around his ankles.

Culver's tired mind could not understand why the man standing next to Dealey was holding a gun on him. Why yet another man, the engineer called Ellison, was also pointing a gun, this one directed towards Culver himself.

15

'Would someone tell me what the hell is going on?'

Kate passed a steaming hot mug of coffee to Culver which he accepted gratefully. He sipped, the liquid burning his lips, but tasting good, warming. He was still soaking wet and had not yet been allowed to change into drier clothes. The faces surrounding him in the Operations Room were neither hostile nor friendly; they were curious.

'What happened to McEwen?' asked one of the engineers whom Culver knew as Strachan, ignoring the pilot's own question. Strachan was sitting in the seat behind the room's only desk, the one usually occupied by Alex Dealey. Culver noted that there were no longer any guns in evidence, but the shift in power was obvious without them.

'We lost him,' Culver answered. His hair was damp and flat over his forehead, his eyes heavy-lidded, an indication of his exhaustion.

'How?' Strachan's tone was cold.

'In the tunnel. He was swept away with the floodwater.' He tasted more coffee before adding, 'There's a chance he's still alive out there. Now would you mind telling me what this is all about?'

'It's about democracy,' Strachan replied, his expression serious.

'Lunacy, more like it.' Dealey was sitting on one side of the room, agitated and looking as if ready to erupt.

Farraday, leaning back against a wall map behind the desk, shirtsleeves rolled to the elbows and hands tucked into his trouser pockets, said, 'Perhaps not, Alex. Their attitude could be the correct one.'

Culver noticed Farraday's shirt collar was open at the neck, his tie hanging loosely against his chest. It was the first time he had seen the senior engineer appear so untidy. Farraday had maintained his own rigid discipline in the shelter, shaving every day, shirt and tie always neatly in place, even if the collar had lost most of its crispness of late.

'That's nonsense,' Dealey retorted. 'There has to be some kind of order, some voice of authority—'

'Some ruling power?' Strachan smiled and Culver thought the smile didn't look good on him.

'Wait a minute,' the pilot interrupted. 'Are you saying *you're* taking control, Strachan?'

'No, not at all. I'm saying there'll be a majority decision from now on. We've seen what bloody power-mad individuals can do, and that all ended with the first bomb.'

Dealey's tone was acid. 'Government by consensus, if I understand you correctly. Well, we had a little example of that just a short time ago, didn't we?' He turned to Culver, who did not enjoy *his* smile either. 'Do you know they had to take a vote on whether or not to let you back into the shelter? They were worried it would be flooded once they opened that door. You were lucky they wanted any information you had gathered.'

Culver looked at Strachan, then around at the others who had managed to cram into the room. He said nothing, just sipped the coffee. The revolver had disappeared from his waistband and he wondered if he had lost it in the tunnel or if it had been taken from him while he lay exhausted on the floor near the tunnel doorway.

Strachan betrayed only a hint of anger.

'From here on everything's to be decided for the common good. If that sounds like Marxist or Trotskyist phraseology, then it's your own blinkered thinking that's telling you so. There aren't enough of us left any more for hierarchy, or government by a few fools. Your kind of politics are over, Dealey, and the sooner you realize it the better it will be for you.'

'Are you threatening me?'

'No, I'm not bloody threatening you. I'm explaining the situation.'

'Do you mind telling me what you've got in mind?' said Culver, impatient with the argument.

'Autonomy for—'

Culver interrupted Strachan. 'I'm not interested. I want to know what you plan to do about the situation we're in.'

Ellison spoke. 'We're going to abandon this shelter, for a start.'

Culver leaned back in his seat and sighed. 'That may not be a good idea.'

'Would you tell us why you think that?' asked Farraday.

This time it was Fairbank who answered.

'Because there's hardly anything left up there, you silly bastards.'

There was a stunned silence before Strachan said, 'Tell us exactly what you found. We've already decided on our course of action, but it would be helpful to know what we've got to face.'

'You've decided?' Fairbank shook his head in mock dismay. 'I thought this was a democracy. What happened to our vote?' He pointed at Culver and himself.

'It's a majority decision.'

'Without proper consultation and, more importantly, without all the facts,' said Dealey.

'The most important fact is that most of us want to leave.'

'It's not safe, not yet,' said Culver, then began to tell them of their expedition, the sheer horror of their discoveries. They listened in wretched silence, each man and woman lost in their own personal despair. There were no questions when he had finished, only a heavy quietness hanging in the room like an invisible, oppressive cloud.

Finally, Strachan broke the silence. 'It changes nothing. Most of us have families we have to get to. I accept that not many may have survived in London itself, but not all of us had homes in the city. We can get out to the suburbs, the home counties, find them.'

Culver leaned forward, wrists on his knees. 'It's up to you,' he said calmly, 'but just remember: there are rabid animals out there, people who are dying and who are just too many to help, and buildings – those left standing in some form – are collapsing all the time. Nothing's solid above us, and the rain is making it worse.'

He drained the last of the coffee and gave the cup to Kate to be refilled.

'Disease is bound to spread,' he continued, 'typhus, cholera – Dr Reynolds has already listed them for you. If that isn't enough, you've got vermin roaming the tunnels, maybe even above ground by now. We saw one or two dead rodents in the station and we saw the damage they'd inflicted. If you come up against a pack of them, you'd have no chance.'

'Listen to him, he's right,' Dealey said almost triumphantly. 'It's what I've been telling you all along!'

'Dealey,' Culver warned, well aware that the man's attempt to dominate, to run things to his order, had led to this confrontation. Law and Order did not exist any more, and Dealey had no force behind him to back up his command. As far as Culver could tell, those who had been aligned with him had soon defected; Farraday was a prime example. 'Just keep your mouth shut.'

Dealey's mouth closed, more in surprise than in obedience. Culver stared at him directly, trying to convey that the situation was more threatening than it appeared; he sensed the mounting tension despite his own tiredness, an hysteria that had steadily risen during the weeks of their incarceration. The fact that these men had used arms as an aid to their 'coup' was an indication of just how high emotions were running. And there was a gleam in Strachan's eye that was as unwelcome as his grin.

'Well, isn't this cosy.' Clare Reynolds pushed her way through the cluster of bodies around the doorway. She cradled a brandy bottle in one arm. 'Thought you two could use some of this,' she said, making her way over to Culver and Fairbank. She uncorked the bottle and poured stiff measures into their coffee mugs. 'You ought to get out of those wet clothes right away. I've treated Bryce's wounds and given him his first rabies shot, but it looks like he's in for a rough ride over the next few weeks. Unfortunately, for him, his incubation period could last from anything to ten days, a month – maybe even two years if he's really unlucky.'

The doctor turned towards the men seated around the desk. 'So how's the revolution going?'

'Take it easy, Clare,' Strachan told her. 'You were just as disgusted with Dealey's imposed regime as any of us.'

'I didn't like his high-handed ways, sure, but his objectives made some sense. One thing that disgusts me above all else, though – and particularly after all that's happened – is the use of force.'

'We didn't use force,' Ellison snapped.

'You used weapons, and in my book, that's force! Haven't you learned anything?'

'We've learned not to listen to bastards like him!' Ellison pointed at Dealey.

She sighed wearily, knowing it was pointless to continue the argument – she had tried that just before and after the take-over. 'Bryce was able to tell me a little of what it's like up there: can you fill in the details?'

Culver repeated his story, giving an even more graphic account of the radiation victims' condition.

'That settles it, then,' the doctor said when he had finished. 'There's no way you can leave the safety of this shelter. If all the other factors don't destroy you – including the flooding in the tunnels – then the vermin will.'

'The water will subside once the rain stops,' Strachan said quickly. 'And it may even have done us a favour.'

All eyes turned towards him.

'It will have flushed out the rats, destroyed their nests,' he told them. 'They won't be a threat any more.'

'Don't be so sure,' said Dr Reynolds. She lit a cigarette. 'These creatures can swim.'

'Not in the conditions out there,' countered Ellison.

'All the tunnels may not have been flooded.'

'She's right,' said Dealey. 'Many of the tube tunnels and sewers have flood doors that would have been closed shortly after or before the bombs dropped.'

'More government precautions to save the élite,' sneered Strachan.

Dealey ignored him. 'And other tunnels would be well above sewer level.'

Clare Reynolds exhaled cigarette smoke into the tightly packed room. 'I think it's time we learned a little more about these Black rats. Did you come across any live vermin, Steve?'

Culver shook his head and Fairbank added a 'Thank God'.

She regarded Alex Dealey coldly. 'And what does – did – the government know about them? You see, I found poisons in the supply store that could only be used against rats, as well as the antitoxin I administered to you and Steve when you first arrived at the shelter. That antitoxin was specifically for the disease carried by this particular strain of mutant Black rat, so I figure their threat was still known and still feared. Was the government aware the problem hadn't been completely eradicated, that these creatures still existed in our sewers?'

'I was just a Civil Servant, Dr Reynolds, and not one to be taken into ministerial confidence,' Dealey replied uneasily.

'Your office was the Inspector of Establishments and you yourself admitted that a large part of your duties involved fallout shelters. You *must* have had some knowledge of it! Look, Dealey, try to understand that we're all in this together; the time for "official secrecy" is long past. Just tell us what you bloody-well know, even if it's only to prevent people leaving this shelter.'

Dealey looked more irritated than intimidated. 'Very well, I'll tell you what I know, but believe me it isn't much. As I implied, my position was not very high in the Civil Service echelon – far from it.'

He shifted uncomfortably in his chair. 'I'm sure most of you know that during the first London Outbreak – that was what the Black-rat infestation of the capital became known as – it was discovered that a certain zoologist by the name of Schiller inter-bred normal Black rats with a mutant, or possibly several mutants, he had brought back from the radiation-affected islands around New Guinea. The new breed soon proliferated and spread throughout London, a stronger and much more intelligent animal than the ordinary rat with, unfortunately, an insatiable taste for human flesh.

'Most were exterminated quickly enough, although the havoc they caused was severe—'

'You mean they killed a lot of people,' Strachan interrupted bitterly.

Dealey went on: 'It was thought at the time that all the vermin had been eliminated, but several must have escaped. In fact, the new outbreak several years later occurred just north-east of the city, in Epping Forest.'

'I seem to remember we were told the problem was solved permanently at that time,' said Dr Reynolds.

'Yes, it was believed to be so.'

'Then how d'you account for those bloody things out there?' Fairbank's eyes were narrowed, anger boiling in his usually genial face.

'Obviously some escaped the net, or had never left the city in the first place.'

'Then why wasn't the public informed of the danger?' asked Strachan.

'Because, by God, nobody knew!'

'Then why the antitoxin, the poisons?' Dr Reynolds asked calmly. 'There's even an ultrasonic machine in the supplies store.'

'They were provided as a precaution.'

Ellison's fist thumped against the desktop. 'You must have known! D'you think we're really that simple?'

Some of Dealey's composure had gone. 'There have been rumours over the years, that's all. Perhaps one or two sightings, nothing—'

'Perhaps?' Strachan was furious and so were others in the room.

'Nothing,' Dealey continued, 'definite, certainly no attacks on anyone working in the tunnels or sewers.'

'Any disappearances?' Culver sipped his coffee-mixed brandy as he awaited the answer to his quietly put question.

Dealey hesitated. 'I have heard of one or two workmen going missing,' he replied eventually. 'But that wasn't unusual. Sewers flood from time to time after heavy rainfall, tunnels collapse—'

'How many exactly?' Culver persisted, remembering Bryce's earlier conjecture that Dealey would know.

'Good Lord, man, I can't give you figures. It was hardly my department.'

'But you were involved in the building of new shelters and extending and updating old ones. Any records of men disappearing while that kind of work was going on?'

'There are always accidents, deaths even, involved in underground excavation.'

'Disappearances, though?'

'This is getting—'

'Why so evasive, Dealey?' Clare Reynolds asked. 'What are you hiding?'

'Nothing at all. It's just that I don't see the point of all this. Certainly, several people have been lost in the tunnels over the years, but as I've stressed, it's nothing unusual.'

'Were their bodies ever recovered?' persisted Culver.

'Not all, but yes, some were.'

'Intact?'

Dealey shook his head in frustration. 'If they weren't found until weeks, perhaps months later, then of course you'd expect the bodies to be decomposed.'

'Eaten?'

A snort of annoyance. 'I'm not denying there are rats

living beneath the streets, but not of the mutant kind. We've never had evidence of that.'

'You said earlier there'd been sightings.'

'They could have been anything – cats, even lost dogs. And yes, I admit, large rats. Not monsters, though, as you're suggesting.'

Clare Reynolds' cigarette was almost singeing the filter, but still she did not extinguish it, conscious of just how low the supply was running. 'Autopsies must have been carried out on the remains that were found, so I'd imagine the existence of the mutant Black would easily have been determined.'

'That may be so, but I was never privy to such knowledge.'

'So *you* say,' remarked Ellison.

'Why should I lie?' Dealey snapped back.

'To protect yourself.'

'From what, exactly?'

The silence had an ominous hollowness to it.

Dr Reynolds quickly stepped in, striding to the desk and regretfully stubbing the meagre remains of her cigarette into an ashtray lying there. 'The real point is that if we're to deal with these overblown rodents we need to know as much about them as possible, and what poisons are most effective.'

'I promise you,' said Dealey, 'I know no more than I've already told you.'

The doctor's words were measured, each one a single capsule, as though she were speaking to someone whose slow-wittedness demanded uncomplicated syllables: 'Have you any idea how many mutant rats are living in the sewers?'

'There can't be a great number, otherwise there would have been much more evidence of them.'

'How d'you explain the slaughter we saw outside?' said Fairbank. 'Just a handful couldn't have done that.'

Dr Reynolds looked around the room. 'Does anyone here know the breeding habits of rodents?'

A small man, unshaven and with skin nearly as pale as the white smock coat he wore, nervously raised a hand, almost as if the sudden limelight would shrivel him up completely. Clare Reynolds knew him as one of the shelter's caretakers-cum-maintenance men. 'It's – it *was* – my job to keep this place free of the buggers, being below ground en'all, with the tunnels nearby, and the drains. Never had any big uns, though, not like you're sayin'.'

'But you have some knowledge of rodents?' the doctor urged.

'No, not much, not really. 'Cept I read a bit about 'em when the Black uns were runnin' riot around London. It made it a bit iffy bein' down 'ere, y'know?' He tried a grin, but the others were more interested in hearing what he had to say than in joining in.

'Well, I know all rats breed five, mebbe more, times a year and can have as much as twelve in a litter.'

'He's talking about normal rats,' Dealey hastened to say. 'As I understand it, the breeding ability of the mutant was nowhere near as great as the ordinary rodent's. One can only assume its very uniqueness played some part in its reproductive output.'

'It's just as well,' someone else remarked. 'Otherwise the sewers would have been over-run with them years ago.'

Other voices murmured mutual alarm.

Dr Reynolds addressed herself to the caretaker once more. 'Have you seen any indications of these larger-sized rats over the years?'

The small man shook his head. 'Can't say that I have. I've

killed off a few of the other kind, but I couldn't say this place has been plagued with 'em.' Scratching his nose reflectively he added, 'Surprisin' really, considerin' the amount of outlets – pipes and cables and tubes and things. Poisons have kept 'em down, I suppose.'

'Have you ever used gas?' Clare Reynolds asked. She had seated herself against the edge of the desk, arms folded, back towards Strachan and Ellison.

Farraday answered the question. 'That wouldn't have been allowed, not with so many people working in the vicinity. Besides, gas is only normally used in sewers.'

Clare craved another cigarette, but she had just used up that hour's ration. 'It's only that I found a proprietary powder among the supplies, the kind that produces hydrogen cyanide when exposed to dampness.'

'I don't see where this is getting us,' said Ellison. 'If we're going to leave the shelter we won't have to bother with putting down poisons. When we get on the outside we'll have guns to protect us.'

Dr Reynolds whirled on him. 'Do you really think that kind of weapon would save you if a pack of rats – or even a pack of rabid dogs – attacked you? It's about time you faced up to the truth of the situation, you idiot—'

Ellison pushed back his chair, but did not rise. 'Look, just because you're a doc—'

Culver did rise, but it was a tired movement. 'You figure out what you're all going to do, I don't give a shit one way or the other. I've told you what it's like out there, so you can make your own choice. As for me, I'm beat.'

Fairbank stood as if in agreement.

Both men made their way towards the door and Culver turned before pushing his way through the throng. 'One thing I remembered when you were discussing the bodies that had been recovered from the sewers over the years.' He ran a hand around the back of his neck, twisting his head to relieve a creeping stiffness. 'I don't know what it means, or even if it's particularly relevant, but I noticed something odd about a lot of the bodies we found on the escalators and in the station itself.'

Kate Garner, already shocked by his revelations, felt a fresh shiver of anticipated dread rush through her. Could there really be anything worse to hear, more suffering to contemplate? Perhaps not, but what he told them added a touch of the macabre to an already horrific account.

'The heads of many of the corpses were missing,' Culver said before leaving the room.

16

Something, someone, was pounding him. His name was being called from a long way off, drawing closer, insistent, piercing the sleepy folds of exhaustion he had drawn around himself.

'*Steve, wake up for God's sake, wake up!*'

Culver tried to push the tugging hands away, unwilling to relinquish the soft respite, but other parts of his consciousness were aroused, alerted, already instigating the waking process. He stirred in the narrow bunkbed and protested at the unrelenting prodding. Still fully clothed, too exhausted to remove them hours before when he and Fairbank had slumped onto the beds – stacked three-high in the men's cramped dormitory – he forced his eyes open.

Kate's face hovered above him, its edges blurred by his own sleepiness. He blinked his eyes several times and the face finally focused.

'Steve, get up, right now,' she said, and her urgency quickly dismissed the remaining vestiges of tiredness.

He raised himself on one elbow, his head almost touching the bunk above. 'What is it?'

Noises intruded from the open doorway – shouts, even screams, and an all-too-familiar rushing sound; Fairbank was awake, too, on the opposite bunkbed, staring confusedly across. Culver recognized the background noise before Kate spoke.

'The shelter's being flooded!'

His stockinged feet were over the side almost before she had time to give him room. Cold water swirling around his ankles completed his revival.

'Where the hell's it coming from?' he shouted, grabbing his boots, the only items he'd bothered to remove before lying down, and pushing his soaked feet into them. Opposite, Fairbank was following suit.

'The well!' Kate told him. 'The artesian well has flooded. The water's pouring through.'

Culver did not take the time to wonder how such a possibility could occur – with the damage sustained to the surface and the sewers below, it required little reasoning to understand how the earth's very structure could easily have been harmed; he stood, Kate rising with him, and stepped out into the corridor, water dragging at his feet.

'Wait!' Kate grabbed his shoulder. 'There's worse—'

But he had already seen with his own eyes.

Water gushed towards him from the opening further down the corridor, the switching unit area, figures thrashing around in the bubbling torrent, fighting against the flow. There were other shapes in that churning mass, though; sleek black projectiles that torpedoed through the water, seeking targets.

Culver watched almost in fascination as one rat reached its victim and clambered up the unfortunate man's leg, claws tearing as they gripped, open jaw reaching upwards, ready to clamp tight when they reached their goal. The man tried to hold the creature away, but its impetus was too great and the victim too unsteady on his feet. Culver saw the rat nuzzle beneath the man's chin, a spurt of blood immediately jetting outwards, the man falling, the water around him churning red.

Kate and Fairbank were behind Culver, the girl clinging to the pilot, the engineer bracing himself against the door-frame.

'How did they get in?' yelled Fairbank.

'Maybe from the well, maybe from the pipe inlets!' Culver was pushed aside as two figures, a man helping a panic-stricken woman, splashed their way down the corridor, something black following in their wake.

Culver, Kate and Fairbank shrank back into the dormitory and watched another of the water-sleek rats skim by. They heard distant gunshots.

'I thought these shelters were supposed to be impregnable,' Culver said to Fairbank.

'This is a communications centre as well as a shelter – I suppose it was never completely sealed off.'

The girl tugged at Culver's sleeve. 'The water level's rising. We have to get out!'

'It'll be okay,' Fairbank told her. 'I don't think we'll be completely flooded.'

'D'you want to stay and take the chance?' Culver asked. He peeked around the doorframe into the corridor again. The flow seemed even more forceful than before. He turned back to say something to the others when suddenly the lights dimmed.

For a few frigid seconds the light fluctuated between dim and bright before settling for bright once more.

Fairbank cursed. 'If the generator goes, we're really in trouble. We won't even have emergency lighting.'

Culver pulled Kate closer to him. 'Where were Dealey and the others when you last saw them?'

'Back in the Operations Room, still fighting it out between them.'

'Okay, that's where we'll head for.'

'Why there, for fuck's sake?' Fairbank demanded to know. 'Let's just get outa here.'

'We need weapons, that's why. We won't stand much chance without them. We can cut through the carrier section, then back to the Operations Room.'

Fairbank shrugged. 'Okay, lead on.'

He waded over to a metal locker and reached for a heavy-duty lamp perched on its top – torches and lamps were kept all around the shelter for lighting emergencies. 'We may need it,' he said and all three hoped they wouldn't.

Culver fought for balance as he stepped back into the corridor. One hand stretched for the far wall as the water, now past his knees, endeavoured to unbalance him. Kate held on to his other arm and Fairbank kept close behind, constantly looking over his shoulder to make sure no dark creatures were swimming towards them. Something nudged the back of his leg and he was relieved to see it was only an empty shoe. Ownerless, it swept by.

Sparks suddenly sprouted from machinery just ahead. 'Christ!' Fairbank shouted. 'If it goes, we'll all be electrocuted!'

The other two heard him but no reply was needed. Culver just hoped that someone had the sense to shut down all the unnecessary machinery. He pushed between two towering racks of telecommunications equipment, pulling Kate in with him. Fairbank, still busy looking over his shoulder, would have passed the opening had not Culver reached out and yanked him in. Figures raced by at the other end of the narrow alleyway they had taken refuge in.

'Looks like they're making for the door to the Underground tunnel!' Fairbank shouted over the noise.

'That might make matters worse,' Culver replied and Fairbank understood what he meant. The flooding in the tunnel could be even greater than before. A deeper sense of dread surged through them, for they realized *that* was their only way out.

Culver pushed on, setting himself only one objective at a time, the acquisition of firearms being the first. Guns would give them some protection against the rats, though they would be useless against too many. Then perhaps they could find high ground – on top of machinery possibly – where they could be above the water level and in a position to hold off any clambering vermin. Culver knew that the Exchange had two other entrances, but both had been sealed by fallen buildings; how the government planners had been so stupid as not to have foreseen such an event, he could not fathom – perhaps they felt the tunnel exit was safeguard enough.

He stepped out from the narrow, machine-created passage into a wider area where the crushing water had become a torrent. On the opposite side was a metal catwalk, just seven or eight feet above floor level, which enabled the engineers to reach the upper parts of communications equipment built into the wall there. If they could get to the catwalk ladder just a few yards ahead of them, then the narrow platform would provide an easy passage for some considerable distance. Culver pointed to the ladder and the others nodded vigorously, failing to see the black vermin that raced towards the pilot.

One was on his shoulders before he had even realized it had clawed its way up his body. Another bit into the hem of his short, leather jacket as he pitched forward into the water.

Kate screamed, involuntarily shrinking back into the slightly calmer current of the passageway they had just passed through. Culver's body thrashed around in the water, two scrabbling black shapes clinging to it, a wild foam created around them.

Fairbank leapt into the mêlée, raising the heavy-duty lamp high and swinging it down onto the back of the creature that was about to tear into the pilot's neck. He thought he heard the rat squeal in pain, but the overall noise was too great to be sure. Its grip loosened and Fairbank, now on his knees, water seeping around his upper torso, swung at it again. The rat fell away, but immediately lunged for its assailant.

Culver coughed water, aware that the paralysing grip around his neck had been released, but not understanding why. He pushed himself upwards, bursting through the foamy surface. Spluttering and gasping for air, he tried to regain his feet, but something else encumbered him, something that dragged at his jacket like a lead weight, one with sharp, scudding claws. Almost without thinking he slipped an arm from the jacket, turned, and used the tough material to smother the thrashing rat. He bore down, water cascading over his back and shoulders, using his weight to keep the lethal-clawed creature below the surface.

The vermin's strength astounded Culver and it was all he could do to keep a grip around its squirming shoulders. He could feel its head twisting round beneath the surface, trying to reach him with those razor teeth, and he was glad the tough leather of the jacket provided some barrier. But his hold was slipping; he could feel the rat slithering from beneath him. Drawing in a huge breath, Culver lunged down, covering the animal entirely with his own body, using his full weight, fighting the current and the rat, both trying their best to dislodge him, natural force combining with animal strength as if in league against man himself.

Culver clenched his hands tighter around the wriggling bundle underneath, resisting the grey, swirling claustrophobia. Huge, single bubbles of air fought their way from beneath the jacket, becoming a frothy stream of effervescence, finally exploding into a gush of larger bubbles as the struggles beneath him grew weaker, began to fade, became almost still. Ceased.

He rose up, his own lungs spurting their protest, falling backwards, rising again, trying to gain his feet. Arms reached for him, and he gratefully used Kate's support to draw himself up. Before he had fully risen, he saw Fairbank's head just above water, resting against a bank of machinery, hands desperately holding away the snapping jaws of a mutant rat. Culver realized Fairbank must have pulled the animal off him, and now the creature had turned its attack on the engineer himself. Culver plunged for the animal, rage burning inside, loathing for these grotesque creatures overcoming the fear.

He pulled at its body, gripping it beneath the shoulders, heaving and taking the weight from Fairbank's bloodied chest. The engineer twisted free, keeping his hands around the rat's throat. They could see its snapping teeth below the surface, the evil slanted eyes staring at them with a malevolence that held no fear, no acceptance of its inevitable fate, no surrender.

The two men pressed hard, Culver using one knee to pin the powerful hindquarters, avoiding the frenzied claws that turned the water white with their scrabbling. They slowly pushed the head down until it was against the floor, both men relieved they could no longer distinguish those glaring, hate-filled eyes. Air rose to the surface and it was fetid, an evil smell befitting the monster it escaped from. Soon the creature no longer struggled, no longer twitched. They released it and the body drifted away with the current.

Culver and Fairbank rose, breathless and shivering, both leaning back against the machinery. Kate allowed them no respite.

'It's getting deeper!' she cried. 'We have to get away from here!'

Culver blinked water from his eyes and looked back along the wide corridor in the direction of the Operations Room. It was not just the rising water that alerted him further, for where the corridor opened out to accommodate the repeater power plant there was total chaos. Figures attempted to run through the water, fleeing from the vermin which skimmed towards them. One of the engineers held what looked to Culver like a submachine gun and was desperately fiddling with its mechanism as though unable to understand how it operated, while a rat stealthily crept along the top of a bank of lifeless television monitors behind him.

Culver shouted a warning, but the man was too far away and the noise too great for him to hear. The rat's front paws slid over the edge of the monitors and it quivered there, held by its huge hindquarters, tensing itself to leap. It sprang, jaws open and aimed at the back of the engineer's exposed neck. The jaws closed almost completely as the incisors crunched into the cervical vertebrae.

The man's mouth opened in a scream, the scream lost in the clamour of other sounds; his back arched and his arms were thrown outwards. The gun, too late, fired. Bullets sprayed, thudding into the ceiling, tearing into machinery, causing minor explosions and spark showers. The firing continued as the man sank into the water, reaching lower targets, his fellow engineers and one or two women who were among them.

The water frothed as he disappeared, the submachine gun becoming silent once more. The man rose just once, his back crimson with his own blood, the rat still clinging fiercely, before sinking to his death. Only the rodent's snout broke surface again, thwarted of its prey by the lack of air; it glided off in search of fresh victims. Of whom there were plenty.

Light abruptly faded, returned, faded again, then remained a dim twilight for long, terrifyingly long, seconds. Something shattered in the complex machinery, an explosion of glaring light and blue smoke. They saw the flame lick and looked aghast at each other.

'This place is finished, Culver!' Fairbank shouted. 'We've got to get out – *now*!'

The lights revived, then flickered before they resumed their normal brightness. Culver saw the dark shapes gliding from the narrow passageway they had themselves used only minutes before.

'Onto the catwalk, quick!' He grabbed Kate and pushed her ahead of him, wading through what had now become a wild bubbling waterway.

Fairbank noticed the rats – three, four, five, *oh Christ, six of them*! – swimming from the gap. Had he looked up he would have seen many others crawling through the wires and machinery behind them. He raced after Culver and the girl, taking big strides in the current, arms outstretched to maintain his balance.

Kate reached the metal ladder leading up to the catwalk and Culver, with a brusque push, urged her to climb. He looked to see if Fairbank was with them and drew in a breath when he saw the closely-packed group of rats bearing down on the engineer.

Clinging to a lower rung of the ladder, Culver stretched out his other arm towards Fairbank. '*Hurry!*' he yelled.

The engineer must have seen the warning in Culver's eyes, for he made the mistake of turning his head to look behind. He staggered when he caught sight of his pursuers.

A deluge of water surging from the opposite direction saved him.

Culver realized that someone, in an effort to escape the flooding shelter, had opened the door to the railway tunnel allowing more floodwater to pour in. Now they did battle with the contraflow, a fresh sweeping tide that met and pushed back at an opposing force, creating a violent meshing, a rolling turbulence.

He just managed to grab Fairbank's outstretched hand before the tidal wave submerged him. The vermin were swept back, twisting and squealing in the foam, kicking out frantically with useless paws as they were smashed into machinery and tossed like flotsam along the wide corridor.

Culver tugged at the dead weight, its pull nearly wrenching him from the ladder. Water cascaded over him, taking his breath away, blurring his vision. Resolutely he drew the floundering engineer towards him while Kate watched helplessly from above. Fairbank half swam, half waded towards the ladder, his feet constantly slipping from beneath him, but aided by Culver's firm grip. He gratefully grabbed a ladder rung when he was within reach and hauled himself forward until he was able to cling there without Culver's help. Bald patches showed through his soaked hair and there were deep lines in his face that had never been evident before. There was a bulbous quality to his eyes that registered shock, yet still he managed a panting grin. He uttered something that Culver couldn't catch and pointed with his eyes to the top of the ladder.

'*You first!*' Culver yelled and Fairbank did not argue.

Kate, already on the catwalk, helped him up the last few rungs. He lay there, gasping for breath, like a floundering fish just hooked from the river.

Culver watched as other bodies were swept past, their

impetus too great for him to reach out and pull them in. The floodwater wasn't too deep yet – perhaps just below chest level – so they would have a chance provided they were not knocked unconscious by unyielding objects. The waters should settle down to a degree once both flows had ceased to fight against each other. The big question was, how flooded would the underground shelter become? Would it be completely filled, or would the level gradually subside? He wasn't keen on waiting to find out.

He climbed the ladder, perching on the edge of the opening for a few moments to catch his breath. Looking back, he saw the water still raged along the corridor from the section where the tunnel door was housed. Anything loose was flowing with it, and that included more bodies. Culver clambered to his feet and pushed his arm through the jacket sleeve that was still hanging loose.

The catwalk was narrow, just wide enough to take one person at a time, the railing on the outside single and frail-looking. The grilled walkway beneath them trembled with their weight.

Fairbank was already up, but still gasping. He squeezed past Kate and began to make his way along the catwalk, heading in the direction of the Operations Room. Culver wiped strands of hair away from the girl's frightened eyes, then nodded after Fairbank. She moved, clutching at the railing with one hand, her fingers never losing contact with it. Culver followed, gently urging her along, his eyes constantly alert. He shouted a warning when he saw the creeping thing on the conduits above Fairbank's head.

The rat dropped, but the engineer was ready. He caught the creature in mid-air, its weight sending him back against the wall of instruments, slashing teeth just inches away from his face. Fairbank heaved the abomination from him, his strength gained from sheer fright, and the rat hurtled over the railing into the waters below.

There were more dark shapes crawling through the pipe network and wires in the ceiling, and the three bedraggled survivors wasted no more time in moving along the thin, precarious platform. Ahead, they heard the sound of machine-gun fire.

Dr Clare Reynolds had just finished her third cup of coffee and fourth cigarette when the water had poured into the canteen. Sick and tired of reasoning with the rebel engineers, who were now adamant about leaving the refuge despite the dire warnings, dismayed at the continuing duplicity of Dealey – a small example of this was his insistence that there were ample drugs and medicines to provide for virtually any situation, any illness or epidemic that might break out among them, all of which was blatantly untrue; yet he had persuaded her to keep quiet over the inadequacies of the medical supplies 'for the good of all', as he put it – Clare had forsaken her rigid rule of cigarette rationing for the moment. What the hell, if the shelter was abandoned, there would be a glut of tobacco among the ruins upstairs and never enough people to smoke it all. She supposed it wasn't much of an example for someone in her profession to be setting, but that had never bothered her in the past, so why now? The message would have to read differently from this point on: DANGER: GOVERNMENT HEALTH WARNING: CIGARETTES AND RADIA-TION CAN SERIOUSLY DAMAGE YOUR HEALTH. And hydrogen bombs can burn you from existence, disease and malnutrition can give you time to think while you fade. She had stubbed out half of her cigarette and lit another.

The powdery ash in the small dish before her seemed

symbolic of all that was left. She stirred it with the glowing tip of her cigarette and it was insubstantial, a miniature pulverized waste. Like her own shattered life.

It was funny how people seemed to dismiss the personal emotions of certain professions – an airline pilot was supposed to think only of his passengers' lives in a crisis, never his own; a priest wasn't allowed to brood on personal problems, only on those of his parishioners – and the medical profession (*vocation*, some would call it) evoked a similar regard. A doctor was not a machine, but they functioned on a level higher than normal human emotion. Or were supposed to. The attitude could be even more outrageous: a doctor would never catch leprosy through treating lepers, would never develop lung disease by helping sufferers of pulmonary tuberculosis, would never catch a cold from a sneezing patient. They were supposed to be immune. She allowed a small ironic smile as she remembered one or two doctors she had known who had succumbed to mild doses of herpes.

Physically and mentally they were meant to be a race apart. But—

(How many psychiatrists had mental breakdowns? Plenty.)

(How many priests committed grievous sin? Enough.)

(How many lawyers despaired at court injustices? Well, there were always exceptions.)

People failed to see beyond the robes of office, the professional façade. Few cared to – they had their own problems, which was usually why they came in contact with the other professions anyway. Only one person in the shelter had concerned herself with Clare's personal loss, and that was Kate Garner. In fact, more than once they had cried on each other's shoulders. No one else had even asked.

She huffed steam onto her spectacles and wiped them with a piece of tissue. There were others in the canteen, but an empty coffee cup and a half-filled ashtray on the yellow Formica table top were her only companions. Still, that was of her own choosing. Although there was a high degree of casualness in her medical manner, she retained a studied measure of aloofness, a mild authority that forbade disintegration on either her part or those around her. It was a role she played to the hilt, a beautiful performance by any standards – Olivier's or Kazan's – but one that was slowly, ever so slowly, beginning to crumble, her dreams the sly and guileful wrecker. For the dreams sent Simon to her, presenting him as whole, complete, approaching in his own easy, restful way, brushing aside with casual waves of his hand each gossamer veil that was somehow not of material but of hazy smoke layers, speaking her name softly, lovingly, and sometimes reproachful that they had been apart for so long, and he would draw nearer; yet she could not move towards him, could only reach out with her arms, her hands trembling and eager, tingling with anticipation, fingertips sending forth an aura that only the Kirlian process could register, strands of loving magnetic energy drawing him inescapably closer to her, until just a few veils drifted between them. In the dreams, his figure, his mutilated body, would grow sharper, its abnormalities focused, the empty eyes where small things glutted, the fleshless grin that was only a grin because the lips were not there to give expression, for they had burned away with other parts of his body, gone with tissue, muscle, leaving bones that were charcoaled black, his clothes tattered and gaping, still hanging loosely from his frame, an incongruous ball-point pen protruding from his lapel pocket, tie dangling like a limp noose from around the bones of his neck as though he had just been cut down from the gallows. And the hand, the skeletal hand that had so casually brushed aside the veils of atomic vapour, would reach towards her, palm outstretched to take her hand, bones clicking – *rattling* – with the movement. The faceless skull that had his hair, although there were only thin, windblown strands left, but they were his colour red, his laughingly carroty red, swaying before her, the mouth opening as if in greeting, the bugs that fell from the widening jaw—

Clare's glasses fell with a clutter onto the yellow table top. Others in the canteen looked around in surprise and resumed their own conversations when she quickly donned the spectacles and tapped her cigarette into the ashtray.

Her eyes blurred behind the lenses and the gesture of fiercely inhaling cigarette smoke enabled her to keep some control. Simon, her husband, her constant friend and never-failing lover, was dead. The cruel dream only confirmed what she already knew, for there was a hurting loss inside her that transcended any need for evidence. It was intuition based – and she had to face it – on a pretty conclusive presumption. Simon, who was – *had been* – a surgeon, a saver of lives, a giver of hope, a cutter-away of malignancy, had been on duty at St Thomas's on the day of the bombs, and she knew, she *positively* knew, he would have had no chance. The initial shockwave would have demolished the building totally. God rest you, Simon my love, I pray it was instant.

When she had woken screaming from the first nightmare, Kate had been there to hold her, to rock her in her arms until the shaking had calmed and the corpse image had retreated to the shadows just beyond her own rationality. Others had stirred in the small dormitory the few women survivors shared, but nightmares and screams in the night were commonplace; they turned on their sides and went back to sleep. She and Kate had shuffled their way down to the canteen where lights were always kept burning (others in the shelter worked on dimmers to conserve energy, and were kept to a minimum during the sleeping hours) and coffee always on the boil. They had talked for hours, Clare laying her particular ghost for that night, not then knowing it was to return on other occasions. Kate's sympathy and her understanding were something to be cherished, their role-reversal a switch that Clare needed and appreciated. Tomorrow she could be stolid, unbreakable (if a little cynical) Dr Reynolds once more; that night she was a frightened, lonely woman who required a shoulder to cry on, a friend to listen.

It had been – how long? Four weeks? – trapped inside this sterile sanctum, an eternity of minutes and seconds, of vacuous moments, of torment-filled hours. Perhaps they were right in wanting to leave. Could life outside – could *death* – be worse than this limbo?

A man at a table nearby (she knew all their names, but couldn't for the life of her remember his at that particular moment) was leaning forward and stroking the hand of a woman opposite. The woman, who had previously worked in the Exchange's large switchboard area, smiled secretly at him, a plain smile that at another time would have held little lure for any man; things were different now, the balance had altered. Any female body was a prize, no matter how awkward, heavy or even advanced in years. The situation had caused jealousies to spring up, rivalry to rear. Its very explosiveness had had much to do with the mutiny – no, mutiny was too strong a word, assertion was better; the assertion of the masses (ha! funny word under the circumstances) over figurehead authority – for it had increased tension, set the men on edge.

The man nearby was running his fingers lightly up and

down the fleshy part of the woman's arm in an overtly sexual manner, and Clare turned her head away, not in disgust, or envy, but because the gesture inspired certain thoughts that she had tried to ignore. Thoughts that concerned her own sexuality.

The relationship between Simon and herself had been fulfilling on many levels, aesthetically and physically. He had never been a marvellous lover in certain terms, never a superstud, a cocksman, but he had been consistent and warming, and rarely, hardly ever, selfish. Their mutual professions were exhausting and demanding (and all-consuming, hence the lack of little Reynoldses) but they had their moments together, and oh such wonderful, giving moments. She had enjoyed their sex, but in the days, the weeks, following the disaster, she had not even thought of her physical needs, for nothing had stirred inside, not even in the loneliness of the sleepless nights, no hunger had caused any secret moistening, no breast tingle. Except in the dreams.

In the nightmares.

When her dead husband had come for her, had raised his skeletal hand to take hers, his body was burnt away, the parts not seared from his bones eaten by the squirming things that moved around inside him. Nothing left—

Except his genitals, the proud and erect penis that pushed from the tattered clothing and was the only part of him that was alive, that was not gristle, was not bitten into. The only part that throbbed with pulsing, life-giving blood.

She pushed the vision away, unnerved, more unsure, more vulnerable than at any other time. It was there in all the dreams, but never realized, until that small discreetly carnal gesture at the nearby table had released it. Oh God, it wasn't that important, *it wasn't that important!*

Clare knew that human survival instincts roused such

feelings, that imminent death inspired procreation in the living, but why now, why had it taken this long? Because certain body appetites had eventually to be nourished, and particular tensions released. But that did not explain the obscenity of her dreams.

And then she understood, or at least thought she did. The world itself had become an obscenity, the things she loved and cherished destroyed or marred, somehow made impure. Contaminated. What was left to respect in the human race when you knew it had pulled the trigger on itself? What satisfaction from a work of art when it was reduced to ash? What joy in a cool breeze when killer particles floated with it? What sustenance from another body when it was cold and rotting? Yet the need was still there, subconsciously stimulated by the annihilation above. They said Jewish couples made love in the tightly-crammed railway carriages on their way to Auschwitz, perhaps their subliminal way of attempting to cheat Death. Roman noblemen had encouraged their gladiators in sexual activities the night before arena combat, those old-time voyeurs confident that the preceding evening's sport would be as exciting as the following day's, so rampant would their fighters be. And hadn't snuff movies been the latest turn-on?

Clare tapped ash once more. She had even examined a corpse, impossible though it should have been, with a healthy erection.

She had to smile wryly at her own maudlin thoughts. Hell, why was she inventing excuses for her own naturally reviving horniness? She had gone a long time without and even grief could not hold it down forever. Ask any widow. Unfortunately, there was no man in the shelter she felt inclined to sleep with. None at all. For, simply, she did not want a penis. She wanted warmth, loving, and touching. But not fucking.

A slight, though not alarming, bewilderment. A small amount of confusion in her emotions as she realized the only person she wanted for that warmth, that loving – and yes, that *touching* – was Kate Garner. The implication did not startle her although it troubled her a little, for lesbianism barely entered her thoughts – at least, it did not taint them. It was solace and caring she sought, and physical gratification played a minor, although integral, part. Doctor Indomitable, as she knew she had been dubbed, had her flaw (if it could be termed as such) and had at last exposed it to herself. She craved – no, too strong a word again – she *wished*, for comfort.

Sadly, she doubted it would be forthcoming, at least not wholly. Kate would provide comfort, but Clare was sure it could only be emotional, not physical. She smiled grimly; *c'est le holocaust.*

She stubbed out the cigarette, breaking it at the filter. Enough of this, Dr Reynolds. Others need your professional services. Time to close tight the self-scrutiny bottle; you can take a few snorts later, in private. Alistair Bryce needed checking again (oh God, how he would soon be suffering!) and there were one or two who needed their nightly sedation (perhaps on this particular night, she would allow herself a couple of pills). Luckily, the dosimeter badges of the three men who had returned from their venture into the grave (some joke, some pun!) new world had not registered any severe radiation, so Bryce's wounds, if not his condition, should be controllable. If not, she held no reservations about helping him ease his way out. She would prescribe her own 'Brompton Cocktail', a euphoric killer made up of heroin, cocaine and gin. Her medical supplies lacked the cocaine, but there were other ingredients that could take its place. No, if there was no choice, she would not let Bryce die in agonizing pain. And then there was still some convincing of others to be done, explaining further to certain stupid individuals the wisdom of remaining insi—

That was the moment Clare heard the shouts of alarm. Motion and conversation froze in the canteen as the few insomniacs and those still on duty (routine was still adhered to, although somewhat sloppily – most of them should have been manning the communications systems rather than passing away the nightshift in the leisure area) listened and wondered. The floodwater announced itself by bursting through the swing-doors.

Pandemonium greeted the announcement.

Tables and chairs were swept back with the tide, cups dancing on the water like floating plastic ducks waiting to be hooked. The wave hit Clare, throwing her backwards onto the next table. She fell to the floor when this, too, was tipped over. She suddenly found herself fighting for air, her head crashing into something, stunning her. Other objects, other flailing arms and legs, were all around, unable to resist the deluge, tossed in its fierce tide.

Once the first wave had made its way down the length of the canteen, smashing itself against the far wall to turn back on itself, the very worst of its force spent, those people who could rise did so. Those who couldn't, the unlucky ones who had been knocked unconscious or whose limbs had been snapped, drowned in a few feet of rising water, unless their companions spotted them and dragged them to safety.

Clare Reynolds rose unsteadily, the choppy floodwater reaching a point just above her knees. Her spectacles were gone and blinking water from her eyes only improved her vision to a degree. A floating table bumped against her and she grabbed one of its upturned legs for support. It afforded little stability and she soon let the table drift away.

The water continued to cascade in from the open swing-doors and she was aware that there were only two ways out: through those doors or through the kitchen area next to it. If the canteen filled to a level of five or six feet, then whoever was trapped inside would most probably die there. She began to wade towards the exit. Others followed, keeping to the right-hand wall for support, pushing away floating chairs and tables, helping the injured.

The lights dimmed and a woman – possibly the same switchboard girl who had been making eye-contact love to the engineer earlier – screamed. Everybody became still for a few heartstopping moments before the power regenerated.

Clare breathed a sigh of relief and edged her way forward, keeping her back to the wall and legs stiff against the fast-flowing current. There was no one behind the wall-length kitchen window which acted as a self-service counter, and she could not remember if any staff had been on duty there when she had helped herself from the chrome coffee machine. Probably not, not at that time of night. Would it be easier to escape from that exit? The floodwater was rushing down the corridor so that its full force pushed against the canteen's swing-doors; the kitchen door was further back and to the side – the pressure would not be as great. It might just be the best bet, even though it meant crossing the worst of the current to get to the open counter.

She turned to the man directly behind her and shouted her intentions over the roar. He wiped water from his face and nodded agreement. Clare did a quick body-count of those in the canteen, several still floundering among the floating furniture. . . . nine, ten, eleven. Eleven. That was it. And a few floating face-downwards. Those who had survived the initial burst looked dazed and unsure. A sardonic thought flitted through her own fear: the choice of whether to stay inside or leave the shelter was no longer theirs. The problem now was, could they get out?

Clare Reynolds heaved herself away from the wall, splashing wildly as she struggled to keep her balance. The current was swilling around her thighs, tugging, pushing, a relentless bully. She almost slipped, went under, but strong hands held her. Clare looked up into the face of the man whom she had spoken to only a few moments before.

'Thanks, Tom!' she shouted and added, 'We've got to get the others to follow. I'm sure we'll have more chance going through the kitchen.'

Others were following already, though, realizing what the doctor had in mind. Those too injured for rational thought were helped by colleagues and a human chain was soon formed across the room. The rising water had begun to swirl around the canteen in a whirlpool effect and the battered group had to avoid dangerous objects rushing at them.

A section of the chain went down, and the two men who had been carrying a semi-conscious woman between them were swept round in the vortex. One of the men managed to rise again, coughing and spluttering, but the other man and the woman disappeared beneath the jumble of canteen furniture.

'Keep going!' Clare yelled at those behind her. 'The water's still rising. We've got to get out before it's too late!'

It seemed an eternity, an inch-by-inch stagger through a foaming maelstrom, clinging to those who fell, preventing them from being swept away, but still losing one, and then two, then more.

Finally they were only a few feet away from the counter and Clare gratefully clutched at the shiny rail that served as a queue barrier. She hauled herself in, others who were near enough following her example, the water spilling almost around their hips. Looking into the bright kitchen interior she noticed that the door at the far end was open wide. No matter, it would still be easier to get out that way.

The man next to her hoisted himself over the barrier and reached for the counter. Several others did the same, one actually ducking below the waterline to slip between the horizontal rails, coming up on the other side spitting water.

Clare had no intention of immersing herself intentionally and stood on tiptoe to slip over the top rail. Tom helped her and as her legs returned to the numbingly cold water she reached out a shaking hand towards the counter. But stopped. And sagged back against the rail. And stared at the black creature as it scurried onto the yellow-topped counter.

Squatting there, sleek and black.

Watching her with deadly, slanted eyes.

Wet fur rising like sharp needles.

Claws splayed into talons.

To be joined on the yellow surface by another of its kind. And another. Another.

Clare screamed as the lights danced their crazy, tormenting flutter.

17

Ellison had never held a gun, let alone used one before that day. It was a new feeling to him and, he discovered, a pleasurable one. Many hours earlier, when they had taken the keys to the armoury from Dealey and had surveyed the range of weapons thoughtfully provided and updated by successive governments who had obviously been nervous of insurrection in the ultimate crisis, he had viewed the weapons with both fear and growing excitement, the dull shine in his eyes matching that of the black weapons themselves, a peculiar affinity in their muted glow.

Farraday, having spent several youthful years in army service (a conscript who had signed on for yet more), and who had maintained a keen interest in military hardware since, had given names to the various guns and somewhat reluctant instructions on how they worked.

There had been but one choice for Ellison. He had viewed the submachine gun with an excitement that almost bordered on sexual arousal, and the feel of its smooth body heightened that feeling. Its loading and operation were relatively simple, and Farraday warned more than informed that the 9mm Sterling submachine gun's effect was deadly, although not highly accurate. There was no denying the sense of power it gave Ellison, a feeling that his body aura had expanded, strengthened, the weight in his hands somehow relating to a new consciousness of the weight between his legs. The psychiatrist who had divined that a gun acted as an extension of the penis might have had something. At least, if not an extension, it was a pleasing accessory.

Included in the small but comprehensive arsenal were self-loading rifles and 7.62mm general purpose machine guns, .38 Smith and Wesson model 64 revolvers, plastic-bullet firing rifles, stun grenades and CS gas canisters. There were other items such as infra-red intruder systems, portable communications apparatus, gas masks and even plastic shields, but it was the weapons that provoked the real interest. Strachan, who had become unofficial leader of sorts' to the engineers, did not bother to arm himself, but others in the group readily picked up weapons, peering down gun-sights and pulling triggers, laughing like schoolboys at the sharp clicks.

The guns had hardly been necessary for their minor 'coup', but Ellison and several others had been worried about the reconnaissance party's return and their attitude towards the take-over, particularly that of Culver, who during the weeks of confinement had remained an unknown quantity. He was friendly enough, but seemed indifferent to their arguments, their complaints. And there was something faintly daunting about the pilot, even though he seldom showed aggression. Perhaps he appeared too self-contained when the rest of them desperately needed collective support. It had been a relief that he had offered no resistance on his return to the shelter, for Ellison was by no means sure he could have pulled the trigger on the man, even though he enjoyed the power that went with the weapon. To threaten was fine, to actually *kill* was something else. However, times had changed (drastically) and Ellison was changing (rapidly). To some, after such mass genocide, one more death would be infinitely tragic, whereas to others it would have become insignificant. Ellison found himself leaning towards the latter point of view. To be ruthless was to survive, and he wanted, and *how* he wanted, to survive.

The nucleus of mutineers, those in fact who had incited the low-key revolt, had returned to the Operations Room to resume discussions with Dealey and the on-the-fence Farraday. Only Ellison had felt the need to carry a gun, not because he thought the confrontation would require its threat, but because it felt good to him.

Now, as water swirled around his waist, he had found a target. In fact, many creeping, darting, swimming targets.

He concentrated his fire on the rats that were above, crawling through the pipe and wire network or over the tops of machinery, the bullets thudding into soft bodies, screeching off metal, embedding themselves in the concrete ceiling. The vermin he hit were knocked squealing from their perches, plummeting down to thrash around in the fast-flowing water, red bloodstains billowing around them like octopus fluid. One creature somehow became entangled in wiring torn loose from its connection by stray bullets, and it writhed in mid-air, jaws snapping frantically, while electricity surged through its furry body.

There were more dropping onto the catwalk over Ellison's head and he waded into the corridor, breaking a path through the still-rising torrent, quickly reaching out for machinery on the other side to support him before he was swept away. He leaned back against a rack, legs braced firmly against the current, and began firing towards the shapes scuttling along the catwalk, only aware of the three people running up there with them as he squeezed the trigger.

Culver pulled Kate down as bullets spat into the ceiling

just a few feet over their heads. Fairbank had seen the figure below pointing the gun towards them as the lights had begun to flicker, and had ducked low, shouting a warning to his companions. He cursed loudly as something tore through the metal gridwork just a few inches from his left leg.

Something caused the narrow footway behind Culver to judder and he quickly turned. The rat was only a short distance away from his legs, a deadly grinning creature whose eyes glinted with malice, even though the lights dimmed. Culver tensed, waiting for the attack, ready to kick out at the vermin when it sprang forward. But the rat did not move. It lay hunched, teeth bared in a silent snarl, eyes glaring, yet no life in them. It lay dead.

Another black creature fell from overhead and Kate screamed as it landed on her back. It squirmed against her, neck twisting wildly and needle-sharp claws scratching at her clothing. Culver raised himself to his knees as the lighting soared to its full strength once more and winced when blood smeared Kate's torn blouse. He quickly realized that the blood was from the creature itself, pumping from its body in several places. Grabbing at the wet fur, careful to avoid gnashing teeth, he lifted the rat and tossed it between the thin bars of the railing, watching the wriggling beast until it disappeared into the water where its death-throes continued.

Mercifully, Ellison had ceased firing and was staring at him in alarm. Culver turned away to tend to the girl, but Fairbank leaned over to inform the man below of his considered, if screamed, opinion of him.

Kate was shaking as she clung to Culver, but when he lifted her chin to look at her face he saw no hysteria, just fear and perhaps despair. There was no time for comfort, no time for encouragement. The floodwater was still rising and the lights were liable to fail completely at any moment. He pulled her into a sitting position and spoke close to her ear. 'We've got to go back down into the water!'

'Why?' Now there was panic in her expression. 'There's nowhere to go, we can't get out!'

'If we're going to stay above water level we'll have to find weapons to fight off the rats! And we'll have to do that before the water rises too high!' He failed to mention the black shapes he could see continuing to climb through the pipe network and wiring.

'Let me stay here!' she cried. 'I can't go back down there!' Culver began to lift her. 'Afraid I can't do that.'

As Kate stood she realized why. She shrank away from Culver, her eyes searching out the black shapes creeping overhead, backing into Fairbank who was preparing to climb down a ladder close by. He glanced around, up, lips forming a single-syllable word, and swiftly lowered himself onto the first few rungs of the ladder. He looked up once more just before his head and shoulders disappeared from view, his gaze catching Culver's and a knowing look passing between them. The understanding was of cold desperation.

Kate slid into the opening after Fairbank and froze when she saw the foaming water beneath her feet. A less than gentle shove from Culver set her moving again. Icy wetness gripped her, closing around her thighs, her stomach, stealing her breath, pulling and tugging in an effort to dislodge her from the ladder. Yet she felt the current was not as strong as before; the waters flowing from separate sources were now fusing with less force. However, it still needed Fairbank's strength to keep her steady once she had stepped onto the floor.

Culver joined them in time to see Ellison take aim at the ceiling again. The engineer released a short spurt of bullets and Culver was surprised when a grimace that could have only been a smile appeared on Ellison's face.

'Where're Dealey and the others?' he called across to the engineer, who lowered the submachine gun towards him before indicating the Operations Room with the barrel. Ellison raised his eyes towards the ceiling again and Culver was strangely reminded of the bloodless eyes of a pike searching for stickleback. Ellison appeared eager to kill and Culver was relieved that only vermin were the targets. Instability, neuroses, and even a touch of madness had become part of the bunker ambience, the effects of grief, claustrophobia, and the knowledge that permanent safety no longer existed. Only the symptoms varied.

There were figures already emerging from the doorway of the Operations Room, struggling through the current and staring with disbelief at the chaos that confronted them. Dealey was among them and he had that same frightened look he had worn when Culver had first laid eyes on him just, it seemed, a few centuries ago. Culver let go of the steadying ladder and made his way towards the group, Fairbank and Kate following close behind, the girl clinging to the engineer for support. Debris floated by – pieces of equipment, paper, books, chairs – spinning with the converging currents. The body of a dead rat, its belly exposed and ripped where bullets had torn through, bumped against Culver's hip and he hastily pushed it from him. He reached Dealey as more gunfire opened up, but this some distance away in another part of the complex. As if encouraged, Ellison resumed shooting.

Culver almost knocked Dealey over as a sudden surge carried him forward into the group; Farraday, close behind the Ministry man, was able to hold them both.

'Can the shelter take it?' Culver shouted, bracing himself against the flow. 'Will it be completely flooded?'

'I'm not su – God, yes, if the flood doors in the tunnels haven't been closed—'

'They won't have been!'

'Then it depends on how heavy the deluge is.'

'Are we above the sewers?'

Dealey shook his head.

'Okay, our best chance is up on the machinery and the catwalks. We'll have to turn the power off, though, before everything blows. And we need guns to protect ourselves from the rats!'

'No, we can't stay here, we must leave!' Dealey tried to move away from Culver, but the pilot held him.

'There's no way. Water's coming through the tunnel exit – we'd never get through!'

'There's another place, another way out we can use!'

Culver moved his grip to the other man's jacket lapels, angrily pulling him close. 'What? You crazy bastard, did you say there's another way out?'

Dealey tried to disengage himself. 'There might be! At least it will get us above ground level!'

'Where is—'

'Oh my God, look!' Farraday was pointing towards the corridor leading to the dining area and kitchen.

For the moment, Culver forgot Dealey and drew in a sharp breath when he saw Clare Reynolds pushing through the water, sliding against the smooth wall for support, leaving a smeared trail of blood in her wake. Her mouth was wide as if in a silent scream and her eyes, spectacles gone, were staring wildly ahead. Her body was slightly arched, head drawn backwards; a black creature clung to her back and chewed into her neck.

Two, three, four – Culver counted five black shapes – glided past her, headed in the direction of the canteen, ignoring the agonized doctor as if the fellow creature already lodged on her had made its claim. Or perhaps they sensed further helpless prey not too far away. More torpedo-like forms appeared, coming from the switching-unit area beyond which lay the artesian well. That had to be the shelter's weak point, Culver surmised; both the floodwater and the vermin must have gained entry from there. Even as these thoughts were rushing through his head, Culver was rushing forward to reach Clare Reynolds, treading high and brushing a path through the water with his hands as if pushing through a wheatfield.

Tiny water gushers exploded before him, beating their own splattering trail towards the swimming rodents, and Culver turned to roar at Ellison, to warn him off, for Clare was too near, too exposed.

Whether the noise in the flooding complex – the meshing water, the shouts, the screams, the fizzing, sparking electrical equipment, the crashing of uprooted machinery and furniture, the crackle of machine-gun fire itself – drowned Culver's voice, or whether Ellison was too frightened or too crazed to hear, there was no way of knowing; the bullets continued to create a field of miniature eruptions between Culver and the doctor, who was feebly trying to reach behind and pull the gorging rat from her neck.

Dark bodies leapt from the water as bullets struck them, high-pitched, child-like screeches piercing the overall wall of sound, throwing others of their kind into mad confusion so that they lost direction, scrabbled around in tight, disorientated circles, squealing their own terror. Two approached Culver, eyes insane, teeth bared, incisors high above the water line.

A spray of bullets pulverized the skull of one and almost tore the other in half. They disappeared beneath the surface in a dark spreading cloud of blood.

Culver moved forward again, wary of the gunfire and praying that Ellison would keep his aim as far away from him as possible. Meanwhile, Fairbank had seen the danger and was trying to reach Ellison. He was only a few feet away when a human body, floating face downwards, spun into him, turning over as it did so to reveal an open crimson mess in its shoulder and throat.

The jolt sent Fairbank reeling backwards, causing him to lose balance, to fall into the turbulent water, the outstretched arms of the dead man becoming entangled in his own so that the corpse sank with him, plunging down in macabre embrace. Fairbank screamed below water and his throat was filled, choking him, sending him spluttering and heaving to the surface, thrashing out blindly to regain his balance.

Culver was still five yards from Clare when her body jolted rigid and holes punctured her chest, rapidly moving upwards, the last appearing in her turned-away cheek before continuing a splattering pattern in the painted plaster behind her. She turned her head, the rat and the searing pain forgotten in the all-encompassing white shock. Although dying's full agony would take a few moments to touch her, red stains swiftly spreading outwards from the deep wounds, Clare was fully aware of what had happened, could see the gunman some distance away (strangely hard-edged clear despite the loss of her glasses), the ugly, lethal machine he held now quiet, Ellison's staring eyes filled with their own shock, the fusing bubbling water, each ripple visible and individual, each spark from the malfunctioning equipment a separate shooting star, a curving pellet of incandescence, each face that watched her sharply defined, each emotion from them sensed by her. She was even aware of the teeth locked into her neck, immobile now for the rat had been shot, too, although not mortally wounded. Fear had gone as though released by the killing wounds, exorcized by the oncoming of death itself. All that remained was recognition, a fleeting insight to what was, what is, what *always* is; the acceptance before closedown. This, coupled with the knowledge that nothing was final.

The intense pain came, but it was brief.

Clare's eyelids covered the already fading scene as she slid down the wall into the water. Only the clinging thing, trapped by its own frozen grip, struggled feebly to rise to the surface once more.

Culver watched in dismay as the doctor disappeared, her white face devoid of expression, the hole in her cheek pumping dark red blood the only blemish.

He dived full-stretch, the impetus carrying him through the meshing currents, reaching her limp, sunken body before it had time to drift. Gathering her in his arms he heaved himself upwards, bursting through the rough surface to gasp in air, hugging her to him, his back against the wall. With horror he saw the rat still clinging to her neck, back legs kicking, raking her, and he reached for it with one hand, trying to tear it loose, incensed by its tenacity. The rat would not, or could not, release her.

In sheer rage, and in the knowledge that Clare was already dead, Culver gripped the giant rodent around the throat with both hands, squeezing as he did so, allowing the woman's body to slip back into the water, using her own weight and his strength to pull the rat from her. Flesh ripped as the creature came away, and a dripping sliver of skin dangled from its jaws. Culver spun wildly, swinging the rat's scrabbling body through the air, smashing it into the wall, feeling rather than hearing small bones break, swinging again and again until the animal hung soft and unmoving in his hands. He threw it away from him with a cry of disgust, then bent down, feeling for Clare's body, clutching at her hair, a shoulder, pulling her to the surface again. He cradled her in his arms and examined her face, gently lifting one eyelid just to make sure, just to confirm, just to assure himself that she really was dead. The familiar coldness crept through him and he let her slip away.

He waited several moments, eyes closed, head resting against the wall, before wading back to the others, soon aware that the water had risen to a point only inches below his chest.

Fairbank had Ellison pinned up against the high wall of machinery, a hand gripped beneath the other man's chin, pushing his head back. He was shouting at Ellison, but Culver could not make out the words. Strachan was trying to separate them both with little success. The others, Kate among them, face screwed tight with this new grief, clung to anything firm they could find – equipment, struts supporting the catwalk, doorframes, anything solid. Culver shuddered as he noticed that above them, clinging to pipes and conduits, the vermin had massed, creating a bizarre black cloud of moving bodies. Many were dropping onto the catwalk and stealthily edging their way along as if wary of the weapon that had been used against them.

Culver knew that he and the others had no choice but to leave the shelter: either the water or the vermin would soon overwhelm them if they remained. He headed for Dealey.

Dealey tried to back away when he saw the look on Culver's face, but there was nowhere to go apart from the Operations Room, which was awash with dangerous floating furniture. He made a sudden break for the ladder leading up to the catwalk and stopped when he noticed the dark moving shapes through the grillwork. A rough hand spun him round.

'*Where is it, Dealey?*' the pilot yelled. '*Where's the other way out?*'

'Culver, above us, look, for God's sake, look!'

'I know. We haven't much time. We've got to leave right now, before it's too late!'

Dealey slipped and would have been swept away had not Culver hung onto him.

'The main ventilation shaft!' the older man screeched. 'There's a ladder inside, rungs set in the wall!'

'Why the hell didn't you tell us before?' Culver raised an angry fist as if to strike him, but checked himself. Maybe later – if they got out. 'Why did you make us go through the tunnel? You knew the bloody danger!'

'We needed to know the state of the tunnels. That was our link with the other shelters.'

'You used us, you bastard!'

'No, no. There's no way down from the shaft, you see, not from the outside! It rises to a tower above ground level and the top is sealed!'

'Christ, we could have . . .'

Culver stopped. There was no sense in arguing, not now. Not with the complex flooding, the water still rising, the rats gathering overhead. 'Let's get to it.'

He looked around, saw Farraday nearby. 'I guess you knew about this too?'

The senior engineer shook his head. 'I had no cause to; maintenance wasn't my department.'

'All right. We'll round up as many people as we can, grab anything that might come in useful on the outside. You take a couple of men and make for the sick bay, get anyone in there to the main vent shaft. Check the dormitories, the test rooms – anywhere you can – but don't take long.'

'What about the dining area and the rest room? There's bound to be people in there.'

'You saw what happened to Dr Reynolds, the rats swimming in that direction. I don't think we can help them.'

Culver glanced upwards. Several black shapes were directly over their heads. *'Fairbank!'* he shouted, but the engineer could not hear over the general noise and was too busy venting his fury on Ellison to notice what was happening. Culver released Dealey and pushed his way over to them. He wrenched the machine gun from Ellison's grasp, knowing little about the weapon but hoping it still had more ammunition in it. Fairbank, Ellison and Strachan watched in surprise as he raised the gun and pulled the trigger.

The effect was explosive. A hail of bullets whined off metal surfaces, smashed into the banks of machinery, scattering the black mutants, hitting many, propelling them into the air, wounding and destroying, but mainly causing panic. And a newfound respect in the vermin for the human aggressor.

Culver stopped firing, his eyes ever-watchful, and quickly told the others of Dealey's disclosure. If their circumstances had not been so critical he thought the three men would have grabbed Dealey and held him under water until he drowned. And he, Culver, might have helped.

'Collect anything you can to use as weapons!' he told them. 'The armoury must be flooded by now, not that we have time to reach it, anyway. Anyone you can find still carrying a gun will be an asset, so go look. *Now!* Get to the main shaft as quickly as you can, but try to find as many others as possible.'

'We can't go looking for them!' Strachan was visibly shaking. 'We must get to the vent right away.'

Culver lowered the gun so that it was aimed at a point between Strachan's eyes. 'I'm just telling you to take the long way round.' He didn't shout, but his words were heard plainly enough.

'We need some protection,' Ellison pleaded. 'Let me take the gun.'

Culver altered his aim. 'No chance,' he said coldly.

Strachan and Ellison saw something in the pilot's eyes that was as frightening as the danger around them; they pushed themselves back in the water, watching Culver all the time, then disappeared into a channel between equipment racks.

Fairbank regarded Culver with raised eyebrows. 'I'm with you, remember?'

Culver relaxed as much as circumstances would allow. 'Yeah, and it's good to have you. Let's move.'

He pushed himself away from that side of the aisle, allowing the current to carry him at a slight angle towards Dealey, Kate and a small group of others who had gathered in the vicinity of the Operations Room. Fairbank followed.

Culver steadied himself by grabbing hold of the same catwalk support that Kate clung to, the arm bearing the submachine gun encircling her shoulders. She leaned against him, her eyes searching his. Her lips formed the name 'Clare' and he could only shake his head.

'Dealey!' he shouted. 'We need torches.'

Dealey pointed into the doorway. 'In there, on the shelves!'

At a flick of the head from Culver, Fairbank dived through, pushing away floating furniture and scanning the shelves lining the walls for lamps, flashlights, and anything else that might be useful as a weapon. His eyes lit on something stashed away on the top of a long, fixed grey metal cabinet in a corner to his left. If a certain part could be broken off, it would make an effective weapon. He climbed onto the photocopier by the cabinet, its surface almost a foot beneath the water, and reached up.

Outside, Culver was moving the group of huddled survivors towards the passageway that would lead them to the main ventilation shaft. There were five others apart from Dealey, Kate and himself: four engineers and the caretaker. They had formed a chain across the corridor leading to the dining area and kitchen, the currents there particularly fierce as floodwater from separate sources converged.

Culver was leading, his hand gripped tightly around Kate's wrist. Behind her came the black maintenance engineer named Jackson, then Dealey. The other three engineers were spread across the open corridor, struggling to keep upright in the current, the caretaker, backed against a wall on the other side, acting as anchor man.

Culver's right elbow was bent, the gun pointing upwards. Every so often he released a round of bullets, sending the gathering vermin scurrying back into darker hiding places. But they seemed less afraid, returning to their previous positions more speedily, slinking forward in packs as if sensing their enemy's vulnerability. Culver groaned when the weapon clicked empty.

The main ventilation shaft was not far away, just along the passageway, then left towards the switching units, but he wondered if they could make it, whether it would be the rising water or the vermin that would defeat their purpose.

He breathed in acrid fumes and began to choke. Smoke spread rapidly across the ceiling and swirled downwards, creating a thick, churning fog. *Oh shiiiiit!* There were other alternatives. They could also be suffocated or burned to death.

The explosion seemed to rock the very foundations of the complex and water either jumped above his head or he slipped down into it – Culver couldn't be sure which.

When his head and chest came clear again, the shelter was almost in total darkness. The red flickering glow from another part of the Exchange, a glow that moved and spread, drawing closer by the second, dimmed only by swilling smoke, reminded him that the worst could always get worse.

18

For Bryce, the reality was more horrendous than any nightmare he had ever known. He had come to after his sedation with the full knowledge that the disease had him. It was too soon for the full symptoms to be evident, but the dryness in his throat, the feeling of burning up inside, and the fierce headache, were the indications and the forerunners of the agony to follow. In a few days' time there would be agitation, confusion and hallucinations; then muscle spasms, stiffness of the neck and back, convulsions and perhaps even paralysis. He knew the symptoms – Civil Defence staff were made aware of them in their training – and he dreaded the inevitable pain he was promised. He would not be able to drink and the inability to swallow properly would cause him to foam at the mouth, to be mortally afraid of liquids, to be terrified of his own saliva. The fits, the madness, would eventually lead him into a coma, a pain-filled exhaustion and, mercifully, death would come soon after.

His hand was numb at the moment, but the memory of Dr Reynolds' quickly administered treatment sent fresh nausea sweeping through him.

After injecting him against the pain, she had squeezed the stumps of his fingers, encouraging them to bleed a little more. Then, using a syringe, she had forced benzalkonium, an antiseptic detergent, into the open wounds, after which, and despite his moaning protests, she had carefully applied a small amount of nitric acid. He was weeping by the time she injected the antiserum around the wounds, and ready to collapse when a further dose was injected into a muscle in his wrist.

And he was pleading by the time she had administered the vaccination, puncturing the side of his abdomen below the ribs fourteen, fifteen, sixteen – he lost count after seventeen – times, quietly explaining to him that the treatment was absolutely vital if he were to survive, ignoring his protests which grew more desperate yet more feeble each time the needle pierced his skin, telling him that each 2ml. subcutaneous injection was an attenuated virus prepared from the brains of rabid animals – as if he really cared. When Dr Reynolds was through, Bryce really couldn't care less about anything, anyone, or himself even; he had swooned back onto the bunkbed and sunk into sweet oblivion.

To wake later, sensing the first pangs of the disease upon him (*knowing* it wasn't only the after-effects of drugs, or the side-effects of the antiserum, that the treatment hadn't worked, that the disease was in him, *feeling* it spreading, flowing with his own blood) and slowly becoming aware that something more was wrong, lying there in the subdued lighting of the sick bay with other ailing survivors, listening to the screams and shouts beyond the closed door, the strange rushing sound, the lapping of water around the cot beds inside the medical room itself. Sharp sounds that sounded like . . . sounded like gunfire.

Bryce sat upright and others around him, those whose sedation allowed, did the same, all of them confused and more than just frightened. A woman shrieked as water drenched the mattress she lay upon.

Bryce pushed himself back against the wall when tiny

waves lapped over onto his blanket. He was still groggy, and for a moment the cot-filled room swung in a crazy pendulum movement. Someone splashed by his bed and he flinched as ice-cold water slapped his cheek. Other figures followed and Bryce drew in his legs, crouching there in the gloom between his own cot and the one above, shying away from the splashes as if they were droplets of boiling water.

The patients were clamouring around the closed door, pushing against each other to be first out.

Bryce sensed what was about to happen but could not form the words to warn them. He raised his mutilated hand, his eyes imploring them to stop, his mouth open with just a rasping cry, a sound too weak to be heard.

The door burst open and those clustered around it were thrown back as floodwater avalanched in. Within seconds Bryce's shoulders were covered and he was forced to scramble from the lower bed onto the one above, while around him figures floundered and fought against the torrent. The iron-framed bunks began to shift, slowly at first, like reluctant, ponderous animals; but soon the pressure became too much and they began to tip, to scatter, to roll towards the end of the room.

Bryce was thrown from the top bunk and the impact as he plunged beneath the surface dismissed the dragging residual effects of the drug. He rose spluttering and coughing, tangled in other arms and legs, pushing against them as they pushed against him. A double bunk toppled onto him and once more he was beneath the water, choking on its brackish taste, the iron frame heavy against his chest.

At first he fought against the weight, but as he struggled a notion sifted through the terror, nudging him in a quiet, stealthy manner. *Why bother to fight?* the thought asked, *why resist when death was inevitable?*

He tried to heave the metal bed from him, its mattress floating down onto his face as if conspiring with the water to smother him.

Wasn't this a better way to die? the inner voice said slyly. *Wasn't this preferable to madness and pain?*

The cot rose a few inches then slumped back as though another weight had been added to it, perhaps someone climbing onto it to keep free of the flood.

One or two minutes of unpleasantness before drifting off to sleep, a sleep deeper and more peaceful than you've ever known, one that could never be interrupted, never infringed upon. Never again tainted with living.

Yes, it was good, it was desirable. But the pain now; how can I accept the pain now?

Easily. Don't resist, that's the secret, that's the way. A few bad moments and then you'll drift. You'll see.

Am I already mad? Has the disease struck so fast?

No, no, not mad. Dying so effortlessly will be the sanest thing you've ever done.

My lungs are tearing. It hurts, it hurts!

Not for long. Breathe in the water, one large swallow, then no more pain.

I can't. I'm afraid.

It's easier than you think.

Who are you?

I'm your friend. I'm you.

Will you stay with me?

Always.

For ever . . .

. . . . and ever . . .

. . . amen? . . .

. . . amen . . .

The last of Bryce's air escaped in a huge, convulsive

bubble, and although he was screamingly afraid, and although his arms and his head thrashed the water, the pain, as the inner voice promised, was not for long.

Soft layers of unconsciousness began to fold over his eyes, like silky gossamer; the discomfort of not breathing relaxed and spiralled away, the anguish tapering with it. The feeling of helplessness was not so disagreeable and the suffering was beginning to subside, to torment less and less and less . . .

It was as the voice said: Easy.

No longer to be a refugee from the holocaust with no certain future, no longer a victim of the disease which spoiled the mind as well as the body. No grief now, little sorrow. A fading sadness. Peacefully, softly drifting. His inner voice had not lied. The weight from his chest gone. Floating. Upwards. Rising. Upwards. Something pulling? Hurting him? Hands on him? No, not that, not now! It was settled! It was accepted! Leave meeeeeee . . .

He burst through the bubbling surface, water jetting from his lungs, and tried to free himself of the hands that had yanked him from the restful peace. The choking muffled his protests as the two men held him; the pain returned, racking his muscles.

'Punch his back!' Farraday yelled. 'He's choking!'

Dazzling light blinded Bryce as he felt someone move around him. A sudden hard blow arched his back and he spluttered water and sickness over the two men. Another blow and he was retching, desperate to suck in air, involuntarily fighting for breath where just a moment ago it had been a relief to find it blissfully unnecessary.

Webber, one of the two engineers who had accompanied Farraday to the sick bay and who was now standing behind Bryce, slapped the Civil Defence officer between his shoulder-blades, using the flat of his hand this time and not his fist. Bryce's own body reaction was clearing his throat and lungs, making outside force no longer necessary.

'Looks like we got to him just in time,' Webber shouted to Farraday. The second engineer, Thomas, was helping the woman who had fallen onto the bunkbed, the added weight that had pinned Bryce to the floor. He dragged her towards the door, the deluge less violent now that the water level inside the sick bay matched the level outside. Yet it was strong enough to make them stagger and fall. Encumbered by the dead weight of the hysterical woman, Thomas flailed around in the gloom beneath the waterline, tugging at the arm that hugged his neck. He broke the hold and pushed himself upright, the woman rising with him. She clung to him, a hindrance that could drown them both. He changed his mind about rescuing her.

Thomas pushed her away with a hand around her throat, then smashed a fist into her upturned face. Teeth broke under his knuckles and she fell away from him, sinking, a spasm of bubbles breaking the uneven, choppy surface. Aghast at what he had done but nevertheless relieved to be rid of her, Thomas headed for the door, ignoring the shouts from behind.

Farraday had witnessed the incident and he raged inside, unable to help, his own hands full with Bryce, who was sagging as though eager to drown, unwilling to help himself. To Farraday's surprise, the woman blustered to the surface just a few feet away, her eyes dazed but still pleading.

Still helping Webber keep Bryce on his feet with one hand, Farraday reached out for the woman with the other, grabbing one arm as she began to sink again, and pulling her over to him. Her head rested against his chest and she seemed momentarily calmed, as if trusting him to save her.

'Let's get out!' Farraday shouted to Webber. 'We can't help any more!' He called for the others to follow, hoping they would hear, averting his eyes from the rear section of the sick bay, afraid of seeing something that would compel him to wade down there and help. These two, Bryce and the woman, were enough.

They began moving towards the door, a tightly packed foursome, fighting the undertow, careful not to trip over unseen loose objects.

Bryce allowed himself to be carried along, neither helping nor hindering. His mind was in a peculiar turmoil, a jumbled mixture of regret and elation. He knew what it was to die and it wasn't so frightening.

Not actually scary at all, was it?

Perhaps just a little bit.

But infinitely better than living with excruciating pain.

Oh yes, anything was better than that.

And let's not forget the gross indignity of madness.

No, let's not forget that.

Ah, pleasant death.

Yes.

With no true oblivion.

No.

Then where are you going?

I . . . don't know. They're help . . .

Do you want to be helped? Is that what you really want? More torture? Would you welcome insanity, would you enjoy it?

I . . .

Would you?

Leave me alone!

But I am you, how can I leave you?

'LEAVE ME ALONE!'

'It's okay, Bryce, we've got you. There's another way out of the shelter. We can make it.'

He stared into the face of Farraday, barely recognizing the senior engineer. He tried to speak but did not know what to say.

'It's all right,' Farraday told him. 'Just try to help us, try to walk.'

He did as he was asked, closing out the distant inner voice that was no longer soothing but angry, telling him what a fool he was being.

'I don't want to die.'

'Save your breath, man.' Farraday's own breath came in short, sharp groans, the effort beginning to tell on him. 'We can't hear you, so don't try to speak. Conserve your energy.'

Through the open doorway, the light seemed less bright and Farraday supposed the power was fluctuating again until he noticed and smelled the rolling smoke. Thomas was standing just outside the doorway, gaping down the corridor, his damp face a mask of dread, unsteady as water surged around his chest.

By the time they themselves reached the door, Thomas was rapidly heading for the switching units, seeming to swim and wade at the same time. Farraday peered towards the source of Thomas's obvious distress, the thick billowing smoke stinging his eyes, forcing him to squint. He just had time to observe flames licking from the test room area when the complex rocked with thunder and searing white light rushed towards him, melting the protective film over his eyes, stripping the skin from his face. He fell back, carried by the blast, and water smothered his flaming hair, steam rising in a brief cloud from his burnt face. He shrieked and black water eagerly raced in, reducing the sound to a bubbling gurgle.

The others had fared no better and, to Bryce, it was just the continuation of the long nightmare. He had been partly protected by the senior engineer who stood directly in front of him and who had taken the full brunt of the explosion. Farraday's weight had been thrown against him, forcing him down, away from the flames, extinguishing the burning bandages on his mutilated hand, instantly soothing the scorching white heat that had exposed all the nerves on one side of his face, vaporizing the fire that had gristled his right ear. The water welcomed him back.

The tidal wave that followed, tightly packed into the narrow corridor, picked up all four of the burnt survivors and hurtled them along in a boiling stream, catching Thomas as it went, scraping their bodies along the walls, smashing into the machinery that finally blocked the tidal wave's path.

His neck was broken and other bones had snapped, yet Bryce could hear the voice again, homing in from a distance, soon drawing near.

Are you ready now? it asked, just a little sulkily.

He could feel himself spinning, another bone crunching somewhere in his arm as it hit something solid, and although he turned and twisted, he was not giddy, nor confused.

Have you had enough?

Oh yes.

Then breathe in the water.

I have. I'm filled with it.

A sigh. *Well, not much longer.*

I can still sense.

Yes, but you can't feel.

No, everything's numb.

Pleasant?

Very.

I told you. Any fear?

A little.

It'll pass. Very soon.

Where am I going?

You'll see.

Is it nice?

No answer.

Is it nice?

It's different. Nice doesn't matter.

I trust you.

No answer, but this time an answer wasn't necessary.

Bryce followed the voice that no longer spoke, drifting lazily after the sound-shadow into a strange, deep void, a total absence that was all, to find that it was true: Nice did not matter. Nice didn't matter at all.

Their bodies were churned and broken as they found their own, separate deaths, each one different, individual.

Water gushed through the complex, and the fire followed at a slower, yet no less lethal pace.

19

Culver searched for Kate, the red glow emanating from the fire in another part of the complex his only source of light. A huge wave had just passed over them, tossing their bodies like corks on an ocean, but now the level had settled to its former roughness once again. Smoke descended as if to join forces with the floodwater in absolute destruction. He glimpsed Dealey braced against the wall, his face red but eyes white. The black engineer, Jackson, was next to him, the others gone, presumably swept back along the corridor their human chain had straddled.

'Kate!' Culver cried, afraid for her. She emerged from the dark water a few feet away from him, sweeping her head to one side to free her face and hair from the wetness. She sucked in air and immediately began to cough as acrid smoke rushed in. He plunged towards her, a hand encircling her waist, and pulled her back against the wall for support. He held her steady until the coughing had subsided, relieved that the smoke had begun to drift upwards, no longer disturbed by other forces. It was a brief respite, for he knew that the shelter would soon fill with the choking fumes, just as it might soon fill completely with floodwater.

There seemed to be hardly any energy left in Kate as she slumped against him. Her forehead nuzzled against his cheek, and she said, 'It's no use, is it, Steve? We haven't a chance.'

He was tempted to drag her over to the catwalk and climb up, to lie there and pray that the flames and smoke would die away, that the floodwater would gradually subside. That the mutant vermin would choose to ignore them.

'We've got one last shot,' he told her, 'and we're going to take it.'

The shaft was their *only* chance.

A small ray of hope came literally from Fairbank, who shone the flashlight at them from the Operations Room doorway.

'I'm coming over!' he shouted, his voice barely audible over the confusion of sounds.

'Wait a minute!' Culver called back. 'There's a bad pull there; we'll help you across!'

'Okay! I've got a lamp as well as a waterproof flashlight. I'm going to toss it over.'

He switched on the second light and reached across the corridor as far as he could without getting caught in the treacherous currents. Culver had moved closer on the other side of the opening and caught the lamp deftly as Fairbank gently lobbed it over. He passed it back to Dealey.

'Keep it on us! Jackson, grab my arm and don't let go!'

Once he felt his upper arm gripped, Culver moved away from the relative protection of the wall. The current tugged at his legs immediately and he leaned into it, his other arm stretched towards Fairbank. The engineer, clutching the rubber-insulated flashlight and something else in his left hand, reached out to Culver with his right. He had to make his own way for at least a foot, then their fingers curled around each other's wrists and Culver pulled as Jackson drew him in.

They caught their breath on the other side and eventually Fairbank gasped, 'This bloody water's getting higher.'

Culver felt the choppy surface just below his armpits. 'We haven't got much long—'

A scream from Kate and they turned to see the dark shapes streaming towards her lit clearly by the lamp Dealey held. There were three of them, yellow eyes just above the waterline, perhaps sensing the most vulnerable in the group, the easy prey.

Fairbank's speed was remarkable. He leapt forward, the water barely slowing his movement, torch in his left hand, the other object now transferred to his right, raised high. He brought the blade down hard and swift, decapitating the leading rat, pulling the weapon clear and striking again, catching the second rat across its back, severing the spine.

The rat squealed, the cry eerily infantile, and blood gushed from the wound in a dark fountain. The cutter was more difficult to pull free this time, but the third rat veered away as its companions sank. It found the shadows and hid itself, keening for others who had been scattered by the thundering noise and who now crouched in other places, squealing and afraid of the smoke and approaching flames. They found each other in the dark, regrouping, massing together, for their combined force was their strength.

The four men gathered around the girl, Culver tried to soothe her, the others anxious to be on their way.

'We've no time to lose, Culver,' Dealey said agitatedly, his head close to the pilot's, the lamp beam constantly moving, searching the area around them.

Curious, Culver ignored him. 'What the hell did you use there?' he said to Fairbank.

The engineer grinned and held his prize aloft, shining the torch onto it. 'Guillotine blade,' he announced. 'The guillotine was kept close to the photocopier in the Ops Room. I managed to break off the blade.' He swished it in the air like a straight, thick-backed cutlass.

'Come on, we've no time for this!' Dealey urged.

'Link arms, like before,' Culver ordered. 'Let me have the lamp. You behind me, Dealey, Kate in the middle between you and Jackson. Fairbank, you take the rear. The idea is to all keep together.'

They moved off, aware that the smoke was becoming more dense, the water-level higher, but unaware that the rats were regrouping above them.

It wasn't long before Culver and the others found themselves inside the ventilation plant, spurred on by the threat all around, the red glow becoming a brighter orange, shadows dancing on the walls and ceiling, fiery highlights bouncing off the water's black surface. There was less smoke inside the plant room itself and the floodwater was calmer. It was quieter in there, too.

'Over there!' Dealey pointed. 'That's the central air duct.'

Culver's beam lit up the shaft. 'Can we get through? Isn't there machinery inside?' he asked, frowning.

'No, the plant itself is really in a building above us. That's where the filters, cooling and heating units, and humidifiers are. This is just the main shaft for circulating the air; other, smaller ducts run off from it.'

The water level was almost up to their shoulders as they waded and half-swam towards the wide shaft.

'Any ideas on how we get inside?' Culver asked, for the ventilation grille itself was not in sight. It was something they had all pushed to the back of their minds, directing their efforts on one problem at a time, unwilling to think too far ahead lest they become totally discouraged. The fact that the entry point to the ventilation shaft was under water had now to be faced. They grouped around the shaft, bedraggled and feeling trapped. Culver tried to remember what the grille had looked like, how it was sealed.

'Is the grille screwed into the shaft, or is there a lock?' he asked Dealey.

The reply was despairing. 'There's a lock to give the maintenance people easy access. I don't have that particular key.'

Culver exchanged the lamp for Fairbank's insulated flashlight and plunged it down, hoping it really was waterproof. The beam glowed beneath the surface, diffused but strong enough to see by. His head and shoulders followed and he found the metal gridwork before him. He searched for the edges, his fingers running along the rim. He soon found the lock and examined it closely, the torch and his head only inches away. He rose to the surface, releasing the last of his breath and gasping in another deep lungful.

'We're lucky the opening isn't screwed into the wall – I think I can break it open,' he told the others who were watching anxiously. Holding a hand out towards Fairbank, he said, 'Let me have the blade.'

The engineer handed him the makeshift weapon, realizing what he was about to do.

Noises came from outside, shouts, splashing, a frenzy of movement. They shone the lamp and the flashlight towards the door just as Strachan appeared; Ellison was close behind, and there were other figures jostling one another to get into the ventilation room. Strachan beamed his own torch in their direction and shouted with relief when he saw them.

A scream from outside changed his expression.

The men – there appeared to be no women among them – bundled through the door, some falling, tripping those behind. A flurry of activity outside increased the panic.

Culver understood what was happening and dived beneath the water, taking the guillotine blade with him. He found the grille lock and tried to insert the length of metal into the crack beside it, using the thin blade-edge. The task was too cumbersome with the torch in one hand and the metal in the other. He quickly re-surfaced and thrust the dripping flashlight into the startled Jackson's hand.

'Take a deep breath and come down with me!' Culver instructed him. 'Hold the beam on the lock while I prise the grid open.'

He disappeared again and felt the long crack between door and frame with his fingers. The light appeared almost immediately and he guided Jackson's hand towards the lock. Using both his own hands, Culver slid the blade fractionally into the slit just above the lock, then worked it in, using only slight pressure to open the gap wider, pushing the metal blade in further as he did so.

When it was two or three inches inside, he used more pressure, pushing the blade at an angle towards the shaft wall, praying the metal would not snap. The gap widened, just a little. He eased the pressure, then tried again. The lock resisted and the blade quivered in the eerie, watery light. His breath was leaving him, but he knew he hadn't a second to lose; Strachan and the others had been followed and there were no prizes for guessing by what. The ventilation room would soon be overwhelmed by vermin.

A sudden greater use of force, regardless of breaking metal, and the door sprang open, its release quickly cushioned by water – so that it stood ajar just six inches or so.

Culver pulled it wide, snatched the torch from Jackson, and swam through, rising up on the other side gasping for air. And the air was so sweet.

He stood inside the shaft, pointing the beam upwards,

drawing in deep breaths of this new, fresher air. A metal ladder was set in the wall, not with separately mounted rungs as Dealey had supposed. The ladder went straight to the top, a height of some sixty or seventy feet, perhaps more; there were openings on either side, smaller shafts, metal arteries from a major vein.

Another grille obscured the top and he noticed the ladder led to a small trapdoor set in it.

He dropped back down into the water and slid through the opening, emerging among a ring of expectant faces on the other side.

'It's okay,' he told them. 'We can make it.' He handed the blade back to Fairbank and pulled Kate closer to the shaft. 'Take a deep breath and go straight through the opening. You'll find a ladder to your right – start climbing straight away!'

He turned to Jackson, giving him the torch. 'You go with her and keep the light on the opening inside the shaft.'

Activity near the doorway caught his attention.

The water's surface was a churning pink foam and he realized that several of Strachan's party had been caught there, the rats dragging them down, tearing them to pieces beneath the water. These strange mutants had adapted to sewer life in a way he would not have thought possible, the foul waters, whether sluggish with slime or rushing with rainfall, holding no fears for them, just another part of their underworld environment. At least those dying men were distracting the vermin, unwillingly giving the others a chance to get clear.

'Move!' he yelled at Kate.

She vanished and Jackson quickly followed. The others in the group clustered around Culver.

'*Hold it!*' He raised a hand as if to ward them off. 'One at a time or we've all had it!' He tugged at the nearest man to him. 'You next, make it quick!'

The engineer eagerly complied.

As the next man went through, Culver saw that there were no more than a dozen left in the ventilation plant. There was no way of knowing how many others were still alive but trapped in other parts of the complex, and no time to reflect upon it. There was nothing more that he and the others could do; to attempt to rescue any more would probably prove fatal for them all.

One of the men standing on the fringe of the group suddenly cried out. His eyes showed surprise, but he kept motionless except for his head, which slowly peered down into the black water swilling just below his chin. His face abruptly creased in agony as he screamed, the cry filling the room, rebounding off the walls. He fell backwards, arms beating at the water.

Another man, close to him, shouted and lunged down. He quickly came up, his hands full with a writhing, black-furred creature. The rat's incisors snapped at the air, its frantic scrabbling too powerful for the man to contain. It fell onto his shoulder, wicked, pointed head twisting to gouge his cheek. The spurting blood drove the rodent to a new frenzy.

As the others watched dumbstruck, Dealey was already sinking below the surface, nose and breath held. He found the opening and pushed his clumsy body through.

'The bastards are coming from beneath!' Fairbank held the blade high and shone the lamp down into the water. He slashed down and a murky shape below changed direction. He slashed again, keeping up a constant thrashing, more to scare off the creatures than to injure them. Blood oozed from one that was not quite swift enough.

The men were bunched together forming a rough semicircle, their backs to the shaft. Culver found himself next to Ellison who, like Strachan, held a flashlight.

'Put the torches under the water,' Culver ordered. 'It might just dazzle them enough to keep them away.'

They did so and shuddered when the dim light revealed shadowy forms swimming below the waterline, like giant piranhas milling around the two men who had fallen, darting in to shake and worry their victims, backing off only when their jaws were full of ripped flesh.

Fairbank kept the lamp above the surface, afraid it would be extinguished in the water. 'Oh, Jesus . . .' he said as the light showed the mass of humped shapes gliding towards them.

'You two – together!' Culver snapped at two engineers between Ellison and Strachan.

'I can't swim,' one of them said pleadingly.

'Move, you silly fucker!' Culver roared.

His companion pulled him down and their shapes disappeared through the opening.

'Give me the torch,' Culver said to Ellison, who looked at him suspiciously before doing so. 'Go through,' Culver told him. 'You too, Strachan. You can keep your light.'

The two men wasted no time in arguing. Bubbles rose where they had been standing.

Now only Culver and Fairbank remained outside the shaft. Just beyond the foaming patch where the unfortunate victims were under attack, the surface was covered almost totally, scarcely a break between them, by gliding dark humps, an army of vermin, now unhindered, streaming through the doorway like a thick, black oil slick, spreading outwards.

No words were necessary: both men swallowed air and dived.

Fairbank went through first and turned to help Culver.

The pilot was almost inside when something dragged at his ankle. He whirled beneath the water as sharp pain shot up his leg. His hands found the bottom of the frame and he pulled himself into the shaft, his right leg held back by the rat that had sunk its teeth to the bone of his ankle.

Culver kicked out with his other foot, but the water would allow no force. The blow glanced off the vermin's back.

Fairbank pulled at the leg, slicing down with the blade at the same time. The lamp, its light gone as soon as it was below the surface, had been discarded, but Culver had the presence of mind to keep his light on the creature. The blade sank into the animal's shoulder, but not deep enough to shake its grip. Fairbank tugged the leg through and drove the cutter down again into the rat's back. Inky fluid almost blinded him.

He let go of Culver's leg and pulled at the metal grille, closing it as much as the rat and Culver's foot would allow. Something heavy struck the outside and he felt a sleek body brush against his fingertips. A sudden nip made him quickly withdraw them from the meshwork.

Culver managed to get his foot below the bottom rim of the opening, the rat still clinging, its neck stretched over the strip of metal, the rest of its body outside. Even though visibility was poor, Fairbank was able to understand Culver's intention, and he struck quickly, pressing down on the flat side of the blade with one hand, slicing through the creature's spinal cord at the neck.

The rat squirmed for several seconds before becoming rigid, then limp. In desperate need for air, Fairbank helped Culver prise the teeth from his ankle. The pilot kicked the corpse back through the opening and punched out at another long snout that was wriggling its way through the narrow gap. Surprised, the rodent backed off.

Both men pulled the grille shut, feeling the tremors as their attackers darted forward and struck the other side. They snatched their fingers free before they could be bitten off, then rose to the surface together.

A clamour of relief burst out around the shaft as they emerged and hands clapped them on the shoulders and back. The two men shielded their eyes against the glare of torches. Several rungs up on the ladder, Kate laughed and wept at the same time, hysteria close, a trembling weakness threatening to dislodge her.

Culver brought the cheering to an abrupt halt. 'We're not out of it yet!' he told them, the words unusually loud in the confines of the tower, noises from the shelter itself completely cut off. 'There's no way we can keep the grille closed, so start climbing that ladder – *fast!*'

He saw there were already three figures perched on the ladder, Kate being the highest. He just hoped it would take all their combined weight. 'Jackson, get past Kate. You're going to have to smash a way out through the top.'

They began moving upwards, those below crowding around the foot of the ladder, anxious to be clear of the water. A bright flash from above, followed almost immediately by a deep rumbling. For a heart-stopping moment they feared the worst, another nuclear attack. But they soon realized the reverberation was thunder, the white light its precursor. They continued the journey to the top of the ladder.

'Those rats are going to be in here at any second,' Fairbank muttered to Culver as they watched the others climb.

'If we just had something to keep the door tight against its frame . . .'

'A belt? We could thread a thin belt through the grille,

hold it closed from this side. We wouldn't need much pressure to keep it shut.'

'You want to put your hand outside to push the belt back in?'

'Not such a good idea, right?'

Strachan drew close, unscrewing the bottom of the rubber torch he held. 'Just an idea,' he said.

The light went out and Culver shone his own torch on the engineer. The tight-fitting bottom section of Strachan's flashlight came away and he held it in the palm of his hand, exposing the tough length of curled wire inside. He dropped the main section into the water.

'We can shape this so it'll fit around the grille,' he said. 'It isn't strong, but maybe we can keep the grille shut long enough for all of us to climb out.'

'It's an idea,' Culver agreed. 'If we push it through near the top, one of us can stand and still hold onto it. Let me have it.'

'No, you come down with me and hold the light.' Strachan pulled the spring out, then bent it into a curve.

They took deep breaths and allowed themselves to sink. The rats outside were thumping their bodies against the grille, aware that their prey was just beyond the thin barrier. Teeth gnashed at the wire as it was threaded through.

The other end came back a few notches lower and Strachan quickly twisted it around the part still connected to the torch base. He gave the loop a testing tug then straightened, his fingers still holding on. Culver checked the improvised lock before rising himself.

'It looks good,' he said, after taking a breath.

'Yeah,' Fairbank commented. 'The only question is, who hangs onto it while the rest of us get clear?'

'Or how long will it take for the water to cover whoever that person is,' Culver added, noticing that Strachan was stooping to maintain the hold, his chin touching the water's surface.

'You two go,' Strachan said. 'I'll hold it for as long as I can.'

Culver and Fairbank glanced at each other and the latter shrugged. 'Who's arguing?' he said. He offered the blade to Strachan. 'You want this?'

'No. When I climb that ladder I want to get up fast. That thing's going to get in the way.'

'Anything you say.' Fairbank reached out for a rung, the heavy blade gripped precariously between his teeth.

'You sure?' Culver said quietly to Strachan as Fairbank climbed.

'Get going, they're getting impatient out there. I can feel the clever buggers pulling at the grille with their claws. Thank God they need air and can't keep it up for too long.'

Culver briefly clutched the engineer's shoulder as he pushed by him. 'Okay. See you up top.'

'Culver?'

The pilot turned, one hand on a rung above his head.

'What the fuck are these monsters? How could they have grown like this?'

Culver shook his head. 'Maybe Dealey has more answers.' He began to climb.

Above, Jackson was pushing at a fine wire mesh that covered the top section of the shaft. It swung open easily and he went through. He found himself in a space about five feet high, louvre-type struts on either side, the roof slightly curved. Strong metal bars crossed the wire mesh from side to side, giving a firmer base to stand on. He could hear the rain outside as he listened at the opening, but could see nothing. It was strange to realize it was night time out there, for the last few weeks had been a world of constant artificial light. Kate joined him and breathed in the wonderful night air, its clean dampness so much fresher than the air inside the dark tower.

There were five separate strutted sections, each no more than a foot wide, and Jackson pushed at one, testing its strength. 'I think I can kick them out,' he said to Kate.

'Hurry then,' she replied, moving aside to give him room.

Jackson lay with his back against the metal bars and kicked with both feet. The struts he had aimed at held, but he felt them shift with the blow. A second, more concentrated kick splintered them. A third created a gap. He aimed higher next time and repeated the process.

Progress on the ladder had come to a halt, the space at the top of the shaft too confined and the mesh, despite the bars, too weak to support them all. Dealey, just behind an engineer whose head and shoulders were poking through the opening above, looked down into the well and felt nauseated. They were an awful long way up. He closed his eyes, resting his head against a ladder rung, his fists clenched tightly around the uprights. He was already wondering how they would get down on the outside.

At the bottom, Strachan strained to keep a grip on the wire loop beneath the water, twisting his head every so often to suck in a breath, the level now well past his chin. The rats outside were frantically scrabbling at the grille and several had managed to widen the gap at the lock side and were pushing their claws through, excited by the blood tingeing the water around them.

Strachan tensed even more when he felt something catch the wire loop on the other side. The loop jerked as razor-sharp teeth bit into it. It snapped.

Strachan wasted no time. He lunged for the ladder as the door began to swing away from him.

Just ahead of Ellison, who was above Fairbank and Culver, the engineer who had earlier announced that he couldn't swim clung to the ladder, his lips moving in silent prayer, eyes gazing through the rungs at the rough concrete directly in front of him, refusing to look either up or down, and wondering if he should have mentioned that he couldn't stand heights either. More brilliant light suddenly filled the upper levels of the tower, followed closely by the deep, rumbling thunder which seemed to shake the very ladder he rested on. He pressed closer to the wall. The thunder faded and a new noise caught his attention. A scraping sound.

Set in the wall beside him was a rectangular air duct, covered, as was the one now below water, with a metal grid. Beyond the grid, he assumed, were the filters to purify the air that was sucked through. The scraping seemed to be coming from inside.

He peered closer, nervous of looking but too nervous not to. He thought he heard movement inside. Thankful that the metal grid covered the opening, he looked even closer, squinting his eyes to see into the small, regular-patterned holes.

Lightning from outside invaded the upper part of the tower again, not quite penetrating its depths, but creating enough reflected light for him to see.

It seemed that a hundred yellow-gleaming eyes were staring out at him, black, hump-shaped bodies crammed into the tiny space behind them. As one, they leapt forward, crashing into the grid and rattling the metal in its mounting.

The engineer howled in fright, reflexively backing away. His foot slipped from the rung, his hands lost their grip. He fell outwards, his cry continuing to a higher pitch, ending only when he plunged into the murky waters below.

Strachan felt, rather than saw, the descending body. He squeezed against the ladder, shoulders hunched and body tensed. A foot caught him a heavy blow on his scalp and he went down, only his tight hold on a rung saving him from falling to his knees.

He felt movement around his legs, smooth bodies bumping against them. The small, confined chamber abruptly exploded into a violent, thrashing cauldron of motion and sounds. The fallen engineer's gurgled shrieks merged with the high-pitched squealing of rats.

Strachan tried to heave himself upwards, but something held his leg. Teeth punctured his thigh.

He pulled, using all his strength, mouth open wide but only a thin, keening sound emerging. He began to rise and then another weight attached itself to his lower body. The pointed jaws closed on the loose parts below his groin and, as he rose, inch by inch, he could feel them tearing away, a fraction at a time, tendons and blood vessels stretching, separating, bleeding. He moaned at the men above to help.

Fairbank had tried to grab at the man who had fallen from just above him and in the process had lost the precious blade. He studied the seething foam below with consternation, blood spurting from the froth in scarlet geysers.

Culver looked down into Strachan's wide, pleading eyes, the pupils completely surrounded by whiteness. The engineer was screaming, the sound too soft to be heard over the clamour. One hand gripped a rung while the other reached towards Culver, fingers outstretched and twitching, a gesture of entreaty.

Culver started to descend, ignoring Fairbank's warning not to.

Strachan sank lower, forcing Culver to climb down further.

He crouched on the ladder, legs bent, clinging with one hand and reaching for Strachan with the other.

Their fingertips touched and slipped into each other's palms. They gripped.

A rat, seeming to grin as it emerged from the water behind the engineer's shoulder, sped up Strachan's arm and onto Culver's as though their joined hands were nothing more than a ship's mooring chain. It was on Culver's shoulder before he had a chance to react.

By instinct alone, he had turned his head away as the mutant reached him. Teeth sliced through his ear and cut into his temple. He cried out as he let go of Strachan, pushing against the rat's underbelly, lifting it clear and throwing the animal away from him in one swift movement.

The rat twisted in the air, emitting its strange infant cry before it splashed back into the disturbed water.

Strachan's shoulders were almost under the surface when, with a supreme effort, he hauled himself clear again.

Culver felt faint when he saw the mass of black, feeding shapes covering the engineer's back, torso and lower limbs. The water was red beneath him.

It seemed that Strachan was almost smiling as he dragged himself upwards, but the smile became frozen, the eyes resumed their fearful stare, as he realized there was no hope for him. He began to slide down again, the weight of the vermin dragging him back into the glutinous, heaving throng.

His shoulders went under. His chin. His face turned upwards just before he sank. His eyes remained open as water covered them. His mouth did not close as water rushed into it. His face became a white blur beneath the surface, a pale, screaming ghost. It faded in a cloud of deep vermilion.

A hand clutched Culver's shoulder and his head jerked around.

'There was nothing you could do,' Fairbank said. 'Now let's get going before they come after us.'

Culver nodded after the briefest of pauses, and both men resumed their ascent, soaked boots constantly slipping on the already wet iron rungs. As they passed a duct set in the wall by the ladder they heard scuffling sounds, and something pressed from behind the grid, scratching furiously to get at the climbing men. Fairbank spat into the opening. Culver could not take his eyes away, but nevertheless kept moving.

Lightning flashed just before Culver climbed through the trapdoor in the wire mesh at the top. He looked down into the deep well, the thrashing sounds still loud, spiralling up the shaft with the squealing, the shrill cries of the mutant vermin.

He closed the opening on the unholy place as if it were the gateway from hell itself. The creatures would climb the ladder, but not before they had finished their underwater feast.

Thunder boomed again as he crawled to the narrow opening in the tower where Fairbank waited. He looked out into the driving rain, seeing nothing else because of it, only the lights shining upwards from below.

Lightning flashed and he was able to see that the buildings had collapsed all around the ventilation shaft, and their bulk had protected the tower from the blast. The tower itself was contained in some kind of stockade, the walls mostly broken now and covered in debris. The rubble was just twelve or thirteen feet below, an easy drop.

He nodded to Fairbank to go first, the night shuddering with thunder, and the engineer grinned, his expression just visible in the shining beams from outside. Fairbank clung to the sill for a moment before releasing his grip.

Culver watched as lightning forked the sky, a lightning the like of which he had never before seen, for it streaked the blackness in five different places simultaneously, the landscape of destruction frozen in monochrome. Electricity charged the air, yet it was vibrant, infinitely preferable to the dank decay beneath him.

He slid from the edge and dropped out into the dark, rain-filled night.

Three: Domain

The black creatures moved easily through the ruins, seeking human prey, a keen, feverish excitement running through them in the knowledge that food was abundant and easily obtained. They sensed their victims' helplessness and showed no mercy; man, woman and child falling to their slashing teeth and claws, weakened bodies finding little strength against the vermin's vicious might. Even the new-formed communities afforded the survivors little protection against the sudden and overwhelming attacks, for the rats were instinctively aware of the shift in power, the balance so abruptly and unexpectedly in their favour.

They had found a huge source of food near the Mother nest, a warm, living supply that had sustained them for many days and nights; but as that flesh had putrified the vermin had sought fresher nourishment, meat that was still moist, succulent with juices, filled with blood that had not dried solid, and inside the skulls, the saporous organ that had not yet been liquefied to slimy pulp by death's decay. The vermin grew bolder in their seeking, more daring in their gluttonous fervour, still preferring the night but less timid of the daylight hours. They ruled the lesser rodents, their cunning and strength so much greater than that of their inferior kin; and they in turn were ruled by others: strange, obscene creatures that skulked in the darkness below, that slithered on gross, misshapen bodies among bones and rotted corpses, communicating in high-pitched mewling, *protected and fed by the giant Black rats, mutants among mutants, the grotesque among the hideous. Weaker than their sleek Black army yet dominating them, feared and favoured, obeyed and exalted as though they held some progenitive secret within their ill-formed shapes, these monsters quivered with a new excitement, an expectancy; sluggish bodies restless, deformed limbs and snouts occasionally thrashing the filthy earth they existed in, the mewling noise reaching a frantic peak before slowly subsiding, finally abating.*

They would look towards a far corner of the inner chamber within the dark underworld they inhabited, many of them with sightless eyes or no eyes at all, and the fervour would build inside them for long moments, dissipating gradually, sinking but not fading completely.

They waited and received the thoughts of the Mother Creature, sensing its anguish, feeling its pain. They waited and, in their way, they rejoiced.

20

The cold water trickled to a halt and the woman clucked her tongue. She twisted the tap off and placed the meagrely filled kettle on the electric stove. She left it to boil on the stone-cold ring.

Walking through to the hallway, the woman picked up the telephone receiver and flicked open the book lying beside it on the narrow hallstand. She found a number and dialled.

'I've already complained twice,' she said into the mouth-piece. 'Now the water's gone off completely. Why should I pay my water rates when I can't have bloody water?'

She flushed, angry with herself and the noiseless receiver. 'You've made me swear now, that's how angry I am,' she said. 'Don't give me any more excuses, I want someone round today to sort it out, otherwise I shall have to speak to your supervisor.'

Silence.

'What's that you say? You'll have to speak up.'

The phone remained dead.

'Yes, well that's more like it. And I'll have you remember that civility costs nothing. I'll expect your man later this morning, then?'

The earpiece could have been a sea-shell for all the noise it made.

'Right, thank you, and I hope it isn't necessary to call again.'

The woman allowed herself a *humph* of satisfaction as she replaced the receiver.

'I don't know what this country's coming to,' she said, pulling her unkempt cardigan tight around her as a breeze – a warm breeze – flowed down from the stairway. She went back into the kitchen.

As she rinsed the teapot with water from the cold kettle, the woman complained to her husband seated at the pine kitchen table, newspaper propped up against the empty milk bottle before him. A fly, its body thick and black and as big as a bee, landed on the man's cheek and trekked across the pallid landscape. The man ignored it.

'. . . not even as though water's cheap nowadays,' his wife droned. 'We have to pay the rates even when it's off. Should never have been allowed to split from normal rates – it was just their way of bumping up prices. Like everything else, I suppose. Money, money, it rules everything. I dread doing the monthly shop. God knows how much everything's gone up since last time. Afraid you'll have to give me more housekeeping soon, Barry. Yes, I know, but I'm sorry. If you want to eat the way you're used to, you'll have to give me more.'

She stirred the tea and quickly sucked her finger when cold water splashed and burned it. Putting the lid on the teapot, she took it over to the kitchen table and sat opposite her husband.

'Tina, are you going to eat those cornflakes or just sit and stare at them all day?'

Her daughter did not even shrug.

'You'll be late for playschool again if you don't get a move on. And how many times have I told you Cindy isn't allowed at the table. You spend more time speaking to that doll than you do eating.'

She scooped up the dolly that she herself had placed in her daughter's lap only minutes before, and propped it up on the floor against a table leg. Tina began to slide off her chair.

The mother jumped up and pulled the child erect again, tutting as she did so. Tina's small chin rested against her chest and the woman tried vainly to lift it.

'All right, you go ahead and sulk, see where it gets you.'

A small creature with many eyelash legs stirred from its nest in the little girl's ear. It crawled out and scuttled into the dry white hair of the child's scalp.

The woman poured the tea, the water almost colourless, black specks that were the unbrewed tea leaves collecting in the strainer to form a soggy mould. Silverfish scattered from beneath the milk jug as she lifted it and unsuccessfully tried to pour the dots of sour cream into the cups.

'Sammy, you stop that clattering and finish your toast. And will you put your school tie on straight; how many more times do I have to tell you? At ten years of age you think you'd be old enough to dress yourself properly.'

Her son silently gazed at the green bread beside his bowl of cornflakes, the cereal stirring gently as small creatures fed beneath. He was grinning, a ventriloquist's dummy, cheek muscles tightened by shrinkage. A misty film clouded his eyes, a spoon balanced ungripped in his clawed hand. A length of string around his chest tied him to the chair.

The woman suddenly heaved forward, twisting her chair so that the ejected vomit did not splatter the stale food. She retched, the pain seeming to gut her insides, her stomach jerking in violent spasms as if attempting to evict its own internal organs.

The excruciating pain was in her head too, and for a brief

second it forced a flash of lucidity. The moment of boundless thunder, the quietness after. The creeping sickness.

It was gone, the clearness vanquished, muddy clouds spoiling her mind's fleeting perspicuity. She wiped her mouth with the back of her hand and sat upright. The hurt was easing, but she knew it would linger in the background, never far away, waiting to pounce like Inspector Clouseau's Chinese manservant. She almost managed to smile at the memory of old, better times, but the present – her own vision of the present – closed in on her.

She sipped the tasteless tea and flicked with an impatient hand at the flies buzzing around Tina's head. Her husband's pupil-less stare from the other side of the table irritated her, too, the whites of his eyes showing between half-closed lids a silly affectation he assumed to annoy her. A joke could be taken *too* far.

'What shall we do this morning, everyone?' she asked, forgetting it was both a work- and school-day. 'A walk to the park? The rain's finally stopped, you know. My goodness, I thought it never would, didn't you, Barry? Must do some shopping later, but I think we could manage a little walk first, take advantage of the weather, hmm? What do you say, Sammy? You could take your roller skates. Yes, you too, Tina, I wasn't forgetting you. Perhaps the cinema later. No, don't get excited – I want you to finish your breakfast first.'

She leaned across and patted her daughter's little clenched fist.

'It'll be just like old times, won't it?' Her voice became a whisper, and the words were slow. 'Just like old times.'

Tina slid down in her chair once more and this time disappeared beneath the table.

'That's right, dear, you look for Cindy, she can come to the park, too. Anything interesting in the news today, Barry?

Really, oh good gracious, people *are* funny, aren't they? Makes you wonder what the world's coming to, just what on earth you'll read next. Manners, *Samuel*, hand before mouth.'

She scraped away surface mould from a drooping slice of bread and bit into it. 'Don't let your tea get cold, pet,' she lightly scolded her husband, Barry. 'You've got all day to read the newspaper. I think I'll have a lie down in a little while; I'm not feeling too well today. Think I've got flu coming on.'

The woman glanced towards the shattered window, a warm breeze ruffling the thin hair straggling over her forehead. She saw but did not perceive the nuclear-wasted city outside.

Her attention drifted back to her family once more and she watched the black fly, which had fully explored the surface of her husband's face by now, disappearing into the gaping hole of his mouth.

She frowned, and then she sighed. 'Oh, Barry,' she said, 'you're not just going to sit there all day again, are you?'

Tiny, glittering tear beads formed in the corners of each eye, one brimming over leaving a jerky silver trail down to her chin. Her family didn't even notice.

They had laughed at him, but who had the last laugh now? Who had survived, who had lived in comfort, confining though it might be, while others had died in agony? Who had foreseen the holocaust years before the Middle-East situation finally bubbled over to world conflict? Maurice Joseph Kelp, that's who.

Maurice J. Kelp, the insurance agent (who knew better about future-risk?).

Maurice Kelp, the divorcee (no one else to worry about).

Maurice, the loner (no company was more enjoyable than his own).

He had dug the hole in his back garden in Peckham five years ago, much to the derision of his neighbours (who was laughing now, eh? Eh?), big enough to accommodate a large-sized shelter (room enough for four actually, but who wanted other bodies fouling his air, thank you very much). Refinements had been saved for and fitted during those five years, the shelter itself, in kit form, costing nearly £3,000. Accessories such as the hand- and battery-operated filtration unit (£350 second-hand) and the personal radiation-measuring meter (£145 plus £21.75 VAT) had swollen the costs, and fitted extras like the fold-away wash basin and the own-flush toilet had not been cheap. Worth it though, worth every penny.

The prefabricated steel sections had been easy to assemble and the concrete filling-in had been simple enough, once he had read the instruction book carefully. Even fitting the filter and exhaust units had not proved too difficult, when he had fully comprehended what he was supposed to be doing, and the shelter duct connections had proved to be no problem at all. He had also purchased a cheap bilge pump, but mercifully had had no reason to use it. Inside he had installed a bunkbed with foam mattress, a table (the bed was his chair), a heater and Grillogaz cooker, butane gas and battery operated lamps, storage racks filled with tinned and bottled food, dried food, powdered milk, sugar, salt – in all, enough to last him two months. He had a radio with spare batteries (although once below he'd only received crackling noises from it), a medical kit, cleaning utensils, an ample supply of books and magazines (no girlie stuff – he didn't approve of that sort of thing), pencils and paper (including a good stock of toilet paper), strong disinfectants, cutlery, crockery, tin opener, bottle opener, saucepans, candles, clothing, bedding, two clocks (the ticking had nearly driven him crackers for the first few days – he didn't even notice it now), a calendar, and a twelve-gallon drum of water (the water never used for washing dishes, cutlery, or drinking, without his Milton and Mow's Simpla sterilizing tablets).

And oh yes, one more recent acquisition, a dead cat.

Just how the wretched animal had got into his tightly-sealed shelter he had no way of knowing (the cat wasn't talking), but he guessed it must have crept in there a few days before the bombs had dropped. Rising tension in world affairs had been enough to spur Maurice into FINAL PREPAR-ATIONS stage (as four or five similar crises had since he'd owned the shelter) and the nosy creature must have sniffed its way in as he, Maurice, had scurried back and forth from house to shelter, leaving open the conning-tower hatch (the structure was shaped like a submarine with the conning-tower entrance at one end rather than in the middle). He hadn't discovered the cat until the morning after the holocaust.

Maurice remembered the doomsday vividly, the nightmare impressed onto the back of his brain like a finely detailed mural. God, how frightened he'd been! But then, how smug afterwards.

The months of digging, assembling, equipping – enduring the taunts of his neighbours! – had paid off. 'Maurice's Ark' they had laughingly called it, and now he realized how apt that description was. Except, of course, it hadn't been built for bloody animals.

He sat bolt upright on the bunkbed, nauseated by the foul smell, but desperate to draw in the thinning air. His face was pale in the glare of the gas lamp.

How many would be alive out there? How many neighbours

had died not laughing? Always a loner, would he now be truly alone? Surprisingly, he hoped not.

Maurice could have let some of them in to share his refuge, perhaps just one or two, but the pleasure of closing the hatch in their panic-stricken faces was too good to resist. With the clunking of the rotary locking mechanism and the hatch airtight-sealed against the ring on the outside flange of the conning tower, the rising and falling sirens had become a barely heard wailing, the sound of his neighbours banging on the entrance lid just the muffled tapping of insects. The booming, shaking, of the earth had soon put a stop to that.

Maurice had fallen to the floor clutching the blankets he had brought in with him, sure that the thunderous pressure would split the metal shell wide open. He lost count of how many times the earth had rumbled and, though he could not quite remember, he felt perhaps he had fainted. Hours seemed to have been lost somewhere, for the next thing he remembered was awaking on the bunkbed, terrified by the heavy weight on his chest and the warm, fetid breath on his face.

He had screamed and the weight was suddenly gone, leaving only a sharp pain across one shoulder. It took long, disorientated minutes to scrabble around for a torch, the absolute darkness pressing against him like heavy drapes, only his imagination illuminating the interior and filling it with sharp-taloned demons. The searching torch beam discovered nothing, but the saturating lamp-light moments later revealed the sole demon. The ginger cat had peered out at him from beneath the bed with suspicious yellow eyes.

Maurice had never liked felines at the best of times, and they, in truth, had never cared much for him. Perhaps now, at the worst of times (for those up there, anyway), he should learn to get along with them.

'Here, moggy,' he had half-heartedly coaxed. 'Nothing to be afraid of, old son or old girl, whatever you are.' It was a few days before he discovered it was 'old girl'.

The cat refused to budge. It hadn't liked the thundering and trembling of this room and it didn't like the odour of this man. It hissed a warning and the man's sideways head disappeared from view. Only the smell of food a few hours later drew the animal from cover.

'Oh, yes, typical that is,' Maurice told it in chastising tones. 'Cats and dogs are always around when they can sniff grub.'

The cat, who had been trapped in the underground chamber for three days without food or water or even a mouse to nibble at, felt obliged to agree. Nevertheless, she kept at a safe distance from the man.

Maurice, absorbed more by this situation than the one above, tossed a chunk of tinned stewed meat towards the cat, who started back, momentarily alarmed, before pouncing and gobbling.

'Yes, your belly's overcome your fright, hasn't it?' Maurice shook his head, his smile sneering. 'Phyllis used to be the same, but with her it was readies,' he told the wolfing, disinterested cat, referring to his ex-wife who had left him fifteen years before after only eighteen months of marriage. 'Soon as the pound notes were breathing fresh air she was buzzing round like a fly over a turd. Never stayed long once the coffers were empty, I can tell you. Screwed every last penny out of me, the bloody bitch. Got her deserts now, just like the rest of them.' His laugh was forced, for he still did not know how secure he was himself.

Maurice tipped half the meat into a saucepan on the gas burner. 'Have the rest later tonight,' he said, not sure if he was talking to the cat or himself. Next he opened a small can of beans and mixed the contents in with the cooking meat.

'Funny how hungry a holocaust can make you.' His laughter was still nervous and the cat looked at him quizzically. 'All right, I suppose you'll have to be fed. I can't put you out, that's for sure.'

Maurice smiled at his own continued black humour. So far he was handling the annihilation of the human race pretty well.

'Let's see, we'll have to find you your own dinner bowl. And something for you to do your business in, of course. I can dispose of it easily enough, as long as you keep it in the same place. Haven't I seen you before somewhere? I think you belonged to the coloured lady two doors along. Well, she won't be looking for you any more. It's quite cosy down here, don't you think? I may as well just call you Mog, eh? Looks like we're going to have to put up with each other for a while . . .'

And so Maurice J. Kelp and Mog had teamed up to wait out the holocaust.

By the end of the first week, the animal had ceased her restless prowling.

By the end of the second week, Maurice had grown quite fond of her.

By the end of the third week, though, the strain had begun to tell. Mog, like Phyllis, found Maurice a little tough to live with.

Maybe it was his weak but sick jokes. Maybe it was his constant nagging. It could have been his bad breath. Whatever, the cat spent a lot of time just staring at Maurice and a considerable amount of time avoiding his stifling embrace.

Maurice soon began to resent the avoidance, unable to understand why the cat was so ungrateful. He had fed her, given her a home! Saved her life! Yet she prowled the refuge like some captive creature, shrinking beneath the bunkbed, staring out at him with baleful distrusting eyes as if . . . as if . . . yes, as if he were going mad. The look was somehow familiar, in some way reminding him of how . . . of how Phyllis used to stare at him. And not only that, the cat was getting sneaky. Maurice had been awakened in the dead of night more than once by the sound of the cat mooching among the food supplies, biting its way into the dried food packets, clawing through the cling-film-capped half-full tins of food.

The last time Maurice had really flipped, really lost control. He had kicked the cat and received a four-lane scratch along his shin in return. If his mood had been different, Maurice might have admired the nimble way Mog had dodged the missiles directed at her (a saucepan, canned fruit – the portable own-flush loo).

The cat had never been the same after that. It had crouched in corners, snarling and hissing at him, slinking around the scant furniture, skulking beneath the bunkbed, never using the plastic litter tray that Maurice had so thoughtfully provided, as though it might be trapped in that particular corner and bludgeoned to death. Or worse.

Soon after, while Maurice was sleeping, Mog had gone onto the offensive.

Unlike the first time when he had awoken to find the cat squatting on his chest, Maurice awoke to find fierce claws sinking into his face and Mog spitting saliva at him, hissing in a most terrifying manner. With a screech, Maurice had tossed the manic animal away from him, but Mog had immediately returned to the attack, body arched and puffed up by stiffened fur.

A claw had come dangerously close to gouging out one of Maurice's eyes and an earlobe had been bitten before he could force the animal away from him again.

They had faced each other from separate ends of the bed, Maurice cringing on the floor, fingers pressed against his deeply gashed forehead and cheek (he hadn't yet realized part of his ear was missing), the cat perched on the bed-clothes, hunch-backed and snarling, eyes gleaming a nasty yellow.

She came for Maurice again, a streaking ginger blur, a fury of fur, all fangs and sharp-pointed nails. He raised the blankets just in time to catch the cat and screeched as the material tore. Maurice ran when he should have used the restraining bedcovers to his advantage; unfortunately, the area for escape was limited. He climbed the small ladder to the conning tower and crouched at the top (the height was no more than eight feet from hatch to floor), legs drawn up and head ducked against the metal lid itself.

Mog followed and claws dug into Maurice's exposed buttocks. He howled.

Maurice fell, not because of the pain, but because some-thing crashed to the ground above them, causing a vibration of seismic proportions to stagger the steel panels of the bunker. He fell and the cat, still clutching his rear end, fell with him. It squealed briefly as its back was broken.

Maurice, still thinking that the wriggling animal was on the attack, quickly picked himself up and staggered towards the other end of the bunker, wheezing air as he went. He scooped up the saucepan from the Grillogaz to defend him-self with and looked in open-mouthed surprise at the writhing cat. With a whoop of glee Maurice snatched up the bedcovers and raced back to the helpless creature. He smothered Mog and thrashed her body with the saucepan until the animal no longer moved and tiny squeals no longer came from beneath the blankets. Then he picked up a flat-bottomed cylinder of butane gas, using both hands to lift it, and dropped it on a bump where he imagined Mog's head to be.

Finally, he sat on the bed, chest heaving, blood running from his wounds, and giggled at his triumph.

Then he had to live with the decomposing body for another week.

Not even a triple layer of tightly-sealed polythene bags, the insides liberally dosed with disinfectant, could contain the smell, and not even the chemicals inside the Porta Potti toilet could eat away the carcase. In three days the stench was unbearable; Mog had found her own revenge.

And something else was happening to the air inside the shelter. It was definitely becoming harder to breathe and it wasn't only due to the heavy cat odour. The air was definitely becoming thinner by the day, and lately, by the hour.

Maurice had intended to stay inside for at least six weeks, perhaps eight if he could bear it, all-clear sirens or not; now, with no more than four weeks gone, he knew he would have to risk the outside world. Something had clogged the ventilation system. No matter how long he turned the handle of the Microflow Survivaire equipment for, or kept the motor running from the twelve-volt car battery, the air was not replenished. His throat made a thin wheezing noise as he sucked in, and the stink cloyed at his nostrils as if he were immersed in the deepest, foulest sewer. He had to have good, clean air, radiation-packed or not; otherwise he would die a different sort of slow death. Asphyxiation accompanied by the mocking smell of the dead cat was no way to go. Besides, some pamphlets said fourteen days was enough for fallout to have dispersed.

Maurice rose from the bed and clutched at the small table, immediately dizzy. The harsh white glare from the butane gas lamp stung his red-rimmed eyes. Afraid to breathe and more afraid not to, he staggered towards the conning tower. It took all his strength to climb the few rungs of the ladder and he rested just beneath the hatch, head swimming, barely inflated lungs protesting. Several moments passed before he was able to raise an arm and jerk open the locking mechanism.

Thank God, he thought. Thank God I'm getting out, away from the evil sodding ginger cat. No matter what it's like out there, no matter who or what else has survived, it would be a blessed relief from this bloody stinking shithouse.

He allowed the hatch to swing down on its hinge. Powdered dust covered his head and shoulders, and when he had blinked away the tiny grains from his eyes, he uttered a weak cry of dismay. He now understood the cause of the crash just a week before: the remains of a nearby building, undoubtedly his own house, had finally collapsed. And the rubble had covered the ground above him, blocking his air supply, obstructing his escape exit.

His fingers tried to dig into the concrete slab, but hardly marked the surface. He pushed, he heaved, but nothing shifted. Maurice almost collapsed down the ladder, barely able to keep his feet at the bottom. He wailed as he stumbled around the bunker looking for implements to cut through the solid wall above, the sound rasping and faint. He used knives, forks, anything with a sharp point to hammer at the concrete, all to no avail, for the concrete was too strong and his efforts too weak.

He finally banged dazedly at the blockage with a bloodied fist.

Maurice fell back into what was now a pit and howled his frustration. Only the howl was more like a wheeze, the kind a cat might make when choking.

The plastic-covered bundle at the far end of the shelter did not move but Maurice, tears forcing rivulets through the dust on his face, was sure he heard a faint, derisory *meow*.

'Never liked cats,' he panted. 'Never.'

Maurice sucked his knuckles, tasting his own blood, and waited in his private, self-built tomb. It was only a short time to wait before shadows crept in his vision and his lungs became flat and still, but it seemed an eternity to Maurice. A lonely eternity, even though Mog was there to keep him company.

They thought they would be safe in the vast sunken chamber which had once been the banqueting hall of the hotel close to the river. They could almost feel the pressure of thousands of tons of concrete and rubble above them, bearing down, threatening to break through the ceiling and crush them. By rights, that should have happened when the first bomb had dropped, but because of some quirk in the building's structure, or perhaps because of the way the mighty building had toppled, the ceiling had held. The great chandeliers had fallen, impregnating those early diners seated below with a million shards of fine glass; and most of the huge mirrors had tumbled or cracked. Parts of the ceiling had collapsed, rubble descending in grinding, crushing avalanches, the openings soon sealed by more debris from above. Most of the hall's stout pillars had withstood the pressure.

Darkness followed within seconds, and the rumbling, the shifting of the earth itself, continued. As did the screams, the cries for help, the sighing moans of the mortally injured. When the city's death rattle terminated, the other sounds went on.

Those in the banqueting hall who had survived the

eruption, or who had not been knocked senseless by falling masonry and glass or rendered immobile by shock, cowered on the floor, many beneath tables and chairs, others against pillars. A strange calmness fell upon them, a still numbness not uncommon in times of massive disaster, and those who could crawled towards the helpless injured, drawn by whimpers and pleading. Lighters and matches were lit. A waiter found candles and placed them around the devastated dining hall; there was no romance in their glow, just a dim appraisal of human and material damage.

It did not take long to discover there was no apparent escape route from the hall: all exits had been blocked by rubble and there were no outside windows. There was access to the kitchens and, mercifully for many, to the bar, but no exit from them. The dining hall and its smaller annexes were buried beneath thousands of tons of rubble. They were trapped, the price paid for not heeding the warning sirens and fleeing with those less composed than themselves. Most of those not transfixed by sheer funk had realized that if nuclear warheads really were about to fall, then there was virtually nowhere in the capital that could be deemed safe. It would be better to take the last sip of wine, to taste the last expensive morsel of food, in elegant surroundings, and with grace. For just a few, even conversation continued in a light vein.

The blast and its consequences had dispelled all such fanciful affectations.

Cut and bruised, dazed and fearful, those who could examined the candlelit stronghold around them. For some it came to represent an impregnable shelter where they could wait until rescue came, sustained by a carefully rationed food supply from the kitchens, heartened by the ample stock of alcohol from the bar; for others, more pessimistic, it represented a vast inescapable prison.

They learned to live a frugal existence, caring for the injured, endeavouring to ease the way for the dying. Corpses were wrapped in tablecloths and deposited, after all drink was removed, inside the bar area, the double doors tightly sealed afterwards. It was decided that no tunnelling through the debris would be attempted until at least two or three weeks had passed, for only radiation fallout would welcome their release. They knew that precious air was seeping down to them, for the candle flames were strong even days after the explosion, and often stirred with secretive breezes. And when water began to trickle through the debris and they guessed it to be rainwater from outside, they knew there were gaps that could be followed and widened by rescue teams with correct equipment.

So they waited in their newfound community where title held little authority, wealth had no use, and the shared ambition was to survive; a thrown-together cooperative with no social and soon no moral barriers – although as to the sexual aspect of the latter, some discretion was still practised: such encounters, enhanced by Death's skeletal shoulder-tapping, were undertaken in the more remote and darker nooks of the dining hall. Dysentery became rife, despite precautions, and claimed several lives; food poisoning (not to mention alcoholic poisoning) almost took more; infected wounds led to fevers; and suicides reduced their numbers by four. When nobody came to rescue the survivors after three weeks, anxiety mounted. At the end of the fourth, with supplies rapidly depleting, carefully rationed candles running low, and the floor awash with water, it was decided an attempt on their own part to reach the outside had to be made. A tunnel was to be dug.

The stronger of the men collected any tools they could find to dig with – broken table legs, long carving knives, even heavy soup ladles – and selected a point where the water appeared to flow more forcefully than others. They cleared what they could with bare hands, then struck at the more resisting blockages with their implements. They were soon forced to try elsewhere, the barrier before them too solid, and then had to abandon the next 'dig' when more debris than they had displaced collapsed in on them. More headway was made with their third attempt.

The earlier tunnels had been tried near the wide entrances to the dining hall; the latest one was where a section of ceiling had caved in, leaving a barely noticeable fissure. The gap was swiftly widened and, although the earth was damp, no water ran from it. The first man, who used to be a waiter in the once renowned and rather grand hotel squeezed through, pushing a candle before him. It was claustrophobic, but then their very existence had been so over the past month. He pressed on, digging at the rubble with a short-bladed butcher's chopper scavenged from the kitchen. Shouts of encouragement came from behind and he grinned in the gloom, sweat already clogging the dust that settled on his bare arms and shoulders. His enthusiasm almost caused another fall and he forced himself to be more patient when the danger had passed.

He stopped again when he heard something ahead of him. He listened, sure it was not from behind, the sound of others following his path. Perhaps he had been wrong, for now he heard nothing. He began to dig again, pulling brickwork away and burrowing through powdered rubble. Then he was certain he heard noises from ahead.

He called for his companions to be quiet and he waited there. The scraping noise did not seem too far away.

The ex-waiter gave a gargled whoop of joy and shouted back to the others that he was sure rescuers were on the way, digging to meet them, obviously careful not to disturb the debris too much with their digging machines lest more danger was created.

He called out, and the others behind called with him. There was no reply except a scratching sound. He frowned. Now it sounded like . . . like . . . gnawing.

Scraping, slithering. Definite movement. He pushed forward.

Presently he came to another blockage and he almost wept with frustration. But then, no, he saw it was only wood, a partition, a screen or perhaps the back of a fallen wardrobe amid the jumble of masonry and rubble. He could see only a small section of the blockage, for it was framed by the rough tunnel itself. He heard more scratching and wondered why the rescuers did not just punch a hole through the wood. He called out again and the noise stopped.

He spoke eagerly and the scratching resumed and the wood bulged, only there was no comfort in the sound this time, for it was not human digging, it was more like the sound of claws scrabbling to break through and that high-pitched squealing was not human, but was the sound of animals, animals with sharp, scratching claws and with enough strength to push the wood inwards, to make it bulge and crack and . . .

He began to back away and the man behind wondered what he was playing at, cursing the shoes that scuffed his face, the others behind him demanding to know what was going on.

The ex-waiter found he could retreat no further, that the next man was blocking his retreat. He stared beyond the candleflame at the cracking wood, a slow scream beginning.

A sliver of wood broke inwards with a crack. A talon-like claw gripped the edge of the newly formed hole. More splinters fell away. A long pointed snout appeared and yellow teeth gnawed a bigger opening. The rat's head and gleaming eyes were the most heart-wrenching manifestation of evil he had ever seen.

His scream escaped as the rat pushed through and closed the short distance between them with a swift, scuttling movement. The light vanished as the candle was dropped and he could only feel the creature eating into his face, his hands useless against the thick, hairy body.

The vermin had known there were humans close by, their keen sense of smell, their acute instincts, attracted by the distinct aroma of living flesh and human excrement. The digging noises had alerted them and given direction.

They poured through the opening, some eating their way through the body of the first man, others tunnelling their way around him, finding more humans, aroused to an intense frenzy by their own bloodlust. They swept along the tunnel, killing and feeding until they reached the huge cavern where the people waited.

The survivors tried to hide in the darkest corners of the dining hall as the black hordes swept down. At first they did not understand what these creatures were, seeing only a flowing devil's spawn, an invasion of demonic beasts, perhaps returning to their hell's womb in which they, the survivors, had been incarcerated. The desperate screams of the tunnellers had forewarned of the irruption, petrifying the people in the dimly lit hall. They scattered and hid as the dark beasts scampered through the narrow opening and descended the rubbled slope, their traumatized minds unable to cope with this new nightmare, to recognize the demons for what they were. The fear would have been no less if they had.

Only when their very flesh was being shredded by flailing teeth and claws did they fully realize that vermin were to be their final adversity, not radiation poisoning, not disease, not hunger and not despair. They hid, but the rats sought them out; they barricaded themselves behind upturned tables and chairs and the vermin squirmed their way through. The kitchens offered no refuge and those who hid in store cupboards only prolonged the waiting, lengthened the torment as razor-sharp incisors gnawed away the barriers. Those who escaped into the walk-in freezer store with its rancid meat might have found some protection had not others belatedly tried to gain entry, pulling open the big metal door and allowing their attackers to storm through.

One elderly man hid inside an oven, cramming his body in, pulling the door closed, holding on to it for dear life, panting and sobbing, legs drawn up in foetal position. Unfortunately for him, the enemy was within. His old heart had given warning twice in the past and it finally lost patience with its host who would not avoid excitement. The old man suffered an undignified death, stuffed in an oven, now his coffin, his feet and arms feebly beating at the iron walls.

An elderly woman pushed open the double-doors to the bar, the stench of the more-recently dead of no concern, and slammed them shut behind her. She stood alone in the total darkness with her back to the doors, listening to the frightening noises outside, her frail legs barely able to hold her weight. A bump against the door made her start; something slid down the other side. More bumping at the base of the doors as though someone was struggling there. The woman stumbled away, hands groping the blackness, heading for the mound of old and new deceased who were wrapped in tablecloth shrouds.

She fell against something and her probing hands found the nose, an open mouth, of an upturned face beneath its thin covering of cloth. She crawled onto the pile of bodies, burrowing down, pulling them around her, flinching as cold hands brushed her arms, as rigid lips kissed her cheek, as the receptive cadavers crowded in on her, hugging her close as if to steal her warmth. Like the corpses, she tried not to breathe lest the sound give her away, but it seemed that her heart beat loud enough for them all. Encased in the stifling bundles, she waited, silently mouthing prayers not remembered since childhood, corpses tight around her as if conspiring to keep her hidden. She might well have eluded the attention of the predators had not other fugitives burst through the doors. The voracious rats quickly overwhelmed them, dragging them to their knees. The concealed woman tried to close her mind to the shrieks.

A quietness eventually fell. Most of the people had been swiftly killed; those still alive could only moan helplessly as the vermin fed.

The woman thought she was safe. Until she heard the rummaging among the mound of corpses in which she lay, the scrabbling of claws, strange childlike sounds. Weight shifted around her. Something nuzzled against the loose fat above her hip. Something began nibbling at the side of her neck.

21

She scratched at the itch on her cheek, her eyes still closed, her other senses still captive of sleep. The insect moved on in search of less resisting prey. Kate's full awakening was sudden, eyelids snapping open like released blinds, sprung by returning fear. The white blanketing mist did not disappear with the blinking of her eyes.

It was several minutes before she was aware that the rain had stopped and the sun had turned the earth's wetness to rising vapour. Her fear quietened.

They had escaped the underground refuge and its unnatural vermin. Flight through the rubbled city had been a continuation of the torment, terror of being pursued driving them on through the rain, each jagged streak of lightning making them flinch, the ensuing thunder causing them to cringe. They had stopped only when they found a clearing, each of them dropping to the ground, drenched, exhausted, with little will left to carry on. She had crawled into Culver's arms, and some time in the night the rain itself had wearied and finally, after so many weeks, relented. The day's heat was clammy and insects droned in the steamy air; the sky was a bright, white haze, only a faint colouring indicating the sun's position.

Kate glanced at her watch: nearly eleven-twenty; they had slept the morning away.

Culver lay like a dead man next to her, one arm thrown across his face as if to shield his eyes from the sun's nebulous presence – or perhaps to cover them against further horror. Without disturbing him, she raised herself on one elbow and looked around.

The mist was almost impenetrable beyond thirty yards or so, although occasionally warm air currents disturbed the swirling veils to reveal glimpses of the destroyed landscape beyond. Kate shivered, even though her body was soaked in perspiration.

The area they sheltered in had once been a park, a green, path-patterned oasis surrounded by tall, once-gracious buildings. To one side had been the older law offices of Lincoln's Inn, a complex comprised of buildings dating as far back as the sixteenth and seventeenth centuries, a high wall separating it from the park. The wall no longer stood, nor did the legal ghetto, for she knew they had climbed through its ruins the night before. She was sure, although she could not see them, that the other buildings which bounded the park would be gone, too, and that the nearby scrubbed stonework of the Law Courts – the huge gothic Royal Courts of Justice – would be nothing but crushed rubble. The park, with its tennis and netball courts, cafeteria, and seat-fringed lawns, had always bustled with life, especially around lunchtime and particularly in the spring and summer months when local office workers poured into it for a brief respite from the city itself; now the grass and leafless trees – those still standing – were scorched black and the only bustle was that of milling insects, their constant droning replacing the sound of voices, of laughter.

And she noticed that the peculiarity was not just in the number of insects, but in the unusually large size of many of them. Maybe they were the meek who would inherit the Earth.

Culver stirred, groaning a little as he wakened. Kate turned to him.

His eyes flickered open and she saw alertness spring into them. There was something more, too: the spectre of deep dread was visible for just an instant as he looked into the drifting mists. Kate quickly touched his face.

'It's all right, we're safe,' she said softly.

He relaxed only slightly and stared up at the white sky. 'It's hot.'

'Humid, almost tropical. The sun must be fierce beyond the mists.'

'Any idea of where we are?'

'I'm pretty sure it's Lincoln's Inn Fields.'

'Uh-huh, I know it.' He raised himself on both elbows. 'It used to be pleasant.' He turned his face towards hers and she saw the question.

'I'm all right,' she told him. 'A little battered, a little bruised, but alive.'

'Did we all make it?'

'I don't know – I think so. Wait – Strachan didn't get out.'

Memories rushed in and his eyes narrowed as if from pain. 'An engineer fell. Two others went down before we even got into the shaft. And Farraday, the others, Bryce . . .'

'I don't think they had a chance. There were explosions before we got to the ventilation plant. And fire . . .' Kate shrugged.

She felt Culver appraising her and was conscious of the bedraggled mess she presented, with her torn clothes, tangled, matted hair and grime-smeared skin.

Culver saw the softness of her features, the sadness in her brown eyes. The man's torn shirt she wore was too large and made her look small, vulnerable, and younger than her years. As yet, the ordeal had not etched irreparable lines in her skin and the dirt on her face combined with the ripped clothing to give her a waif-like appearance. He pulled her to him and, for a little while, they rested in each other's arms.

Eventually, she asked him: 'What happens now, where do we go?'

'I think Dealey may have the answer to that,' Culver replied. Despite the rain having fallen for so long, he could still smell the acridity of the scorched grass. Nearby, a blackened tree rested its length along the ground like some discarded giant charcoal stick. Vapour rising from the ground added to the haunting desolation of the scene.

'He seems to be a man who likes secrets.'

Culver's attention was drawn back to the girl. 'It's engrained in him.'

'You'd think he'd have forgotten his civil service training under these circumstances.'

'It's precisely these circumstances he's been trained for. The "them and us" syndrome carries on, no matter what, only I think now there are more of "them" than "us" left. That's the way it's always been planned.'

'Do we have a chance?'

'While we've got him we do. He was the only reason I got into the Kingsway Exchange, remember?'

'He needed you then.'

'Devious as he is, I don't think he'll desert us. Besides, I don't think he'll want to travel alone through what's left of this city – the dangers are too great.'

'Dangers?'

'The rats, for one.'

'You think they'd come out into the open?'

He nodded. 'They'll have a field day. Take a look at these insects: they've thrived on radiation and while there may not be much vegetation left for them to eat, there's plenty of other food around.'

She did not ask what he meant by 'other food'.

'Those that needed to may well have adapted fast. As for the rats, they must be instinctively aware they have the upper hand – look at the way they attacked us in the shelter. They may still feel uncomfortable in broad daylight, but they only have to wait for nightfall. Then, as we well know, there's the problem of rabid animals. And working a way through the ruins will be treacherous; break a leg or ankle and you're in real trouble. No, Dealey's better off in a group and he knows it. Which reminds me, my ankle's hurting like hell.'

She moved down to examine the injured limb and winced when she saw the ragged holes in his blood-soaked sock. Even the top of his boot had blood-smeared puncture marks. Untying the lace, she eased the boot off then began to gently roll down the torn sock; she was relieved to find no swelling.

'When did the rat get at you? Can you remember?'

'Clearly,' he answered. 'It was just before we closed the opening to the vent shaft. Fairbank got me through.'

'We need to clean the wound.'

She reached into a pocket and pulled out a crumpled but unused handkerchief. 'I'll wrap this around it for now and pull the sock back up to keep it in place. We'll have to find somewhere to bathe it, and we'll need antiseptic.'

'Thank God Clare kept us regularly dosed against their disease.' A shadow passed over Kate's face as she thought of the doctor's terrible death. She busied herself with the handkerchief, folding it carefully to make a rough dressing. 'Your ear's been cut through too, Steve,' she informed him, 'and there's a nasty gash in your temple. They'll need looking at.'

Culver touched the wounds, then closed his eyes, quickly opening them again when his thoughts became even more vivid. He stared into the surrounding fog and Kate became aware that he was trembling. She assumed it was a reaction to the previous night's events and quickly changed position to put an arm around his shoulder.

'You did what you could for all of them, Steve. Don't let it prey on your mind. You can't be responsible for all our lives.'

His words were sharp as he pulled away. 'I know that!'

Kate did not allow the rebuttal; she moved with him. 'What is it, Steve? There's something more that you won't tell me. Clare mentioned something to me back there in the shelter, when you were sick. You were delirious, talking, calling out for someone. Clare thought it was a woman, a girl, someone who meant a great deal to you and who drowned. You've never told me, Steve, not in all the time we were inside the shelter; can't you tell me now?'

Kate was surprised to see a smile appear, albeit a bitter one.

'Clare got it wrong. It wasn't someone close and it wasn't a girl. It was a machine.'

She stared at him in confusion.

'A goddam helicopter, Kate. Not a person, not a wife or lover; a Sikorsky S61 helicopter.' His short laugh expressed the bitterness of his smile. 'I crashed the bloody thing because of my own stupid carelessness.'

She was relieved, but could not understand why the memory still haunted him.

As if reading her mind, he added, 'I crashed her into the sea and eighteen men went down with her.'

It made sense to her now: his frequent remoteness, the aloofness towards the happenings around them and the decisions that had had to be made, yet the reckless bravery to save others, the risks he took. For some reason he blamed himself for the deaths of these eighteen men and, a natural survivor, he disdained his own survival. He had no death wish, of that she was sure, but his 'life' wish was not so strong either. So far it seemed to be the survival of others that drove him on, starting at the very beginning with Alex Dealey. She hesitated for a moment, but she had to dare to ask, had to know how justified his guilt feelings were.

'Will you tell me what happened?' she said.

At first, when the coldness crept into his blue-grey eyes, she thought he would decline; then his gaze swept past her, staring intently into the mist as if seeing the destruction beyond. Whatever inner battle was taking place, it was soon resolved. Perhaps his own guilt feelings paled into insignificance against this vast obscene backdrop, itself a devastating indictment of *mankind*'s culpability; or perhaps he had just wearied of his self-inflicted penance and felt admission – confession? – would expel its demons. Whatever the motive, he lay back against the scorched grass and began to tell her.

'Years ago, when the North Sea oil boom really took off, the big charter companies found themselves desperately short of helicopter pilots to ferry oil-rig crews back and forth. Bristow's could take an experienced single-wing pilot and turn him into an experienced chopper pilot in three months, with no charge for the training; an agreement to work for them for at least two years was the only stipulation. I signed on, went through their training, but unfortunately didn't quite manage to fulfil the contract.'

He avoided her eyes and flicked at a fly that was buzzing close to his head.

'The money and conditions were great,' Culver went on, 'so was the company. There wasn't much risk involved because flying wasn't permitted under extreme weather

conditions; occasionally an emergency would take us out at
such times, and now and again bad weather caught us
without warning. The morning my chopper went down into
the sea started perfectly: sun shining, calm waters, little
breeze. I guess if it hadn't been like that, none of us would
have survived.'

He fell into silence once more and Kate thought he had
changed his mind, had decided the memory was best left
undisturbed. He looked at her as if asking her trust and, by
lying close beside him, head resting against his shoulder,
she gave it.

'I had a full load,' he finally went on. 'Twenty-six passengers – engineers, riggers, a relief medical team – and everyone seemed cheered by the fine weather. I remember the
sun dazzling off the water as if it were no more than a huge
placid lake. We took off and flew at a height of fifteen
hundred feet towards our designated oil rig. We were soon
over it and flying past, gradually descending to our inbound
level . . .'

Kate raised her head and looked at him in puzzlement.

'Sorry,' he said. 'Standard procedure for rig landing is to
fly five miles beyond, descend to two hundred feet and head
back, preferably with the wind behind. The rig shows on
radar, although the blip disappears from the scanner when
it's within a mile's range; after that you rely on sight.

'Everything was normal, no problems at all. I was still on
the outbound course, levelling off, when we ran smack into a
thick sea mist.'

He shivered, his body becoming tense, and Kate held him
tight.

'It was sudden, but no cause for alarm. I turned the
machine and headed back in the direction of the rig, flying
even lower to keep visual contact with the sea. I should have

risen above the fog bank, but I figured we were close to the rig and would soon be clear of the mist. But you see, the fog was shifting and moving in the same direction – that's why it had come up on us so swiftly when we were outbound. Then, without any warning, I had nothing at all to focus on.

'I should have switched to instrument flying, but I was confident I could rely on my own instincts to take us clear; all I had to do was maintain a constant altitude. The Civil Aviation Authority has a term for it: "Pilot disorientation", an overwhelming compulsion for a pilot to believe in his own senses rather than what his instruments tell him. They say it's a common phenomenon, even among the most experienced aircrew; all I know is that my stupidity cost the lives of those men.'

'Steve, you can't blame yourself.' She tugged at his collar as if to shake sense into him.

'I can, and I do,' he said quietly. 'Every pilot who has lost his aircraft and killed his passengers and who has himself survived feels the same way, even when no fingers are pointed at him. It's something there's just no refuge from.'

She saw it was pointless to argue at that moment. 'Tell me what happened,' she said, and this time there was no reluctance on his part to continue.

'We hit the sea and bounced off. We hit again and the floor was ripped out. One of the flotation tanks must have been damaged, too, because next time we hit, the copter flipped over and sank.

'I found myself outside, lungs full of freezing water. Don't ask me how I got out, I don't remember; maybe through an escape hatch, or maybe I just floated through the ripped floor. I was semi-conscious, but I could see the helicopter below, sinking fast, disappearing into that deep, never-ending gloom. I broke surface, coughing water, half-drowned, that murky vision already working its own special torture. I tried to get rid of my lifejacket, tried to tear it off so I could go back down, help those still trapped inside the helicopter, anything to relieve me of my guilt there and then, even if it meant my own death; but other hands grabbed me, held me there. My junior captain had escaped, too, and was clinging to me, one of the surviving riggers helping him. They stopped me diving and sometimes I curse them for it.

'Only eight of us made it. Other bodies were recovered later, but most went down with the Sikorsky. We were lucky that another helicopter was preparing for take-off on another rig close to the one we were headed for; when we lost radio contact and disappeared from the radar scanner, it was sent out to search for us. By the time it reached our last point of contact, the fog bank had drifted on and we were visible. They winched us aboard just in time; any longer and the cold would have finished us, even though the weather itself was mild.'

Culver sighed deep and long, as though some of the pain had been released with the telling. His voice became flat, unemotional. 'The wreckage was never recovered, so the investigators couldn't be sure if instrument failure had been involved; but from my own account and my co-pilot's, "pilot disorientation" was assumed. The CAA rarely classes it as a sign of incompetence or negligence, so no action was taken against me. It was my fault, of course, but not officially, and no one voiced any accusations.'

'And yet you blamed yourself,' said Kate.

'If I'd followed the book, those people would still be alive.'

'I can't answer that, Steve. It seems trite to say that accidents will always happen, even to the most careful. The fact that you weren't accused, not even in private, surely absolves you from any responsibility.'

'The company didn't ask me to complete my contract.'

'Do you really wonder at that? My God, they wouldn't be so heartless.'

'It may have been the best thing for me, to fly that same route, to try to carry on as normal.'

'How could your employers know that? It could have been the worst thing to have done. I can't believe you've been so foolish as to allow guilt to shadow your life for so long.'

'It hasn't, Kate. Oh, it was bad for a long, long time, but gradually the thoughts found their own little hideaway at the back of my mind. I wasn't too well received at other companies after the crash, despite the inquiry's findings, and I was desperate to get back in the air. I needed to find my own peace.'

The perspiration that trickled from his forehead was due to something more than humidity. 'Thank God an old friend came along just at the right time. Harry McKay and I learned to fly together and we'd kept in loose contact over the years. He suggested our own charter company; he'd handle the business side, I'd do the flying. Harry had a little money of his own and knew where he could find more. We'd be up to our ears in debt for a few years, but it would be our own company and eventually all the profits would be ours. Debt or no debt, profit or no profit, I jumped at the chance. From that moment on we were so busy that I was able to keep those bad memories suppressed, even though I was always aware they were lurking on that shelf, ready to slip down—'

'Or be taken down and dusted off? Is that what you do from time to time?'

He twisted his head to see her face. 'You're harder than you look,' he said.

'No, I just hate to see someone indulge themselves in self-torment. You were cleared by the inquiry and by your own company, even though everybody loves a scapegoat. It seems to me you've been punishing yourself because the authorities didn't. Maybe you'll take this world destruction on your shoulders, too. Sure, you can take my part of the burden as well. I don't need it.'

'You're being bloody—'

'Silly? Am I really? Isn't guilt supposed to be a primary condition of the human psyche?'

He smiled. 'Is this meant to shake me out of my self-pitying stupor?'

Kate tried to turn away, her anger flaring, but he held her. 'I'm sorry,' he said. 'I know what you're trying to do and I'm not mocking. I'd even go as far as to say I'm grateful. But just telling you about it has already helped. It's as if I've let something go, set those memories free. Maybe I was the gaoler of my own memories all this time, when all they wanted was to be set loose. And what you said about this world destruction is partly true: it doesn't minimize what happened on that day, but it kind of overshadows it.'

She relaxed against him. 'Haven't you spoken about the accident to anyone else before?'

'Couple of people, Harry for one. Usually in drinking sessions.'

'Was the other person a woman?'

'No. As a matter of fact, it was a doctor. Not a shrink. Just an ordinary GP. You want to hear about it?'

She nodded against his shoulder.

'About a year after the accident I developed sore testicles – at least, that was what it felt like to me. You can smile, but when that happens to a man he fears the worst. I let it ride for a while, but it got no better. Finally, I went to see my doctor and he diagnosed an inflamed prostate, said it was due to stress. I offered that flying was a stressful occupation, but he was smarter than that. He explained that after the helicopter went down and all those lives had been lost, I had kept my emotions in check, had never allowed the breakdown that should have naturally followed – not necessarily a huge, hysterical breakdown, you understand, but perhaps a brief nervous collapse. I hadn't allowed it and the body won't be fooled. The inflamed prostate was a physical manifestation substituting for a mental one. The damage wasn't permanent, just a little uncomfortable for a while, and eventually it passed.'

'But the anguish didn't.'

'No, I told you – it found its little place to rest on. I guess the point I'm trying to make is that my only penalty for a stupid mistake was sore balls, when it was death for all those others, misery for their families. Doesn't that strike you as hilarious?'

'You suffered more than that. And it's never stopped for you, no matter how much you kept the hurt inside. You talk of penalties without realizing that life itself doesn't punish us; it's something we confer on ourselves. We create our own atonement. We manufacture our own crucifix and nail ourselves to it.'

Culver was momentarily too surprised to answer. Whether or not he agreed with Kate's philosophy, he knew he had misjudged her. He should have realized there was more to her by the way she had adapted inside the shelter, how she had helped Clare Reynolds nurse the sick, himself included, how quickly she had accepted – no, adjusted to – the hideous and traumatic change in all their lives. And she had proved she was no fluttering, fainting damsel in their escape from the shelter.

'Why are you looking at me like that?' Kate asked. 'Haven't you heard a thing I've been saying?'

'Oh yes, I've heard.' He kissed her forehead. 'And you may be right. How come you didn't mention all this before?'

Her exasperation rapidly vanished. 'How come you didn't tell me about the crash before?'

Culver was about to reply when movement caught his eye. 'It'll have to keep. Looks like the others are stirring.'

'Steve . . .' She pulled at him as he began to rise.

He looked down at her quizzically and she returned his kiss.

A frightened voice called out. 'Oh God, where is everybody?' Culver answered. 'Take it easy, Ellison. You're safe enough.' He pulled on his boot and reluctantly got to his feet, gazing down at Kate as he rose. He gently touched her hair before walking over to the engineer, limping slightly as he went. Kate followed.

The others were waking, disturbed by Ellison's shout. They stared around them, startled by the mist. Culver did a quick check as he approached: Ellison, Dealey, Fairbank stretched out beneath a fallen tree. Jackson and one other engineer, a man he knew as Dene. Five of them, he and Kate, making seven. Had they lost others in their flight through the ruins? He didn't think so; the rest had probably drowned or been torn to pieces by the vermin back inside the shelter. Or maybe even burned to death: the choice of death was varied.

Ellison looked relieved to see him. 'What is this place?' he asked, rising.

'As far as we can make out, it's what used to be Lincoln's Inn Fields,' Culver replied. 'What's left of it.'

Ellison tried to penetrate the mist. 'The rats . . .?'

'Stay calm. We left them back in the shelter. We're safe for now.'

Dealey had risen only to his knees as if the world was still unsteady. 'This fog – is it a dust cloud?'

'Use your head.' Culver grabbed his arm and hauled him up. 'Can't you feel the heat, the humidity? After all that rain and with the sun beating down, the place has become a steam bath. And if that makes you uncomfortable, just wait until the insects start biting.' He turned towards the fallen tree. 'How're things, Fairbank?'

The small stocky engineer yawned, then grinned back at him. 'Things is hungry.'

'That sounds healthy enough. Jackson, Dene?'

The two other engineers looked less happy. They rose and joined the others, eyes warily watching their surroundings.

'Any injuries?' Culver asked of them all.

'Do bruises and grazes count?' said Fairbank, reaching the group.

'Only rat bites and broken limbs are eligible.'

'Then I'm not even in the race.'

'Check yourself, anyway. You never know what you did to yourself back there.'

Each man examined his clothing for tears and his skin for abrasions. There were cuts and plenty of bruises, but no bites.

'We were lucky,' Fairbank said.

'Luckier than those poor bastards we left behind,' Jackson remarked angrily and a silence fell over them.

It seemed natural that Dealey should break the silence. 'We must get away from here. I believe it's still not safe to be out here in the open.'

Each man, soul-weary and afraid of what lay ahead for them, studied the dishevelled Ministry man with quiet, brooding disdain, as though now holding him solely responsible for the deaths of their colleagues and friends left behind in the Exchange. Kate sensed and shared their contempt, yet oddly felt a tinge of pity for Dealey. He stood among them, a small, balding, middle-aged man, his clothing torn, his face and hands filthy, his shoulders – his *whole* demeanour – stooped and tremulous, and she knew it was wrong of them to attribute so much blame to him. The grand folly was universal.

She broke the tension, anxious to avoid the confrontation that was looming and which would be so pointless. 'Will it be possible to get out of London?' she asked, not just of Dealey but of all of them.

Dealey, no fool and aware of their resentment, was grateful for her question. 'Yes, yes, of course. But there is an easier way than going overland. And there is still a safe place for us here in the city—'

'What city, you—' Jackson took a step towards Dealey, but Culver held his arm.

'Easy,' he said. 'I think I know where Dealey means. First, though, we've got a few minor things to take care of. I could do with some food, for one, and I think we need to rest up a little more before making plans. Besides, I've got a rat bite that I need treated before I do any more walking.'

'We can't stay here,' Dealey insisted. 'This very mist may be thick with radiation.'

'I doubt it. The most critical time is over and besides, the long rainfall must have flushed most, if not all, the radiation away. Anyway, we've spent a whole night in the open; if we were going to be poisoned, it'll have happened by now.'

'But there's been no All-clear.'

'Christ, get it into your head, Dealey: there's never going to be an All-clear. There's no one left to give such a signal.'

'That's not true. There are other shelters, many of them; the main government shelter under the Embankment will still be intact, I'm sure.'

'Then why no communication from them?'

'A breakdown somewhere. EMP, collapse of the cable tunnels – any number of things could have broken our communications with other stations.'

'Let's cut out the crap,' Ellison interrupted. 'Right now we need food and maybe something for self-protection, if we can find anything. I don't like the idea of travelling unarmed.'

Jackson agreed. 'This looks like as good a place as any to rest up in. At least it's open ground and man, I'm sick of confined spaces.' He turned to Dene who nodded in agreement.

Fairbank just grinned approval and Kate said, 'You need something on that wound, Steve. It looks clean enough and there's no puffiness around the bite, but you never can tell.'

Culver frowned at Dealey. 'I'd rather we all stayed together, but if you want, you can go your own way. It's up to you.'

After a moment's hesitation, Dealey said, 'I'll stay.'

Culver hid his relief: the civil servant had too much valuable 'inside' knowledge for them to have let him leave. 'Okay, let's decide on who our scavengers are going to be.'

'I'll be one,' Fairbank promptly volunteered. 'And you won't be the other,' he told Culver. 'We'll try and find antiseptics, medicines and analgesics along with some food, while you rest that leg. I know the area and where to head for; let's hope we can burrow our way into some of the shops.' He wiped sweat from his face and neck with his hands, then glanced at Jackson and Dene. 'You two game?'

'Sure, we know the area too,' Jackson said for them both. Dene, a thin, sallow-complexioned man in his early twenties, appeared less certain, but did not feel inclined to argue. However, he thought of something that the others seemed to have overlooked. 'How we gonna find our way back in this fog? I mean, the streets won't exactly be the same, will they?'

'Is your wristwatch the type with hands?' Culver asked. The engineer nodded. 'You can just see the haze of the sun. Got it? Okay, south is midway between the hour hand and twelve o'clock. It'll give you a rough bearing on where the park is; once you locate it you'll soon find us. Try and get back within the hour and save us some worry.'

'If you can find anything left to burn, a fire might help us,' Jackson suggested.

'We'll manage something. Just be careful and don't take any chances.'

Fairbank clicked his tongue against his teeth and pointed. The three men set off together, backs to the sun, heading towards the area that had once been High Holborn.

Culver and the others watched the mist swallow them up. It was an eerie and foreboding sight, and the immense emptiness they left behind had little to do with unoccupied space.

Culver shook off the feeling, concentrating on the task in hand. 'Kate, will you help Ellison collect wood – branches, fencing, anything that hasn't burned to charcoal – and bring it here? Any paper would help too – search the litter bins. And keep within shouting distance.'

Ellison appeared ready to object, but evidently thought better of it. He walked away, a hand brushing flies from the air before him, and Kate went with him.

Culver slowly turned to face the last man left with him. 'Just me and you now, Dealey. I've got one or two questions and you're going to give me straight answers. If not, I'll break your bloody neck.'

22

Alex Dealey shifted uncomfortably against the tree stump, its blackened, jagged shape rising above him like an accusing finger pointed at the night sky. Not far away, the fire that had been kindled earlier in the day and constantly fed with anything that would burn, hued the mist orange. The blaze was welcome not just for its warmth against the sudden chill of the night air, but because it held the all-prevailing darkness at bay, and with it, its terrors. The others, except Culver and the girl, who it would appear had found warmth and comfort in each other, stayed close to the protective glow, gazing into the brightness, conversing in low-murmured voices. Occasionally laughter broke the quiet tones, although never raucous, always subdued, as if the men were afraid the sound might carry to hostile ears. Dealey stayed apart from the group, his hunched shoulders covered by one of the blankets the three engineers had brought back with them from their forage into the ruins, for their resentment of him was obvious, unequivocal, and discomforting. Fools. Ungrateful bloody fools.

He pulled the blanket over his head, holding the sides tight under his chin so that he resembled a huddled monk, only his nose and the tip of his chin caught in the fire glow. He smelled of insect repellent and antiseptic ointment, these too salvaged from the ravaged city, and a plaster covered a cut on his forehead, another a larger wound on the back of his hand, both injuries sustained in their escape from the shelter. The three engineers had been gone longer than expected, causing concern among those who had stayed. There had been no need to worry, though, for their delay had been caused by the amount of useful items they had managed to scavenge.

Quite a few of the shops had been destroyed by fire, while others had been completely buried by the debris of office blocks they were housed beneath; some, however, although badly damaged, could be reached by cautious digging. Two café-restaurants, a hardware store and a pharmacist had been unearthed, and Jackson had remembered an up-market bedding centre from where they had retrieved sheets and blankets in which they could carry their prizes. The men were ashen-faced when they returned, not even the accumulation of dirt disguising their skin's paleness, and had refused to speak of the harrowing sights they had witnessed, only Fairbank mentioning that piles of bodies had been blasted into corners or against rubble mounds like so much litter by fierce winds. They had come across no living person.

The fire, lit with a lighter taken from a corpse by Ellison, had been a beacon to them in the humid mists once they had found their way back to the desolated square in which the blackened park was situated, and they had proudly, if quickly, displayed their spoils. Four short-handled axes, honed to a lethal sharpness, two hammers, and six long knives had been brought back as utensils or weapons, whichever purpose they lent themselves to at any time. Flashlights, already battery-loaded, thin rope, spoons, scissors, two can-openers, paper cups, a miniature camping stove along with a Calor gas cylinder, had been retrieved from the hardware store. From the pharmacist (which had proved the hardest to enter, but considered worth the risk and effort) came bandages, Band-aids, cotton wool, antiseptic cream, insect repellent, bicarbonate of soda, glucose tablets and vitamin pills, water purifying Sterotabs and, considered extremely important, three rolls of toilet tissue. Fairbank discreetly handed Kate two small packages which Dealey guessed contained tampons (he also suspected birth control pills were wrapped up with them, for he knew that Dr Reynolds had strongly encouraged all the surviving women in the shelter to use the contraceptive tablets thoughtfully provided by the government among the medical supplies).

The few battery-operated radios they had come upon were either completely dead or had only emitted heavy static. As for food, they had taken whatever canned items they could find, but not too much for it would prove too cumbersome and, once they travelled on, finding further supplies should not present too great a problem. The three engineers had expressed delight at how much canned food was kept by the café-restaurants as they produced their tinned harvest of beans, soup, chicken breast in jelly, ham, sausages, tongue, peas, asparagus, carrots, peaches, pineapple chunks, condensed milk, and coffee. Cans of Coke and lemonade were also brought along in case they could not find an adequate source of water. They had all laughed when Culver had admitted he was glad they had decided not to bring back a *lot* of food.

Fairbank received loud commendations when he produced two bottles of Black Label Johnnie Walker.

Food was heated in its tins on the small stove while Kate treated and dressed the various wounds among the group. They were all grateful for the insect repellent, for the air was plagued with pests. Equal shares of food were dispersed among the plastic cups and nobody seemed to mind the agglutination of meat and vegetables; they ate as though this was their first meal for weeks and was to be their last for a similar period. The dessert followed in new cups and Coke was drunk straight from the tins. Jackson almost upstaged Fairbank with his whisky by producing four packs of cigarettes from his trouser pockets like a magician manifesting cute rabbits from thin air.

The alcohol, the cigarettes, and the filled stomachs contrived to create a mood of calmness, a natural enough counter-balance to the tension they had endured for so long. They spoke of their future hopes rather than the past tragedy, each one unconsciously trying to evoke some aspiration, something that could be salvaged from their shattered lives.

Dealey had not shared in the conversation, but had sat moodily staring into the fire.

Dusk fell swiftly, more swiftly than was natural for that time of year, and the steam, slowly dissipating throughout the long afternoon, fell low as if humbled by the incredible sunset that followed. They stood as one and gazed into the western sky, their upturned faces bathed in the reflected flare.

The huge, swift-rolling clouds, a confused combination of alto-cumulus and nimbo-stratus, were coloured in violent shades of red, orange, and yellow, their bellies streaked a dazzling gold, their ragged heights pure vermilion. They moved like mountains across the sky, vivid and powerful, overwhelmingly beautiful, and as the survivors watched they felt the earth itself could ignite once more by being so close to their boiling fury. Even though the sun's fiery brilliance was diffused by clouds and atmospheric dust, they could not look directly at it, for its intensity was too blinding, its effulgence too destructive; the sun, too, seemed outraged by the satellite planet which had dared to re-create a facsimile power to its own.

Jagged glittering streaks patterned the sky like thin, dashed brushstrokes; these were not clouds but dust particles, coalesced and held aloft by warm, rising air currents. In the far distance some were descending vertically like heaven-thrown javelins.

The sky to the east was no less stunning, although its redness was more crimson, its clouds a deep amber in parts. All movement was in that direction as if sucked in by some giant vortex beyond the horizon. The spectacle was both awesome and frightening.

As they watched, spellbound, the red boiling anger gradually subsided, for the sun was sinking further into the horizon, turning the dusk into a softer, less frenzied vision, a warm richness subduing the violent-tossed clouds so that their hurried drifting became graceful, flowing rather than rushing.

The sun disappeared – and again, its descent seemed unnaturally fast – casting in its wake a shimmering radiance that lit the underbellies of the clouds so they seemed glutted with blood. Darkness encroached, a definite curve, vignetted only slightly, moving steadily but warily forward as if afraid of being scorched. With it came a half-moon, indistinct and rust-stained, peeping only occasionally through the clouds, as though reluctant to bear witness to the spoiled earth below.

The temperature had cooled with the sun's fading, but only slightly; still the group moved closer to the fire and Dealey wondered if a primitive fear had been reborn. There was a silence between them for some time, each person intimidated yet uplifted by what they witnessed. Gradually, conversation resumed and more food was cooked and con-sumed. The second whisky bottle was emptied.

Evening became night and stars were hidden behind clouds and dust that layered the upper atmosphere; the elusive half-moon changed from russet to a pale sanguine (like the last of Christ's blood on the Cross, Dealey had thought, the final trickle that had run like water; perhaps the moon reflected the blood spilt below). Dealey moved away from the fire, tired of the others' attitude towards him, resenting their scorn. They didn't – *couldn't* – understand his importance to them, how he and he alone had seen them through the worst of the disaster, guided them through those early days, organizing, administrating – *taking on the damned responsibility*! The events of the day, with its discoveries, and the relief from the violence of the preceding night, had obviously enhanced their drunkenness, for they treated him as though he, personally, had pressed the button that had precipitated this third and final world war. It was a mood that classified government circulars dealing with what was termed the 'ultimate confrontation' had warned against. Civil unrest, aggression against the authoritative body. Subver-sion, anarchy, revolution. Events inside the Kingsway shelter had proved the correctness of the government view. And even now, when he had led this miserable few to safety (in that his knowledge had provided the escape route) they treated him with disrespect.

He shivered, glad of the blanket, for the warm clamminess of the evening had finally given way to the night's chill. He had watched Culver and the girl leave the fireside, they too taking a blanket with them (for warmth or cover?). It was obvious why they wanted to be alone. Wonderful aphrodisiac was death.

He shook his head, the movement lost beneath the blanket. Culver could have been a useful ally, yet he chose to side with the ... the – Dealey refused to allow the word to form in his mind, but the thought was there anyway – the rabble. The pilot's interrogation earlier in the day had been discourteous to say the least. Harsh, even brutal, might be more appropriate.

—*Exactly how many entrances to the main government headquarters below the Embankment were there?*—

—*Would some still be accessible?*—

—*Could the shelter have been flooded?*—

—*Specify the separate tunnels leading to it*—

—*When was the shelter built?*—

—*Before which World War: this one, the last one, or the first?*—

—*Had the government been prepared for this war?*—

—*How long before the bombs dropped was the evacuation into the shelter taking place? Hours, days, weeks?*—

—*How many days?*—

—*What number of people could the shelter hold?*—

—*Jesus, how were they all chosen?*—

—*Apart from government and military personnel*—

—*What skills and what trades?*—

—*Why those? What bloody influence did they have on the government? What made them so valuable?*—

—*Planners? What the hell could they plan except how to make money from the ashes?*—

—*How long could everybody exist down there?*—

A pause. An angry, tight-lipped pause. And then

—*Would they, this small group of survivors, be allowed in?*—

Dealey had answered the questions, calmly at first, but eventually becoming outraged, himself, by Culver's anger. He, Dealey, was only a minion, he didn't run the bloody show, he wasn't privy to every government document or decision. If he had been, he would have been inside the headquarters his bloody self! He just wished they would all get it into their thick skulls that he was nothing more than a glorified bloody building inspector! That was the only reason he had keys and inside knowledge. All right, he was intended to be one of the privileged few, but wasn't included in the early evacuation and, as it turned out, he was lucky to have survived at all. And someone had to take charge down there, in the Exchange, otherwise the survivors would have degenerated into a disorganized, defeatist mob!

His outburst had meant nothing to Culver, for the questioning was not yet over. The pilot was curious about the rats.

Unlike before, when Dealey had been questioned inside the shelter on this special breed of vermin, he finally (and it was obvious to Culver, with no remorse over his previous lie) admitted that he knew they had not been entirely eliminated, nor could they be unless the whole of London's underground network, the sewers, the canals, the railway tunnels, and all basement areas were filled with poison gases or compounds, and even then there would have been no guarantee of total eradication. The task would be too dangerous and too immense. And the vermin could always flee into the surrounding suburbs. Even so, the numbers were thought to be so small that there would be no real danger to the community as a whole and certainly a massive purge on the vermin would cause unnecessary panic in the capital's populace. Far better to be vigilant and act swiftly and silently should there be evidence that they were growing in numbers.

Culver had not been satisfied. Dealey knew more – or at least, suspected more – than he was saying. The time for secrecy had long passed and, Culver warned, the others in their group might not be as tolerant as he if they suspected Dealey was still withholding information. The older man had protested that there really was nothing more to tell. Except . . . Except . . . yes, there was a certain rumour circulating in various ministerial departments, a rumour that did not rouse much curiosity and therefore had died as swiftly as it had begun.

Dealey had been vague about the story for he honestly did not recall the details, but the pilot had pressed him further, his eyes keen and searching. Something about . . . let me see . . . about a certain kind of rat – several, in fact, of this mutant species – in captivity. It was said that they were under observation in a government research laboratory, possibly – no, probably – being allowed to breed. The only interesting part of this rumour was that the creatures were apparently undergoing some extraordinary genetic transformation. There were two types of mutant vermin, he had explained, the kind resembling the normal Black rat, and another, which was a grotesque. It was the grotesque that the scientists were particularly interested in.

He had been afraid the younger man would strike him then. Why hadn't he told them all this before? Why had the government been so secretive about the mutants; what was there to fear? Culver had actually drawn his fist back and Dealey had stepped away, his own arm raised for protection. That movement may have saved him from the other man's wrath, for the rage disappeared from Culver's eyes and his fist dropped limply to his side. The anger was replaced by disgust.

There had been no further questions. Culver had walked away to sit by a blackened, branchless tree and had not spoken another word until Ellison and the girl returned with firewood.

Dealey was relieved (there was enough hatred directed towards him) that the pilot did not mention their conversation to the others later in the day; he was also somewhat contemptuous. Well, Mr Culver, who was withholding information now? Did he consider they already had enough to worry about? WAS IT NOT IN THE PUBLIC INTEREST? With privileged knowledge came responsibility; perhaps you've learned that today. Dealey had allowed himself a covert smile.

The fire still burned brightly, for the men around it kept the flames fed with more scavenged wood, but the heat did not reach Dealey at his huddled position against the mutilated tree. Beneath the blanket, his eyelids began to close, his chin began to drop to his chest.

Sleep took him in slow stages, for trepidation did battle with fatigue: the night and darkness were something to fear. And so were his dreams.

He was descending a steep, spiral staircase, the steps made of stone, worn and rounded as though many centuries of footsteps had preceded his. He thought the descent would never end and his head was giddy with the constant circle; his legs were becoming numb, his back aching with the constant jarring. One hand reached out for the wall at his side and his fingers recoiled at the slimy wetness of the stonework. The stickiness was yellow-green, the colour of phlegm, and suddenly he was descending the throat of some massive beast and the twisting corridors he finally found himself in were its intestines. Something or someone was waiting for him, somewhere ahead. He did not know if it would be in the creature's abdomen – or in its bowels. His feet slipped in the viscous fluid that lined the curling tunnel and the odour of rotting dead grew stronger with each step. At one stage hysteria seized him, flicking out from the darkness ahead like a lizard's tongue, and he turned in its grip as if to flee, but the fleshy corridor behind had shrunk so that there was no way back. He was drawn into the darkness, no longer capable of movement by himself.

They were waiting for him in a vast underground hall, perhaps a cavern, perhaps a crypt, and they grinned, but made no sound as he entered. Isobel was there, wearing the billowing, flowery dress he detested so much, the ridiculous straw hat with its cherries on the brim, and pink gloves that were meant for washing dishes and not the Queen's garden party, an invitation to which she still waited (yearned) for. His sons were there, even the eldest who should have been overseas, blown to pieces on foreign soil, and their wives and children with them, all grinning, even the baby. There were others that he knew in the crowd – colleagues, his immediate superior at the Ministry, neighbours, and there was the ticket collector at his local railway station, and an archbishop he had once met at a dinner function, although he hadn't worn his full canonicals then – but most were strangers. Although they *all* bore one marked similarity. It was easy to spot, no problem at all, and he remarked upon it as they surged forward, surrounding him, grinning, grinning, grinning, revealing their teeth, the two long ones in front, the incisors, drooling wet, glistening sharp; for the heads were those of rats, even the baby's who turned from suckling its mother's swollen breast to grin at him, its jaws smeared with the blood that came from its mother's nipple . . .

He wrenched away from the rat that nibbled at his arm, but the others crowded in on him, locking him tight among them, and Isobel leaned forward to kiss him, only her lips were bared and the teeth ready to sink into him. She ignored his rebuff and nuzzled his cheek, her smell choking him so that his throat constricted and he could hardly breathe. She drew blood and licked at it with a hairbrush-rough tongue.

She guzzled and the sound sickened him even more. His clothes were gone and they grinned at his shame. They poked his soft, overblown flesh, making appreciative noises. They bit pieces from him as though tasting delicacies; the mouthfuls became larger, more substantial, and soon they were eating into him, ignoring his protests, and as his hands touched his own face he felt bristling fur, stiffened whiskers, and his teeth were like theirs, sharp and deadly, and his hands turned to claws and they raked his own body. And even being one of them could not save him, for they stripped him of meat and fought over his heart, until he decided he'd had enough, it was a dream and it was time to leave, time to wake up before they devoured him completely. He forced his consciousness to assert itself and reluctantly, sluggishly, it obeyed, drawing him away, back through the slimy, twisting corridors, up the spiral staircase, family, friends and others snapping after him, still grinning, enjoying the game, upwards, upwards, higher and higher, a light ahead, closer, a bright light . . .

Awakening.

Awakening to another bad dream.

23

They stood like grey spectres in the mist, unmoving yet somehow tenuous, like shadows cast on shallow water. They were silently watching the sleeping forms spread around the still-glowing embers of the fire.

Dealey nervously rose to a sitting position, careful not to make a sound, at first wondering if this was merely a continuation of his dream. The blanket, which had remained over his head as he had sunk into his uneasy sleep the night before, slid onto his shoulders. He tried to count the spectral figures, but could not be sure if some were only stunted tree trunks, the morning mist – although not as dense as the previous day's – contriving to deceive. He was tempted to call out, to greet them or at least alert the others of his own group, but the cry stayed in his throat: there was something menacing in the vaporous silhouettes' unmoving, silent stance. Dealey pressed his back against the charcoaled tree stump.

An insect droned in front of him before touching down on his eyebrow, immediately sucking moisture gathered there. Dealey blinked, twitching his face to frighten the fly off, afraid to slap it away. The insect, fearlessly large, refused and its host was forced to jerk his head. The fly angrily droned away, but now a trickle of sweat running into the crevice by the side of his nose sought to torment him. Cautiously he lowered his head and brushed his face against the hand resting on his upraised knees, blaming the sweat on humidity and not fear.

One of the figures was moving, drawing nearer to the recumbent bodies, becoming more visible. Dealey held his breath as the tall black man leaned over a heaped blanket, studying the sleeper beneath. The man wore a shapeless see-through plastic mac, buttoned at the neck like a cape, and in one hand he carried a rifle, in the other, a rusty butcher's knife. He stood erect once more, then moved on to another sleeping form. This time he used the blade to draw back the blanket.

The other figures were emerging from the mist, becoming more distinct. One of them picked up the whisky bottle lying close to the embers and drained the last few dregs. The bottle was dropped back onto the blackened earth. The sleepers were beginning to stir.

Dealey counted ten ... twelve ... fifteen, at least fifteen figures approaching the makeshift campsite, and there were two, no, three small crouched shapes moving among them. Dogs! Oh, God, they had dogs with them! Weren't these people aware of rabies?

He opened his mouth to shout, in part a warning, in part a greeting, and something smooth and hard slid along his throat. He choked as pressure was exerted, the iron bar pinning his neck against the tree stump behind. In the corners of his eyes he could see filthy, white-knuckled hands on either side of the metal bar and he knew his captor was behind the stump, arms stretched around it. Dealey felt his tongue begin to fill his mouth from the pressure.

His companions were sitting up and looking around in surprise. Dealey watched, pinned to the tree, as one still sleeping man was kicked. Ellison awoke with a shout and tried to rise; a foot against his chest flattened him. Jackson saw and protested, but the big black man pressed the discoloured butcher's knife into his cheek. Fairbank reached for the short-handled axe lying close by, but a boot pinned his wrist against the grass stubble and another kicked the tool away. Dealey began to gurgle, his eyes staring like those of a ventriloquist's dummy in a garish-pink painted face, his tongue pressing between his teeth. His heels began to kick at the ground and he tried to slide beneath the bar, but the aggressor was too strong.

The tall black man looked his way and waved the rifle. With a last spiteful jerk, the pressure against Dealey's neck was released. He slumped over, hands trying to soothe his bruised throat. A less-than-gentle nudge with the iron bar sent him scrambling to join the others. He stumbled to his knees not far from the two black men, Jackson and the raincoated man, and stole a quick look around at the intruders, twisting his head and massaging his throat as he did so.

They were a strange group, their presence made more sinister by their apparel and the assortment of weapons they carried. Much of their clothing was tattered and stained with filth, although several wore shirts and jackets that still bore the sharp creases of newness; he assumed that these had only recently been taken from partially-destroyed stores. Like the tall black man, some wore unbuttoned raincoats as if expecting the rains to return at any moment. One or two wore floppy-brimmed women's hats. Ripped T-shirts, sweaters and jeans were the main dress, and shawls were draped around the shoulders of a few. There appeared to be more blacks than whites among the group, and all carried shoulder bags or cases of some kind.

There were three women with them, two West Indian

girls, who could only have been teenagers, and an older, white woman with bedraggled yellow hair and an expression that was as stony hard as any of the men's. She wore a patterned skirt, red the dominant colour although there was no brightness to it, which almost reached the bottom of her calves; below were ankle-length socks and sneakers. A loose-fitting blue sweater and a large, light-blue silk scarf, serving as a shawl, adorned her upper body. She coughed into a hand and the sound was throaty, full of bile. The two teenagers had on tight-fit jeans and sweaters, one wearing a man's jacket despite the heat.

Dealey saw now that the rifle the tall man held was, in fact, only an air-rifle, although in his grip it looked lethal. A telescopic sight was even mounted on its top. As he glanced around, he saw that others had similar weapons, while some had handguns tucked into waistbands or pointed at the figures on the ground. By the look of them, these too were only air-pistols. The rest of their armoury consisted of knives and long stout sticks – pickaxe handles, he assumed. A frightening, unruly-looking bunch, he thought, and flinched as a dog trotted up and sniffed his feet. The animal looked as mangy as the rest of them, but at least no foam speckled its jaws and no madness glinted in its eyes. It appeared to be reasonably well-fed, too; but then acquisition of food should have been no great problem as they themselves had found. When the dog turned away, disinterested, he noticed the sores and scabs on its sides and belly; parts of its body were also free of any hair.

Dealey turned his attention back to the people and realized they, too, were in a poor condition. One side of the tall black man's face was covered in sores and an eyelid was half-closed with an angry swelling; yellow, pus-filled spots flecked his lips. Others of his group bore the same marks.

The youngest of the girls clutched her stomach as if it pained her and several of the men looked equally uncomfortable. Roughly tied bandages decorated several arms and wrists; dressings could be seen on legs through torn trousers. One, a youth of no more than nineteen, rested on crutches, favouring a foot swaddled in discoloured wrappings so that it was swollen to three times its normal size.

Unlike the creatures of Dealey's dream, none of them was grinning. But the threat they exuded was the same.

It was Jackson who spoke first. 'You gonna take this blade outa my face, brother?' He used soft tones, as if gentling a wild beast.

There was no change of expression as the other man flicked the knife across Jackson's cheek with a swift, easy movement, drawing blood. The prone engineer swore and touched his face; he drew the hand away and stared at his bloody fingers in disbelief.

'I ain't your brother, pigshit,' the other man said quietly. Someone sniggered.

Dealey began to rise, still clasping his throat, and two of the intruders moved closer. 'Who are you?' he asked, hoping the authority in his voice would carry some weight.

'Keep your mouth shut,' he was told. 'We askin' the questions, you givin' the answers.' The tall black man raised the rifle, so it was pointing at Dealey's head. 'This is a .22, almost as powerful as the real thing. It hits target, it can kill.'

'There's no need for this, I can assure—'

A pickaxe handle struck Dealey on the back of the legs and he tumbled to the ground, crying out sharply.

'I tol' you to shuddup,' the black man warned. The man who had hit Dealey stepped back and allowed the end of the thick stick to rest on the ground. There was an unhealthy pallor to his face and a redness to his eyes.

'I wanna know how you escaped the bombs,' the black man said. 'How come you weren't blown to pieces?'

'We were—' Dealey began to say.

'Not you.' He prodded Jackson with the gun barrel. 'I want the nigger to tell me.' His entourage enjoyed the humour.

'Hey, come on, man,' the engineer protested. 'Why you talkin' to me like this?'

'Jus' answer the question, pigshit.'

'We were below ground in a shelter before the bombs dropped.' He eased the end of the barrel away from his body, afraid the gun might go off. The other man allowed the movement.

'What fuckin' shelter? You govmint men or somethin'?'

Jackson realized his mistake. 'No, no, we're just engineers, man. We worked in a telephone exchange, under the streets, that's all.'

'He said it was a shelter, Royston,' the yellow-haired woman volunteered. 'I heard him call it a shelter.'

The dark man's eyes narrowed suspiciously. 'Yeah, I heard. You one of them crazy bastards who set this up?'

Jackson's eyebrows arched in surprise.

'Are you kiddin' me? I'm a fuckin' maintenance engineer, that's all. We're all telecom engineers, 'cept for . . .' He avoided looking towards Dealey. 'Come on, what's this about, man, we're all in the same trouble.'

'I figure different. You look kinda healthy, nigger. You all look kinda healthy. A lil dirty, maybe, but in pretty good condition, considerin'. We ain't seen many like you.'

'There are others?' Dealey could not help but ask. 'How many have you seen?' He received a warning tap from the handle. 'No, please, this is important. You must tell us.'

'I don't need to tell you shit.' The man called Royston – Christian name or surname, it was unimportant to Dealey, at that particular moment – strolled over. 'What you think anyway, everybody's dead? Well most are, boy, an' them that ain't oughta be. But you still ain't tol' me why you lookin' so plump and healthy. You know somethin' we don't?'

He squatted beside Dealey, the wrinkled plastic mac opening out and spreading around him, and said confidentially, 'Take a look at us, man. We got scabs an' coughs and cuts that won't heal. We got the shits and some of our brothers have died jus' from bad colds, know what I mean? See that lil sister over there? She got runnin' sores all down her body. See the guy on crutches? His foot stinks so bad we can't go near him.' His voice became almost a whisper. 'Half of 'em is dyin' an' they don't know it.'

'Are there no hospitals, no medical centres?'

'You don't hear me, mister. There's nothin', no hospitals, no help, no nothin'. The only good thing is there's no law, 'cept in what we carry.' He tapped the rifle barrel with the blade. 'We take what we want an' we do what we want, you understand?'

Dealey nodded slowly, realizing only brute force governed now. 'Are there no troops in the city?'

Royston allowed himself a short laugh and Dealey winced at the stale breath. 'Nothin'. There's nothin' left anywhere, not in the whole fuckin' world. We come from th'other side of the river thinkin' somethin' had to be left over here, but all we foun' was the dead and the walkin' dead. Sure, a few other groups like us, survivin' on what they can, killin' to get it if necess'ry. Jus' law of the jungle, what you might think is right for me, huh? So here am I gassin' an' you ain't answered one question yet.' He touched the top of the knife against Dealey's nose and his voice became harsh. 'How many of you aroun' here an' where do we find this shelter?'

'Look what I caught!' The interruption came from some

distance away and all heads turned to locate its source. Two figures came through the mist and one of them was Kate. Of course, Dealey remembered, she had drifted off with Culver the night before to find their own sleeping space. The other figure, a white man wearing trousers several times too large for him and an equally baggy jacket with just a vest beneath, was propelling her forward with one hand entwined in her hair. In the other hand he carried a curved meat-hook.

The smile behind Royston's eyes was not pleasant. He rose from his crouched position.

The other men in his group looked on with keen interest, while the blonde woman with the silk scarf regarded Kate with undisguised hostility, as though she posed a threat.

'Found her sleepin' just a little way off,' her captor announced with a grin. A red handkerchief was tied around his forehead to keep straggly hair away from his eyes. Like the others, he hadn't shaved for quite some time and there were blemishes on his skin that might have been healing burns.

'She on her own?' the man called Royston asked.

'Reckon so. She was sound asleep when I crept up on her.'

Dealey looked off into the mist. Culver, where was Culver?

The big black man stood in front of Kate. 'Not bad,' he appraised, running the back of his fingers down her cheek. 'Not great, but not bad.' He allowed his hand to stray beneath her chin, touching her neck, sliding into the open shirt collar. He felt her breast and squeezed hard.

Kate recoiled from his touch, hitting out with clenched fists. The man still gripping her hair forced Kate to her knees, while the others, wary of the men they guarded, chuckled in anticipation. Over the past few weeks they had learned that everything, anything, they could find was for the taking: food, clothing, shelter, bodies, and lives – all were included. There was no control anymore, just survival.

Royston carefully laid the air-rifle on the ground, but kept the knife blade pointing upwards, and approached Kate once more. She glared angrily at him, but fear was in the expression too. Royston laid the blade flat against her cheek and the cold steel was as repugnant as his touch. His face was only inches away and she thought the smell was from the sores and scabs on his skin and not just his breath; his ulcerated lips moved slowly, as if it hurt to talk.

'You need a lesson, white lady. You ain't got the say no more.' He twisted the blade so that the sharp edge was pressing into her cheek. Kate tried to pull away as blood seeped onto the discoloured metal but the hand in her hair held her firm.

'What the fuck you doing?' Jackson screamed, outraged by the reflection on his own race as much as the assault on the girl. He sprang forward and kicked at the other black man, sending him reeling and following through by grabbing the knife-wielding hand. Baggy Trousers let go of Kate and caught Jackson from behind, using the meat-hook to snag his shoulder, and pulled back. Jackson screamed as the curved point sank into a muscle. He was hauled off and he curled up into a tight ball as they attacked him with vicious kicks.

The two young blacks watching over Fairbank, one of them wearing a floppy-brimmed woman's hat, dared the stocky engineer with their stares to make a move. Another, a white man of considerable girth, but of tender years, held a thick arm around Dene's neck and pressed the barrel of an air-pistol into his temple. Ellison was similarly guarded and Dealey remained immobile on hands and knees.

'Stop it, you're killing him!' Kate pleaded.

'Hold it!' The big black man was on his feet once more and Kate sobbed with relief when the beating ceased. Her relief was premature.

Royston stooped to pick up the rifle and said, 'This mutha's goin' to learn the hard way. An' maybe we'll git some questions answered at th'same time. Bring him over here!'

He strode towards the remains of the fire and kicked at the ashes with his boot. Beneath the white dust, embers still glowed fiercely. 'C'mon, git him over.'

Baggy Trousers and another man caught Jackson by the elbows and dragged him to the wide circle of smouldering ashes.

'Okay, shove his face in there,' Royston pointed at the shimmering embers.

'No!' Kate screamed, rushing forward. Royston barely looked as he slapped her to the ground. He nodded to his men and stood behind the half-conscious Jackson, legs apart and gun butt resting against a hip, barrel pointing skywards.

The faces of Baggy Trousers and his accomplice were grim as they drew the kneeling engineer closer to the fire. At its edge, they leaned him over so that he was off balance. They began to force his head downwards.

Culver crept forward, crouching low, using the gradually thinning mist as cover. In one hand he held the small axe he had taken with him the night before. He and Kate had left the others chatting around the fireside, both wanting privacy, a chance to talk together. They had found a fallen tree and snuggled down beside it, Culver spreading the blanket they had brought with them and wrapping it around them when they had settled. The axe was in case any unwelcome visitors of the kind that had black fur and sharp teeth should come upon them during the night. Although it would have afforded little protection, the weapon gave him some comfort.

They had kissed, touched, a mild making of love, for both found themselves still exhausted, their fatigue preventing emotions reaching any peak; but they were content within each other's arms, happy to talk in low-murmured voices, to explore and to confide. Sleep had not taken too long to overcome them.

Culver had been the first to awake the following morning and had gently untangled himself from Kate's arms; she had stirred, mumbled something, and he had kissed her damp forehead, telling her to sleep on, it was early. Culver had walked off to relieve himself, carrying the axe as a precaution; now that it was daylight he was more cautious of rabid animals than of rats.

Near the centre of the park he had found a partly-demolished shelter. Ridiculously modest, he had stepped inside and was unzipping his jeans when the stench hit him. He took a step back in disgust and his foot slipped on something wet. His stomach heaved when he searched the gloom beneath him.

The people might have taken shelter just before the bombs had dropped – it had been around lunchtime and the park would have been crowded – or they might have crawled and staggered there afterwards. The corpses, what was left of them, were in one stagnant heap, spreading over the floor like a bulky, rumpled carpet. Yet the bodies were alive with movement. Greyish-white movement.

The maggots must have consumed most of the flesh, yet still they wriggled among the bones, forming glistening patterns in their well-ordered, almost ritual quest for sustenance.

He fled from the shelter, holding his mouth as though

unwilling to further defile their mausoleum with his own vomit. The sickness poured from him in gut-wrenching spurts. And even when his stomach was empty, the muscles there still contracted painfully, expelling empty air as if purging more than just bile from his body. It was a long time before he was able to stagger away and find another place to relieve himself.

The park itself was littered with debris blown into it from surrounding buildings and, even though it was in a sheltered position, no tree, bush, or blade of grass had been left unscathed. He avoided swarms of gross insects, knowing they bred among corpses. The mist was rising more rapidly, for the ground and ruins were becoming dry despite the weeks of heavy rainfall. Culver shakily made his way back to the fallen tree he and Kate had nestled beneath.

He was surprised to find her gone and assumed she had wandered back to the others around the campfire, thinking he had done the same. Following on, and pondering over their plan for the day (in an effort to shut the crawling tomb from his mind), Culver heard the voices before catching sight of the intruders. Something in their tone warned him that they were not friendly.

Culver crouched low, the mist still thick enough to conceal him unless he got too close. He saw them and tension filled him, easily dismissing the earlier memory. He watched as the tall black man, garbed in a ridiculous see-through raincoat, touched Kate, and Culver's hand clenched tight around the axe. Jackson sprang at the man when he held a knife against Kate's cheek, sending him to the ground, and then was himself attacked by two others.

The black stranger shouted something and Jackson was dragged towards the ashes of the fire. The girl had been knocked down and her assailant had turned his back towards him before Culver realized what was about to happen.

Jackson's face was only inches away from the smouldering embers when anger – more than just anger: it was a ferocity that filled every extremity of his body and sent seething pulses through his head – spilled from Culver in a silent scream, making his whole body tremble, his lips baring to reveal clenched teeth, a grimace of sheer hatred. Hadn't they been through enough without their own kind, survivors like themselves, subjecting them to this perverse treatment? Hadn't the destruction taught them anything? Had the madness only bred fresh madness? He restrained the cry and silently ran forward.

Culver was among them before they were even aware of his approach; the tall black man still had his back to him.

At last releasing the cry, Culver swung the axe in a sideways arc and the metal head cut deep into the raincoated man's spine, severing it completely. He had to tug hard to pull the axe free.

Royston screamed, a high, animal sound, his arms splaying outwards, throwing the weapons. He collapsed immediately and lay prone on the ground, unable to move, able only to die. His hands and feet twitched convulsively and a whining came from his scabbed lips.

Culver did not linger; his next target was one of the men holding Jackson over the ashes, a man who wore a red handkerchief around his forehead. The edge of the axe caught him beneath the chin, snapping his head upwards, toppling him onto the hot embers. Culver felt something *thwack* against his leather jacket and saw the other man pointing a gun at him. It occurred to him in an instant that he had been shot, yet there had been no gunfire and no pain.

He swung the axe again; the gun fell as the intruder who had brandished it clutched a fractured wrist.

Jackson fell face forward into the ashes and rolled over screaming, embers glowing in his dark skin.

Culver could not help him: there were too many of the enemy to contend with. He ducked as a rifle aimed at him, feeling a stinging along his cheek. The man with the rifle rushed him, using the weapon as a club.

Fairbank took advantage of the distraction. He grabbed the axe still lying nearby, bringing the blunt end up into the stomach of one of his guards. The other received the sharp end across the bridge of his nose.

The fat man holding Dene released the pellet from the air-pistol into the engineer's temple. Dene sank to his knees, hands clasping at the wound. He slumped face forward to the ground and lay there silent and still. The fat man hastily snapped open the weapon and pushed in another pellet.

Ellison attempted to run from the three men coming towards him. They easily caught him and he lashed out with fists and feet, but quickly succumbed to their concerted assault.

Catching sight of the man rushing towards Culver, Dealey threw his arms around the passing legs. The would-be assailant fell heavily and Culver stepped forward and brought a foot down hard against the back of his head. Something crunched and he hoped it was the man's nose; better still, his neck. He quickly scanned the chaos, the axe poised before him to ward off further attack.

Kate was dragging Jackson out of the fire, slapping burning embers from his face. Fairbank had just hacked at the leg of a fat man who had been waving an air-pistol in the air, his target undecided. The gun went off, the *phut* heard over the screams of the women and the excited barking of the dogs; a gusher of blood had erupted from his thigh. The injured man went down – on one leg, whimpering as he tried to stem the flow. Three other men and women stared with uncertain looks; the attack on them had been so swift and so devastating that they were perplexed. And now they, too, were afraid.

It was the blonde woman with the blue silk scarf and long skirt who broke the deadlock: with a screeching roar, she threw herself at Culver. Jagged fingernails tore at his face, only his up-flung arm protecting his eyes from serious injury. They went down in a struggling heap, Culver's back sending up a shower of ashes.

The three men advanced, spurred on by the woman's fury. Fairbank was suddenly before them, brandishing his axe, slapping the metal head against the palm of his hand, challenging them to come closer. They hesitated, lifting their own weapons, an iron bar, a pickaxe handle, and a knife. Their progress was more cautious.

Culver brought a knee up hard between the woman's legs, sending her over him. She writhed on the other side of the ashes, sucking in air, but already scrambling to get back at him. Culver pushed himself up, embers falling from his leather jacket, and half turned to meet the attack. Her screwed-up face was only a foot away and, still unbalanced, he struck his fist into it, following through and rolling clear of the heat. His knuckles were bloody when he regained his feet.

He saw Fairbank ward off an iron bar with the axe. Another man was about to bring a stout piece of wood down on the engineer's unprotected head. Culver took two paces and leapt, twisting his body so that it struck the assailant sideways on. They fell together and Culver was on his feet instantly; his boot caught the prone man on the chin. A third, knife-wielding, man backed away, reluctant to become involved. The two coloured girls were clinging to each other and shrieking, keeping well clear of the fight. Culver turned to help Fairbank and saw that the man with the iron bar had also disengaged from the fray for the moment. Fairbank's smile was uninviting.

Culver joined him and said quietly, 'We'd better get away from here while we can.'

'That's a fact,' Fairbank replied.

They quickly observed the plight of their companions; Ellison appeared to be in the worst trouble.

'Dealey, help Kate,' Culver ordered. 'Start running, towards the river. You know where to go.'

Dealey rose and stumbled towards Kate, who was kneeling beside Jackson, still brushing ash from his face. The three men beating Ellison were caught unawares as Culver and Fairbank laid into them. Two went down immediately, although not seriously hurt; the third staggered back as Fairbank struck him with his left fist. Culver and Fairbank scooped up Ellison and dragged him after their retreating companions.

'Dene!' Fairbank shouted.

Culver glanced around and found the prostrate body of the young engineer. 'Keep going, I'll check him out.'

Fairbank, axe raised in his right hand, his left supporting Ellison, staggered away while the pilot hurried over to Dene's limp form. He knelt and turned the engineer over onto his side. Death was now familiar enough to be easily recognized.

Footsteps approached and he looked up to see the assailant with the iron bar bearing down on him. He threw the axe and it struck the man in the chest, although not blade-first; the impetus, however, was enough to bring a halt to the attack. The iron bar fell to the ground as the man clutched his chest, his legs beginning to buckle.

Culver was up and running again, racing through the ravaged park and wishing the mist had not thinned out so much; its cover would have been welcome. He caught up with the others and relieved Kate of the severely burnt maintenance engineer, who was groaning aloud. Dealey was supporting Jackson on the other side. They moved as quickly as possible, a stumbling, awkward run, passing the maggot-filled tomb Culver had come upon earlier, skirting around empty tennis courts, the wire fencing surrounding them strangely untouched by the blasts.

Jackson tripped, went down, almost dragged Culver and Dealey with him.

'Keep going!' Culver yelled at the others, waving Kate away. 'They'll be coming after us!'

'We must hide,' Dealey said as they lifted Jackson to his feet.

'Soon as we put some distance between us,' Culver told him.

Rubble spilled down from varying heights to meet the edge of the park and they found themselves climbing, choosing the lower valleys, uneven passes in the debris. Culver noticed that one of Jackson's eyes was completely closed and a large part of his face had been burned raw; there were darker lumps enmeshed in his skin, pieces of charcoal that had seared their way through to the flesh beneath and become affixed there. His left shoulder was covered in blood. At the top of a rise, Culver turned to see if they really were being followed. Running figures were just visible in the swirling mist. He dropped into the ravine below, helping Jackson, aware that he had been seen: one of the figures had stopped and pointed at him.

Another sight had been engrained on his mind: the fallen city, just mounds of broken earth and shorn buildings rising above the low-lying, drifting mist, like clipped mountains above clouds.

For Kate and Alex Dealey, it was the clearest view of the destroyed capital they had yet had, and for the first time the enormity of what had happened struck them like a physical blow. Dazed, and more deeply disturbed than ever before, they staggered on through the hollows and dips, over the ridges and huge concrete outcrops. The heat made their exertions exhausting, their bodies soon becoming soaked with perspiration. Even the dust they stirred up in their flight contrived to choke and slow them. Glass fragments shimmered in the wreckage like glittering diamonds caught in the sun's rays, the wispy vapours unable to hold back the light completely.

Culver's bitten ankle was hurting like hell and he knew it was not sweat seeping through the bandage and sock. At one stage he put a hand to the stinging in his cheek and his fingers came away bloody. He knew he had sustained other injuries in the struggle, but he would discover what they were later – if there was a later for any of them.

Kate cried out when she missed her footing, but hobbled on, too afraid even to look back.

The valley ahead widened out and Culver knew they must be in what was once a broad thoroughfare leading to the Aldwych; beyond that was Waterloo Bridge and the river. Fairly close to that was the only place he felt they could be safe.

But at this rate, he knew they were not going to make it.

24

'In here!'

Culver pointed at the opening, a hole created by a large concrete slab leaning crazily against a shop-front. Much of the building above the shop had slid down the chunk of concrete and around its sides; the gap was formed between the slab and a landslide of rubble. Culver and Dealey helped Jackson, who was still moaning with pain, while Fairbank held on to Ellison, whose steps were still unsteady after the beating he had taken.

They made for the opening as Culver quickly scanned the landscape behind. He couldn't see their pursuers, but he could hear them: a pack of screaming banshees, howling for blood. Revenge was all they had, their only motivation; that and survival.

Dealey hesitated at the entrance. 'It isn't safe in here. The whole structure is loose, unstable.'

Culver gave him a shove. 'Take Jackson, follow the others. Waste one more second and the mob'll see us.'

Dealey reluctantly did as instructed, bearing the whole of the black engineer's weight, both of them crouching to get through the gap. The pilot backed his way in, eyes on the route behind them. He ducked from view when the first head came into sight over a small crest of debris, praying he hadn't been observed. They had been lucky earlier, his attack taking the intruders by surprise and effective only because of that surprise. This time these people were not out to steal or torment or question: they were out to kill.

Dust sifted down, blinding him for a moment. He brushed it away, blinking rapidly. Something creaked above him, then concrete ground against concrete. Dealey was right: the whole place was ready to collapse.

He moved further in, the figures of his companions barely visible in the dim light. Something shifted around them. The groans of a dying building. No, the reflex spasms of a building already dead. Pounding rain had worked on the remains over the weeks, weakening it further, changing broken concrete into pulpy mush. He could hear water dripping all around.

Voices from outside. Culver and the others froze, listening. Shouts, angry and something more. Excited. Eager for the chase. A new sport born out of the chaos. The human hunt.

'Keep still!' he hissed and they, the hunted, did not move.

Dealey breathed in dust and putridity and wondered what lay about them in the darkness. He squinted his eyes, peering into the gloom, knowing they were inside a shop for beyond the opening they had stepped over a short sill, the edge of which must have been a display window. In the distance, far at the back of the shop, he could see a glimmer of light. Another opening, a means of escape, at least. He could just make out broken display racks and the littered floor beneath them. Ah, a bookshop. He knew the one, had browsed through it in ... in better times. What value the written word now?

Jackson groaned beside him and Dealey could feel a new wetness sinking into his own clothing, a sticky flowing that had nothing to do with his own body damp. The engineer was bleeding over him. He shifted, repulsed by the seepage, and Jackson groaned aloud. Frightened the sounds could be heard outside, Dealey clamped a hand to the injured man's mouth. Jackson's semi-closed eyes opened wide with the sudden sharp increase of pain in his charred lips; he screamed against the darkness and pushed against whoever was trying to stifle him. He was free and terribly afraid. There were moving shadows all around, hands reaching for him, fingers touching his burnt skin. He screamed again, and tried to escape. Something tried to hold him; he knocked it away. He had to get out. There was a light, an opening. He had to get through it. There were rats down in the shelter! Large black rats! Rats that could tear a man to pieces! He had to get out!

Culver lunged at the distraught engineer, knowing it was already too late, that those outside could not have failed to have heard. Mad with pain and panic, Jackson threw the pilot to one side, intent only on reaching the source of light, desperate to escape the dark hole in the ground where he could smell the burning of his own flesh and hear the screeching and scuffling of night creatures. He staggered towards the triangle of light, slipping on objects scattered on the floor, almost falling over more bulky shapes lying in the dust.

He was nearly there and already the air seemed cleaner. He sobbed with relief. But he could see shapes coming through, figures filling the opening, blocking the light, taking away the clean air. There were shouts and they reminded him of earlier sounds, the jeering as his face had been lowered into the heat, the sneering curses of men and women who had become worse than rabid animals, who had become like the vermin that roamed the underground world, mutilating not just to live, but for the pleasure it gave them. He roared, plunging towards the figures in the opening, pushing at fallen beams to get to them, wanting to feel *their* flesh open beneath *his* fingers.

The others heard the grinding sound and sensed the shift in weight over their heads.

'It's giving way!' Dealey screeched.

There was no need for further words. They moved as one away from the tearing, grinding noise above them, slowly at first, almost cautious as if haste would precipitate the avalanche; but as the rending and cracking became a co-ordinated rumble and the walls creaked outwards, they began to run blindly towards the rear of the building.

There had probably been screams from those trapped at the entrance, but they could not be heard as the rest of the building collapsed section by section about them. The inclination of Kate, Fairbank, Dealey, Ellison and Culver was to huddle beneath furniture or against pillars, but the crashing masonry and timbers followed them, driving them onwards, allowing no respite, jaws of an alligator snapping behind leaping toads. It was an insane jumble of movement and noise.

Kate fell, was up, not knowing if unseen hands had helped her, running, sliding, but never stopping, constantly moving ahead of the enormous surge, prodded by its cloudy draught. Towards light ahead, a sliver of light, a thin fraction of yellow-white. A door, still upright, slightly ajar, the building's lower portions protected by other buildings on the opposite side of the road, they themselves shorn of their upper floors.

Someone was pulling at the door from the inside, opening it wide, sweeping aside the clutter at its base; and Fairbank – she thought it was Fairbank – was ushering her through, telling her, she thought, to keep on running, the instructions inaudible, and she was outside, others crowding behind her, all of them running away from the crashing building, climbing the long slope of rubble opposite, not stopping until there was no breath left, no more energy to carry them on, until clouds of dust covered and choked them, making them fall and hide their faces, lying there and hoping, desperately praying that they were far enough away, that they could not be reached by crushing rubble. Waiting for the rumbling to diminish, to fade away, to stop.

And eventually, the tremors did stop.

Kate raised her head and wiped dust away from her face and eyes. Her body was at an angle, the horizon of the slope she had tried to climb ending abruptly fifty or sixty yards above her, broken parts of the building it had once been standing like monoliths along the ridge. Someone groaned nearby and she twisted to see a figure coated in what appeared to be white powder but which was, in fact, pulverized masonry, slumped as she was, and just beginning to move. It was Ellison.

Kate sat up. Below her was Dealey, he, too, barely recognizable under the dust layers. Much further down, Fairbank was beginning to rise, wiping his face with one hand, the other still clutching his axe, and turning to survey the demolition, much of the building's outer shell still standing – at least on their side. There was no sign of Jackson and no sign of their pursuers and no sign of—

'Steve?' It was a mild question asked of the dust clouds. 'Steve!' This time Kate screamed the name.

The three men with her on the incline jerked to attention and looked at the rubble below with dismay. No, not Culver, they needed him! The sudden loss made it clear in all their minds just how *much* they needed him. Dealey sat down on the slope and ran a hand through his thin and now powdery hair, his brow knotted in exasperation. Ellison shook his head in despair; he hadn't liked Culver, yet had to admit there was something very reassuring about his presence. So much so, he wondered if they could survive without him. Fairbank's usual cheerful countenance was a mixture of grimness and incredulity, his eyes disbelieving, his mouth set straight, held rigid; Culver had come through too much to be killed in this stupid way. Kate was in shock, her senses numbed for the moment. She stared into the billowing clouds, listening to the smaller sounds of the fall-in's aftermath, the settling of stonework and glass, the sliding of objects and gravel; the tail-end of her scream had left her mouth open and her fists clenched tight before her.

The dust clouds slowly dispersed, taking with them the surrounding mist, until the scene was only thinly veiled by floating particles.

Kate broke down when Culver appeared from behind a mound that had once been a car, now half-buried in debris. Brushing powder from his head, shoulders and arms, he strode up the incline towards them.

'Thought you'd lost me, huh?' he said.

It seemed that Kate's tears would never stop. The others sat some distance away, uncomfortable and anxious to move on, while Culver cradled her in his arms and did his best to stem the outpourings of her misery.

'I thought you were dead, Steve,' she managed to say between sobs. 'After everything else, I couldn't stand that.'

'It's nearly finished, Kate. We're nearly clear of all this.'

'But that can't ever be so. There's nothing left for any of us.'

'We're alive. That's all that matters. You may think it's impossible, right now, but you've got to put everything else out of your mind. Just think of living and getting through this mess; think beyond that and you'll go mad.'

'I'm close to it, Steve, I know I'm close to madness. I don't think I can take any more.'

He kissed the top of her head. 'You're the sanest one among us.'

Her trembling was gradually subsiding. 'But what's left for any of us? Where can we go, what can we do? What kind of world's been left to us?'

'It might just be a peaceful one.'

'You can say that after what we've been through this morning? And last night?'

'This morning was to let us know that a holocaust doesn't necessarily change the nature of all men for the good. We've seen enough to know self-preservation can bring out the worst.'

The tears still flowed, but the shuddering sobs had stopped. 'We realized that inside the shelter.'

'Yeah,' he mused, 'there was a certain lack of camaraderie. But it grew from fear and desperation.'

'Those people this morning didn't look desperate. They looked as if they were enjoying themselves.'

'Let's just say we've been knocked back a few thousand years to a time when other tribes are the enemy and certain breeds of animal are dangerous. We got through it then, we'll do it again.'

'You're hardly convincing.' Some of the colour was returning to her cheeks.

'I know. I don't believe it myself. But our ancestors may have had the right idea about one thing: they spent most of their time considering how to live, not why they were living. They were too busy finding food and building shelters to concern themselves with despair.'

'Thank God I found the oracle to take care of me,' she sniffed. Culver smiled. 'All I'm saying is, concentrate your mind on here and now, and nothing else. The rest is too big to contemplate. Use Fairbank as an example: it's as if he's on autopilot. Maybe he'll crack up eventually, but it won't be until he's got time to, when he's in safer and more stable surroundings. As far as I understand him, he's not interested in yesterday, nor tomorrow. Only now, this moment, today.'

'It's unnatural.'

'Not for him. And not for these times.'

'But we have to think ahead if we're to live.' Her crying had stopped, and he wiped away the wetness, smearing the dirt on her cheeks.

'We think as far as a destination.'

'We have one? You mean out of London?'

'Closer. You feeling a little better?'

She nodded. 'I'm sorry. I thought I'd lost you . . .'

He kissed her lips. 'I'm the bad penny.'

'You look terrible.'

'You're no picture.'

'Are the others watching?'

'They're trying not to. Why?'

'I need you to touch me.'

'That's good. You're thinking for the moment.'

'I'm thinking for several moments.'

'Does a good cry always make you feel raunchy?'

'More often than not.'

'That's worth knowing.'

He kissed her then, and there was more than consolation in the touch. They broke away by mutual consent, neither one prolonging the sweet torment. A little breathless, Culver beckoned to the others.

'Ready to move on?' he asked them.

'Waiting for you, pal,' Fairbank answered.

'Move on to where? I've been beaten almost to a pulp, dragged through the ruins and nearly crushed to death.' Ellison spat dust from his mouth in disgust. 'How much more do you think I can take?'

'None of us can handle much more, that's pretty obvious,' Culver told him, 'so you just be your usual charming self and we'll see what we can figure out.'

He looked out over the hazy ruins and wished he could see the full extent of the damage. The mist was clearing, but it was still impossible to see the small hills surrounding the rubbled city. He wondered what lay beyond.

'All right,' he said finally. 'We can try to make it out of what's left of the city on foot, finding food and shelter as we go. It doesn't look as if we're going to get any help from official sources and I doubt we'll find any Red Cross soup kitchens set up along the way.'

'But where *is* the government help?' Ellison snarled. 'Just what the fuck are they doing about all this?'

'The devastation has been beyond all expectation,' Dealey began to say. 'It was all underestimated. No one foresaw—'

'No jargon, Dealey, no bloody officialese excuses!' Ellison's hand hovered threateningly over a brick by his side.

Fairbank stirred. 'Cut it out, Ellison. You're getting too much to stomach.' His words were all the more ominous for their quietness. He turned to Culver. 'What about the main government headquarters, Steve? Wouldn't we be better off there?'

'That's what I was coming to next. Our friend from the Ministry here and I had a quiet chat yesterday, and he disclosed some interesting details about the place. It seems it's impregnable. Bomb-proof, radiation-proof, and famine-proof.'

'Yeah, but is it flood-proof?' Fairbank rumbled darkly.

'Each section can be sealed by air-tight doors,' Dealey said.

'You can get us in?' Ellison asked eagerly.

'He knows the entrances,' said Culver. 'We'll worry about getting inside when the time comes.'

'Then you think we should make for the shelter,' Kate said.

'Yep. Literally go to ground. It's our best bet.'

'I agree.' Dealey looked at them all individually. 'It's what I've advocated all along. Wait until the radiation has passed, then link up with main base.'

Ellison now had second thoughts. 'How do we know it really is safe? There's been no communication from them.'

Dealey answered. 'The fault must have been from our end, or somewhere between. Remember, we've had no contact with any of the other shelters, either. I think it's not only in our own interest to report to government headquarters, but it's also my duty as a civil servant.'

Fairbank gave him a tired handclap.

'It's a feasible choice,' said Culver. 'Agreed?'

The others nodded.

'Jackson?' said Kate.

Culver held her arm. 'He's dead, you know that. He had no chance in there.'

'It seems so cruel, after all he'd . . .' She let the words trail off, aware that they all sensed the futility.

Without further words, Culver helped her up and they all began to clamber over the ruins. They concentrated their efforts on not stumbling over treacherous masonry and avoiding fragile-looking structures, steering well clear of any open pits and fissures. Not far away, and protruding through the low mist, were the supports of the elegant Jubilee Hall, beneath which had been the trendy shops and stalls of Covent Garden. Its very bleakness forced Kate to look away, for she had always known it as a lively bustling square, a favourite haunt of both tourists and young Londoners. The Aldwych was gone, its semi-circular buildings flattened, as was the once magnificent Somerset House, much of it tumbled into the Thames which it had backed on to. Surprisingly, protruding from the rubble was the steeple of St Mary-le-Strand, only the tip broken off. It presented an odd and perhaps ironic sight amid the devastation, but Kate, following Culver's advice, did not let the thought linger.

Climbing, sliding, and brushing away swarms of oversized insects, they steadily made their way towards the river. A walk that would have taken no more than five or ten minutes in normal times took them the best part of an hour. They became almost immune to the unpleasant sights they came upon, their minds learning to regard the image of mutilated, swollen and rotted corpses as part of the debris and nothing to do with human life itself. Vehicles, overturned, burnt out, or simply askew in the roadway, had to be skirted around or climbed over, their ghoulish occupants ignored. Nowhere did they find walking, moving people; nowhere was there anyone like themselves. They wondered if it were possible for so many to have been destroyed, yet when they looked around at the damage to the inanimate, they understood that very few people could have lived through such destruction.

'How much further?' Ellison complained. He was panting and one hand was clutched tight against his side as though ribs had been damaged in the beating.

'The bridge,' Culver said, his own chest heaving with the effort. His cheek was caked with darkish blood and he had realized earlier that a pellet from an intruder's air-rifle must have scythed a path across it. The wound throbbed, as did the rat-bites in his ear and temple, but no longer stung. The pain in his ankle was sharper, but did not hinder him too much.

'If we can get to Waterloo Bridge there's a staircase leading down to the Embankment. We can get to one of the shelter's entrances from there.'

They journeyed on and were shocked when they reached Lancaster Place, the wide thoroughfare leading up to Waterloo Bridge itself. They should have expected it, but somehow hadn't. And one more defilement to their city should not really have surprised them. The bridge was gone, collapsed into the river.

They looked towards its broken structure with new bitterness. The open space from bank to bank looked insanely empty. On the other side, the National Theatre was a mound of rubble.

'Please, let's not stop now,' Dealey implored, fighting his own inexplicable sense of loss. 'The steps may still be intact. They're in a sheltered position.'

They walked forward and it was strange, so very strange, like walking a gangplank towards the edge of the universe. The great, wide bridge stretched out over the river as if yearning to fingertip-touch the similarly outstretched section on the other side. Vapour rose from the swollen river, thicker here, and hanging heavily.

They looked towards the west and saw the broken shaft of Cleopatra's Needle.

'Oh, no,' Dealey moaned, for he was examining the area beyond the snapped monument.

Culver's forehead sank onto the wide balustrade overlooking the Embankment road.

'Steve, what is it?' Kate clutched at his shoulder. He raised his head.

'The railway bridge.' He pointed. 'Hungerford Bridge.'

They saw that it, too, had collapsed into the river. The metal struts had broken in several places and it hung as if by threads, dangling into the river like a sleeping man's fishing rod, still loosely connected to the section on their side. This section had fallen onto the roadway, completely blocking it. The others looked uncomprehendingly at Dealey and Culver.

'There was an enclosure, a compound, beneath the bridge,' Culver told them. 'A thick brick wall with barbed wire on the top. A mini-fortress, if you like. It's been destroyed by the bridge.'

His face set into grim lines and it was Dealey who explained. 'The main entrance to the shelter was inside that enclosure.'

25

From a distance the wreckage had looked simple, just a
collapsed iron bridge, broken in sections so that one part
formed a waterchute into the river, the midstream portions
mostly submerged, concrete supports shattered in half. Close
up, it was a complicated tangled mess of bent and twisted
steel girders, scattered red brickwork, huge chunks of
masonry, and riddled with cables and wires. A segment of
railway line rose from the disorder like a ladder into the sky.
An engine lay on its side among the jumble, carriages behind
piled up in zigzag fashion, the rear compartments ripped off,
the top of one protruding from the river. Culver made a point
of not looking into the broken windows; he had seen enough
dead for one day without searching out more. He guessed
the train driver had made a desperate dash to reach the
station, Charing Cross, in the hope that he and his passengers might find a last-minute refuge. Had the train been
delayed on the bridge when the sirens had sounded, or was
it far back on the southern side of the city? He imagined the
race across the river, passengers chilled by the rising and
falling sirens, helpless and depending on the driver to get
them to safety. The murky grey-brown water below, the
panoramic view of London, Big Ben and the Houses of
Parliament to the left, St Paul's in the distance to the right,
renowned landmarks of an historical city that would soon

cease to exist. What must have gone through their minds in those last moments? Impotent rage, unable to help themselves, unable to run, hide, to be with loved ones? Or total, shocking fear that blanketed all thought, that paralysed their senses? It was obscenely terrible, the thought of their sterile waiting. The sudden emptiness as the sirens stopped, the terror of fellow passengers and the *chuggajig* of metal wheels somehow not filling the silent void. The incandescent flash that would have seared their eyeballs had they looked directly into it. The thunder that followed.

Culver shuddered. It was as though the souls of the dead were revealing their story to him, their horror still existing in the complex of torn metal, the last thoughts of the dying collected there, waiting to be absorbed by receptive minds. He shook his head, a physical act to disperse the notion.

'I know this place,' Kate was saying. 'The down-and-outs used to sleep under this bridge. There was a mobile soup kitchen every night. But I was never aware of any compound.'

Dealey spoke with some satisfaction. 'Nobody was meant to. It's surprising how anonymous and innocuous these enclosures are.' He corrected himself. '*Were*. The tramps actually wrapped themselves in cardboard and slept against the very walls of the compound. They presented a perfect camouflage. The bridge overhead was thought to be adequate protection in the event of a nuclear explosion.'

'Looks like someone goofed again,' Ellison said bitterly. 'Is there any way we can get through to the entrance?'

'You can see for yourself. It's buried beneath hundreds of tons of rubble,' Dealey replied.

'But there are other places.' Culver was alert once more. 'You told me there were other entrances.'

'This was the obvious one, the one I planned to use. It was the most protected. The others are mostly inside government buildings, and they, of course, will have been covered by the ruins, just as this has.'

'They must have realized what would happen,' Fairbank said. 'They had to have other escape routes.'

'In the main, the other exits are outside what was considered the danger zones.'

Culver frowned. 'Wait a minute. Yesterday you told me there were other, smaller points of access along the Embankment.'

'Yes, yes, that's true. But I'm not sure that we can get into them, even if they aren't covered by debris.'

'Can't we just knock?' Fairbank asked wryly.

'You don't understand. These entrances are meant for maintenance inspection and are really only narrow shafts and tunnels.'

'We're not choosy.'

'I'm not sure we'll find a way into the main complex.'

'It's worth a try,' said Culver.

'How the hell do we get past all this?' asked Ellison, indicating the massive debris before them, then pointing towards the even bigger mass that was the destroyed Charing Cross railway station. 'I don't have the strength to walk around that lot – I think a couple of my ribs are fractured.'

'We'll work our way through here,' said Culver. 'It might be dangerous, but it'll save time. Are you up to it, Kate?'

She gave him a nervous smile. 'I'll be fine. It's strange, but I feel so exposed out here.'

'That's what comes from living underground for so long.'

'Yesterday it was different. I felt free, liberated, glad to be out of the shelter. Since this morning, though, since we were attacked . . .' She did not bother to complete the sentence, but they all knew what she meant; they shared her feelings.

Culver took her hand and led her towards the beginnings

of the wrecked bridge. The others followed and began to climb, Fairbank giving assistance to Ellison in the more difficult places.

'Keep away from anything that's loose,' Culver warned. 'Some of this junk doesn't look too solid.'

The smell of oil and rusting metal was everywhere, but it was a relief from the other odours they had been aware of that day. Culver chose the easiest route he could find, wary of touching anything unstable. The climb was arduous in the damp heat, but not difficult. Soon they were on a level section, overlooking the continuation of the road they had just left. Culver paused, giving Kate a chance to rest and allowing the others to catch up.

Below, the wide roadway curving slightly with the river was jammed with scorched, immobile traffic. Another road, equally wide, veered off to the right towards Trafalgar Square. The mist was minimal now, but Nelson's Column could not be seen. Victoria Embankment, running alongside the Thames, was relatively free of debris (apart from vehicles), for the offices on the north side had been set back from the thoroughfare, gardens and lawns between. As expected, the buildings were no more than crushed ruins: the Old War Office, the Ministries of Defence and Technology – all were gone. The Admiralty at the beginning of the Mall should have been visible since nothing obscured the view but, of course, that had vanished too. He briefly wondered if all the works of art in the National Gallery, which was on the far side of Trafalgar Square, had been destroyed beneath the deluge. What significance did they have in the present world, anyway? There would be little time to appreciate anything that was not of intrinsic material use in the years ahead. As he knew they would be, the Houses of Parliament and Westminster Abbey, at the end of the road he faced, had been totally destroyed. Peculiarly, the lower section of the tower housing Big Ben was still erect, sheered off at a hundred or so feet; the top section containing the clockface protruded from the river like a tilted, rock island. And again, surprisingly, only the southern end of Westminster Bridge had collapsed. It defiantly spanned the river, just failing to reach the opposite bank.

The sun's fierce rays sucked up moisture from the Thames, so that it looked as if the water were boiling. Somehow it appeared to him that here were the intestines of the city's torn body, exposed to the light and still steaming as all life gradually diminished. Masts of sunken, ancient boats, those that had been converted into smart bars and restaurants, jutted through the rolling mist. Pleasure boats, their surfaces and passengers charred black, drifted listlessly with the current, the longboat funeral pyres of a modern age. A stout wall, still unbroken, lined the riverbank, and the waterline was high, lapping over the small quaysides that were situated near the broken bridge. Much of the gardens on the other side of the road from the Embankment wall were buried beneath fallen office blocks, but here and there a tree stuck through the debris, protected from the worst of the blast by the very buildings shattered around them, leaves washed clean of dust by the constant rain, and flourishing under the humid conditions. Culver's eyes moistened at the sight.

Someone tapped his arm. Dealey pointed into the distance. 'Look there, you can just see it as the road curves.'

'D'you want to tell me what I'm looking for?'

'Don't you see it? A small, rectangular shape set in the pavement quite near the river wall.'

Culver's eyes narrowed. 'I've got it. Like a tiny blockhouse, is that what you mean?'

'That's it. That may get us inside the shelter.'

Culver shook his head. So many everyday sights, ignored, not even wondered at, all part of the big secret. He recalled mild curiosity when coming upon the odd ventilation shafts around the city, but always assuming they were for the Underground railway system or low-level car parks. It was only when viewed subjectively that they obtruded from the general background and took on a special significance – like the stockade over the Kingsway telephone exchange and the one they now stood over, crushed beneath Hungerford Bridge. He supposed the art of concealment was to make something commonplace, unnoticeable.

'Let's get to it,' he said and, containing their eagerness, they scrambled down from the wreckage.

The going was easier once they were on the ground, only human remains, carrion for colonies of feverishly crawling things, marring their progress. They had still not become used to the legions of insects, but fortunately the swarming droves were concentrated on less resistant entities.

They were passing over a long grating set in the pavement, when Fairbank brought them to a halt. He knelt, peering down through the iron slats.

'Listen!' he said.

The others knelt around him and saw there were thick pipes running horizontally a few feet below ground level.

'What are they?' Kate asked, slightly out of breath.

Dealey told her. 'Ventilation pipes, conduits containing cables, wiring. The complex is directly below us.'

Fairbank hushed them again. 'Listen!'

They held their breath and listened.

It was faint, but definite. A humming vibration.

'Generators!' Ellison proclaimed excitedly.

They looked at each other, a gleaming in their eyes.

'Jesus, they're functioning.' Fairbank was triumphant. 'There are people down there!'

He and Ellison let out whoops of glee.

'I told you,' Dealey said, surprised at their outburst, but smiling nevertheless. 'I told you this was the main government headquarters. Didn't I tell you that?'

'You told us that.' Kate was laughing.

'Wait!' Culver held up a hand. 'Is it me, or is the sound getting louder?'

The group listened more intently, Fairbank putting his ear against the grille. 'Seems like the same pitch to me,' he commented after a few seconds. He twisted his head to look up at Culver.

But Culver was watching the sky.

The others noticed and followed his gaze.

The humming became a drone, a sound different from the one below them, and the drone grew louder.

'There!' Culver stabbed a finger at the sky.

They saw the aeroplane at once, a dark smudge in the hazy sky, flying low from the west. Slowly, as if sudden movement would disperse the image, they rose to their feet, their faces upturned and with stunned expressions, none of them daring to speak.

It was Dealey who broke the silence, but only with a whisper. 'It's following the river.'

The aircraft was drawing nearer and Culver saw it was small, light.

'A Beaver,' he said, almost to himself.

The others looked at him in puzzlement, then quickly returned their gaze.

'An Air Corps Beaver spotter plane,' Culver expanded. 'On bloody reconnaissance – it has to be!'

The tiny aircraft was almost over their heads. Fairbank and Ellison began to shout as one, waving their arms to attract the pilot's attention. The others instantly joined in, leaping in the air, running back along the Embankment in a vain attempt to keep up with the machine, calling at the top of their lungs, flapping their arms, desperate to be noticed.

'Can he see us, can he see us?' Kate was clutching at Culver. 'Oh God, make him see us!'

Then it was gone, taking their spirits with it. They watched until it became a smudgy speck. They waited until it could no longer be seen.

'Shit, shit, shit!' Fairbank.

'He couldn't miss us!' Ellison.

'He may not have spotted us through the mist.' Dealey.

'It's clearer here. There's a chance.' Culver.

Weeping. Kate.

Culver put an arm around her shoulders, hugging her close. 'It doesn't matter whether he did or not. We're safe now. Once we're inside the shelter, we'll be okay. And there's a whole tunnel network down there – a way out of London.'

'I know, Steve. It's just that for a moment we almost had contact with . . . with . . .' She found difficulty in choosing the right word. 'I don't know – civilization, if you like. Something beyond all this.' She gestured at the ruins.

'We'll have real contact soon, I promise you that.'

'Do you suppose the plane will come back?'

'Who knows. The pilot might choose another route; he'd want to cover as much ground as possible.'

She nodded and wiped a hand across her nose. 'It's my day for crying.'

He smiled. 'You've pulled through so far. Just a little longer.'

They returned to the grille set in the pavement and passed over it, no longer interested in the faint thrumming sound emanating from its depths.

Reaching the grey-stoned block, they studied its rough surface, walking all around, bemused at first and soon worried.

'Terrific,' Fairbank said, wiping sweat from the back of his head. 'No opening. How the fuck do we get inside, Dealey?'

The object, massive and dark, a strange monolith, remained impassive and seemingly impregnable. At least twelve feet long and five or six feet wide, it resembled a huge tombstone. Or a sacrificial altar, thought Kate.

'There's a hole in the top,' Dealey announced simply.

The others looked at each other and Fairbank grinned. The stone blockade was six feet high, perhaps more, and the engineer had scrambled up before anyone else could move.

'He's right,' Fairbank called down. 'There's a part at the end here that isn't covered. It's cunning, you'd never know. And there's a door.' He pulled the axe free of his belt. 'It looks as if it's locked, but I think I can handle that.' White teeth split his grime-covered face in a grin as he surveyed them from his lofty perch. 'Care to join me?'

Culver stood below helping up the others, Fairbank pulling from above. He scrambled up after them and looked down into the opening.

'What is this thing, Dealey? It can't be newly built.'

'No,' Kate said. 'I've passed this spot many times over the years and never even given it a second glance, never even wondered what its purpose was.'

'It was an air-raid shelter during the war,' Dealey told them, brushing away a buzzing fly and wiping his face with a discoloured handkerchief. 'At least, it led down to an air-raid shelter. I explained to Culver yesterday that the original underground chambers, built many, *many* years ago, have been expanded through the decades.'

'Well, we can see how much for ourselves,' said Ellison, growing impatient. 'For God's sake, let's get inside.'

'Right,' Fairbank agreed. He slipped down into the opening, and examined the lock. 'Don't you have a key?' he called back to Dealey, who shook his head.

'Not for this place,' he said.

'Okay, it shouldn't be too much of a problem anyway.' He swung the axe.

It took no more than four solid blows to open the door. It swung inwards and a chilling coldness sprang out like an escaping ghost.

Culver shivered. The dank cold seemed more than just released air. It brought with it a sense of foreboding.

26

The coolness inside was a relief from the humid atmosphere above ground. They descended the stone steps, Fairbank in the lead, axe tucked back into his belt. The air was musty, the smell of disuse, and the concrete walls were rough to the touch.

Fairbank paused. 'There's no light down here.' He rummaged in his pockets and passed back two small bright tubes. 'Picked these up yesterday,' he told them. 'Figured they might come in handy for lighting fires.' He flicked on the cheap throwaway lighter he had kept for himself. The flame, weak though it was, gave some comfort.

Culver passed his over his shoulder to Ellison, who was bringing up the rear.

'I've got one,' the engineer said. 'Maybe you'd better pass it down to the front, though, and let me have one of those midgets.' He handed the lighter to Culver, who passed it on. 'It's the one I found yesterday,' Ellison explained. 'The flame's stronger.'

They continued, the lighter casing growing hot in Fairbank's hand. Their footsteps were hollow-sounding and loud. It was a long climb down and, inexplicably, Culver's unease increased with every step. He wondered if the others felt the same. Just below him, Kate let both hands slide against the close walls, as if afraid she might stumble and fall. Her hair was tangled, dark in the feeble lighter glow, and her shirt was torn and still covered with dust. He squeezed her shoulder and she briefly touched his hand with her fingertips, but did not turn around.

Fairbank eventually stopped and brushed away cobwebs from the opening before him.

'There's a big room here.' His words had a slight echo. He waved the light ahead of him. 'Seems to be empty.'

They crowded in behind him, branching out so that their lights covered more of an area. Other rooms led off from the first chamber and Ellison poked his head through a doorway to one.

'Nothing,' he pronounced, disappointed.

'This one too.' Fairbank was at another doorway.

'They're all empty,' said Dealey, walking to the far end. 'This is just part of the old air-raid shelter system. As you can see, it hasn't been used since the last war.' He reached an opening and called back to them. 'This way.'

They quickly hurried to him and he led them through what seemed a labyrinth of corridors with empty rooms branching off. He finally stopped beside a square doorway set into the wall two feet from the floor.

'We'll need your axe again to force it,' he said to Fairbank.

The engineer slid the sharp end of the tool into the crack, close by the lock. He exerted pressure and the door easily snapped open. Inside they could see thick piping, some at least a foot in diameter, and heavy cables. The thrumming was louder, more distinct than when they had listened at the grille above ground.

'Maintenance entry,' Dealey said by way of explanation as he stepped through.

Inside, the narrow corridor with its wall of pipes and cables extended in both directions. Dealey took them to the right.

'You sure you know where you're going, Dealey?' came Ellison's voice from the rear.

'Not a hundred per cent, but I think this way should take us close to the new complex.'

The darkness and the narrowness of the passageway began to have a claustrophobic effect on Kate. Outside she had felt exposed; down there she felt threatened. She kept close to Culver, who was now in front of her.

Dealey had stopped once more and was kneeling, holding the small flame towards a two-by-two-foot grid in the floor. He inserted his fingers between the meshwork and pulled; it swung open like a trapdoor. They saw metal ladder rungs disappearing downwards.

'It should take us down to shelter level.' The warm glow from the tiny flames softened Dealey's features, but to Culver the man looked ten years older than when he had first laid eyes on him. Odd that he'd only just noticed.

Culver squeezed past Fairbank and knelt on the opposite side of the opening to Dealey. 'How far down does the shaft go?'

'I'm not sure. We must be fairly near.'

'Is it safe?'

Dealey looked at him sharply.

'Vermin, I mean,' Culver said.

They all tensed in the silence that followed.

Finally, Dealey said, 'There's no way of knowing. But what other choice do we have?'

'The usual. None at all.'

Culver went in first, exchanging his weaker lighter for Fairbank's and wincing at the hot metal. He climbed down, holding the lighter between thumb and index finger, his other fingers curled around the upright support so that both hands were used. The shaft was circular and metallic, and the hum of machinery grew louder the lower he went, although it was still muted. He heard the others climbing into the shaft after him. It seemed a long time before he touched down in another passageway, this one wider than the one he had just left. Some of the piping and cables ran along its ceiling. There was water on the floor.

Dealey reached him, then Fairbank, followed by Kate. Ellison arrived clutching his side and breathing heavily. 'Christ!' he uttered when his feet became soaked.

'Maybe this place was flooded, too,' said Fairbank.

'I doubt it,' Dealey replied, touching the walls. 'They're not damp. Very cold, and I suppose dankish, but you'd expect that at this temperature. Not soaked, though. I think the water on the floor is just seepage, nothing to worry about.'

'Nowadays, when a government man tells me not to worry, I worry,' Fairbank retorted without rancour.

Culver held his light to the left, then to the right. 'Which way?'

'It probably doesn't matter. These maintenance corridors skirt the headquarters; they're part of a larger system that protects the main shelter. Either way should lead us somewhere useful.'

'Okay, let's take the left.'

They went on, splashing water, all of them becoming chilled with the cold. There were one or two turns in the passageway, but never right-angled, only bearing to the right, then reverting to the previous direction. Culver guessed they were still heading west, although he admitted to himself he could be entirely wrong. They passed ladders leading up into other shafts and, here and there, large junction boxes into which the cables and wires disappeared, to emerge on the other side. The flames the men carried were fading.

Fairbank's was the first to shrink to nothing. He tossed it away and they heard the *plop* as it struck water.

Dealey's was next.

Soon they were groping their way along, barely able to see, hands against the walls for guidance. The idea of trying to find their way in total darkness terrified them all. Culver heard the trickling of water just ahead, but there was not enough light to see where the sound came from. He discovered its source when the ground felt different beneath him. He crouched.

'There's a drain here.' He felt with his fingers, cold air was rising from the slats. 'Looks like quite a big one.'

'It'll lead down to the sewers,' said Dealey. 'Being so near the river, there must be a constant seepage into the tunnels.'

'Steve, let's keep moving while we still have light,' Kate urged.

He straightened and they moved on.

Ellison stared miserably at his sinking flame and drew in a sharp breath when it finally went out. A little further on, Culver stopped again and cupped a hand around his lighter, the only lantern they had left.

Ellison bumped into Dealey. 'What the hell are you doing?'

'Shut up.' Culver was peering ahead into the darkness. 'I think I can see a glow.'

They crowded round him. 'You're right, Steve,' said Kate. 'I see it, too.'

'Thank God for that,' Ellison breathed.

Their pace quickened and soon the faint glow in the distance grew stronger, became a long sliver of pale light. As they approached, they were able to distinguish a door. It was slightly ajar, the light coming from inside. The corridor ended there.

The door was solid, made of thick metal painted green.

There were flanges around its sides, like the doorway of the Kingsway exchange, to provide a tight seal when closed. Culver pushed against it, cautious for some reason. Beyond he could see dimly lit grey walls, another passageway. The heavy door resisted his push. There was something behind it.

He shoved a little harder and something moved inside.

Culver looked around at the others, then snapped the lighter shut. He put it in his pocket. Using both hands, palms flat against the smooth surface, he eased the door wider. The light illuminated their faces. When there was enough room, he slipped through.

The body – what was left of it – was slumped against the door, one hand, much of the flesh gone, still gripped tight around the six-inch bar that was the door's handle. Culver felt himself sway a little, even though he should have been accustomed to such atrocities by now. It could once have been a man, although it was hard to tell. The corpse had been fed upon. The head was missing.

One hand holding the door open – the corpse seemed determined to push it shut – Culver quietly called the others in. 'You first, Dealey. You next, Kate, and don't look, just keep your eyes straight ahead.'

Of course she looked and immediately moved away, her chest heaving.

'Oh shit,' said Fairbank when he saw the headless body.

Ellison visibly sagged and Culver thought for a moment the engineer would crumple. Ellison leaned weakly against the wall and said, 'They're down here.'

Nobody disagreed.

He staggered back towards the open door. 'We'd better get out. We can't stay here.'

Culver caught him by the shoulder and allowed the door

to close. It did not shut completely, but stayed ajar, just as they had found it. The corpse's hand released its death grip, the arm slumping to the floor.

'We can't go back,' Culver said steadily. 'We don't have the light. And besides, the rats may be out there.'

'You think this . . .' Dealey averted his gaze '. . . this person was trying to keep them out?'

'I don't know,' Culver admitted. 'Either that, or he was trying to escape.' He had decided that the body was that of a man, for the tattered remnants of what looked like olive-green overalls or a uniform of some kind still clung to it.

Fairbank seemed fascinated by the spectacle. 'The head,' he said, 'why's the head gone?' The stench was there, but it was not powerful, not cloying. The man had been dead some time, the worst of the smell long since dispersed. 'It's like the Underground station. Remember the bodies we found? Some with heads missing?'

'But why?' asked Dealey. 'I don't understand.'

'Maybe the rats shrink 'em.' Nobody appreciated Fairbank's macabre humour this time.

'Can't *you* tell us why?' Culver was looking directly at Dealey.

'I swear I know nothing more than I've already told you. You must believe me.'

'Must I?'

'There's no point in my lying. There would be absolutely nothing to gain from it.'

Culver conceded. He looked along the corridor, noticing for the first time the blood smears that stained its length. 'I guess that answers one question,' he said, pointing. 'He was trying to escape from the inside. They had him before he even reached the door. He must have crawled along as they tore him apart.'

Kate had covered her face, her head against the wall. 'It's never going to end. We're not going to live through this.'

Culver went to her. 'We're not inside yet. The rats may have attacked and been beaten off. This place can hold hundreds of people, Kate, more than enough to defend themselves. And they have the military to protect them, too.'

'Then why him, why this one body?'

'Maybe they didn't know he was out here. It's just a corridor, probably one of many. They may not have even known he'd been killed.' An overwhelming sense of dread was building up inside him as he spoke. It had been growing since first they had smashed open the door above ground, and now it was sinking through every nerve cord, through every organ in his body, turning them to lead, filling his lower stomach with its draining heaviness.

'There's another door here!' Fairbank was standing further down the passageway, pointing to a recess on his right.

Culver gently eased Kate away from the wall and took her with him, the others already making towards Fairbank. The door was similar to the one they had just left, only wider and higher. It was open.

With increasing trepidation, they stared into the interior of the government headquarters shelter.

She stirred, restless, perceiving a faraway danger.

Her obese body tried to shift in her nest of filth and powdered bones. The sound of running water was lost to her, for she did not possess ears, yet something inside could receive the high-frequency mewlings of her subject creatures. There was no light in the underground chamber, but her eyes had no optic nerves anyway. Yet she was always aware of movement around her.

The huge, swollen hump of her body moved in a deep breathing motion, swelling even more so that dark veins protruded from the whitish skin, skin so fine it seemed the network of ridges must burst through. Her jaws parted slightly as air exhaled with a high wheezing sound; the breath also came from another source, another, misshapen mouth in a stump by the side of her pointed head. There were no teeth inside this mouth and no eyes above it. A few white hairs grew from the snout, the one that enabled her to smell, but the protuberance had little other use. Her limbs no longer supported the gross weight and her claws – there were five on each paw – were brittle and cracked, grown long and curled from lack of use. Her tail was stunted, merely a scaly prominence, no more than that. The Mother Creature resembled a giant, pulsating eyeball.

A mewling sibilation escaped both snouts and she tried to thrash around in her bed of slime, but her weight was too much, her limbs too feeble. Only dust stirred, the bones ground to white

389

powder by her soldier rats, the sleek black vermin who guarded and protected her with their own lives. Whom she now called to her.

There were other movements in the dark, cavernous chamber. They were the twitching, writhing motions of her fellow-beasts, those who resembled her in appearance, different from the servant and soldier vermin. Many had been produced from her own womb. And many had mated with her.

Like the Mother Creature, most were captive of their own malformation, debilitated by their own grotesqueness. And some were dead, others were dying.

She screeched, the sound of a screaming child. She was terribly afraid.

But she sensed her black legions were coming to her, winding their way through the flowing corridors, bringing food, the skulls into which her twisted tusks would bore holes so that the spongy flesh inside could be sucked out, swallowed.

She waited impatiently in the darkness, obscenely gross, body quivering, while her offspring, six of them and each one peculiarly shaped, like her yet unlike her, suckled at her breasts.

27

They walked through the carnage, their stomachs sickened, yet their minds somehow numbed. Perhaps their personae had already begun to adapt to such mayhem, such staggering destruction. Horror and revulsion touched, felt, insinuated itself into their consciousness, but some inner defence of the psyche, a natural yet mysterious barrier against insanity, prevented those feelings from penetrating their innermost selves.

The people of this mammoth sanctum, fugitives from the holocaust above, had been caught by surprise, unaware that another and just as deadly enemy lay within.

The first chamber that Culver and the small group of survivors found themselves in was low-ceilinged but capacious, its concrete interior dimly, though adequately, lit. It housed vehicles, many of which were strange to their eyes. Their colour, uniformly, was grey, none bearing markings of any kind. They stood in neat crammed rows, dead things like granite statues, that seemed incapable of motion. The windows of each were small affairs, mere slits in the metal bodywork, heavy-glassed and sinister. Among them were four turretless tanks of a design that none of the group had seen before. The main shells were small, unable to accommodate more than two passengers, and the long, sleek gun muzzles extended far beyond the limits of their hulls. Other vehicles resembled army scout cars, their wheels, like the tanks', on tracks; they had few apertures and entry seemed to be through the roof. The shapes of the rest were more conventional only in that they had doors on either side and they did not run on tracks; instead, each vehicle had six extremely wide wheels.

All the vehicles (Culver had counted eighteen in all) appeared to be empty.

At the end of the long bay were two massive iron doors, both shut.

Dealey had explained there were curving ramps leading up to ground level behind the doors; there were two more sets along the way, the final pair of doors opening out into a secluded and protected courtyard. It had been Ellison's idea to leave the shelter there and then, using the ramp and possibly taking one of the vehicles, for by that time they had discovered other bodies, corpses so savagely mutilated that they were barely recognizable as human. The group had passed between the vehicles, carefully avoiding featureless cadavers that sprawled in the gangways, making for the exit. Controls for opening the huge doors were set inside a small, glass cubicle, and the panes were smeared with dried blood. Ignoring the two bodies – though the term 'bodies' was hardly appropriate for the matter that lay on the cubicle floor – Fairbank tried the switches set in the wall, assuming they would open the exit doors. Nothing had happened; the mechanism was inoperative.

They went through an area marked DECONTAM UNIT, not lingering to examine the racks of silver-grey, one-piece suits, the machines that resembled metal-detecting doorways, or the gruesome things that lay on the shower floors.

It was beyond the decontamination area that Culver, Fairbank, Ellison and Kate began to gain some idea of the immense size and complexity of the government's war head-quarters. Dealey kept quiet while they expressed surprise, the horror of what lay around them momentarily lost in their astonishment.

They had found themselves in a long, sixteen-foot-wide corridor with many other passageways branching off from it. Straight coloured lines swept along its length, here and there a particular shade veering off into another corridor; they were directional colour codes and on the wall was a list of sections, all in groups and each group assigned a particular colour.

They quickly scanned the list, which ranged from CLINIC to LIBRARY, from GYMNASIUM to THEATRE, from PRINT ROOM to FIRE DEPT. There appeared to be a television and radio centre, offices with a secretarial pool, a works area (whatever that encompassed), dormitories and even a station. The latter sign puzzled them and Dealey explained it was the terminal for the railway line that connected the shelter with Heathrow Airport.

'It's a whole bloody city down here,' Ellison had said in awestruck tones.

They had taken the central corridor and, as they had progressed, so corpses became more in evidence. They passed a dormitory and, out of curiosity, Kate glanced in. She immediately swung away, slamming her back against the corridor wall, closing her eyes but unable to banish the sight imprinted on her brain. The room was similar to the dormitories in the Kingsway exchange, only longer and wider, able to accommodate many more people; the bunks were three-tiered and, apart from a few stiff-backed chairs and lockers at the far end, there was little other furniture. The mass of body remains was by that far end, piled against the lockers as though those sleeping or resting had fled there, trapped by the monstrosities that had surged through the open doorway. Many had not even managed to leave their beds.

They came upon curiously small two-seater cars, abandoned in the passageways, and which appeared to be operated electrically. There were cameras at regular intervals set high on the walls. For every hundred yards or so, there were radiation meters, alarms and push-button intercoms. Dealey tried one or two of the latter, but they were lifeless. Yet the lighting and air-conditioning appeared to be functioning normally and the muted, pastel colours of their surroundings, obviously chosen for their calming effect, belied the tragically ironic fate that had befallen the occupants of the shelter.

With each section the group passed through, their apprehension grew, hysteria beginning to rise and bore through that self-protecting emotional barrier.

The carnage was everywhere, no area, no passageway, no room unblemished. It was a journey through a nightmare, a pilgrimage into Hades. And with each step, each turn of the corridor, the atrocity grew worse, for the dead became legion.

At one stage, Kate moaned, 'Why? Why weren't they protected? There must have been weapons. There must have been a guard force, an army of sorts . . .'

The question was soon answered, for they had come to an inner core of the enormous complex.

They were at a T-junction, the corridor extending left and right, disappearing into a curve, suggesting that the shelter's centre was circular. The door directly ahead was set at least five feet back into the wall and they wondered if this was an indication of the wall's thickness. In front of the broad, metal door was a small desk mounted into the floor itself, an elaborate but compact console on its surface. There were two cameras set in the corners of the alcove and a range of various coloured push-buttons set on one side. The sliding door had been jammed open by two bodies, and from what was left of their clothing, it was obvious they had been army personnel.

Culver stopped to pick up a lightweight weapon, a snub-nosed machine gun. 'A MAC II,' he told the others. 'An Ingram. I've seen them before.' He pointed it back along the corridor, warning his companions to stand clear, and pulled the trigger. It clicked empty. 'Pity,' he sighed, and dropped the weapon to the floor.

'What is this place?' Fairbank asked, looking through the jammed door.

Dealey was pressing the buttons of the small desk console, glancing at the door as he did so. 'Nothing appears to be operating,' he remarked, 'apart from the lighting and ventilation. The systems have either been shut down or destroyed.'

'Answer the question,' Culver told him.

'This place? This is the operation centre for the shelter. If you like, it contains the vital organs of the whole complex. The generator and boiler rooms, communications and cypher, living quarters for, er, certain persons, the War Room itself. A refuge within a refuge, if you like.'

'You said living quarters. You mean there's an élite among the élite?' Culver had asked the question.

'Of course. I don't think I need tell you who would be among that special group.'

Culver shook his head.

Kate clutched at him. 'I think we should leave, and I think we should leave *now*.'

'There will be weapons inside,' Dealey said quickly. 'And there may be other survivors.'

'As well as the vermin that did all this?'

'They've gone, I'm sure of it. We've had no sight of them since we entered the shelter. I think we can assume they did their worst here, then moved on . . .'

'To fresh pastures,' Fairbank finished for him.

'That may be exactly the case.'

'But how did they get into here in the first place?' Culver was perplexed. 'How could they possibly have infiltrated such an installation? It makes no sense.'

'Perhaps we'll find the answer inside.' Dealey went to the gap between door and wall. He disappeared through it, not waiting for a reply.

The others looked at each other and it was Fairbank who shrugged, then followed. 'What've we got to lose?' he said.

Kate reluctantly allowed herself to be helped through by Culver, gingerly stepping over the torn bodies that had prevented the door from closing. Inside, the smell of death was almost choking, even though it was old and had lost much of its pungency.

And it was inside, among the human corpses with missing limbs, many headless, organs gouged out, that they found the dead rats.

Now they sat in the vast, circular War Room, exhausted both mentally and physically, each of them trembling, their eyes shifting constantly, never relaxing their vigilance. They all clutched weapons in their laps, wrested from fingers that seemed unwilling to release their grip even though the guns had not managed to save them. Two of the group held Ingrams, which seemed to have been the standard arms for military personnel inside the shelter, while Kate and Dealey had pistols, 9mm Brownings; Ellison had managed to find a

Sterling submachine gun from the armoury – it was a weapon he had grown fond of after his earlier acquaintanceship.

They were on a balcony overlooking row upon row of matt black benches, each containing six or seven separate working units, all of which were complete with television monitors, computers, telephones, teleprinters and switching consoles. Giant screens in the curving walls dominated, even though they were blank. One had been punctured by bullet holes. Dealey had told them that when live, the screens would have shown different areas of the world, indicating nuclear strikes and strategic deployment of military task forces. A particular screen was kept solely for visual contact with Allied Heads of State and their executives, the pictures to have been beamed from satellites unless atmospheric conditions interfered, in which case contact would be maintained through cable. The ceiling lamps were recessed and subdued, each section of the benches having individual built-in lighting. Around the walls and below the screens were various other pieces of machinery, including a bank of computers and television screens. A coffee machine, dated by comparison to the hardware around it, lent the only touch of humanity. Just off the War Room was a tiny television studio containing the bare essentials for broadcasting (which included a soft-upholstered armchair and loose, deep blue drapes as a backdrop, all presumably designed to give an air of calm, even comfortable, authority). Who the hell would be sitting in front of their TV sets while the world around them had been reduced to smouldering ashes was anybody's guess. The studio, they assumed, was for broadcasting to the nation, for quite near them on the balcony was another camera, angled towards the long control table they now sat at; this was obviously used for televised conversations with the

Allies. Next to the television studio was a conference room, its walls and ceiling soundproofed. This was probably where the more 'delicate' decisions concerning the future of the human race would have been discussed and made. There were many other rooms and corridors leading off from the main concourse, the War Room itself the hub of a concrete-walled wheel, but as yet they had not investigated any of these, nor did they feel inclined to. They had seen enough.

The early Christians might well have suffered similar massacres in their own Roman arenas, mauled then torn apart by animals for the gratification of their rulers' bloodlust, but could even those occasions have been on such a grand scale? This modern arena below was almost overflowing with human remains, as though a large number of the holocaust survivors had fled here when the rodent invasion had begun, perhaps still believing that their leaders would now save them from this new, unforeseen disaster. They had been wrong. Nothing could save them from the fury of these mutant beasts, not even the rapid-fire weapons of the soldiers. How could it be so? How many, *just how many*, rats could have caused such massive slaughter? And how could they have got inside the top-security shelter?

It was Alex Dealey, looking weary and dispirited, all trace of pomposity gone, outweighed by adversity, who attempted to supply the answers. He was slumped in a swivel chair, leaning forward over the long table before them, one hand on his forehead, shielding his closed eyes.

'The rats were already inside the shelter,' he said quietly. 'They were inside, waiting. Don't you see? There are sewers below here, miles of underground tunnels, weirs that control the flow of rainwater and effluent. The rats must have roamed the network for years, scavenging where they could, feeding off the city's waste. Oh dear God.' His other hand slowly went to his forehead and he seemed to sink within himself, his shoulders shrinking. 'Food is kept below the main shelter level, a huge cold-storage chamber. It was rarely exchanged, only added to. Hardly any of it was perishable, you see? Any that was, was kept nearer to hand where it could be easily replenished. For years the rats have had an ample food supply.'

'Surely it was checked from time to time?' Culver asked incredulously.

'There was no need, it was considered safe from harm. I suppose it was given a cursory examination at regular intervals, but you would have to see the vastness of the store itself to realize much was left unseen. All foodstuffs were tightly sealed, as was the storeroom itself; the thought of entry by vermin was hardly considered.'

'Not considered at all, it appears,' ventured Ellison, shifting in his seat to ease the stiffness of his ribs.

'Poisons were laid and traps were set. Nobody would have realized the unique cunning of the scavenger they were dealing with.'

'Obviously not.'

Culver was still puzzled. 'There had to be some evidence of these creatures. Somebody must have noticed something.'

Dealey looked up and shrugged. 'Why? These headquarters have never been occupied. Certainly maintenance work has been carried out, new, more-advanced technology installed as the years have gone by, and inspections have always been made at regular intervals; but it's obvious that this breed of rat has kept well-hidden. Its own instincts would have warned it of the treatment it would receive from its old enemy. Remember, too, the extermination of these mutant creatures over the past decade has been carried out ruthlessly and on a grand scale. There have been pogroms against them, if you like.'

'Not ruthlessly enough by your earlier account.' The others looked at Culver with curiosity.

'What do you mean by that, Steve?' Kate asked.

'When I had my little private chat with Dealey yesterday, he told me there was considerable scientific interest in the mutant Black rat. So much so that they tried to breed them in laboratories.'

'I said that there were rumours, nothing more. But that has nothing to do with these creatures in the sewers. Nobody could have known they existed.'

Fairbank was scratching his temple with the snub-nosed muzzle of the Ingram. 'All right, so how come these bloody things didn't attack the maintenance guys or whoever did the checks on this place?'

'I told you: they were probably deeply afraid of men and much too wily to reveal themselves.'

Fairbank swept the gun around the room below. 'They got over their shyness fast.'

'After the bombs dropped, yes. It could be they sensed they had the upper hand. Perhaps their numbers had grown to encourage that belief, also. Another point: they may have considered the mass evacuation into the shelter as an invasion of *their* territory. My theory is that all these elements were involved.'

'They were threatened, so they attacked.' Kate's statement was flat, toneless.

'It's all we can assume.'

'They went up against firepower,' said Fairbank. 'And against an awful lot of people. They must have felt pretty confident.'

'Or they had a stronger motive.'

Once again, all eyes turned to Culver.

He shook his head. 'I don't know, it's just a feeling I've got. There's something more, something we don't know about.'

Ellison was impatient. 'I still don't understand how it was possible for the rats to overwhelm them. Doors could have been sealed, the rats could have been contained, or closed out of any number of different sections.'

'Remember the doors where all those vehicles were housed? The big metal doors to the ramps? They didn't function. Like most things around here, apart from the lighting and ventilation, they were inoperative. I'm sure if we examined the main power switching area we'd find machinery or wiring destroyed, either by the trapped survivors when they used guns to protect themselves, or by the rats gnawing through vital cables. It's not unusual: it's a speciality even of normal vermin. There are all kinds of safeguards in this complex that need power to function.'

'Why the lights and ventilation, then?'

'They're on completely different systems which obviously haven't been harmed.'

Dealey slumped back in his chair, wiping both hands down his face, the Browning placed in front of him on the table. 'It's my belief that the survivors were attacked very soon after the first bombs had dropped, when the people were in mortal fear and disorganized. Can you imagine the scenes inside this shelter at the time? Panic, remorse, total disorientation. Even the trained military personnel would have been traumatized. The survivors were confused and almost defenceless.'

'How many . . . how many would have been here?' Kate's gun was held rigid in her lap as though she were afraid to release it even for a moment. She wanted to leave immediately, but like the others she was totally drained of strength. And they needed answers before they ventured further into the shelter.

'It's impossible to say,' Dealey told her. 'Hundreds, possibly. We've seen enough dead to know there were a large number of people. Not everybody who had access would have reached the shelter by the time the bombs exploded, and of course, many – *many* – may have escaped when the rats attacked.'

Culver was hesitant. 'The, er, apartments we passed in this part of the complex: you said they were meant for certain persons.'

Dealey nodded. 'That was why I was so relieved that they appeared to have been unoccupied. I'm sure the Royal Family were evacuated from London long before the crisis finally erupted.'

'And the Prime Minister?'

'Knowing her, she would have remained here in the capital, inside these headquarters, from where she could direct operations.'

'Do you think there's a chance she and her War Cabinet got out?'

There was a long silence from Dealey. He lifted his hands from his lap and let them drop again, making a muffled slapping sound of despair. 'Who knows?' he said. 'It's possible. It depends on how much they were taken by surprise, or how well they were protected. I have no intention of examining all these bodies to find the answer.'

Culver found the irony of the situation incredible. A failsafe refuge had been constructed for a select few, the rest of the country's population, apart from those designated to other shelters, left to suffer the full onslaught of the nuclear strike; but the plan had gone terribly wrong, a freak of nature – literally – destroying those escapers just as surely as the nuclear blitz itself. *The stupid bastards had built their fortress over the nest, the lair – whatever the fuck it was called – of the mutant Black rats, the very spawn of earlier nuclear destruction.* If there really were a Creator somewhere out there in the blue, he would no doubt be chuckling over mankind's folly and the retribution paid out to at least some of its leaders.

Fairbank had risen from his seat and was staring down at the ghastly scene below. Among the human remnants were inanimate black-furred shapes. He rested his hands on the balustrade. 'I don't understand. They managed to kill a lot of rats down there before they were overwhelmed. But take a close look at some of those animal carcases. They're unmarked, and they're not in such an advanced stage of decomposition as the others. A lot of these fuckers died more recently.'

Culver joined Fairbank, interested in the engineer's speculation. 'Hell, you're right,' he said.

Kate and Ellison barely showed concern, but Dealey rose to his feet. 'Perhaps we should take a closer look,' he suggested.

They descended the short staircase into the main concourse, repulsed by the strong odours that assaulted them, and wary of what might skulk among the ruins.

'Here,' Culver pointed.

They approached with caution, for the rat looked as though it had merely fallen asleep while feeding. Only when they drew close did they notice that its eyes were half-open and had the flat, glazed stare of the dead. Culver and Dealey leaned towards it while Fairbank kept a cautious vigilance on their surroundings.

'There's dried blood around its jaws,' Culver remarked.

'It was eating flesh when it died.'

'There's no marks, no injuries.' He prodded the stiff-haired carcase with the gun barrel, using considerable effort to turn the animal over onto its back. There were no hidden wounds.

'What the hell did it die of?' Culver asked, puzzled.

'There's another over there,' Fairbank said.

They went to it, carefully avoiding the mouldering decay scattered across the floor. There were few insects so far below ground and that was at least something to be thankful for. Culver knelt beside the sprawled carcase and repeated the same operation. Bullet holes punctured the creature's underbelly and they realized its outer shell was a mere husk; underneath it was rotted almost completely away.

Moving on to yet another, the three men discovered this body, too, was unmarked. They averted their heads from the ripe smell.

'Could they have been poisoned?' Culver stood, his eyes ranging over other carcases. There had been more in the other sections and passageways, but the group had not stopped to inspect them closely, assuming they had been killed by the humans they were attacking; it was possible that many of these had also died from causes other than mortal wounds.

'It's possible,' said Dealey, 'but I don't see how. Why would they take bait when they had all the food they needed? It makes no sense.'

He was deep in thought for a few moments and was about to comment further when Kate called from the balcony. 'Please, let's go! It isn't safe here!' One arm was clasped around a shoulder as though she were cold; the other held the gun.

'She's right,' Culver said. 'It's not over. There's something more in this hell-hole. I can feel it like I can feel an icy draught. The dead haven't settled.'

It was an odd thing to say, but the others sensed its meaning for they shared the same intuitive awareness. They climbed back up the steps, their pace now quickened, urgency beginning to return, renewed fear overcoming weariness. The discovery of the dead yet unmarked rats had rekindled their apprehension, its mystery instigating further, unnerving dread. The vast underground bunker had become an enigma, perhaps a deathtrap for them all. It was as if its concrete walls were closing in, the tons of earth above bearing down, pressing close, a huge oppressiveness weighing on their shoulders.

Striving to crush them into whatever lay beneath the underground citadel.

28

The condition of the power plant explained much to them, for it had been reduced to nothing more than a blackened shell, its complex machinery just charred, useless husks. They averted their eyes from dark mounds on the floor, shapeless forms that had once walked and talked and been like themselves.

'Now we know,' said Dealey. There was the sadness of defeat about him. 'They did battle with the rats here. Bullets, an explosion – a chain reaction – devastated this place. All their careful planning, all their ultimate technology, destroyed by a simple beast. They finally discovered who the real enemy is.' He leaned against a wall and for a moment they thought he would sink down. He steadied himself, but did not look at them.

Ellison was shaking his head. 'So that's why there was no communication; everything was knocked out.'

'Communications, machinery – even the doors couldn't be opened,' said Fairbank. 'The first one we found could be opened manually from the inside. And the second was jammed by those two trying to get out. But the others must be sealed tight. Christ, they were all trapped inside their own fortress!'

'Surely all the doors aren't electronically controlled,' said Kate.

'I'm afraid they are.' Dealey still did not look up. 'Don't you see? This was a top-secret establishment, the most critically restricted place in the country; exit and entry had to be centrally controlled.'

Ellison had become even more agitated. 'There have to be other doors jammed open. Some of the people down here must have escaped, they couldn't all have been killed.'

'Escape into what? Into the radiation outside?'

'I still don't understand why the lighting still works,' said Kate.

'Light was the most valuable asset down here, the most protected by back-up systems. Imagine this place in total darkness.'

They tried not to.

Dealey went on. 'The headquarters has four generators, each of which is designed to take over should the others malfunction. If number 1 fails, 2 automatically comes into operation; if 2 then fails, 3 takes over and so on to 4. It's unlikely that all should shut down at the same time.'

Fairbank secured the axe in his belt more tightly. 'I've got no faith in "unlikely" any more. And I think we're wasting time here; let's move on and out.' He looked directly at Culver.

'You know the place, Dealey,' the pilot said. 'Just how *do* we get out?'

'There may be other blocked doors, as Ellison said. If not, we'll have to go back the way we came.'

Kate shrivelled inwardly at the idea, for she had no wish to retread those same abhorrent corridors.

'Let's start looking, then,' said Fairbank. 'This place is troubling my disposition.'

They passed on and suddenly the foul mélange of smells became almost overpowering. Kate actually staggered at the noxious fumes and Culver had to reach out and steady her as he fought down his own nausea. It was Fairbank, grubby handkerchief held to his nose and mouth, who called them forward. He was peering into a wide opening from which came the now-familiar thrumming noise.

'Take a look at this!' he shouted, and there was both fear and excitement in his voice. 'It's bloody-well unbelievable.'

They approached, Culver taking the unwilling girl with him. He covered his face with a hand, nearly gagging when he drew close to the opening; the others were undergoing the same discomfort. He looked inside with considerable consternation, he, too, reluctant to witness more horror, and his eyes widened, his mouth dropped. His spine went rigid.

The ceiling of the generator room was high, accommodating the four huge machines and the largest diesel oil tank Culver had ever seen, its top disappearing into the roof itself. Overhead was a network of pipes, wiring and catwalks. The walls were uncovered brickwork with only piping and mounted instrument-gauges to break up the monotonous pattern. The lighting here was dim; several areas had their own individual sources of light, most of which were switched off. It was uncomfortably warm inside there, a factor that added to the putridness of the atmosphere.

The spacious floor area was an ocean of stiffened, black fur.

Kate reeled away, falling, but instantly scrambling to her feet, ready to run.

'They're dead!' Culver shouted and she stopped. Still afraid, she went back to the four men.

It was an eerie and ugly sight. And, even though the piled bodies were those of a mortal enemy, a strangely pitiful one. The rats lay sprawled against and over each other, hundreds upon hundreds, many with jaws open, bared yellow incisors glinting dully, others with half-open eyes glaring wickedly, although glazedly, at the human intruders. Still more had managed to crawl along the rafters, the piping that networked the ceiling, and lay there as if ready to leap; but those, too, were lifeless, menacing only in appearance.

'What the shit happened to them?' said Ellison in a low breath.

The others were too stunned to reply. Slowly Culver walked into the generator room until he was at the very edge of the great mass of inanimate fur. A rat stared up at him with a rictus grin, taut-curled claws just inches away.

Fighting his repulsion, Culver kneeled close. Again, he saw dried blood staining the lower jaw. Culver rose, quickly scanning the humped-back shapes, as Dealey stood by his side.

'I don't understand,' Culver said.

'I think I do,' the other man replied and Culver looked at him curiously.

'They're diseased,' said Dealey. 'The blood is from their saliva. They've been wiped out by some illness, a plague of some sort. With luck it's killed them all.' He leaned over to prod the nearest rodent with the tip of his gun barrel.

'What kind of plague?' A different wariness was disturbing Culver.

'Impossible to tell. I could hazard a guess, though.'

'I can take it.'

'Possibly anthrax.' He eased the carcase he was prodding over onto its back and made a small grunting sound. 'No pustules, and this chap hasn't any swelling of the abdomen, so I'll guess again. I'd bet on it being pneumonic plague.'

Culver quickly stepped back.

Dealey straightened, but there was no overt concern in his expression. His shoulders were still slightly stooped as though the savage intrusion upon his sacred citadel, the surviving bulwark of his own authority, had finally dispirited him, made him realize just how fragile and ultimately vulnerable that authority had been. The destruction of the city had not shaken his faith, but the annihilation of those in power, his overlords who were to rule from this surrogate National Seat of Government, had devastated him. It was, to him, the loss of his own potency.

'I thought only humans could catch pneumonic plague,' said Culver, slowly backing away.

Dealey wearily shook his head. 'No, animals too. They catch it from their own disease-carrying fleas.'

'Then we . . .?' Culver left the question unfinished.

'We have yet another reason to leave immediately,' Dealey said, nodding.

'Bastards!' Ellison suddenly screamed from the doorway. He raised the Sterling submachine gun to chest level and began firing into the mass of stiff-furred bodies, the brick-walled chamber erupting into a cauldron of explosive sounds. Black bodies leapt into the air as though still alive. Culver and Dealey hastily jumped to one side, while Kate clasped her hands to her ears, dropping the gun she had been holding. Unable to restrain his own fury, Fairbank joined in with Ellison, the small Ingram, its firing not as loud as the Sterling, bucking in his hands with its rapid recoil.

Culver let them spend their anger and hatred, watching the vermin's dark bodies twitch and jump, their flesh torn open by the frenzy of bullets. Small limbs were severed, heads exploded. A two-foot long tail scythed into the air like a tossed snake. Ellison's weapon emptied before Fairbank's and he let it clatter to the ground in disgust. Fairbank ceased firing, a strange, icy grin on his face. The sudden silence was as startling as the thunder preceding it.

Culver walked back to them while Dealey stood and shook

his head as if to clear it of echoes. 'If you're finished, let's—' the pilot began to say when Kate screamed.

'They're moving! They're still alive!'

She was pointing over his shoulder and Culver whirled, his eyes searching the heaped bodies.

He saw no movement.

And then he did.

Parts of the dark ocean were shifting, black shapes slowly disengaging themselves from the whole, creeping forward, slowly, painfully. Resolutely. Yellow eyes glittered. Hissing sounds came from cruel mouths.

Dealey turned and began to retreat when he saw the converging shapes. Kate backed away to the other side of the hallway.

The creatures were dying, some stirred by the shattering noise, others by the bullets themselves thudding into their bodies. The nearest had reached the edge of the mass, was sliding over corpses onto the floor, its long, pointed head weaving from side to side, jagged teeth bared and blood-stained. Others slid down behind it.

Culver raised the Ingram and split the first creature in two with a quick burst of bullets. The others came on, pushing themselves across the floor, sliding smoothly through the spreading blood of their companions. He fired again, the impact scattering the crawling vermin, and Fairbank joined him, aiming his gun into the mass.

They stopped. Watched.

Still there were shapes moving forward.

'What's keeping them coming?' yelled the engineer.

Culver's reply was grimly calm, although he felt anything but. 'Hate,' he said. 'They hate us as much as we hate them. Maybe more – they're the ones who've always had to hide. Thank God there's hardly any strength left in them.'

'Let's thank God from the outside, huh? They may be dying but they still want to get at us.'

They let one more burst rip into the undulating bodies, then hurried through the door.

'I don't want to waste time looking for doors that may not be open,' Culver told the others. 'So let's just head back the way we came. Agreed?'

The others nodded assent and he took Kate by the wrist. 'They can't reach us,' he assured her. 'They're dying, weak; we can easily outrun them.'

She gratefully leaned against him and the five of them began their journey back through the maze of corridors, Dealey in the lead, anxious to put as much distance between themselves and the plague-ridden vermin as possible. They closed their minds to the terrible sights they had to face once more, their tiredness gone for the moment, overcome by coursing adrenalin, and tried not to think of the deadly disease they had just come into contact with. Through the War Room they went, not pausing for a second, almost oblivious to the macabre scene around them. The mutant rats had been diminished, rendered helpless, but still they felt their deadly threat. They yearned to breathe clean, fresh air again, to empty their lungs of death's odours; they needed to see the open sky, to feel a natural breeze brush their skin. They hurried, breaking into a run whenever a clear stretch of corridor, uncluttered by human remnants, presented itself. Through the shelter's central core, slipping into the opening created by the two unfortunates who had jammed the door, into the various sections, stumbling here and there, but never stopping, never pausing to draw in breath.

Finally they reached the decontamination area. They sped through and found themselves in the vast vehicle pool.

Culver brought them to a halt. 'Torches! We'll need torches.'

'And I know where I can find some.' Fairbank dashed off, weaving between the strange-looking parked tanks and vehicles, heading for the small glass cubicle at the far end of the chamber by the doors.

'You know, some of the survivors may have had a chance if they weren't too panicked,' Culver commented as they watched Fairbank disappear.

'How?' asked Dealey.

'Inside these machines. They could have easily shut themselves in and waited out the rats.'

'And then escaped into the tunnels?'

Culver shrugged. 'It's possible.'

'But as we said before: the atmosphere would have been thick with radiation, especially if the attack took place at the very beginning.'

'It was just a thought.'

Fairbank was returning with two heavy-duty flashlights of the kind that had been kept in the Kingsway complex. 'Here you go,' he said, handing one to Culver. 'I spotted them earlier. Guess they kept them handy for emergencies.'

The group moved towards the wide door leading to the corridor, which in turn led to the smaller outer door to the underground bunker. Culver remembered how sickened they had all been on finding the headless corpse still clinging to the green metal door; the sight barely stirred them now. He allowed Fairbank to go through first, both men switching on the flashlights. The last to enter the dark, concrete corridor, he kept his hand on the door.

'Do I close it, or not?' he said to the others. 'If I do, there's no getting back inside.'

Ellison said, 'If you don't, any rats left alive can follow.'

Kate shuddered. 'No matter what, I'm not going back inside that slaughterhouse.'

Culver looked at Dealey and Fairbank.

The former gave a small nod of his head and the engineer said, 'Shut the fucker.'

He closed the door.

The corridor was bright with the flashlights, water on the floor reflecting the beams. The coolness of the atmosphere hit them like an incorporeal wave, turning perspiration into icy droplets; air-conditioning inside the shelter had kept the temperature low, but the difference in the outside tunnels was substantial. Each of them shivered. It was a relief to be away from the grim sight of the human massacre and the dead and dying creatures who were the perpetrators; but the chill darkness that surrounded them created its own sense of ominous menace.

Dealey broke the uneasy silence. 'I suggest we use the first upwards outlet we come to, rather than look for the ladder we came down on.'

'We don't need a vote on it,' said Fairbank, already leading the way down the corridor. He moved fast and was soon well ahead of the others.

'Don't get too far ahead!' Culver called out. 'Let's stick together.'

'Don't worry, I'll stop at the first ladder,' came the hollow-sounding reply.

Kate kept close to Culver, striving to keep her mind free of the day's terrors, not contemplating what the rest of it might bring. They trudged down the dank corridor, splashing water, the noise they made amplified around them, the tenseness a shared, unifying sensation. They heard trickling water and passed over the drain they had discovered on their way into the shelter. Ellison's breathing was coming in short, sharp gasps; with every step it felt like someone was jabbing his ribs with a knife. He needed to rest but, although he was sure the worst was over, he refused to consider the possibility while still in the confines of the damp passageways. Perhaps when they reached the next level they could take a break. Perhaps not. Dealey was last in line, constantly casting his eyes around the pitch blackness behind as though expecting the shelter door to be flung open and hordes of squealing rats to burst through. His imagination, thoroughly aroused by now, conjured up further, grotesque visions: in his mind's eye he saw the corpses inside the shelter stirring, gathering up their scattered pieces, moulding them back into grotesque, barely-human forms, rising, many without heads, for they were lost forever, stumbling through the complex, bumping sightlessly into one another, scrabbling their way to the exits, humps of rotted flesh falling from them, staggering out into the dark corridors fringing the underground bunker, searching for those who still lived, *seeking revenge for their own deaths on those who had survived* . . .

He moaned aloud and tried to wipe the fatigue-induced visions from his mind with shaking hands. He had never thought it possible to experience a nightmare while still awake, for a dream to come so alive when one's eyes were not closed. Sometimes, though, reality created the worst living nightmares.

Running footsteps ahead, coming towards them. A blinding light, freezing them in its glare like fear-struck rabbits paralysed by on-coming headlights.

Fairbank almost ran into Culver.

The engineer leaned against the wall, shining the light back in the direction he had come. He was gasping for breath. 'They're ahead of us,' he managed to say. 'I heard them squealing, moving around. They're above us, too, take a listen!'

They waited and the noise grew. Slithering sounds. Scratching. Squealing. Coming from the corridor ahead of them. And then, just faintly, they heard similar noises overhead. They became louder, exaggerated by the acoustics of the passageways.

'Back!' Culver said, pushing at Kate to make her move.

'Back where?' Ellison shouted. 'We can't get back into the shelter! We're trapped here!'

Culver and Fairbank, shoulder to shoulder in the narrow confines, pointed the Ingrams and flashlights into the tunnel ahead, waiting for the first sighting. It soon came.

They swarmed from the darkness just beyond the range of the beams, a squealing thronging multitude of black-furred beasts, scurrying forward into the glare, eyes gleaming. The vermin filled the corridor, a flowing stream of darkness.

Culver and Fairbank opened fire at the same time, bringing the rush to a sudden, screeching halt. Rats twisted in the air to land on the backs of others, who were themselves in death-throes. Yet more took their place, more advanced, bodies snaking low to the floor, powerful haunches thrusting them forward. Culver stopped firing for a moment to yell at the two men and the girl.

'I told you – *move back!*'

They did, slowly, still watching over Culver's and Fairbank's shoulders.

The advance stopped momentarily and the two men rested their weapons. Bloodied creatures wriggled on the floor no more than fifty yards away.

'Steve!' Kate was near to breaking. 'There's nowhere to go! It's hopeless!'

'Find the drain,' he said to them. 'It can't be far behind us. Find it quickly.'

More shadows rushed forward and the two men opened fire again. Bullets ricocheted off the walls, showering sparks, creating a bedlam of flashes and leaping animals.

'*Give us one of the lights!*' Ellison was screaming in panic.

Without pausing, Culver handed his flashlight over. Ellison grabbed it and stumbled away, aiming the beam into the puddles at their feet. The shooting stopped. The group continued their retreat.

'Here they come again,' Fairbank warned. The rats were relentless in their attack, jumping over the backs of their injured companions, only the narrowness of the passageway itself preventing the group of survivors from being overwhelmed. Both Culver and Fairbank had the same question in mind: How much ammunition did they have left?

'It's here, I've found it!' Ellison called out.

The rats were still huddling together in the full glare of the torches, hemmed in by the rough walls, neither retreating nor advancing. Culver told Fairbank to raise the beam above ground level for a moment. The two men drew in sharp breaths when the light travelled over the quivering humped backs, for the black creatures stretched far away into the tunnel, well beyond its curve.

'Oh, shit, beam me up, Scotty,' Fairbank said in hushed awe.

'Culver, we can't get it open. It's stuck!'

The pilot turned and saw Ellison and Dealey struggling with the drain cover, Kate holding the light for them. He reached for the axe tucked into Fairbank's belt and said, almost in a whisper, afraid anything louder would encourage the vermin to continue their attack, 'Start firing the moment they break.'

Fairbank did not risk looking at him; he merely grunted affirmation, finding the advice totally unnecessary.

Culver knelt beside the two men and handed the Ingram to Ellison. 'Help Fairbank,' he said, then examined the edges of the drain. 'How far down are the sewers?' he asked Dealey, still in a low voice.

'I've no idea,' Dealey's reply was equally quiet. 'I think there are channels below us, running into the main waterways, but I don't know how far down they are, or even if they'll accommodate us.'

Culver bent low and listened, but although he could hear the water trickling down the walls he could not tell whether it was running into a stream. He inserted the sharp side of the axe head into the gap between the grating and its surround. Before trying to lever it up, he scraped out mud.

Fairbank's whisper was harsh. 'They're coming forward again! Taking it slow this time, just creeping along. The bastards are stalking us!'

Culver shoved the blade in as far as it would go. 'Dealey,' he hissed, 'push your fingers through on this side of the drain. Pull when I give you the word.'

'*Hurry it up!*' Ellison's voice was a frantic whisper.

The light Kate was holding shook madly.

'Okay, *now!*' Culver leaned on the blade with all his weight and Dealey heaved upwards. For two dreadfully long seconds nothing happened. Then Culver felt something beginning to shift. The drain cover came up with a squelchy sucking and water ran more freely into the widening gap. After the first few inches it swung up more easily and Culver grabbed at its edge pulling it wide. The lid clanged against the passage wall, the signal for all hell to break loose again.

He snatched the flashlight from Kate and shone it into the

opening. The drain was roughly two foot square, large enough for them to climb into. About ten feet below he saw sluggish moving water.

Culver had to shout to make himself heard over the cacophony of muffled bullets and screeching rats, and even then the others could only guess at his meaning. He tugged at Dealey.

'There are no rungs! You'll have to drop down into the water – it shouldn't be too deep! Help Kate when she follows!'

Dealey needed no second bidding. He was horrified at having to jump into such a black, unknown pit, but even more horrified at the idea of being eaten alive. He lowered himself onto the edge, then sank his overweight stomach into the hole, using elbows to hold himself in that position. There was little room to spare, but he managed to scrape through. With an intake of breath, he slid down, hanging onto the edge with his fingertips. Closing his eyes, Dealey dropped.

His belly and chin scraped against rough brickwork and the fall seemed to last an eternity. He cried out as his feet plunged into cold wetness, but the sound was abruptly cut off when he touched the slimy channel bed. He found himself on hands and knees in flowing water, the level just reaching below his hunched shoulders. His figure was bathed in light from above.

'It's all right!' he shouted upwards, almost laughing with relief. 'It's shallow! We can make it through here!'

He thought he heard a shout from above and then another body was blocking out the light. Rising, Dealey realized the roof of the channel was arched, rising to no more than four feet at its apex. He now stood inside the drain shaft through which he had dropped. Loose chippings and water fell onto his upturned face as Kate's feet slid towards him. He reached up and took her weight, endeavouring to lower her gently, the effort almost too much.

Above, one of the guns had stopped firing.

Culver looked anxiously at the two men and saw Fairbank throw his Ingram away.

'That's it!' the engineer shouted. 'Empty!'

'Get back here!' the pilot told him, tucking the small axe into his own belt. 'Dealey, here comes the flashlight! For God's sake, don't drop it!' He let the torch fall and was relieved when it found safe hands.

Ellison came with Fairbank, still firing along the tunnel. Fairbank dropped to one knee beside Culver and leaned close. 'We can't hold them back any longer! One more rush and that's it!'

'Give me the light!' Still pointed towards the vermin, the flashlight was handed to him. The firing had become more sporadic, the rats advancing, then stopping, Ellison having the sense not to waste bullets. 'We'll get Ellison down there first, then you,' Culver said to Fairbank, keeping his voice low in between bursts of fire. 'I want you to stay inside the drain to support me when I come through. I'm going to have to pull this cover shut before I come down.'

'That's not going to be easy.'

'What the fuck is these days?'

Fairbank grunted and stood with Culver, who reached around Ellison and took the gun. 'Get in the hole!'

Ellison could not take his eyes off the sprawl of dark, inert bodies and their more lethal companions – those who still crept forwards. 'They know. They know they can take us. Look at them! They're getting ready for the final attack!'

It was true; Culver sensed it. The bristling, quivering motion among the packed bodies was building to fever pitch.

Instinct, cunning, maybe just determination – something told these creatures that their enemy had become more vulnerable.

'Get into the drain,' Culver said evenly and Ellison moved away. The pilot faced the rats, gun in one hand, flashlight in the other. 'Is he down yet?' he called quietly over his shoulder.

'Nearly,' Fairbank replied.

'You next.'

'Okay, but first back up until you're on this side of the hole. It'll make things easier for you.'

Hands reached out and guided Culver around the opening. Fairbank clapped his shoulder and wriggled into the drain.

'Make it quick,' he said before dropping from view. 'I'll be waiting.' He was gone and Culver was alone.

Alone except for the creeping mutants.

He gently eased himself into a sitting position, gun and flashlight held chest-high, then slid his legs over the edge. Now comes the tricky part, he thought.

The rats sensed their prey was escaping. The squeals rose to high-pitched screeches as they surged forward.

Culver squeezed the trigger, knowing he would never contain this charge. Bullets thudded into rushing bodies, spinning them over, ripping them apart. But still they came, splashing through the water, a solid, heaving mass.

With a cry of fear, Culver pushed himself off the edge, his elbows catching his weight before he dropped down completely. He kept firing and the rats kept coming, pushing past those that fell, brushing aside their wounded, pure fury storming them forward.

Culver's feet scrabbled around below him until firm hands grabbed his ankles and guided them. He triggered one last spray of bullets, then knew he had no choice. He dropped the flashlight, grabbed the drain cover and ducked.

He felt the support beneath him dropping too, giving him room to manoeuvre in the confined space. He stayed crouched just beneath the grating, knowing it had not sunk properly into its home.

'Take the gun!' he called down, lowering the weapon as far as he could. Someone, probably Fairbank, took it from him. The drain was brilliantly lit by torchlight.

Culver lifted the cover just a little, pulling his fingers from the opening immediately when something sharp brushed their tips. Using the flat of his palms, he tried again. The weight above him was tremendous and he knew the vermin were swarming over the cover. He could hear their squeals only inches away from his face. He felt talon-like claws through the slits of the drain cover, tearing into his hands, and he ignored the pain, using all his strength to lift and slide the lid round. Fairbank's shoulders trembled beneath him, but the stocky engineer held firm, assisting him as much as he could.

The cover closed with a firm, satisfying thud. The rats frantically scraped at the other side, their screeching reaching a crescendo. Culver could not see them, but he felt their hot, fetid breath on his face. He allowed himself to slowly collapse and Fairbank sensing it was all right to do so, gently lowered him. Other hands supported him and he gratefully sank into the running water.

He rested there, head back against the slimy brick wall of the channel, brownish water flowing over his lap, his hands clasped around his knees, breathing in deep lungfuls of stale air, his eyes closed. The others sprawled in similar positions, too exhausted to care about the soaking. They listened to the scrabbling, the frustrated scraping above them while trying to regain their breath, their composure. The squeals from the enraged vermin sent shivers running through them.

Presently, Dealey voiced what they all knew. 'They'll find other ways into the sewer.'

Culver opened his eyes and was relieved to see the flashlight he had dropped had been saved. Fairbank held the Ingram above water level, his face a taut mask, eyes staring and particularly white against the contrast of his dirt-grimed face. Kate's head was against her knees, loose, bedraggled hair falling around her face. He resisted the urge to reach out and touch her, knowing there was precious little time for comfort. Ellison and Dealey held the torches, the latter also clutching the Browning automatic; there seemed to be barely any strength left in either of them.

Culver stretched out a hand. 'Let me have the gun.'

Dealey hardly had to move to give it to him, so close were the walls of the channel. 'It got wet when I fell into the water; I had it in my pocket.'

Culver took the gun, praying it would still fire. 'Ellison – the flashlight.'

Without argument, the engineer passed it over.

'Any idea which way we should go?' Culver asked Dealey. The sound of his voice sent the squealing above their heads into a new furore.

'No. I don't have much idea of the sewer network and I'm completely disorientated anyway.' He glanced up nervously into the opening above.

'Then we'll move in this direction,' Culver indicated with the Browning to his left. 'That's the way the water's flowing, so it must lead somewhere.' He rose, crouching because of the low ceiling, and climbed over the others. 'I'll lead. Kate, you stick close to me. Fairbank, you bring up the rear.'

They all scrambled to their feet, desperately tired and

limbs aching, but keen to be moving. They waded after Culver through the filthy water, the foul smell considerably less unpleasant than the other odours of that day. It was difficult to walk, for the sluggish water leadened their feet, and the constant crouching put added stress on their legs. Yet it was a relief when the sounds of the vermin faded behind them.

They splashed onwards, water trickling through to the channel from other, smaller outlets on either side. The curving walls were covered in lichen and repulsive to touch; here and there, brickwork had fallen inwards, leaving dark impenetrable gaps. Soon a new sound reached their ears and they paused to listen.

'It's rushing water,' Dealey said. 'There must be a main sewer ahead of us.'

'And a way out,' added Ellison.

'Yes, there has to be.'

Their pace quickened and the rushing noise quickly became a mild roar. They stumbled on, ignoring the small things that bumped against their shins, the occasional pocket of gaseous fumes, constantly slipping on the smooth floor beneath the water, but rising to their feet instantly, not stopping to regain breath or rub bruised knees. It wasn't long before they entered the bigger centre channel.

It was at least twelve feet across, the ceiling curved and high. On either side of the swift-moving stream, its spumescent surface littered with debris, were causeways wide enough to walk on. As they shone the flashlights in either direction, they saw other conduits and outlets spilling their contents into the main sewer.

They stepped up onto the causeway on their side, each of them feeling a sudden lift in spirits at this new sight.

'We're lucky,' Dealey said over the noise. 'This tunnel

must have been completely flooded when the rainfall was at its worst.'

'I can't see any ladders.' Fairbank was shining his torch more carefully in one direction, then the other. Culver did the same to add more light.

'There'll be some further along. I would think there's a storm weir in that direction . . .' Dealey indicated the water's flow '. . . so we may find a way out along there.'

Culver felt a hand slide round his waist and looked down to see Kate gazing up at him.

'Are we safe now?' she asked, her eyes imploring.

He couldn't lie. 'Not yet. Soon, though.' He briefly pulled her to his chest and kissed her hair. 'Keep your eyes open,' he told them all. Then he was moving on once again, the others filing close behind.

The rushing water reminded him of the flooded Underground tunnel and his mind wandered back further, to the desperate race against the fallout, the journey along the railway track – the first encounter with the mutant rats. And his first sight of the terrified, frozen girl who was Kate. He thought of the long, trouble-strewn days inside the Kingsway shelter, the first expedition into the shattered world above. The dying, begging people. The rabid dog. Bryce. He remembered the fight back against the floodwaters, the rebellion inside the shelter itself. And then the invasion of rats, the flooding of the Exchange, the terrible struggle to escape. He thought of Dr Clare Reynolds.

Strangely, this day and the day before were just a mad, turbulent blur, with no order, no sense. An insane jumble of visions and stenches. Mixed with death.

One element was common throughout, apart from the weeks of waiting inside the shelter: since the first bomb had dropped he had been running, running, running. Even now he had not stopped and he began to wonder if he ever would, for there would be more danger to face in the new world outside, where only the insects and scavenger beasts could thrive. Perhaps there were no more places left where people could rest.

'Hey! You missed something! Over there.' Fairbank was casting his beam towards the opposite causeway.

Culver aimed his own flashlight in that direction and saw the opening, a passageway beyond. He could just make out stone steps further back. 'Any idea where it could lead?' he asked Dealey.

'Impossible to say. It's not a channel or a drain.'

Culver stared down into the spume-flecked water. 'We can't risk crossing here. We'll have to go on.'

'Not much further, though,' Kate said excitedly. 'Look, there's a gangway across.'

Deep in thought, Culver had missed both the opening and the small, causeway-connecting bridge in the near distance. They hurried towards it, and found the structure was made of iron, narrow in width, and with just a spindly handrail on one side.

'It has to be fairly close to that passageway for a reason,' commented Ellison. 'It's gonna take us out of here, I know it.'

Culver led the way across, testing the bridge's safety with every step. The metal surface was rusted but firm, although the handrail itself wobbled uncertainly. They hurried back the way they had come, this time on the opposite bank, and soon reached the opening. The passageway was at least eight feet high and wide enough for two men to walk along comfortably side by side. The glistening wet stone stairway at the end of the passage was easily visible in the illumination of both flashlights.

It led upwards, into the ceiling.

Kate clutched Culver's arm. 'It's the way out! It has to be!'

Fairbank whooped with glee and even Dealey managed to smile.

'What the hell are we waiting for?' cried Ellison, and Culver had to restrain him from charging forwards.

'There's a whole network of sewers, conduits and pipes all around us – not to mention passageways such as this. Those rats could be anywhere by now: above, behind or ahead of us. It's their territory, so let's just take it quiet and easy.'

He moved to the foot of the steps and shone the torch upwards. Just beyond ceiling level was another opening, a doorway. He began to mount the stairs, taking them slowly, one at a time. The others, heeding his warning but nevertheless impatient, crowded behind him.

Culver reached the top and saw the door itself was old and rotted, a rusted metal sheet battened to its surface. It was open about two feet. He shone in the beam and saw another long corridor. Like the previous one, puddles covered the floor and its walls were of old, crumbling brickwork. It appeared to stretch a long way.

Culver pushed at the metal and the door ground protestingly against the stone floor, shifting only a few inches. Wary of what could be on the other side, he slipped through. No half-eaten corpse held the door open.

The others came in after him, shivering anew with the dank cold. Culver examined the lock and found an open bolt, rusty with years of dampness.

'This is an entrance for the sewer workers and inspectors,' declared Dealey. 'It probably leads to an exit along the Embankment, or somewhere in the vicinity.'

'I thought they used manholes,' said Fairbank.

'Of course not. They have to bring in equipment for repairs and suchlike, as well as large work crews.'

'Why would the door be unlocked?' asked Culver.

'Negligence probably. You can see the door's been warped out of shape by dampness. I doubt anyone found it necessary to lock it anyway. Sewers aren't generally frequented by trespassers, are they?'

'No,' Culver agreed, 'but I'd feel safer if we got it closed. Remember what's chasing us?'

Fairbank lent his weight when Culver put his shoulder to the door. It closed reluctantly, the movement echoing back from the far end of the passageway. Culver shot the rusty bolt with some satisfaction.

Their footsteps were less hurried as they tramped along the lengthy corridor, not because their fear had left them – although it was not quite as acute as before – but because weariness was finally asserting a stronger grip, adrenalin losing its power.

Another door greeted them at the far end, and this one was locked. A hefty kick from Culver opened it.

They found themselves in a spacious room with several doorways around the walls.

'Ah, now I think I understand,' said Dealey.

The others regarded him curiously.

'We've come back to a part of the old World War Two shelter. This must be the second level, just below the section we first entered. I was wrong about the passageway we've come through; it wasn't for sewer workers. It was meant as a means of escape should whoever inhabited this shelter be trapped. The whole region is catacombed with chambers such as this. When you consider how long ag—'

'Take a look!' The coldness in Fairbank's voice startled them all. He was sweeping his flashlight along the floor.

At first they thought the objects lying there were just debris, pieces of mislaid junk left by previous generations of occupiers. When they looked closer the chill inside them all deepened.

The first object to take on an identity was a severed arm, all but one of the fingers missing. The next was the remains of a head, one empty eyesocket bored into and enlarged as though something had been dragged out. A piece of putrid flesh that may once have been a thigh lay close by. The human parts lay scattered around the floor, white bones reflecting the torch lights, dried and shrivelled meat lumps standing alone like strangely shaped rocks on a desert of dust.

The familiar dread returned, only this time more potently, for they were weakened, exhausted, close to total hysteria. Culver caught Kate as she sagged. She did not faint entirely, but that unconscious state was not far away.

Ellison began to head back towards the door through which they had just arrived and Culver brought him to a sudden halt.

'No!' The pilot's voice was firm, almost angry. 'We're going on. We didn't come across any rats on our way into the old shelter, so I figure it's our safest way out. Nothing's making me go back into the sewers.'

The words rebounded off the empty walls, as if to mock him.

He continued determinedly, 'We're going to walk straight through this, right to the other end of this room. There's a doorway there and with any luck, a stairway beyond. Just look straight ahead and don't stop for anything.'

Culver set off, supporting Kate, keeping her walking, her head tucked into his chest. The arm around her shoulder clutched the Browning, its muzzle held erect, ready to swing down into action. He kept the flashlight in his other hand aimed directly at the far doorway. Someone behind stumbled and he looked around to see Dealey on one knee, a skull, with the back of its cranium cracked open like a hatched egg, rolling to a stop a few feet away.

'Get up and keep walking,' Culver commanded, his voice tight. 'Don't stop for anything,' he repeated.

But they did stop.

As one.

When they heard the child crying.

29

The group stood as a rigid tableau among a macabre land-scape of human remnants, listening to the pitiful crying. Culver closed his eyes against both the sound and the new pressure. He wanted to be free of this sinister madhouse, this vault of atrocities, but there was no clear escape, no relief from the mental tortures it inflicted upon them. His only desire was to take Kate's hand and run, never stopping until daylight bathed their faces, until clean air filled their lungs. Yet he knew it wasn't possible. He would have to find the child first.

They listened, feeling wretched with the plaintive cry. The wailing was high-pitched, possibly that of a little girl.

'It's coming from over there,' someone said at last.

They looked to the right, towards an opening that had been boarded up with heavy planks, the bottom section broken inwards. The wood appeared to have been gnawed.

The crying continued.

'I don't think it's wise to stay,' said Dealey, looking around anxiously at the others.

'Then go to Hell,' said Culver in a low voice.

He felt a slight resistance from Kate when he moved away; then she was moving with him. The others reluctantly joined them at the boarded doorway. Culver and Fairbank shone their flashlights through the gaps between the planks of wood and peeked in. The far wall was at least forty feet away and the room itself was bare of furniture, like the chamber they stood in. Fairbank aimed his beam low and tapped Culver's shoulder.

The stone floor of the room had collapsed inwards, leaving a ridge of jagged concrete around its circumference, with broken, exposed joists protruding. Below was a pit filled with rubble.

The sad, despairing cries tore at their nerves.

'The kid's somewhere below,' Fairbank said.

Culver called out. 'Can you hear us? Are you on your own?'

The crying stopped.

'It's all right. We'll come down to get you! You're safe now!'

Silence.

'The poor little sod is terrified out of her mind,' said Fairbank.

Culver began to pull at the planking. The rotted wood came away easily, breaking into long, damp splinters. The crying began again.

It was an eerie sound, the emptiness of the surroundings giving it a peculiar resonance, as if it came from a deep well.

'It's okay!' Culver shouted again. 'You're going to be all right!' Echoes of his voice bounced back.

There was quiet from below once more.

The two men pulled away the wood, creating a hole large enough to climb through. They shone the lights in, the others peering over their shoulders.

'Construction work on the new shelter must have caused the fall-in,' Dealey said. 'With the continuous dampness over the years, the vibration from the new works, it's a wonder the whole bunker hasn't fallen in.'

Culver indicated the dark chasm before them. 'Maybe the nuclear bombs caused the final collapse.'

'Steve, please don't go down there.' Kate spoke in a low whisper, and there was an urgency in her request that disturbed Culver.

'There's a kid inside,' he said. 'It sounds like a little girl, and she's alone, Kate. Maybe others are with her, too injured to speak, unconscious, maybe dead. We can't just leave her.'

'There's something wrong. It ... doesn't feel ... right.' The first sound of the crying child had sent a harrowing and uncanny sensation spilling through her. There was something unnatural about the voice.

'You don't really think I can walk away.' Culver's statement was flat, his eyes searching hers.

She averted her gaze, not replying.

'How can you get to her?' Ellison was still agitated, hating Culver for wasting so much time in this God-forsaken hole. 'You'll break your neck trying to get down there.'

'There could be a way through the sewers,' Dealey suggested. 'Underneath here must be the very basement of the old shelter, close to the sewer network.'

Culver shook his head. 'There's no way I'm going back there. Look.' He pointed the flashlight. 'There's a broken joist over there sticking up from a pile of rubble. The top end of the joist is leaning against the wall, just below the overhang. I think I can make it back up that way. Getting down is no problem; the ceilings are low in here; it's an easy drop.' He turned to Fairbank. 'I'd like to borrow the Ingram.'

The engineer surprised him by shaking his head. 'Uh-huh. I'm coming with you. You'll need a hand with the kid.'

Culver nodded gratefully and handed the Browning to Dealey. 'No point in you three waiting. Take them out of here.'

Again he was surprised when Dealey refused. 'We'll wait for you,' the older man said, taking the gun. 'We'll be better off if we all stick together.'

'You're crazy!' Ellison erupted. 'Look around you! Those bloody rats have been here, and they can get to this place again! We've got to leave now!'

He made as if to grab the gun from Dealey, but Fairbank's hand clamped around his arm.

'I've had all the shit I'm going to take from you, Ellison.' The stocky engineer's eyes blazed angrily. 'You always were trouble, even in peacetime, bitching, whining, never happy unless you were complaining about something. Now if you want to leave, leave! But you go on your own, and with no flashlight and no gun. Just don't go stumbling into any hungry rats in the dark.'

Ellison appeared ready to attack the other man, but something in Fairbank's glacial smile warned him off. Instead he shook his head, saying, 'You're all insane. You're all fucking insane.'

Culver gave Kate the flashlight. 'Keep it shining into the floor opening – we're going to need all the light we can get.'

Her quietness disturbed him, but he turned away. 'Ready?' he said to Fairbank.

Muttering something about 'another fine mess', the engineer eased his way through the gap they had created.

Both men paused on the other side, Fairbank shining the light downwards. Apart from rubble, the room looked empty. The light beam reflected off black pools of water in the debris.

'Can you hear me down there?' Culver called out, aware that it was impossible not to be heard.

'The kid may be too scared to answer,' Fairbank suggested. 'God knows what the poor little beggar's been through.'

They thought they heard a shifting sound.

'You want the gun or the flashlight?' the engineer asked.

Culver would have preferred the Ingram. 'Let me have the light.'

With backs to the wall they eased themselves around the overhang, fearful that it might collapse beneath them. Streams of dust trickled into the darkness below. Kate, standing just inside the gap, one leg still in the outer room, helped guide them with her light.

Culver came to a halt. 'Okay, this is where we go down.' They had reached a corner, the flooring wider and seemingly more solid there. He could just make out the iron beam projecting beneath the overhang.

'Hold the torch for a moment,' he said, then lowered himself into a sitting position. He turned onto his stomach and lowered himself, his feet finding the angled beam. He let himself go, boots sliding down the joist, the descent to the heap of rubble not long. Steadying himself, he looked up.

'Throw me the torch, then the Ingram.'

Fairbank did so and clambered over the edge himself. They were soon standing side by side.

'Easy,' acknowledged the engineer, retrieving the weapon.

Culver swept the torch around the room. 'There's nothing here,' he said. 'Nothing.'

He moved forward and something gave way beneath him. Fairbank tried to grab him as he fell, but was encumbered by the gun. Culver toppled, rolling in the debris, the axe in his belt digging painfully into his side. The sound of sliding masonry echoed around the damp walls. Fairbank went after him, and fell also, cursing as he went.

And the crying began once more, high-pitched and fearful, the voice of a terrified child.

Both men looked towards the direction of the cries. They saw a dark doorway, another room. A familiar nauseating stench came from that room.

Dust settled around them as Kate's voice from above called out, 'Are you okay?'

'Yeah, we're all right, don't worry.'

The two men picked themselves up and noticed that, yet again, the crying had stopped.

'Hey, kid,' Fairbank yelled, 'where the hell are you?'

They heard what sounded like a whimper.

'She's in there,' Culver stated what they both knew.

'That smell . . .' said Fairbank.

'We have to get her.'

'I don't know.' Fairbank was shaking his head. 'Something—'

'We have to.'

Culver led the way, sloshing through the puddles, stepping over debris. After a moment's hesitation, Fairbank went after him.

The next-door chamber was wide and long, its ceiling, fallen in many places, low. Parts of the walls had collapsed, too, creating deep, impenetrable recesses. In the distance they could hear a faint rushing, gurgling noise, the cadence of the sewers. Long cobwebs, like soot-filled lace, drooped everywhere. Scattered on the broad expanse of floor before them were humped shapes, yellow-grey in the gloom. Smaller white shapes glowed almost phosphorescently. Dark, less discernible forms lay between.

Both men took a step backwards, Fairbank raising the weapon, Culver reaching for the axe in his belt. The urge to run, to flee from this stinking, horror-strewn cellar, was almost irresistible. Yet it held a peculiar, paralysing fascination. And the distressed whimpers could not be ignored.

'They're not moving,' Culver whispered urgently. 'They're dead. Like the others in the shelter, wiped out by the plague. They must have crawled back here, their lair, to die.'

'All those skulls. Why all those skulls?'

'Look at them. They've been broken into. Through the eye sockets, between the jaws. Look there – holes bored straight through the top of the cranium. Don't you see! They eat the brains. That's why so many corpses we found were headless. The bastards brought them back here to feed off.'

'Those other things . . .'

Culver singled out one of the bloated, yellowish-white shapes. Its form seemed peculiarly blurred, indefinable.

'What the hell is it?'

Culver had no answer to the engineer's question. He moved closer, fascinated, despite himself.

'Oh, sweet Jes . . .' The words faded on his lips.

The bloated creature barely resembled a rat. Its head was almost sunk into the obese body, long withered tusks emerging from the slack jaw. Under the strong light they saw there was a pinkishness to the fine, stretched skin, a smattering of wispy white hair its only covering. Dark veins streaked its body, blood vessels that had hardened and stood embossed from the skin. The twisted spine rose to a peak over its rear haunches; the tail curved round like a lash, its surface hard with scales. There were other projections about its body, these resembling malformed limbs, superfluous and hideous in shape. The slanted eyes glinted under the torch glare, but there was no life in them.

'What is it?' Fairbank repeated breathlessly.

'A mutant rat,' said Culver. 'Of the same strain as the Black, but . . . different.' Dealey's words came back to him.

He had said there were two breeds, born of the same altered gene. 'A grotesque', Dealey had called it. It was an inadequate description. He had implied they were undergoing some genetic transformation. *Oh Christ, so this was the result!*

There was a rustling, not far away.

Nerves taut, ready to snap, both men whirled around, the light beam stabbing at the darkness.

'Over there!' Fairbank pointed.

Shapes were moving. A mewling sound to their left made them turn in that direction. Other movements, scuffling in the darker corners.

'It's like before,' Fairbank said in dismay. 'They're not all dead.'

Culver swept the light over the sluggishly heaving forms. 'They can't harm us. Listen to them. They're weak, dying. *They're frightened of us!*'

A black shape disengaged itself from the mass. It tried to crawl towards them, hissing as it came, but it could hardly move. Fairbank aimed the gun.

Before he could fire, a squealing scream came from a far corner. The two men looked wide-eyed at each other, then towards its source.

'The kid!' exclaimed Fairbank.

The torch beam reached the far corner, but too many other objects were in the way for a clear view.

'Let's get her and then get out!' Culver urged. He held the axe ready. 'Shoot at anything that moves, try and clear a path!'

They set off, both men determinedly keeping panic in check, making for the corner where the piteous crying had resumed. Only now the sound was different, more shrill . . . less like a child's . . . more like . . .

A hail of rapid *phuts* overshadowed the other noises as

Fairbank fired at the obscenely bloated bodies. He could not be sure that they moved, but was taking no chances. The creatures seemed to pop with small explosions.

A Black rat rose up in front of Culver, standing on its haunches so that it looked immense. It snarled and hissed at him, blood-flecked foam dripping from bared teeth, but Culver could see the animal had no strength, only instinctive hatred driving it on.

Blood splattered Culver's hand as he brought the axe down on the thin skull.

The two men kicked ground bones aside as they made their way towards the crying child, scuffing up white powder and looking away from dismembered human parts. As Fairbank stepped over an inert pink form, the creature raised its sinister, pointed head, toothless jaws attempting to snap at his ankle. The engineer stamped down hard and felt bones crunch beneath his foot.

The mewling increased in pitch, became an intense swell of squealing, of helpless ululation . . . infantile wailing . . .

Childish crying . . .

The realization struck Culver like an icicle dagger. He almost stumbled, almost fell among the fearful writhing bodies. He tried to reach out and bring Fairbank to a halt, but it was already too late. They were there. They had reached the far corner. They had reached the Mother Creature's nest.

'Oh . . . my . . . God . . . *NO!*' Fairbank sobbed as they looked down at the throbbing, pulsating flesh and its terrible spawn.

'It can't be,' Fairbank moaned. 'It . . . just . . . can't . . . be . . .'

In another section not too far away, from a hole in the crumbled brick wall, came the sounds of scuffling, of scampering clawed feet.

30

Kate, Dealey and Ellison flinched when they heard the gun-fire. Kate stood perilously close to the edge of the collapsed floor, attempting to shine the flashlight into the doorway through which Culver and Fairbank had disappeared.

'Steve!' she called, but only heard more soft gunfire. And in the pauses, an awful ululation, a strident, piercing screech-ing. She turned to the others. 'We must help them!'

'There's nothing we can do,' Dealey told her. His throat was dry, he could barely speak; the hand gripping the Browning would not keep still. 'Keep ... keep the light ... on the doorway as a ... as a ... guide for them,' he stammered.

Ellison remained on the other side of the broken boards, inside the darkened room, listening to the dreadful sounds, the trembling in his legs making it difficult for them to support his body. His hands were clawed against his face, his eyes staring and seeing nothing but blackness. *They were crazy, crazy to stay here, crazy not to run, to get out while they had the chance, crazy to think they could defend themselves against so many.* Culver and Fairbank were finished. Nothing could save them! The rats would rip them to pieces and then come searching for the girl, Dealey and himself! *Why hadn't they listened to him? The stupid, bloody fools!*

He looked towards the source of light, seeing Dealey's

silhouette, the man leaning forward into the opening, clutching the gun. The gun! He had to take the gun! And the flashlight – he would need the flashlight!

Ellison moved quickly.

Dealey turned as the Browning was snatched away, tried to protest, but was pushed back against the doorway, shards of splintered wood digging into his back.

Gun held forward, Ellison made a grab for the flashlight. *'Give it to me!'* he screamed as Kate tried to pull away.

He caught her arm, yanking her inwards. She fell, tried to kick out at him, but a hand smacked her viciously across the face. She cried out, falling backwards. The flashlight was taken from her.

Dealey tried to intervene and Ellison pushed him away once more. He levelled the gun at him. 'I'm leaving!' The engineer's words were spat out. 'You can come with me, or you can stay. But I'm getting out now!'

'The others . . .' Dealey began to say.

'We can't help them! They've had it!'

Ellison began to back away, keeping the weapon pointed at the two figures, who were blinded by the flashlight. Then he turned and began to run, heading for the door at the other end of the room, away from the mayhem below, away from his companions. And, he foolishly thought, away from the vermin.

31

Fairbank shouted his abhorrence, screamed his fear, as he fired at the huge swollen mass before them. The creature screeched, the sound of a hurt, terrified child, and attempted to lift her obese body, tried to protect herself, her two jaws snapping ineffectively, her useless limbs thrashing the ground, trampling and scattering the tiny offspring that had suckled at her breasts.

Bullets ripped into her, explosions of blood spurting out in dark jets, drenching the two men, soaking the earth around her, covering the blind, squealing things beneath her with its sticky fluid. In a paroxysm of agony, she rose up, exposing her sickening, fleshy underbelly, several of her brood still clinging to the many breasts that dangled there. A frenzied hail of bullets tore her open, a waterfall of blood gushing out, carrying with it internal organs that steamed in the dank atmosphere. Still she moved, still she writhed, falling again, but incredibly shuffling her way towards the two men.

Fairbank's howling cry mingled with the muted crackling of the weapon, his face lit up with the bright flashes, his eyes demented with loathing, with revulsion for the monstrosity coming towards them. The massive, throbbing body began to come apart, the rising curved spine shattering into splinters, bursting outwards like shrapnel; flesh ruptured and parts pulverized as bullets tore through; one barely raised claw was shredded to pulp. Yet still it advanced.

The pointed head, its incisors like curled tusks, the eyes white, sightless, weaved in front of them; a strange stump protruded from her shoulder next to the head, an opening within it which could only have been another mouth, spitting blood-specked drool.

Culver sank to his knees, strength draining from his legs. He stared at the heinous deformity, the misbegotten grotesque, horrified, his muscles numbed. But as her foul breath and her spittle touched his cheek, the shock was punctured.

The flashlight at his knees, he raised the short axe with both hands and, with a screaming roar, brought it down with all his force.

The pointed skull before him split cleanly in two, grey-pink substance inside falling loose, liquid from the opened throat jetting out.

The piercing screech came from the stump next to the cloven head, the toothless jaws wide with the creature's pain, her scaly purple tongue stabbing frenziedly at the air.

Culver struck again, cutting through this other skull, the axe head sinking into the shoulder, into the body itself.

The squirming abomination suddenly went rigid, became frozen just for a few moments. Then slowly, agonizingly slowly, it began to slump, nerve ends twitching, torn, bloated body quivering.

But Culver was not finished. His eyes were blurred and his face dampened by tears as he attacked the litter, the smaller more obscene – *much more obscene* – creatures that the monster had given birth to. He hacked their pink bodies, ignoring their faint cries, striking, pummelling, crushing their tiny bones, making sure each one was dead, beating any small movement from them, shredding them from existence, sundering them of all form, of any shape.

A hand tugged at his shoulder, the grip hard, violent.

He looked up to see Fairbank grimacing down at him.

'The other rats are down here,' the engineer said through tight-clenched teeth.

Culver was hauled to his feet, his mind still confused, still dazed by the slaughter. And by what he had slaughtered. He quickly became aware of the darting black shapes in the rubble of the damp underground chamber.

The rats were in turmoil, leaping from an opening in the brick wall, scampering down the slope of debris, squealing and hissing, looking wildly around, lashing out at each other, gnashing their teeth and drawing blood. They poured through, more and more, filling the room, and somehow oblivious to the two men. The mutant Black rats fought each other, groups turning on an individual for no apparent reason, tearing it apart and gnawing at the body.

Culver and Fairbank could not understand why they were ignored as the animals swilled around the chamber, biting at the other gross forms that lay dying or dead on the floor, high-pitched squeals filling the air, the sound resembling hundreds of excited birds inside an aviary; the noise, the movement, intensifying, rising to a climax, climbing to a thunderous pitch.

Then they stopped.

They lay in the darkness, black-furred bodies quivering, a trembling, silent mass. Occasionally one would hiss, snarl, rear up, but would become passive almost immediately, sinking back among its brethren. The shaking motion seemed to reverberate in the atmosphere itself.

Bathed in blood, grimed with filth and barely recognizable, the two men held their breath.

Nothing stirred.

Slowly, wordlessly, Fairbank touched Culver's sleeve. With a slight jerk of his head he indicated the doorway they had entered by. Keeping the light beam on the floor before them, the two men began gently, quietly, to make their way through the gathered vermin, careful not to disturb any, skirting round when a pack was too thick to step over.

A rodent lashed out with its incisors, hissing at them when they trod too close. The teeth grazed Culver's ankle through his jeans, but the animal did not attack.

At one point, Fairbank tripped and stumbled into a tight group, going down on his knees among them. Inexplicably, they merely scattered, snarling at the air as they did so.

They were just thirty yards from the doorway, both men wondering why they could not see Kate's flashlight shining into the collapsed room behind, when an eerie keening began.

It started as a single, faint, low whine; then other rats joined in, the keening growing, swelling. The sound ended in a startling unified screech and the vermin broke loose again. But they darted towards the bloody, shapeless carcase of the gross monster that the two men had destroyed, the miscreated beast who had nurtured the even more hideous newborn, pouncing on the remains, fighting each other over the scraps, covering the nest completely with their own frantic bodies.

And when there was nothing left of the malformity and her brood, they turned on their kindred, the bloated beasts who were of the same breed but perversely different, savaging them until they, too, were nothing but bloody shreds.

The two men ran, heading for the doorway, kicking aside

those vermin still standing in their path. Culver swung the axe as a rat sprang at him, catching it beneath the throat. It squealed and dropped in a limp bundle to the floor. Another leapt and caught his arm, but the leather jacket ripped and the animal fell away, Culver cracking down with the blunt end of the axe, breaking bone. Fairbank scattered four or five others that had grouped in the doorway itself.

They were through and there was still no light from above, but they heard Kate cry out Culver's name.

Fairbank whirled in the doorway, pressing a shoulder hard against the frame, the Ingram pointed back into the chamber they had just left.

'Culver, give me light!' he shouted.

Culver did so, shining the beam into the next room. The rats were swarming after them.

Fairbank fired, the weapon hot in his hands, his trigger finger stiff with the pressure. The advancing rats danced and jerked as though on marionette strings. 'Start climbing,' he called out over his shoulder. 'I can hold them without the light for a couple of seconds!'

Culver quickly climbed the heap of rubble leading to the fallen joist. His torch lit up Kate standing on the ledge above.

With no time to even wonder what had happened to her flashlight he yelled, 'Catch!' and lobbed the light towards her. She only just managed to hold it; she turned the beam back down into the pit.

The thing they had dreaded most of all happened. The Ingram clicked empty. With an alarmed shout, Fairbank turned to follow Culver, dropping the useless weapon into the dust.

Culver ran two steps up the angled joist, throwing the axe onto the ledge above him and grabbing at the edge just before his boots began to slip down again. Pieces of masonry fell away, but he quickly had both elbows on the overhang. His feet scrabbled for purchase.

He heard screaming from behind.

Kate was kneeling on the ledge, pulling at his clothes, trying to lift him. Dealey, too, had ventured out and had a hand beneath Culver's shoulder. The pilot's boots found a grip, enough to push upwards. He scrambled over the edge, instantly rising to his knees, grasping the flashlight from the girl.

Fairbank was halfway up the slope, his lower body engulfed by biting, scratching vermin. One darted up his back, sinking its teeth into the back of his neck. The engineer rolled over in an effort to dislodge the animal; his mouth was open in a scream, his eyes tightly closed against the pain. The rat fell away and Fairbank started to crawl again, his hands clawing into the rubble, the weight of the vermin chewing into his legs holding him back. He rose to a kneeling position, the rats clinging to his lower body. He tried to push them away and his hands came away bloody, fingers missing.

'*Help me!*' he screamed.

Culver tensed and Kate threw herself at him, knocking him back against the wall.

'You can't, you can't,' she kept saying over and over again.

He tried to free himself, but she held him there, Dealey using his weight to assist her. And in reality, he knew that the little engineer was beyond help.

'*Give me the other gun!*' he shouted and could not understand why they did not comply, why they merely held him tight.

Fairbank was dragging the giant rats upwards with him. They covered him now, making him a creature of black, stiffened fur, a monster of their own kind. His screaming had turned into a raspy choking as they tore into his neck. One side of his face had completely gone, the skin ripped down, taking an eye and most of his lips with it. His nose was nothing more than a mushy protuberance. He tried to raise his arms as if still reaching for the ledge, but they could hardly move with the weight of the rats clinging to them.

Fairbank fell stiffly backwards, crashing down into the rubble, the black pools of water. His blood spread outwards, joining those pools as the vermin pushed and snapped at each other in their struggle to devour the most succulent parts.

Others were aware of the three people on the overhang above and darted up the slope, springing onto the metal beam, attempting to scramble onto the ledge.

32

The thing that would eventually kill Ellison was lying in the darkness. It did not move, nor even breathe. It made no sounds, nor could it. It had been dead for some time. But still it would kill Ellison.

The corpse was that of a sewer worker, a senior repairs foreman, and as a living being the foreman had chosen this shadowy place to die. Others in his small work crew, on the day of the bombs, had elected to return to the surface, to find their families, to put their faith in the authorities. This man had had no such faith. He was old, ready – more than ready – for retirement, not just from the job he had worked at for forty-two years (some said a hundred, others said he was born in the sewers, while still others who did not appreciate his dour, often rancid, humour maintained he belonged there), but from existence itself. He may have been considered perverse in his belief that life was somehow cleaner beneath the streets than above. What he meant, but what he never told anybody, was that there was a wonderful absence of people in this permanently nocturnal underworld. And everything was more distinct down there, more defined, unlike the murky upperworld where there were shades for everything, colour, opinions and race. In the depths, every-thing was black unless illuminated by man-made light; and such illumination made the blackness beyond mere black, deeper in intensity. He had considered himself a simple man (although he was not) with a penchant for absolutes. The tunnels gave him absolutes.

And the falling bombs had provided the ultimate one. There was no more living, only dying.

He had let his workers go, not even offering advice. In fact, he was pleased to be released from them. Then he had found his place in the dark.

The old air-raid shelter was not unknown to him, although strictly speaking it was off-limits to the sewer workers. He hadn't visited it for many years, for past curiosity had soon been diminished by the bunker's very emptiness; but once he was alone, he had sought out the refuge simply because he had preferred death without wetness. True, the old complex was damp and puddled, but there were places where the moisture at least did not run.

So he had settled down in the dark corridor, not minding when the batteries of his helmet lamp had run down, the light slowly eaten by shadows, swallowed by blackness in one quick gulp. He waited and ruminated, having no one to shed tears for (his family were not close) and little regret that it had all come to this. In a way, he was even pleased that his manner of death was of his own choosing, and not specifically laid out by the corporate authority who had ruled his destiny for as long as he could remember. He had heard that the final stages of starvation were not that unpleasant, that the mind, unrestricted, not diverted by physical needs, found a new, freer plane. If only the boring hunger pains and the agony that came from organ deterioration did not have to be endured first.

The days had passed and the old man had tried to remain still, not to maintain strength, but because stillness was close to lifelessness. He lost track of time, so had no idea of when the hallucinations began (or even of when they ended). He enjoyed most (who wouldn't mind swapping anecdotes with God, or floating through space and seeing the Earth as a tiny pinpoint of blue light?), but there were others that terrified, that made him huddle up in a tight ball and hide his face away from sights and sounds that had no place in his dimension. The scurrying noise had provoked the worst visions for, inexplicably, they seemed to draw him back to a dreamy reality. The padding, scuffling of small bodies was very close, coming from a grating that ran the length of the corridor in which he lay. He never dared look, for that would mean testing the truthfulness of the dream, and that truth might bind him longer to the existence he was trying to escape. He had lain still, not breathing, lest those underworld creatures that made such sounds impose *their* truth upon him.

The old man's delirium was timeless, the slide – once the worst was over – into peace, not oblivion, easy and gliding, with almost no line drawn between the two opposites, life and death. The body had straightened before the final but slurred moments, legs sprawling outwards, arms at his sides, and head slumped onto his chest. It was the way he had chosen and it had not been too unkind to him.

He had thought, mistakenly, that at least his way out was of no consequence and no bother to anyone else; but in that, he was wrong.

Had not the sewer worker chosen that particular spot in which to wither away, and had his legs not sprawled outwards, feet pointing east–west, then Ellison would not have stumbled over him, tripped and lost his flashlight, gun, and a little later on, his life.

Ellison burst through the door, his only desire to be as far away as possible from the commotion back there. He knew the others had no chance: there would be nothing left of Culver and Fairbank by now, and Dealey and the girl would not last long on their own. He did not consider that the latter two had even less of a chance without the flashlight and gun he had taken from them. They were fools and the world was no longer fit for such; only the clear-headed and ruthless would survive. He meant to survive; he had already gone through too much not to.

Beyond the room where Kate and Dealey lay stunned was yet another room, this one smaller and square-shaped. The flashlight soon picked out a door directly opposite. He prayed it would not be locked as he hurried over, and his prayer was answered. Thankfully, he pushed it open wide and saw the short corridor beyond, another door at the end. Whoever had originally designed the crazy house must have had a mania for doors and corridors, unless (and more likely) these were added over the decades as the complex was extended. So unnerved at what lay behind and so intent on what lay ahead, Ellison failed to notice the sprawled legs, the opposite-angled feet, just inside the door. Both flashlight and gun were thrown from his outstretched hands and he landed heavily, the concrete floor rushing up to meet him and skinning his hands and knees. His surprised cry changed instantly to one of pain, then anguish when something shattered and there was no more light.

Panic, his old acquaintance and motivator, sent him fumbling around the hard concrete floor in search of the precious light. He recoiled from the stick-like leg he touched, moving rapidly away, coming up against a wall and feeling some kind of grille beneath him. The slats were wide enough for his hand to go through and, for a moment, his fingers dangled in space. He hastily withdrew them, not liking the cool draught of air that embraced his skin.

He found the torch close by, cutting his hand on the shattered glass. He pressed the switch, praying once again, but this time the invocation went unheeded: the light failed to respond.

Ellison began to whimper, occasionally a self-pitying sob breaking loose. The gun. He had to find the gun. It was his only protection. But somebody up there had closed shop: his entreaties were ignored. He searched as much as he could of the corridor, moving around on scraped hands and knees, finding only dried, brittle excreta, presumably the dead person's bequest to the world. Eventually he gave up, knowing madness or vermin would claim him if he remained in that place one minute longer. He moved to the wall on his right, feeling the grating beneath his feet – perhaps the gun had fallen into it – and touching the wall on that side with both hands he moved forward, sure that it was in the right direction, his fingertips never leaving the wall's coarse surface, blinded by bubbling fear as well as lack of light.

A corner. Moving away, keeping to the wall. A doorway. The doorway he had seen from the other end just before he had tripped. He found the handle, twisted, opened the door, went through. He had no way of knowing what kind of room he was now in. He could only keep to the wall, moving to his right, going around a long way it seemed, although he understood that blindness made distances longer, not stopping until he had found another opening. He entered this one, still keeping to the wall, stumbling onwards, travelling further into the labyrinth, unaware that if he had chosen the left-hand path, he would have come upon a staircase leading upwards.

33

Fairbank's screams resounded in their ears long after he was dead. As they fled from the room with its precarious ledge, the vermin leaping upwards, falling back, trying again, claws sinking into broken masonry, scrambling over the edge to give chase, the two men and the girl could not close out those horrifying shrieks from their minds. Dealey and Kate had had to drag Culver from the room, and only when the screaming stopped had he allowed them to. For a few seconds he had stood in the doorway, axe still clasped in one hand, staring down at the heaving mass covered in Fairbank's blood. A rat had appeared nearby, its long, pointed snout sniffing the air as its claws had struggled for purchase. Another had arrived at its side and Culver had used his boot to send them reeling back down.

As they hastened across the chamber, Culver only half-hearing Kate's explanation of the missing flashlight and gun – the absconded Ellison – the vermin were steadily surmounting the overhang, ignoring the shrill combat of others who fought over the remaining human fragments. Still more found other routes from the basement chamber, their senses keen, bloodlust roused and still not sated from weeks of plenty.

Strong emotions other than fear were coursing through Culver: the deep grief for the engineer, the rending sense of having failed him, loathing for the beasts themselves coupled with a wild anger at them. It seemed that the mutant vermin were in a conspiracy with the powers who had ordered the all-out destruction of mankind: what those lunatic powers could not kill off, the rats were happy to clear up.

Kate held the flashlight Culver had thrown up to her, and she kept it pointed at the doorway Ellison had disappeared through, almost as if the beam would provide a straight, safe path to run along. They reached the doorway, passed through without pause, conscious of the squealing sounds close behind. They traversed the smaller, square-shaped room they found themselves in, heading for an open door opposite. The first of the chasing rats was no more than twenty feet behind.

Culver pushed Kate and Dealey inside, going with them and quickly turning to slam the door shut. Bodies crashed into it on the other side, rocking the wood in its frame. More thumps followed as the giant rats leapt at the door. Culver could see the wood bend inwards with each thump. He stiffened when he heard scratching. Then came the determined gnawing.

'Get down to the other end!' he shouted. 'I'll hold them for as long as possible, then I'll make a break for it!' He kept his foot and shoulder to the door, feeling it move judderingly against the frame.

Kate backed away, keeping the light on Culver, on the door he struggled to keep closed against the Hell's demons outside, almost falling over something at her feet, moving away so that the circle of light grew, took in all the doorway, the beginnings of the corridor walls, Dealey, white-faced and shaking like a man with ague, the similarly white-faced corpse that smiled down into his chest.

She screamed, backed away fast, sent something behind her scudding across the floor, almost falling over it. She turned and saw the other flashlight lying there, its glass smashed. It was next to a long grating beneath which were pipes with valves, stopcocks of some kind. She imagined the wide-spaced slats of the grille were so that maintenance men could reach through and adjust the valves. And there was the Browning lying in the shallow trench, propped up against the piping. The gun and flashlight were there in the corridor, but where was Ellison?

Her scream had caused Culver and Dealey to turn and see the starved body of a man wearing overalls, a helmet with a fitted lamp by his side. His emaciated expression seemed oddly pleased with his demise.

'Steve, the gun,' Kate said, pointing the torch through the grating. 'Ellison must have dropped it down there.'

'Can you reach it?'

'I think so. I think my hand can go through.'

The door bulged and, near the floor, the first splinter cracked inwards. Culver pushed his body hard against the wood. 'Try and get the gun,' he told Kate.

She knelt beside the opening and, keeping the light on the Browning, slid her fingers through the slats. Her whole hand sank in and she pushed further until her wrist was inside too. Further still until she was stopped by her elbow. Her fingertips could just touch the gun butt.

'Hurry!' Culver urged.

Kate was careful not to topple the weapon, knowing it would never be reached if she did so. Her fingers slid down on either side and she closed them firmly like pincers, making sure she had a good grip before slowly drawing her hand upwards.

The black creature darted forward and bit into her hand before she was even aware of its skulking presence.

Kate's screams jolted the two men like rapid blows from a

hammer. They could only see her crouched silhouette, the flashlight lying on its side, shining towards the far door. Her shoulders were jerking as though she were being pulled, her head thrown back in resistance. They guessed instantly what held her there.

More splinters loosened at Culver's feet, but he was unaware of them. He ran to the struggling girl, her agonized screams dismissing any other danger from his mind. Scooping up the flashlight, he knelt beside her and grimaced when he looked down through the grating.

A rat, so big it filled the gap between the piping and the floor of the shallow cavity, had locked its jaws into Kate's hand and was tugging at it, its head moving in a swift shaking motion. Other rats were squirming beneath the piping, approaching Kate from the other direction. The concrete trench resembled a long, narrow cage filled with squealing, hissing creatures, their thin heads protruding through the bars, teeth snapping at the air, eager to reach the girl.

Culver beat at the heads nearest to her kneeling body with the axe as they tried to bite into her. They screeched as their snouts burst open.

'*Steve, helpmehelpme!*' Kate shrieked. '*OhGodthey're-hurtingme!*'

Culver grabbed her wrist and wrenched it upwards. The rat came up with the hand, its eyes protruding, its skull pressed against the bars. He tried to hit at it, but the grille was too narrow, the angle too awkward for the blow to be effective. The beast's teeth were clenched tight into Kate's hand.

Over the deafening uproar of squealing vermin and Kate's screams, Culver vaguely heard Dealey shouting.

'They're breaking through the door, Culver!'

He turned, shining the flashlight in that direction. The

lower portion of the door was beginning to give way, the wood bulging inwards. He saw slivers fall away, a black protuberance poking through, yellow teeth gnashing at the rough edges.

'Get over here and hold the light!' Culver yelled at Dealey.

The older man blanched when he saw the creatures eating into Kate's mangled hand. Even as he watched, a rat snipped off two fingers, retreating with his prize as another took its place. Blood flowed from the wounds, covering the vermin's heads, smearing their evil, yellow eyes, while Kate writhed, her screaming descending to shocked agonized moans. Culver thrust the flashlight at Dealey, then grabbed Kate's wrist with both hands. He pulled with all the strength he possessed, hoping the sudden jolt would dislodge the clinging rats.

It was no use. He tried to batter the first creature's head against the struts, but the rat still clung, its eyes shining frenziedly. Culver realized the teeth were locked into the bones of the hand – *what was left of the hand* – and nothing would loosen that grip, possibly not even death. He searched for the gun, but it was lost beneath black wriggling bodies.

'Culver!' Dealey was pointing the flashlight at the door once more. Culver glanced over his shoulder, still tugging at the wrist, and saw the rat's head pushing through the hole it had created, only its shoulders restraining it. Splinters fell away in a different section nearby and long talons appeared, scratching at the wood.

He sensed Dealey beginning to rise, making ready to run for the far door. He caught his arm.

Kate was moaning repeatedly, her eyes closed in a half-faint, her head rolling from side to side. Her hand was in shreds, all the fingers gone now, but the rats still pulled, still tugged, still gnawed at the bloody remnants, cracking fragile bones.

Dealey stared pleadingly at Culver.

Kate's body went rigid with further excruciating pain.

Wood split behind him.

Culver swiftly unbuckled his belt, drawing it from the jeans loops. He placed the axe on the floor, then slipped the belt around Kate's arm just below the elbow. He curled the leather over, tied a half-knot and pulled it tight so that it sank into the flesh. He completed the knot.

And picked up the axe again.

Kate's eyes opened just as he raised it high. She looked at him, momentarily puzzled. Realization pushed its way through the pain and her eyes widened unnaturally and her lips curled back over her teeth as she opened her mouth to howl.

'*Noooooooooo . . .!*'

The axe flashed down, striking her arm just above the wrist. Bones shattered, but it took another blow to sever the hand completely.

Mercifully, Kate fainted.

There was turmoil below as the rats fought over what was left of the hand. Culver picked up the limp girl and stood, the white-faced Dealey rising with him. A quick glance told them that the rat at the door was nearly through, only its haunches wedging its struggling body in the opening. It frantically scrabbled at the floor, snarling its frustration, saliva dripping from straining jaws as it tried to force a way in. More wood fractured close by and, where before there had only been a claw, there now appeared another sleek black head.

And all the while, the starved corpse of the man smiled into its chest.

Culver carried Kate to the far doorway, Dealey leading.

They hurried through just as the determined rat broke loose into the corridor, another following, then another, a stream of rampaging devils. Dealey slammed the door on them and fell away as their bodies pounded the other side.

They found themselves in a square-shaped room, another doorway opposite, to one side. But as Dealey flashed the light around they caught sight of a stairway.

'Thank God,' breathed Dealey.

They did not linger. Behind them, the door was already cracking, the smell of fresh blood keen in the vermin's senses. Although Kate was not heavy, Culver was at exhaustion point. A trail of blood from the stump of her arm followed them to the stairway and formed tiny pools on the steps as they climbed.

Once, twice, Culver stumbled, and only Dealey's helping hand prevented him and the girl from tumbling down. The second time, Culver lost the blood-splattered axe, and he had to tell the other man to place it back in his hand.

They staggered upwards and found themselves in a narrow, door-less passageway. It extended in both directions.

Squealing, scurrying sounds from below: the rats were in the room they had just left.

The two men chose a direction at random, hurrying along the passage, Culver having to move at an angle to allow room for Kate's inert body. They could hear the mutant animals on the stairs.

Culver and Dealey's breathing was sharp and rasping, their chests heaving rapidly with the exertion. Both men were ready to drop, a feeling of hopelessness, of defeat, beginning to overcome them, sapping their will and thus their remaining strength. So desperate were they that they almost missed the narrow opening. Only a fresh breeze, so different from the stagnant air they had grown used to, halted

Culver. He called Dealey back and looked into the opening. He blinked his eyes to make sure. Faint daylight softened the darkness above.

'It's a way out!' Dealey gasped. 'Oh, dear God, *it's a way out!*'

He brushed past Culver and began climbing the stone steps. Culver lowered his burden, supporting Kate in a momentary standing position; he crouched and let her slump over his shoulder. He straightened, an arm clutched around her legs, the other gripping the weapon, and began to climb, the fresh air already beginning to invigorate him, cooling the perspiration that covered his body, the breeze's sweetness a beckoning hand.

The narrow stairway curved round, spiralling upwards to lead them from the twilight depths into the bright sunlight of another world, a silent shattered landscape that offered little hope, but at least could still give comfort from maleficent darkness.

Panting for breath, they reached a strange-shaped enclosure, its ceiling high but its grey-slab walls close, a heavy wooden door set in one side. The door had a small, metal-strutted opening in its top section, and from there the sunlight poured in.

Dealey rushed at it and pulled the handle. 'It's locked!' he cried in dismay. He grabbed the struts and rattled the door in its frame.

Culver laid Kate on the stone floor and stepped towards the door, unceremoniously thrusting the other man aside. He smashed at the lock with the flat end of the axe. The lock was old, its mechanism stiff with lack of use; the wood around it chipped away and the lock itself soon clattered to the floor. But still the door would not open. It gave a fraction of an inch, but no more. Culver saw a wide but thin bar on the other side.

He stepped back and kicked, and kicked, and kicked. The gap widened, the metal bar bending outwards. A short, sharp blow from the axe loosened it completely from its mounting. The door burst open just as they heard scrabbling on the stairway.

'Get her out!' Culver shouted as he positioned himself at the top of the stairs. He allowed the first rat to reach the top step before he kicked at the open jaws, sending the animal slithering back down again, colliding with those who were just rounding the final bend. The next he sliced open with the axe. The next had its eyes slashed as the blade swept across its thin skull. It reared in the air, falling backwards with a helpful kick from Culver into those below. It lashed out, squealing in pain, flailing the other rodents with claws and teeth, causing confusion, itself coming under attack from the creatures, blocking the narrow stairway in a mêlée of furious bodies. Giving Culver time to run through the door and slam it shut.

His foot struck the padlock that had held it closed and sunlight stung his eyes as he desperately looked around for another method of keeping the door shut. He was on a wide stone stairway, the steps rising beyond the small structure he now pressed against. Behind him was the walkway along the Embankment and in the near distance stood the rectangular blockhouse they had used to enter the shelter. Rain-battered litter lay scattered around the steps and walkway, scarves, hats, bags – items discarded by tourists at the first sound of sirens so many weeks before. There was nothing among them that would hold the door closed.

'Culver!' Dealey called from the Embankment wall. 'There's a small boat down here. We'll be safe on the river!'

It was a chance. The only chance they had.

'Get Kate onto it!' he shouted back. 'I'll hold them as long as I can.' He could still hear the rats tearing their fellow creatures to pieces inside the small building. Dealey struggled with Kate down the ramp leading to the pleasure-boat jetty, water lapping over onto the landing stage. Culver waited a few moments, giving them time to get aboard the craft there, then pushed himself away from the door, leaping down the steps two at a time, trusting in God that he would not slip. He raced to the ramp and looked back in time to see the door swing open and the rats come surging out. Absurdly, he noticed something else: the building they had just fled from was the base of a monument; above, still proud although headless, Boadicea rode her stone chariot, her outstretched arm left intact, continuing to wave her spear defiantly at the collapsed Houses of Parliament.

He ran down to the jetty and looked in dismay at the large, empty pleasure boat still moored there, moving list-lessly on the swollen river.

'Over here!' came the shout and he saw Dealey standing in a smaller boat further down towards Westminster Bridge. He made for it.

'Cast off!' he called out, aware that the vermin were scampering down the ramp, several leaping through the railings to get at him.

The boat would have accommodated no more than fifteen to twenty people on the benches set around its interior. A tiny white-topped cabin covered the bow, its paintwork scorched and bubbled, protection against the spray or foul weather for those tourists lucky or quick enough to find a place inside. Steering was from the stern, a simple but no doubt effective rudder fixed there, its bar ending close to an equally basic gearstick. In front of both was a pale green box that covered the engine. Not the most gracious looking of boats, it seemed to Culver in those desperate moments the handsomest craft he had ever laid eyes on. It was already a few feet away from the quayside, drifting lazily out into the current, and he had to take a running leap to reach it.

He landed on the small area of deck, sprawling over the engine box and quickly turning to face whatever followed. Two rats leapt at the same time. One just reached the side and tried to clamber over. Culver dislodged it easily with a slashing stroke of the axe. The other had scuffled over onto the bench, jumping from there onto the engine covering. It skidded around to face Culver, hissing venomously.

Culver struck and missed as the quivering animal ran to one side. It came at him as a bundle of powerful, squirming fury, knocking him back onto the bench, rending his face with needle-like claws.

Culver sank down, the weapon falling to the deck. He pushed upwards and over, using the animal's own momentum. The rat flew over the side, splashing into the muddy water.

Culver was on his feet immediately and at the rudder and gearstick in two quick strides. Kate lay huddled on the deck, her eyes closed, her face white with shock. He knew she would not yet be in pain – the nerve ends had been cut away and shock was its own analgesic – and was relieved to see her arm was now only seeping small amounts of blood.

From the quayside, the vermin plunged into the water and glided towards the drifting craft.

'How do we start it?' Dealey was close to weeping. 'There's no key, there's no damned key!'

Culver groaned, his shoulders sagging. There was now hardly any mist on the water, although the sun was hazy-bright above, and he could clearly see the sleek black shapes smoothly moving towards them. Given time, he might have been able to open up the engine and bypass the ignition; but there was no time – the leading rats were already sinking their claws into the boat's hull.

He stooped to pick up the axe and spotted the boat-hook lying beneath the bench. 'Dealey, use that to keep them off. We may get away yet!'

Leaning over the side, he swiped at a body in the water. The distance to the water level was frighteningly short, but at least the current was taking them away from the quayside. Red liquid stained the river as the axe found its mark. Dealey had picked up the long, stout pole and was just in time to push back a rat that was clambering over the side. Another appeared in its place and snapped at the pole, sinking its teeth into the wood and refusing to let go. Dealey had to use all his depleted strength to shake off the rat, shoving it back into the water where it thrashed the surface into a foam, still refusing to release its grip. Only as air escaped its lungs did the animal relinquish the hold to swim back to the surface. Meanwhile, other vermin had taken advantage of the struggle.

They scrambled up the side of the boat, using their powerful haunches to thrust themselves from the river.

Culver moved backwards and forwards, never stopping, knowing if he battled with one rat for too long, then others would quickly steal aboard. He thrust, cut and hacked, his face grim and a part of his mind cold, almost remote from the action. Dealey helped him, his movements more clumsy, less swift. He had learned a lesson, though, and that was to keep his jabs with the boat-hook sharp and short, never allowing the vermin to gain a grip.

The river bank drew further away, but still they came, a skimming black tide of them. The boat was drifting upriver with the tide, moving towards the bridge with its missing span on the opposite side of the river. Beyond he could see rising from the river the peculiar rockface that was the fallen section of the ancient clock tower.

Culver realized that if the current took them fast enough they might just outdistance the swimming vermin. If only they could keep them off the boat, if only . . .

He froze.

He had looked up, just for a moment, a quick glance at the bridge itself. Black shapes were darting along its balustrade and the pavement below – he could just see the moving humped shapes. Many were peering through the ornate mouldings. They were lining up above him, bustling, jostling each other for position, long snouts descending, front paws already stretched downwards, balancing themselves. Tensing themselves. Readying themselves to drop down as the boat passed under the bridge.

34

It was hopeless. They had no control over the small craft as the current lazily carried it towards the bridge. Still warding off boarding vermin, Dealey caught sight of Culver and wondered why the man was not moving, why he was staring ahead of them, regardless of the danger they were in. He followed the pilot's gaze and he, too, became still.

He could not speak, he could not curse, he could not even weep. Dealey had become too numbed by it all. To survive the holocaust, to struggle through the terrible aftermath, to thwart disaster at every turn – and now this. To be destroyed by creatures that skulked in filth. A bitterly ironic death.

Culver turned, as if to warn him, and saw that he already knew. Something passed between them. A recognition of shared, impending death? That, and something more. A sudden, cognizant touching of spirits, a startling and rare *knowing* of each other. For Dealey, who was and always had been a pragmatist, it was a spontaneous and staggering insight not just into another's psyche, but also into his own, giving an acute awareness of his own being. The moment passed, but the sensing was indelible.

A dripping, sleek-furred rat appeared over the stern, and Culver attacked it with a grim deadly ferocity, slicing its skull in half and pushing the broken body back into the river with the end of the axe. Feeling that same chill rage, Dealey turned his attention back to the creatures beginning to clamber onto the deck. His anger grew as he attacked them, for he had been driven beyond fear, had reached the stage for which the very animals he did battle with were renowned; trapped, cornered, he turned on his aggressors.

Jamming the hook at the end of the pole deep into the mouth of one that had jumped onto the engine covering, he pushed against it so that the rat skidded off the smooth surface onto the bench at the boat's side. Dealey followed through, leaning over and lifting the stunned creature before it had a chance to recover. The effort took considerable strength, but he did not have time to wonder where that strength came from. Teeth sank into his ankle and he roared with anger and pain, stabbing down at the animal, battering its skull and body, forcing it to release him. The pole hook bent, broke off, and he used the jagged piece of metal that was left to stab into the rat. A jet of blood gushed as an artery in its neck punctured and the rat fled squealing. Yet another was already lunging for him. It caught him in the stomach, sending him back over the engine covering, the pole flying from his grasp. He felt his clothing tear, teeth entering his abdomen. He sank his fingers into the wet fur, digging deep, trying to push the burrowing creature away.

A shadow covered the sun and the mutant rat was wrenched from him.

Culver had the creature gripped around the neck. He pulled it back, regardless of ripping Dealey's flesh, and exposed its belly: he brought the axe down with a deep, chopping movement, then tossed the writhing animal aside.

He did not linger; he turned, lashing out, scything, racing along the deck, inflicting wounds, severing limbs and heads, never resting, never pausing, never allowing himself the time to think.

Dealey clutched the wound in his stomach for a moment, then reached for the fallen pole, picking it up with both hands and joining Culver in the fray.

Although soon only seriously wounded or dead vermin remained inside the boat, others continued to clamber over the side. The water all around had become black with them. And the bridge was only yards away.

Culver bludgeoned a rat that was stealthily approaching Kate, the stump of her arm lying exposed and enticing on the wet boards of the deck. She opened her eyes as he lifted her, only a brief flash of recognition in them before she sank back into protective oblivion. She was terribly, dangerously, pale. Culver, in a quick moment of tenderness, kissed her lips before gently placing her on the engine box. Then he was back, fighting, yelling, keeping the boat clear.

He sensed the huge bulk of the bridge looming over them, looked up, saw the first of the rats beginning to drop, landing with a splash in the water just ahead. The boat drifted closer. He saw their quivering, excited shapes above, crawling over the buttress near the Embankment, across the supports, poking their bodies through the thick ornamental balustrade and balancing on its broad top.

Impatient, another leapt outwards and managed to land slitheringly on the top of the pleasure boat's tiny cabin. It glared down at the two men, but did not attack.

Culver raised the axe, holding it across his chest in both hands, ready for the final onslaught. Once the boat was under the bridge, the vermin would fall on them in an avalanche. He prayed the end would be swift.

An eerie silence fell. Their squealing stopped, so did their trembling. It was as before, in the basement chamber, the lair in which the grotesque creature had suckled her young;

the vermin had fallen silent then, just before they had gone mad with bloodlust. It was about to happen again.

Dealey offered up an unspoken but fervent prayer, and Kate softly moaned, still unconscious.

The rat on the cabin roof watched Culver. Its haunches began to quiver, the unsightly pointed hump above them tensing. It bared its teeth and hissed.

The roaring, whirring sound came fast, breaking the unnatural quietness with a swiftness that stunned both men and beasts. Over the deafening noise came gunfire and Culver and Dealey watched open-mouthed as chippings sprayed off the old bridge. The vermin scattered. Many were thrown screeching into the water below, bodies rent by bullets. Others leapt into the river for safety, but still the gunfire followed them, spewing tiny, violent fountains, many of those fountains a deep red.

Confused, deafened by the noise, Culver and Dealey crouched in the boat as it drifted beneath the bridge. Rats fell onto them and once more they were beating them off, the squealing audible now they were beneath the bridge, the roaring above muted. But this time the vermin were terrified, demented by the sudden turmoil, scuttling around the boat in disarray, those in the river disorientated, swimming in circles.

The two men stood before the recumbent girl, striking out at those who came too close, defending rather than attacking. Culver caught sight of the same rat still perched on the cabin roof, and still watching him. Unlike the others, this creature was not panicked. Its gleaming eyes showed that it was not even afraid. It shuffled close to the edge of the cabin roof. Its fur bristled, swelling its body. It launched itself into the air.

The rat's powerful haunches sent it clear of the engine

covering on which Kate lay. Its flight seemed peculiarly slow to Culver, the action – and his reaction – almost leisurely. Its black shape grew languidly in his vision, claws outstretched so that he could count each one, jaws opened to reveal every yellow fang, the two incisors stained and jagged from use, eyes slanted wickedly, intent on his.

And the axe was coming up from behind Culver, a lazy, arcing motion, sweeping high to meet the floating beast.

Culver's arm juddered with the impact and he fell backwards under the animal that had been split down the middle, through the skull and shoulders, the blade travelling alongside the spine, stopping only when it reached the big bones of the mutant rat's pelvis.

Culver lay there as the creature's life substance flooded over him. He pushed the opened body away, barely able to lift it.

Daylight dazzled him as the boat passed from beneath the bridge. Yet something still blotted out much of the clear blue sky and he could not understand why, could not understand the thunderous roaring.

Dealey was near him, pointing, shouting something, but the other sounds were too great. A rush of wind, a gale-force breeze, rocked the little boat. Culver dragged himself to his feet and staggered, gripping the side of the boat to steady himself. He looked up once more.

'Pumas,' he said, the word lost in the whirlwind. He suddenly understood why they had not seen or heard the helicopters before that moment: the tilted hulk of the Big Ben tower had hidden their approach from upriver.

The three helicopters hovered over the river, one close to the boat below, their wheels retracted, their huge blades creating a maelstrom. Two of them hailed down bullets from specially mounted 7.62mm general purpose machine guns onto the bridge and into the river, while the third manoeuvred its draught to push the boat with its three human occupants away from the bridge.

The same word kept forming on Dealey's lips: *'Incredible-incredibleincredible!'*

Culver stumbled over him and grabbed his shoulder. 'It's not over yet!' he shouted close to Dealey's ear. 'They're still coming aboard! We've got to keep fighting them off!'

As if to prove the point, two rats appeared just in front of them, sliding over the side. The two men acted as one, kicking out at the beasts and sending them toppling back into the water. But more leapt onto the boat, using it as a place of refuge from the rainstorm of lead. Culver and Dealey attacked them before the bedraggled vermin had a chance to recover. There were still too many, though. More and more clambered over onto the benches and deck.

'It's no good, we can't hold them!' Dealey shouted, once again panic-stricken.

'Get onto the cabin roof!' Culver told him over the roar. He leapt onto the engine covering, Dealey following suit. The older man awkwardly climbed onto the small roof while Culver picked up the unconscious girl. It was difficult, but Culver managed to pass her up to Dealey, who dragged her to momentary safety. The pilot kicked at three rats that had mounted the box, one managing to grip his jeans and tear off a shred as it fell back into the well of the deck. Culver sprang up onto the cabin roof and knelt there, ready to swing at anything that followed.

Dealey, half-sitting because standing would have been too precarious on the rocking boat, tapped Culver's shoulder and pointed.

Culver looked up at the giant shadow that filled the sky above them. A man was being lowered down to them.

Culver thanked God that the Puma helicopters had been fitted with both machine guns and winches. Feet dangled just above their heads, and then the man was down, Culver and Dealey helping to steady him.

'*Not a great time for a pleasure-boat ride,*' the winchman yelled, and saw the two men were too weary to speak. '*I can only take one . . .*' He noted the rats below, the man with the axe still striking at those trying to reach the cabin roof. '*Okay, I can stretch it to two, but we'll have trouble up top! Let's get the girl into the harness!*'

They could hardly hear his words, but guessed his meaning. Together they lifted Kate and secured her in the harness loop, the helicopter maintaining a steady hover above them, skilfully following the motion of the boat. '*All right, one of you get behind and put your arms around my shoulders! You'll have to hold tight, but we'll soon get you up there!*'

Culver indicated at Dealey to do just that. Dealey shook his head.

'*You go!*' he yelled.

'*Don't be bloody stup—*' Culver began to say.

'*I don't have the strength to hold on! I'd never make it!*'

'*Come on, either one of you,*' the winchman shouted impatiently. '*One of the other choppers will pick up whoever's left. I'm signalling for lift now before those bloody monsters start chewing my toes!*'

Dealey slapped Culver's shoulder and took the axe from him. He even managed a weary smile.

Culver barely had his arms gripped over the winchman's shoulders before a thumb was offered skyward and their feet left the cabin roof. They soared upwards, moving rapidly and steadily away from the boat. He looked down anxiously and held his breath when he saw the black shapes swarming onto the white roof. Dealey was standing, swinging the short axe with both hands, knocking the vermin aside, sweeping them overboard or back down onto the deck. But for every one ejected, another took its place. He saw Dealey's ever diminishing figure go rigid with pain as his thigh was bitten into. Another rat scurried up his back, forcing him to reach behind to dislodge it, the weapon falling from his grasp.

'*Dealey!*' Culver shouted uselessly.

The second Puma swooped in, a winchman already swinging at the end of the wire. His feet never touched the cabin roof; he scooped up the blood-soaked man and pulled the rat from his back all in one movement. They swung away from the craft, two black forms still clinging to Dealey's legs. Their own weight sent the rats crashing back into the river, flesh and material stretching then parting under the pressure. Culver closed his eyes as the two figures were winched upwards. The third helicopter hovered low, using up its ammunition on the vermin. Gunfire ravaged the boat and the mutant rats that filled it, and when the bullets burst through its fragile hull, reaching the fuel tank, the little craft exploded into a thousand pieces. Culver opened his eyes in time to see the pall of black smoke billow up into the air, a miniature replica of the explosions that had destroyed the city so long, so very long, ago.

Reaching hands helped them into the helicopter, Culver hauled in first, then the girl, the winchman climbing in last.

Culver was quickly guided to a seat and he sank down gratefully into the cool shade. The big door slid shut, the interior of the helicopter still noisy but less than before. He watched as Kate was carefully lifted onto a fixed cot-stretcher and another officer, a medic he assumed, examined the stump of her arm. The man did not flinch; he had obviously treated worse injuries during the past few weeks. From a case, he swiftly took out a small phial which he broke open to extract a syrette. Expertly, and without cutting away her jeans, he plunged the needle into a muscle in Kate's thigh, holding the syrette there for a few seconds while its fluid drained. He noticed Culver watching.

'Morphia,' he explained. 'She's lucky we got to her before she came out of shock. Don't worry, she's going to be okay – it looks like a clean severance. I'll dress it and release the tourniquet for a while. Does she have any other wounds?'

Culver shook his head, tiredness beginning to overtake him. 'Cuts, scrapes, that's all. Oh yeah . . .' he remembered, '. . . we've been exposed to pneumonic plague.'

The medic raised his eyebrows in surprise. 'Okay, I'll give her a quick once-over. How about you? Need some sedation?'

Again Culver shook his head. He gazed at Kate's wan face, its lines softened already as the drug began to take effect; he wanted to go to her, comfort her, beg her forgiveness for what he had had to do, but she would not hear. There would be time later. He knew there would be much more time for both of them. He turned away, looking at the tiny windows in the door, the hazy blue beyond. Another face appeared before him: the winchman.

'Flight Sergeant MacAdam,' he introduced himself.

Culver found it difficult to speak. 'Thanks,' he finally said.

'Pleasure,' came the reply.

'How . . .?'

'You were spotted early this morning.'

'The plane?'

The winchman nodded. 'We thought you might have been from government HQ. Were you?'

'No . . . no, we were trying to get into . . . into it.'

The man looked keenly interested. 'Did you manage to? Christ, we've had no word from headquarters since this whole bloody mess started. What the hell happened down there?'

'Didn't . . . didn't anyone get out?'

'Not a bloody soul. And nobody could get to the HQ from the outside – all the main tunnels are down. Those bastards hit us harder than anyone expected. Some of the survivors may have got out into the city, who knows? We haven't been able to search, first because of fallout, and then the freak rainstorms. We've been patrolling this stretch of the river ever since word got back that your party had been seen. But there was supposed to be more of you. Where're the others?'

'Dead,' Culver said flatly, thinking of those who had escaped the Kingsway shelter as well. He suddenly remembered Ellison. Torchless, weaponless. Inside the shelter. 'All dead,' he reaffirmed.

'But what did you find down there? What was inside?'

The medical officer intervened. 'Let him rest, Sergeant. He can be questioned when we get back to Cheltenham.'

The winchman still looked questioningly at him.

'Rats,' Culver said. 'Nothing but big bloody rats.'

MacAdam's face was grim. 'We've heard stories . . .'

'People managed to get out of London?'

'Oh yeah, plenty got out.'

Culver sank further back into the seat. 'But where to? What to?'

The winchman's face was still grim, but it held a humourless smile. 'It isn't quite as bad as you obviously think. The lunacy was stopped, you see, stopped before everything was destroyed. Sure, the main capitals are gone, the industrial cities, many of the military bases; but total destruction was brought to an abrupt halt when the separate powers realized the mistake . . .'

'Sergeant,' the medic warned.

'What mistake?' Culver asked.

'You rest now; you need it. We'll soon have you back at

base where you'll be taken care of. You'll find it's still chaotic, but some order is beginning to return under military rule. And they say a new coalition government's about to be formed any time . . .'

The sergeant stood, patting Culver's shoulder. 'You take it easy.' He turned to go.

'Who started it?' Culver shouted after him. 'Who started the fucking war? America or Russia?'

He wasn't sure if he heard right, the noise of the rotor blades almost drowning the reply. It sounded like 'China'.

The winchman was standing at the cockpit opening, the same humourless smile on his face. Culver thought he heard him say, 'Of course, there isn't much left of it any more.'

Culver returned his gaze to the small windows, eager for their light, surprised, but too weary to be further shocked. The gloom of the Puma's interior depressed him; there had been too many sunless days. His mind roamed back, seeing images, scenes he would never be free of.

And he thought of the final irony. The slaying of those who had long before plotted out their own survival while others would perish, choiceless and without influence. The slaying of a weakened master-species by a centuries-repressed creature that could only inhabit the dark underworld; mankind's natural sneaking enemy, who had always possessed cunning, but now that cunning – and their power – enhanced by an unnatural cause. He thought of the giant, black-furred rats with their deadly weapons, their teeth, their claws, their strength. And again, their cunning. He thought of the even-more-loathsome, bloated, slug-like creatures, brethren to and leaders of the Black monsters of the same hideous spawn. And he thought of the Mother Creature.

The medic, intent on treating the girl's wound, glanced around in surprise when he heard the man laughing. He quickly began to prepare a sedative when he noticed tears flowing down Culver's face.

Culver thought of the Mother Creature and her offspring, her tiny, suckling litter. The government headquarters had been attacked so ferociously because the Black rats had believed their queen to be under threat. The poor fools had been wiped out as soon as the shelter became occupied, the mutant vermin disturbed by the terrible sounds of bombs, alarmed at the sudden invasion. The onslaught had been instant and merciless.

Culver tried to stop laughing, but he couldn't. It was all too ironic. And the greatest irony of all was the Mother Creature's children. The little creatures who fed at her breasts.

He wiped a shivering hand across his eyes as if to wipe out the vision. He and Fairbank had been distraught with the discovery. Through their shock, the possibilities had assailed them, the implications had terrified them.

For the small, newborn creatures had resembled human ... *human*! ... embryos. They had claws, the beginnings of scaly tails, the same wicked, slanting eyes and the humped backs. But their skulls were more like the skulls of man, their features were those of grotesque, freakish humans. Their arms, their legs, were not those of animals. And their brains, seen clearly through their tissue-thin craniums and transparent skin, were too large to belong to a rat.

His shoulders shuddered with the laughing. Had mankind been created in the same way, through an explosion of radiation, genes changed in a way that caused them to evolve into walking, thinking, upright creatures? Another dreadfully funny notion: had mankind evolved not from the ape, as the theorists, those wretched interpreters of it all, thought? Had mankind ... had mankind evolved from these other foul creatures? And had that same course of evolution been unleashed once again?

He wanted to stop laughing, but he could not. And neither could he control the tears. It drained him, it nauseated him. And presently someone was leaning over him, aiming a needle, anxious to release him from the hysteria.

The rats went back.

They swam to the Embankment and leapt from the water, black skins glistening in the bright sunlight. Others, those on the bridge, ran squealing from the thunderous, death-dealing crea- ture in the sky. They gathered in the open, trembling, confused by the violence against them and by the loss of the beasts below who had ruled them. And something else was gone. The Mother Creature and her strange litter, the new alien breed that the Black rats had yearned to destroy, for they were not of their kind, no longer existed. The difference of these newborn was beyond understanding and had sent fear coursing through the black mutants.

But they had not been allowed to kill them. The Mother Creature was all-powerful, controlling their will, ruling them and allowing no dissent. Her own special guard had dealt with those who rebelled. And the guard had been felled by the sickness.

Still the rats had protected their matriarch, governed and conditioned by her thoughts. Now those thoughts were no longer in their heads. And their numbers had grown small.

They returned to the gloomy underworld, safe there below the ground, away from the sun. They soon found the human who hid among them in the darkness, his burbling anguish – his smell of pungent fear – drawing them to him. They scratched on the door he hid behind. Then began to gnaw at the wood. They took pleasure in his screams.

When there was nothing left of him, they roamed the dark tunnels, content to stay, to rest, to procreate.

When they were hungry, they left the dark, ever-nocturnal underworld, silently creeping into the open where the night sky and fresh breezes soothed them. They slithered among the rubble of the old city, seeking sustenance and easily finding it.

And only when the first haze of dawn broke did they slink back into the holes, back into the tunnels below, reluctant to leave this new, free territory. This new world that was to become their domain.

Ash

JAMES HERBERT'S FINAL NOVEL

James Herbert's best-loved character, David Ash,
the sceptical detective of the paranormal, returns in the
long-anticipated novel *ASH*. There are reports of
strange goings-on in an isolated castle.
Many suspect that it is haunted . . .

extracts reading groups
competitions books new
discounts extracts
competitions
books
new
events books
extracts
new reading groups
interviews
events extracts books
discounts
new books events
events new

www.panmacmillan.com

extracts reading groups
competitions books extracts new